My hu_____

and other _____

Catherine MacDonald

Copyright © 2018 Catherine MacDonald

All rights reserved, including the right to reproduce this book, or portions thereof in any form. No part of this text may be reproduced, transmitted, downloaded, decompiled, reverse engineered, or stored, in any form or introduced into any information storage and retrieval system, in any form or by any means, whether electronic or mechanical without the express written permission of the author.

This is a work of fiction. Names and characters are the product of the author's imagination and any resemblance to actual persons, living or dead, is entirely coincidental.

The views expressed in this work are solely those of the author and do not necessarily reflect the views of the publisher, and the publisher hereby disclaims any responsibility for them.

ISBN: 978-0-244-36695-7

PublishNation
www.publishnation.co.uk

catherinemacdonaldauthor.com

Chapter One

It's funny how the major dramas of life often creep up and bash you over the head when you're occupied with the most trivial and mundane activities. One Tuesday in April, I was breakfasting with my husband, Ian, in our London flat; both of us deep in the morning papers, contemplating a day of meeting friends, shopping, and the usual insignificant household tasks. Nothing had prepared me for what was about to happen. I had not the least suspicion that I would face a threat to my whole way of life – and perhaps that was just as well.

'I'm not feeling great...'

Ian dropped the *Telegraph* crossword, and the paper rustled to the floor in slow motion, making an ominous, sighing sound. I raised my head in surprise, and then the mounting alarm in his eyes was reflected in my own. His skin was fading to ash, coated with a waxy sheen of sweat, and a sharp pulse of panic convulsed me.

'Ian! Does your chest hurt? Try to relax: take a deep breath!'

He gulped, one hand clenched upon his breastbone, and I grabbed for the telephone, punching at keys with clumsy fingers which seemed to have lost their normal sense of feeling. Expletives peppered the air as Ian fought against a rising tide of pain.

'I think my husband is having a heart attack!' I stuttered, the words sticking in my throat as the 999-operator picked up my call.

'Okay, love. Try to keep calm. I need to ask you a few questions and then I'll tell you what you can do to help him.'

Thank God for the Emergency Services. The professional, competent manner of the operator was like a comfort blanket, helping to calm the agitation which trembled through my limbs. He dealt swiftly with the essentials and promised to stay on the line until the ambulance arrived. Then I dropped to my knees beside my stricken husband, still clutching the handset and hoping I could convey a sense of reassurance to him.

'It's all right, dearest. An ambulance is coming. Breathe slowly and deeply; you are going to be fine, I promise.'

But my confidence wavered as I watched his chest pulsate with rapid, shallow breaths. Ian fumbled for my hand, and the chill of his fingers served only to increase my alarm. His grey eyes were fixed on mine, holding an urgent appeal as he grappled with shock and panic.

'My love – I need to tell you that the last years with you have been the happiest of my life,' he murmured, and I was blinded by a mist of tears as I detected the fatalistic tone in his voice. All my instincts roused me to fight; roused me to make him fight too.

'Don't speak like that, Ian, don't! We have plenty more years ahead of us; just wait and see.'

I kissed his hand with greedy lips, as if I could somehow pass on my own life and vitality to him until help arrived. Fright scattered my thoughts, but then I was recalled to the insistent voice on the phone and forced myself to pay attention to the advice at the end of the line.

'Aspirin...'

I clambered to my feet, relieved that there was one positive thing I could do to help. The medicine cabinet in the guest bathroom was the usual repository of unwanted or untried medicaments and lotions, which I never got around to clearing out. Now I scrabbled amongst bottles and packets until I found what I needed, before racing back to the slumped figure at the breakfast table.

'Swallow this darling. The operator says it could help.'

I pressed the tiny tablet into Ian's unresponsive hand. He grimaced, then did as I instructed, although tea slopped on to the carpet as he lifted his cup with shaking fingers to wash the tablet down, and he swore as the hot liquid splashed his trousers. I didn't care: nothing else mattered now. I wanted to smother him in a cloud of loving words and caresses before it was too late. Where on earth were the paramedics? How would I bear it if my husband died before help could reach us?

The voice on the telephone nagged at me, but apprehension had shaded the edges of my vision with wavy blackness, and I was drowning in stress and dread of what might be coming next. Ian clasped my hand as if it was the only thing keeping him from the next world, and his wedding ring dug painfully against my fingers with the force of his grip, but I wasn't going to complain.

'I love you,' he breathed, his voice scarcely more than a raspy whisper, and I grasped at this sentiment.

'I love you too, darling. Stay strong for me, please…'

The shrill pealing of the doorbell galvanized me with relief. I stumbled into the hall, fumbling with the locks, and finally flinging the door wide open as if I was welcoming guests to a party. No guests were ever more welcome than the green uniformed duo who loomed in the doorway, laden with bulky equipment.

'Mrs Inglis? Where is your husband?'

I sank on to a chair as the medics assumed cheerful control, and at last I could bid the operator a thankful farewell. My legs felt floppy as a puppet with no-one to work the strings, but the trembling and weakness ebbed away as I watched the deft co-ordination of the men. It was an inexpressible relief to relinquish my responsibility for Ian to people who knew what they were doing.

'Has he had a heart attack?' I blurted out, and one of the men smiled up at me as he unbuttoned Ian's shirt, before placing little discs on his chest and tummy.

'Can't say for sure,' the paramedic replied. 'It looks like a heart problem, but he's still with us, and we need to get him into hospital pronto. How old are you, Ian, mate?'

Ian winced at this familiarity, which was not to his taste. He muttered 'seventy-two' in a testy tone, which cheered me – this was how he would react in normal circumstances. Time began to move at its usual speed again. I stopped feeling that I was taking part in a tragedy and began to view myself in a hospital drama instead; hoping that the ending of this episode would be upbeat and positive.

'You don't look that old. He's kidding us, eh Stu?'

'You don't look a day over sixty, Ian. Regular spring chicken, I'd say.'

The two medics were working with rapid efficiency; carrying out procedures which they had done so often they had become automatic. It wasn't long before they were ready, and then they hoisted Ian on to a portable trolley, with accompanying grunts and grimaces, finding his tall and muscular frame wasn't easy to move. They began to manoeuvre the trolley towards the door, and I attempted to gather my wits, which had gone walkabout after this dramatic start to our day.

'Where are you taking him?' I demanded. It didn't sound like my voice, and I wondered briefly how a quavering old lady had managed to seize control of me.

'St Thomas's. Do you want to come with us, love? There's room in the ambulance.'

Well, of course I wanted to be with my husband – for my own comfort, as much as his. I was grateful to these strangers, but I wasn't going to let anyone take Ian away from me.

'I'll need to get my bag and coat,' I murmured, dismissing the old lady and concentrating on practical matters, and the paramedic nodded in response.

'It'll take us a few minutes to settle him in the ambulance. We'll wait for you, but don't hang about.'

They disappeared through the door towards the lift – our flat was on the second floor of the building. I dashed to the loo, because my stomach was cramping as though I'd eaten something noxious, before grabbing my outdoor garments. Then I hurtled down the stairs to the road. Ian was being loaded inside the ambulance, while a few passers-by lingered; open-mouthed, and clearly disappointed that there was nothing more exciting to see than a mature gent suffering from chest pains.

Ian was soon strapped in and connected to a machine, which began to utter ominous whirring noises. A print-out emerged; then the siren cut into the peaceful morning, and we set off through the traffic at an impressive, swerving pace. I reached across for the reassurance of Ian's hand. He was frowning at the machine, and I was heartened to see him taking an interest in what was happening around him.

'Is that an ECG?' he asked, and the medic called Stu nodded.

'S'right, mate. Doing that now means the doc will be able to see what's up pretty quick when we get you into A and E.'

He picked up the print-out, scanning it solemnly and giving a little whistle. 'I've seen worse. Let's hope they get you sorted out and back home soon.'

Hope was the right word in the circumstances. Hope flooded through me, and the churchyard pallor of Ian's face began to recede as he accepted that he wasn't about to die. It was a relief to see faint colour returning to his cheeks, but he still looked in shock; his features gaunt and strongly defined. He let out a huge, shuddering sigh, as though nerving himself for the next stage of events.

'This isn't how I planned to spend the day,' he complained in querulous tones. 'Eithne – I shall need you to ring Tom Haverstock to say I can't make lunch.'

'Don't worry about any of that, darling. I will take care of it,' I soothed, and he lay back, closing his eyes as though he wanted to shut us away and pretend it was all a horrible nightmare. There wasn't much to see in any case, although I could sense the streets of London zipping past. I opened my mouth to comment on the exciting roller-coaster ride, but then closed it again. I wasn't supposed to be enjoying any of this.

A sharp corner was succeeded by a burst of acceleration, and we came to a jerky halt outside the hospital. The paramedics shouted instructions, and Ian was rushed to a bay already staffed with waiting experts, leaving me to hover anxiously on the fringes as they carried out their procedures. The jargon was worryingly unfamiliar. Everything seemed so complicated to my untrained eyes, and the equipment and bleeps and pings were a stern reminder that this was a serious affair. But after ten nervous minutes, the sense of urgency was replaced by a more tranquil mood, and some of the staff dispersed to attend to other patients. A Registrar leaned down to talk to Ian, and I craned forward to hear what was being said.

'You don't appear to be in any immediate danger sir, but you have suffered some malfunction of the heart. We'll need to keep you in for further tests. That might take a day or two, but we want to find out what's going on with you, hmm?'

Ian gripped the sides of the trolley, looking as exhausted as a man who has undergone ten rounds in the ring. He summoned a faint, watery grin as he tried to project his usual confident personality, although I could see it cost him a painful effort.

'Thank you, doctor. We need to get to the bottom of this, so we can take steps to ensure it doesn't happen again. My wife has had a real fright,' he added, looking across to where I hovered, with my bag clutched tightly against my chest.

'That's the spirit. Try to relax now. We have the situation under control.'

The Registrar turned to brief a nurse, and I began to remark that I wasn't the only person who'd received a shock but thought better of it. I sidled to the trolley, caressing the hand nearest to me, and holding it to my face; wishing fervently that we could begin the day again, with a different start.

'Don't worry, darling. I think the worst is over,' I murmured, bending down to kiss Ian's forehead. There was a tiny scratch on one cheek where he had nicked himself whilst shaving, and this upset me all over again. Ian was a man who always took great care with his appearance, and it broke my heart to see the netted lion in a helpless, supine state.

The nurse plumped Ian's pillow, and pulled a blanket across his body. She didn't seem the least bit concerned but radiated a brisk and beaming efficiency, which suggested that she enjoyed her work.

'We'll be taking your husband to a cardiology ward now. Perhaps you'd like to go home to fetch him some toiletries, and his pyjamas and dressing gown. I don't suppose you had time to think about all that before the ambulance brought him in,' she said to me. I knew that no matter how ill he was feeling, my fastidious husband would kick up a fuss if he was forced into hospital issue pyjamas, or one of those open-backed gowns which provide the minimum of privacy for the wearer, but I was very reluctant to let him out of my sight after the trauma of the morning.

'Are you sure I don't need to stay with him?' I demanded, my eyes holding a question, and she understood my unease; patting me on the arm as if I was a child needing to be calmed.

'Quite sure. You don't have any cause to worry. Doctor says he is stable, and he's in the best place now. But I know how difficult it can be when you've been married for a long time.'

Well, we hadn't been married for a very long time. I could hardly sit still in the cab on my way back to the flat; my apprehension fuelled by the stark remembrance of two sudden and unexpected deaths which had already robbed me of a lover and a husband during my adult years. I replayed the words of the consultant in my head, clinging on to the positives, and trusting that this time, there would be a reprieve for me.

There was an unsettling sense of life interrupted in the air as I turned the key and tottered into the flat. The remnants of our breakfast adorned the table, and the paper lay crumpled on the carpet where Ian had dropped it. It should have been an everyday scene, but something felt very wrong. Then the memory of Ian's ashen, gasping face hit me all over again, and delayed shock made me come over woolly-headed. The cold, leathery embrace of the sofa offered little comfort as I sank down and pressed my face into the cushions. Scenes from my past life invaded my conscious mind, and I fought to escape the insistent memories of tragedies which were impossible to suppress.

Ian and I were no traditional Darby and Joan, whatever appearances might suggest. Although we had known one another for years, our relationship hadn't been easy or straightforward – it was more like a case of worlds colliding and flying apart again. We first met when I was in my twenties, and Ian his early thirties, and a rapid courtship resulted in our engagement. Then I wavered in my affections, deciding to return to my first love, Nick DeLisle, and Ian reacted with fury to my desertion. There were some years of hostility between us, now thankfully buried in the past.

But Nick, who was a journalist, was killed during a trip to Africa, and I became a single mum, with a son, Nicholas, who never knew his real father. That was a lonely, painful time for me. Eventually, I found solace in a marriage with Peter Leigh, an old schoolfriend of Nick's. We lived quietly in Cheshire, and our two daughters, Olivia and Louisa, were born there. My life finally seemed settled and tranquil, even though it was not the future I'd hoped for.

Ian and I were thrown together by chance almost twenty years later, when he moved into our neighbourhood with his second wife, Laura, and their family. I had no intention of rekindling a relationship with him, but boredom with my life and renewed attraction to my former fiancé proved to be an irresistible combination. Circumstances forced us to confront our feelings. Middle-aged madness overwhelmed us, and we became lovers. Then I discovered I was pregnant…

I lost the baby, and somehow, we managed to keep the truth from our partners. Although my heart was racked by indecision, I came to my senses and ended the affair, and Ian turned his attention back to London and a different existence. He had never liked life in the country, and it wasn't long before he settled his family in the city again. Contact between us dwindled away; leaving behind more painful memories than happy ones.

Nonetheless, I was genuinely surprised and sorry when Ian's wife Laura died some years afterwards, having contracted an aggressive form of cancer. We attended her funeral, where Ian's remote hostility shocked and saddened me – there was a hint of blame for Laura's illness and death in his bearing towards me; as if she had divined the truth and been grievously wounded by what had occurred between us during their brief sojourn in Cheshire. It was an uncomfortable and sobering sensation. Afterwards, I thought I would never see Ian again, and I mourned our lost intimacy. Despite all the difficult times, we had shared a special relationship, and I felt that there were indissoluble links which ought to bind us together.

Fast forward another year or so. Peter, upon whom I depended so gratefully, had finally heeded his family's pleas to retire from Leigh Engineering; the company founded by his father. He travelled to Sweden to negotiate the final stages of the sale of the company to a Swedish conglomerate, and his counterpart invited him on a trip to the north of the country in the private jet his firm had recently purchased.

No-one was aware that the small plane had been badly and carelessly serviced and maintained. As they flew over the vast Swedish forests, a gradual cabin decompression occurred, and all the occupants fell into an unconscious, hypoxic state. Despite the frantic efforts of the Swedish Air Force to intervene, the plane crashed when it ran out of fuel, killing everyone on board.

At least I had the comfort that Peter had known nothing about what was to happen. It was my only consolation. The realisation that another loved one had been torn so suddenly from my life stunned me, and I had a breakdown; unable to cope with the loss.

Throughout my marriage to Peter I had suffered a shackling sense of guilt, because I did not love him with the unconditional adoration I had felt for Nick. The aftermath of the affair with Ian was like a drenching with cold water, which forced me to re-evaluate my life and my obligations. I tried hard to be a better wife, and Peter and I were eagerly anticipating spending more time together when he retired. It seemed terribly cruel to be deprived of our future happiness by such a malign twist of fate.

I must say that Ian behaved very well. He took one look at my abject person at Peter's funeral, scheduled a meeting with my son Nicholas, with whom he had always maintained friendly relations, and began to interest himself in my affairs. My daughters were inconsolable at the loss of their father, and Nicholas had career commitments in Australia which limited his time in England.

Ian used his contacts to help with the interim management of Leigh Engineering. He negotiated new terms with the Swedes, so that we maintained shares in the business and an income, and he took a non-executive directorship himself at Nicholas's request.

He arranged first-rate legal representation, which resulted in a large damages and insurance pay-out for the children and myself in recompense for Peter's death. At least I would have no money worries. And Ian didn't hassle me or do anything except offer affectionate company and support, which helped me to struggle through a fog of sadness and confusion.

Some nine months after the accident, I found myself staying at Ian's house in the south of France, in company with mutual friends.

The house was rambling and comfortably quirky, and I found solace in the beautiful garden, which was exotic and vivid with heavy-scented shrubs and unfamiliar plants. It was comforting to sit in the sun and breathe in the abundant life all around me. The guilt which had plagued me since Peter's death began to dissolve, and I felt that I was slowly reviving in the unaccustomed warmth after my prolonged and icy immersion in grief.

One day, the friends took themselves off for a long day trip which I didn't fancy, and Ian and I were left alone to enjoy the peace of the garden. As we relaxed over a bottle of wine, Ian reached for my hand, and gently reminded me of a promise we had made to one another years ago, when our affair had ended.

'Promise me that if we find ourselves alone in later life, you'll come to me,' he had demanded, and I had promised to do so. It seemed an unlikely prospect, although we meant what we said.

Now he felt that the time had come to ask me to keep my word. I was almost in tears.

'But such awful things happen to the men I get close to! I don't want anything bad to come to you, Ian. You've been so kind to me during these last months.'

'I think that's a risk I'm prepared to take. And don't they say, 'third time lucky', anyway?'

He pulled me into his arms with the gentlest of caresses. It was comforting to feel his body so close to me once again, but his touch revived searing memories, and I felt shaken and faint. Was it another betrayal of my late husband to accept this new intimacy?

'It's too soon,' I murmured. 'I don't think I can do it. Please let's leave things as they are.'

He didn't press me further. But that night, he came to my room, and slipped under the sheets next to me. My body was tense in his embrace; unyielding, and painfully aware of past associations. He held me in his arms, and skin nuzzled skin, but that was all – and to my surprise, I slept deeply and peacefully. My usual restless and unhappy dreams took flight. His warmth was melting the pent-up sorrow inside me, and I felt lighter and more hopeful that I might have another future before me.

He came again the next night, and on the third night, it seemed natural, even appropriate, to make love. It wasn't the selfish, frantic passion of old days, but a deep and considered desire to be close to one another. I burrowed against his body; wanting the reassurance that this liaison might be a lasting one, and his whispered words of endearment reached places inside me which were waiting to be healed.

When the time came to return to England, the friends left without me. I had nothing much to go back for, and I was beginning to realise that Ian needed me as much as I might need him. Our children were adults living their own lives, and we were free to be together without causing pain or problems for anyone else. It seemed to be a fitting end for the complex path our relationship had taken over the years.

I let my house in Cheshire as I was unwilling to part with it altogether, and Ian and I divided our time between France and England. He still had some business commitments in London, and I enjoyed rediscovering the city where I had passed some emotional years in my youth. But I think we were happiest in Provence, where we could lead a simple, harmonious life; treasuring the peaceful present after our turbulent past.

I would have been content to keep things as they were, but Ian pressed me to marry him.

'It makes things easier from a legal point of view,' he told me, stroking my cheek as I sat beside him on the sofa. 'Besides, I would like you to be my wife. It's about time.'

We married at the local Mairie, in a quiet and private ceremony. Our children attended with their partners, and they seemed to be happy for us, although I sensed that Olivia and Sam, Ian's younger son, wore smiles which masked a lurking disapproval. At the time of Ian's admission to St Thomas's, we had been married for eight years. It felt like a lot longer – but in a good way.

The past was behind me. I had to deal with the present situation. A strong cup of tea perked up my spirits – I am British, after all, and it was far too early in the day to hit the gin bottle, although my eyes wandered to the drinks cabinet more than once. As I gulped the hot liquid down, my head grew calmer and my thoughts more rational, and I turned with relief to the tasks which needed to be done. My first action was to change into different clothes. I knew Ian liked to see me looking smart, and the old sweater and trousers I had thrown on when I got up were strictly for the house.

It didn't take long to pack a bag with Ian's belongings, and I handled his clothing with loving fingers; relishing the lingering sense of his person in the smell and feel of the garments. Then I rang Tom Haverstock's number. Tom was loudly and extravagantly sorry to hear of Ian's misfortune, and I twisted impatiently in my chair as he expounded on similar afflictions which had been visited on their cronies. I had to be abrupt to get away.

'Tom – please forgive me, but I haven't spoken to Ian's children yet. I'll let you know how he gets on. Goodbye.'

The Uber arrived, and I made my way downstairs at a more sedate pace than my earlier dash to the ambulance. At this later hour, the streets were noisy and obstructed with traffic, and I was thankful that our first urgent hospital trip had gone so smoothly. At least I could use the creeping journey to alert my step-family to their father's illness. It wasn't quite the Tuesday morning I had planned, either.

Ian's eldest child, Alex, was the product of his first, short-lived marriage to Jane, while Sam and Maudie were his children with Laura.

Alex was my favourite of the Inglis clan, and he lived in Manchester with his wife Chloe, and young son Jack. He was a diffident, charming young man, who had been in a relationship with my daughter Olivia for some years after she left school. Ian's only child resident in London was Sam; an investment banker in his mid-thirties. Sam and I had a cool and distant relationship, because he actively resented the fact that I had married his father, although I thought privately it was time he got over this snit. I dialled his work number and swallowed hard, hoping that he would not be difficult with me today.

A glacial PA fielded my call, but when I explained what had happened, her manner changed, and she put me through at once. Sam's response was abrupt and irritated.

'Eithne? I hope this is important. I've been called out of a meeting.'

I explained the situation as succinctly as I could and was met by a loaded silence at the other end.

'Well, where are you? Shouldn't you be with him?'

There was an explosive edge to his voice which fired me up in an instant.

'Sam! Don't you think I would be with Ian if he was in any danger? I've been assured that he is stable for the moment, and I thought it would be sensible to come back to the flat to collect his things. Can you imagine your father wearing hospital pyjamas?'

I forced myself to breathe deeply to quell my annoyance. Falling out with Sam wouldn't help, but there were times when I longed to give him a sharp put-down. He had inherited the worst characteristics from both his parents, and his combination of Ian's tendency to dominate matters and Laura's self-satisfaction was not to my taste, although his father didn't seem to notice anything amiss. Sam was silent for a while, considering this question.

'No. You're right,' he said grudgingly. 'What do they think it is?'

'Something to do with his heart, but they need to run further tests. He will be kept in for a day or so at least. Can you find the time to visit him? I know he would like to see you,' I said, nobly repressing the fact that I wouldn't.

'When are visiting hours?'

'Afternoon and early evening. I'm going back now to deliver his personal things.'

'It would be more convenient for me to come tonight. But you must let me know at once if he takes a turn for the worse. And Eithne – make sure you get him into a private room.'

My backbone prickled with irritation at his tone of command, and I took a moment or two to calm myself before picking up my phone again. I could get no answer from Alex, and I left a voicemail, trying to make it sound matter-of-fact, because I didn't want to alarm him unduly.

My final call was to Ian's daughter, Maudie, in Scotland.

Maudie had married a Scottish laird and was fully occupied with running an estate which depended on attracting visitors for weddings and hunting n' fishing as much as farming. It was not an easy life, although she was devoted to her husband Alistair, and never complained about her lot. She was a sweet-natured girl, and her agonised voice told me just how distraught she was to hear the news about her father.

'Oh, poor Daddy! Should I come down? I could get a train later today, although I've got a couple booked in to discuss a wedding. I suppose Al might be able to handle it.'

'I don't think there is any need for you to drop everything and rush down here,' I said, adopting a confident, brisk manner in my efforts to reassure her. 'There is every reason to think that your father will make a full recovery. I'll ring you from the hospital with the latest news, and you can speak to him then, if they don't mind mobiles on the ward.'

I was hazy about hospital protocol. We had both been lucky with our health, and I could hardly remember Ian being ill, apart from the usual colds and tummy bugs which visiting grandchildren brought with them. Maudie hesitated, evidently torn between filial concern and the commercial demands of the estate.

'If you promise me that Daddy isn't in danger, I'll come to see him when he's back at home. The twins have some holiday coming up in a fortnight,' she said, heaving an anxious sigh.

'I'll see if the flat is free – if not, we'll squeeze you in with us.'

Ian had bought a second, small flat in the building where we lived, so we could accommodate visitors without disrupting our own lives.

'I love my family, but I don't want them on top of me,' Ian said firmly, and the second flat meant that we could enjoy the children and grandchildren without interrupting our normal routines, which were important to us as we grew older. We sometimes let the flat commercially to short-term visitors, but I didn't think there was anything scheduled in the next weeks.

Maudie's dilemma was almost palpable – I could imagine her twisting her hair round her fingers, in the way she did when she was agitated.

'Okay – I suppose that's sensible. But please keep me in the loop, Eithne. Darling Daddy... I hate to think of him in hospital. He won't be a good patient,' she added, and I smiled, as I pictured my difficult husband confined to a bed and hospital routines.

'No. But I'll make sure he behaves himself, so don't worry.'

Why were the streets so chaotic today? I began to think I should have made the journey on foot, but then the grey and gloomy buildings of the hospital loomed in the distance as my mobile beeped. Alex was calling from Manchester, and I quickly repeated my tale of the morning's drama.

'Poor Eithne. What a terrible shock for you,' he said warmly. 'You must look after yourself, too.'

I was cheered by this unexpected consideration for my feelings. It was typical of Alex to think of me as well as his father. He was a welcome contrast to his brother, and I had been devastated when he and Olivia parted company.

'Might you be able to get down to see him? I know he would like that,' I said, in hopeful tones, but his hesitant tone indicated problems to be overcome.

'Well, I can try. I promised Chloe that I would take Jack to his drama group this evening, and I know she has a Girls' Night which she wouldn't want to miss. But I'll see what I can do. Please give my very best love to Dad. I know you will be doing everything you can for him.'

A different kind of anxiety assailed me as I replaced my phone in my handbag. For some time, I'd been worried about Alex and what was going on in his marriage, and there had been an undercurrent of tension in his voice which made me pause for thought. But that would have to wait. My priority now was my husband.

Chapter Two

I was forced to navigate my way through several floors of the building before I found Ian, because there was genial confusion amongst the staff members I consulted as to his location. Everyone was helpful, but no-one knew where he was. Eventually, I ran him to ground in a four-bedded ward, where he lay immobile and disconsolate on a bed by the window. The sun streamed through the glass, but the light it cast was surprisingly muted and dusty, as though it reflected a shadowy and uncertain hold on life here.

'There you are! You've got a wonderful view of the Shard,' I said inanely, in the way that you struggle to put a better gloss on difficult situations. Ian's response was predictably growly and terse.

'This is intolerable. No-one has been near me for the last hour, and I haven't a clue what's going on,' he complained.

'Well, they can't be very worried about you, then. I expect you will have to wait for the next doctor's round to find out what treatment they have planned.'

We were both unsure how to behave in this unexpected and unnatural environment. Ian shrugged away from my kiss, but when he saw disappointment on my face, his expression softened, and he stretched out a hand to me.

'You look nice. I'm sorry to be such a bear,' he muttered, and I realised it was hard for him, a person who always took control of events, to be catapulted into a situation where he was at everyone else's mercy. I squeezed his hand and perched unsteadily on the side of the bed.

'Don't be silly, darling. This must be horrible for you. But let's hope your stay will be a short one.'

I leaned across, speaking in low tones, because I didn't want the other occupants of the ward to think I was denigrating them in any way. 'Would you like me to see if I can get you into a room on your own?' I breathed, but he shook his head.

'I don't think that's going to be possible. And I have told them we have insurance, but they say I'm better off seeing the NHS consultants here at this stage.'

We sat in silence for a few moments, thinking this over.

'Tom was awfully sorry to hear what happened. He asked me to pass on his best wishes, and he'll reschedule lunch as soon as you are up for it. I've contacted the children, and they all send love. Sam is hoping to be able to visit you this evening,' I said, searching to find something for Ian to look forward to.

It was almost one o'clock. A tray with a congealing mess of mince and cabbage was pushed to one side on the table by his bed, and I wrinkled my nose at it. Ian followed my gaze.

'I tried – but I couldn't,' he said faintly.

'I don't blame you,' I consoled him. But the food was a reminder that I had eaten nothing since our disrupted breakfast, which accounted for the disagreeable, hollow feeling inside me, and I reached for my handbag.

'Shall I get you something from the shop? Could you fancy a sandwich?' I suggested.

'A sandwich will be very welcome.'

He gazed mournfully into the distance, perhaps imagining the heaped plate of roast beef at Simpson's, where he had planned to meet Tom today, and I made my way back downstairs.

As I queued for the till, I looked with interest at my fellow shoppers. The small shop was crowded and busy. Harassed medical staff jostled with cleaners, clutching sandwiches and soft drinks, to be gulped down at a desk before tackling the next wave of demands. Ambulatory patients, looking like girdled dumplings in their bulky dressing gowns, juggled magazines and chocolate bars as they struggled to keep the tedium of their hospital confinement at bay.

I purchased fruit, sandwiches, and a bag of humbugs – Ian's weakness for these was well-known in the family. When I returned to the ward, a slim figure was standing at Ian's bedside, and I hurried up to hear what was being said. The doctor was a young Asian lady, whose shining dark hair was coiled into a long plait. Her white coat did not disguise an exotic presence and a sultry smile, and I hoped her patients' heart rates wouldn't be shooting sky-high because of this goddess-like apparition. She certainly had a regenerating effect on my husband, whose alert demeanour was very different to the apathetic figure I had left slumped on the bed, and a surge of wry amusement took the edge off my concern for him.

'This is my wife,' Ian told her, as I paused; not wanting to interrupt anything of importance.

'I have explained to your husband that we will be taking an ultrasound scan of his heart later today. He is scheduled for an angiogram tomorrow, because the most likely diagnosis is that he has a blocked artery, which will require a stent. If all goes well, he should be back at home very soon,' she said, and relief cannonballed through me. I had been anticipating surgery and a lengthy convalescence, but she made everything sound routine. Ian sighed after her as she moved off to another bay.

'What a lovely girl. And she evidently knows her stuff.'

His eyes followed her graceful progress, and I had to wave his sandwich before his face to recall him to the needs of his stomach. He picked it up, smiling mistily, and obviously remembering how his younger self would have chatted her up in an instant, and I didn't interrupt his few moments of fantasy. He looked down at his sandwich as though he'd never seen one before, and then came back to the present.

'Smoked salmon. Excellent. I am hungry now. It's a relief to know that they can sort me out, and she says the procedure is something they do every day.'

He took an appreciative bite, and I began to eat too, taking a covert look at the other occupants of the ward while I did so. A man aged around fifty occupied the bed opposite. The heaped mound of bedclothes swathed a Michelin tyre body, and he was snoring in a way which didn't bode well for the night.

An elderly gentleman lay in the bed nearest the door. He was attached to a bleeping machine, and I didn't like the pallid look of his skin, or his silent immobility – he was evidently seriously ill.

When he had eaten, Ian went to the bathroom to change into his pyjamas and dressing gown, before settling down with the paper in his bedside chair. I had bought him a fresh *Telegraph*, feeling that the copy at home was tainted with bad luck. The official visiting time had now begun, and I was surprised to see that the two visitors per patient rule was blithely unobserved.

The noise level of the ward rose dramatically. The overweight man's family had brought two screaming toddlers with them, and I was glad that Ian wasn't feeling particularly ill at this point. After one of the children had run across to us for the fourth time, whooping and kicking out at the bed frame, I went to the nursing station to enquire about the possibility of obtaining a private room. You would have thought I had requested a visit from the Queen.

'Those are reserved for patients recovering from surgery, or who require critical care,' a buttoned-up nurse retorted, making me feel as though I was well out of order. She had a point, but I didn't look forward to Sam's reaction when he saw I had failed to get his father some privacy.

Despite the hubbub, Ian eventually put down the paper and slept in his chair, while I stood guard to keep the toddlers at bay. A polite request to the parents to restrain them had been met with abuse, and I decided it wasn't worth escalating matters – or Ian's blood pressure – by complaining to the staff.

The frustrating afternoon wore away. I felt as though we had taken root there; that breakfast had almost been in another lifetime. But about five o'clock, two nurses appeared with a portable scanner, to make the ultrasound of Ian's heart. Blood was taken for testing, his pulse and blood pressure checked, and then the evening meal was wheeled in to the ward. This looked more palatable than lunch, and Ian managed to eat his chicken curry and fruit crumble without complaint.

'What will you do, my love? You must be starving,' Ian said, as he laid down his spoon.

'I'll get something later. I am not a bit hungry, so don't worry about me.'

The day's drama and upheaval had repressed my normal appetite. Now, the unnatural heat of the ward and the background drone of hospital noises made me feel almost jet-lagged, and it was harder and harder to smother the yawns which threatened to erupt as I lolled in my seat.

At least the ward was quieter. The screaming infants had been replaced by two women, and their hissing voices were raised in argument across the helpless bulk of their kinsman, who stared between them, his face vacant and resigned. I began to feel some sympathy for the patient. His visitors would hardly help his recovery, and they certainly didn't improve the atmosphere of the ward.

Perhaps Sam would not be able to make it. I glanced at my watch and felt guilty relief that I would avoid the potential conflict of his company. But the sound of clipped footsteps echoed down the corridor, and my spirits sank when I realised it was my stepson striding up to the bed: the cold, set lines of his face showing what he thought of his surroundings.

Sam wasn't as good-looking as his father, although his expensive suit and air of smug self-possession made him difficult to ignore. All the other people on the ward stopped talking to gape at him as he banged down his briefcase on the floor with an exasperated thump.

'My God, Father! I'm so sorry to see you in here. I told Eithne to get you into a private room.'

He leaned down to embrace his father with exaggerated care, then glanced round with an air of manifest distaste. Ian murmured something indistinct, and I went to fetch another chair, but Sam remained standing over the bed; adopting an air of authority as though he was a consultant himself. He had a long list of questions to put to us, but we couldn't answer very many to his satisfaction, owing to the lack of a definite diagnosis. Sam's frustration was apparent in his barking tone, and after a while I began to lose patience as well.

'Please, Sam – I know you'd like to see your father being treated privately, but it's better to use the NHS at this stage,' I said, trying to keep an equally sharp note from my voice. 'Let's just get him through the next day or so with the procedures here, and we can see a private specialist if it's necessary when he's back at home.'

Sam's expression could have curdled milk. I knew he would take no notice of my opinions, and he turned back to his father.

'I'd like to talk to whoever is in charge here. I'll be back shortly.'

He stomped off to the nursing station, and Ian pulled nervously at his sheets, trying to smooth things over.

'Sam only wants what's best for me. Don't be put out,' he urged, seeing my furious face.

'Don't you think I want that too? But Sam needs to understand that you can't always make something happen by throwing money at it.'

This was the closest I had come to criticising Sam in all our years together, and Ian's face was thoughtful, but he didn't respond. An uneasy silence enveloped us until Sam returned, slightly pink in the cheeks, and with an angry glint in his eye.

'It's hopeless. I can't get any confirmation of what's wrong with you, and there don't seem to be any private rooms available.'

I could have told him that but forbore to inflame the situation. Sam surveyed the ward, throwing the other patients and their visitors a glance which should have slain them all on the spot.

'I am so sorry, Father. Can you bear it in here for a night or two? At least they seem to think that if all goes smoothly with the angiogram, you will be discharged afterwards.'

Ian nodded. His face had gradually grown pinched and grey again, and exhaustion was apparent in the deep furrows of his forehead. I was anxious that he got some rest and respite from Sam's hectoring, so it came as a relief when the bell rang to signal the end of visiting hours. I rose, smoothing Ian's silvery head; my affectionate smile hiding the fact that I desperately needed time to myself now, to come to terms with the upsetting events of the day. My chest felt tense and tight, and I was conscious of the pounding of my own rapid heartbeats.

'I hate to leave you, dearest, but you need to get some sleep. I will be here tomorrow, just as soon as they will let me in. Good luck with the angiogram, and remember that we are all thinking of you,' I said, and Ian held me tightly, returning my caresses, although the thin lips of his son indicated disapproval of this public display of affection. Sam bent down to bid his father a more dignified farewell and emitted a horrified gasp.

'Eithne! I can't believe that Father is still wearing his Rolex. Don't you know how much petty theft goes on in hospitals? You must take it back home with you at once.'

He slid the watch from his father's wrist and presented it to me with an exaggerated flourish, leaving me feeling absurdly like a conjuror's assistant as I stowed it in my bag. Expensive watches held no significance for me, although I was annoyed all over again by the presumption that I was neglecting my duty to his father. The Rolex was insured, but it had been a gift from a company Ian had worked for, and it held some sentimental value for him, although it had been the last thing on my mind until now. The niggly little episode clouded our goodbyes, and it was an effort to keep tears from filling my eyes as we waited for the lift to arrive, although I was determined not to let myself cry in front of Sam.

My comfortable bed and a mug of cocoa were calling to me, but Sam surprised me in a different way as we left the hospital and strolled into a soft and muted London dusk.

'I don't suppose you've had dinner, Eithne. Would you care to come for a meal now, if it isn't too late for you?'

Refusal trembled on my tongue, but the sandwich had been a very long time ago, and the thought of cobbling something together at the flat wasn't appealing. Perhaps I ought to accept his invitation – perhaps this was a kind of peace offering after the sharp words on the ward.

'Won't Emma be expecting you?' I asked, playing for time.

'No. I told her I would grab a bite before going home. Let's take a cab, and we can talk some more about Father.'

The restaurant Sam selected was dim and expensive, and I slid into the banquette as unobtrusively as I could, conscious that I wasn't clad in strappy, glittery evening dress like the other female diners. However, a restorative G and T coursed through me with instant effect, and I began to look forward to my meal, although I was never wholly at my ease with Sam. I regretted Emma's absence, because she could always be relied on to provide a safety net of chatter about their children.

But Sam was more affable now we were away from the hospital. He enquired politely about my own family, and I gave him a succinct summary, before switching the conversation back to Inglis affairs. I knew he was merely feigning interest in my side of things.

'Emma's landed a couple of commissions lately. Her Ma's been drumming up suitable clients,' he announced, and I expressed diplomatic approval. Emma claimed to be an interior designer, although she worked on a very part-time basis, and I felt she was destined to be a dabbler rather than a grafter. She and Sam had three children. Amelia attended nursery school and Simon was still a baby, but they had despatched Oliver to prep school at a regrettably early age. Much was demanded of him as the eldest child, and I frequently felt concerned about the weight of expectation which had settled upon his skinny frame.

'Oliver's been slacking recently. He'll be getting a tutor in the summer hols if he doesn't shape up.'

I could hardly bear the reproof in Sam's voice. Poor Ollie – surely Ian hadn't been like this with his own offspring? I couldn't say what I wanted, which was to urge Sam to cut the poor little lad some slack, so I was relieved when the conversation returned to the patient. Now Sam was intent on further cross-examination.

'Hadn't you noticed anything different about Father recently? Has he been complaining about pain anywhere? When did he last get a proper check-up from his GP?'

His questions hammered at me, and I grew confused. Exhaustion and gin fogged my responses, and I saw that Sam was exasperated. But there was an underlying accusation that I had not been taking sufficient care of his father, and I wasn't going to accept that.

'You know that we walk everywhere in town, and Ian still plays tennis once a week. He is far from over-weight, and the GP considers that he's quite fit for his age, Sam. The only thing he hasn't done is take statins, because they give him an unacceptable level of muscle pain,' I countered, and Sam frowned over his soup.

'The timing of this is most unfortunate. I'm relying on you to keep a closer eye on him in future, Eithne. We're very lucky the outcome isn't more serious.'

Why did I get the feeling that Sam's concern wasn't just centred on his father's health? I picked up my wineglass, but the next question almost made me drop it again.

'I don't suppose you know the details of Father's will?' he enquired, with an unsuccessful attempt at nonchalance, and I felt as though I'd received a blow to my stomach. Ian wasn't about to die, and I considered that this question was in very poor taste.

'Well, only very roughly.'

The hastily dampened avaricious gleam in Sam's eye made me unwilling to divulge such information as I possessed. 'If he predeceases me, I have the use of our flat here for my lifetime, and I am entitled to a quarter share in the French house. But I don't know how he has disposed of his capital.'

This was untrue. I knew that Ian had divided the bulk of his estate between his three children and me, although I would have a lesser share than his direct descendants. I could almost see calculations taking place in Sam's head. He glanced at me, frowning, and then looked away again. With the difference in age, it was likely that I would survive my husband, and no doubt this was another irritant.

After this tetchy exchange, he retreated behind a screen of superficial barbs, and I concentrated on my steak. Eating meant that conversation could be kept to a minimum, although there was one subject I wanted to get his opinion on while I had the chance.

'Have you seen Alex and Chloe recently?' I enquired. 'I have a funny feeling that all isn't quite right there. Alex is always so cagey on the telephone, and they haven't visited us in months.'

Sam's shrug told me that I couldn't expect to hear anything useful from him. He had little time for his half-brother – he and Alex had never been close. And none of us had ever got to know Chloe well; something which caused me increasing pangs of guilt.

She and Alex had a shotgun wedding owing to her pregnancy, and Ian had been exasperated with his son, because he felt the couple were so unsuited. There was a big difference in age, education and family background, and Chloe wasn't interested in getting a job. Her days were spent undergoing beauty treatments and lunching with her girlfriends, and Alex had occasionally applied to his father for a loan to cover an expense which he couldn't meet. I knew he was embarrassed at having to do it. Ian didn't grudge him the money but hated to think he was subsidising a lifestyle which he disapproved of.

'Chloe. She's a total nightmare,' Sam pronounced, sounding smugly pleased at the thought. 'We have very little to do with them, so I can't help you there. Alex made his bed, and he'll have to lie on it.'

I wanted to lean across the table and whack him. Sometimes, I suspected that Sam would like to eliminate Alex from the Inglis world altogether, but that was not going to happen. Ian's divorce from his first wife had been messy, and he had been estranged from Alex as a small boy, but they had established a close bond in later years, and I knew that Ian regretted his absence in Alex's childhood. I didn't think Ian would allow Sam to side-line his half-brother, much as Sam might want to do that.

We finished our meal in silence, and I began to succumb to the urge to close my eyes, because I felt drained by the long and difficult day. Little scenes and sounds from the hospital danced inside my head, and I had to concentrate hard to keep up my end of the conversation.

'Coffee?' Sam enquired, as the dishes were removed. 'I don't suppose you eat pudding – I expect you have to watch your weight.'

His rudeness revived me. I didn't consider myself fat, and was about to utter a sarcastic retort, but he cut across me unexpectedly.

'There's something else I've been meaning to speak to you about for a long time, and after today, I can't put it off any longer. I suppose you realise that I know about you and Father in Cheshire?' he drawled, and now an ugly grimace twisted his mouth as he spoke.

I froze.

'Know what?'

Panic constricted my throat. I forced my eyes to challenge his and was horrified by the calculating disdain I read there.

'Oh, come on, Eithne. I know you had an affair. I overheard Father on the phone to you when we were away on that skiing trip, and then you lost a baby... perhaps that was just as well. I don't think my mother would have given him up. You'd have come off second best there.'

'None of this has any relevance now.'

I hardly recognised the tight voice with which I tried to rebuff him. What was he hoping to gain by dredging up the past, especially today? I scrabbled in my bag, and dropped some notes on the table, but he caught my wrist in a cold grip.

'My treat.'

He thrust the money back at me. 'But Eithne; I don't believe your children know the truth about any of this. I have never let on to anyone, although that doesn't mean I approve of what you did. Would you like them to understand that you cheated on Peter? I hope I'll never be obliged to share your secret.'

My head throbbed painfully. His words amounted to blackmail, but I had no idea why he considered it was appropriate to attack me like this. Wasn't the best way to tackle bullies to stand up to them? I decided to fight, although I felt like a kitten arching its back before a mastiff.

'Are you threatening me, Sam? I can tell you that your father would be very unhappy if he knew about this. Do you want to make him even more stressed, in his current circumstances? That won't help his recovery,' I retorted, making my voice more assertive than I felt. Sam gazed at me, biting his lower lip, as though this aspect had not occurred to him.

'I want to make sure I can count on your support in future,' he said, after a lengthy, considering pause. 'Not just about Father's health, but regarding another project I have in mind. I know that he listens to you...' (and his face showed very clearly that he found this fact both surprising and annoying.) 'That could be important. I need to be confident that you won't interfere when it comes to the finances. But this isn't the time to go into details.'

'You can't just leave things in the air after what you have said!' I protested, but he rose to his feet and made to help me on with my coat. And I suddenly felt exhausted and unwilling to suffer him any longer. I needed the comfort of my home surroundings, and my own company. I stood aside, looking away, while he paid the bill, and allowed him to usher me into a waiting taxi when we walked out into the darkening night.

'Goodnight, Eithne. I'd be grateful if you could let me know how things go with Father tomorrow, so I'll know if I need to visit the hospital again.'

His face was a polite mask, but I was conscious that it concealed dislike and frustration. My farewell was equally cold, and I slumped in my seat, willing the tension in my body to evaporate as the taxi turned homewards.

Sam's threats had unsettled me more than the events of the morning. The affair in Cheshire was now in the distant past, and the two people most likely to be hurt by any revelation were no longer living. But I knew that my children might react emotionally and adversely to the knowledge, and I would do anything to prevent that happening.

Chapter Three

I could hardly complain about my life with Ian. In comparison with many people, I knew that I was very fortunate, but it was a source of constant regret to me that I saw so little of my own children.

Nicholas, the much-loved son from my relationship with Nick, had married an Australian girl, Patti, and although he made occasional noises about 'coming home', I feared that home was now the other side of the world. I had to be content with skyping his family – his two sons, Freddie and Finlay, were growing up fast – and it wasn't a great substitute for rough hugs from cheeky grandsons. Ian had promised me that we would pay them a visit, but that might have to wait now.

My younger daughter, Louisa, had made her home in New England. She had celebrated her veterinary degree by taking time out to travel, and she looked up our old friends in America during her time abroad.

One of these friends was Josh, the son unwittingly fathered by Nick, when he was working in New York during his early twenties. It was Josh whose eruption into our lives had caused such a shock while Louisa was still a schoolgirl. Since then, he had become an accepted part of our family, albeit at a distance.

Lou always had a soft spot for the shy young man who had been searching for his identity, and now, he was happily astounded by the pretty butterfly who had emerged from a stolid, guinea-pig loving chrysalis. She didn't return home, but married Josh, and began a new life with him and their two small daughters, who had inherited her love for animals. I knew that she was settled and happy with Josh, and I was pleased with the unexpected family link, but it was hard to lose another child to a life abroad.

And Olivia flitted from place to place, unattached and often unhappy, although she would never admit it. She had split from Alex when she was in her early twenties, declaring that she wanted to see the world before becoming tied to anyone, and it was impossible to argue with her once she had made up her mind. Peter's death sapped her youthful spirit, and I think she felt that by staying away from England, she might escape some of her sorrow.

Her reaction to the news that Ian and I were living together was a shrug and a satirically raised eyebrow, and the comment that 'she hoped I would be satisfied now.' I wasn't sure what she meant by that and took care not to pursue the topic. She didn't know about our ill-judged affair, but she recognised that there had always been an attraction between us.

The pay-out after Peter's death had given her a degree of financial independence, and she continued her wandering ways. There were times when she began a new relationship, but nothing seemed to satisfy her for long. Now, she was living in Florence with an Italian with whom she was running a restaurant, and I had seen nothing of her since the previous Christmas.

Although I was shattered by the events of the day, I knew that sleep would elude me unless I could dismiss the gloomy thoughts which swamped my mind. Ian's absence was tangible. The flat seemed lifeless without his tall frame and the echo of his deep voice; it was a hostile, uninhabited territory. I longed for sleep but dreaded it too. On two other occasions in my life, I had been forced to come to terms with an unexpectedly empty bed, and the sight of my nightdress on the pillow without Ian's pyjamas lying snugly adjacent brought an unwelcome reminder of wretched nights in the past.

I didn't feel able to cope with more surprise and sympathy, even if the feelings were genuine. However, I sent quick e-mails to my children to let them know about Ian's hospital admission, and the simple act of typing acted as a soporific. When I finally crept under the duvet an enervated and dreamless slumber overtook me, and I was only too willing to succumb.

Next morning, I stretched out a hand, and for a moment, the cool space beside me was confusing. Then the jumble of sirens, corridors and white coats which had invaded my dreams clarified into reality. I scrambled into my dressing gown and dialled the hospital, anxious to know whether Ian had passed a peaceful night, but there was no answer from the ward. Ring back, the switchboard lady told me, the staff are probably busy with breakfast and medications. I cursed the fact that I'd forgotten the charger for Ian's mobile when I packed his gear the previous day, and there was no way I could contact him directly.

I found myself averting my eyes as I picked up yesterday's paper from where it lay creased on the floor – it was a painful reminder of our unwanted drama. But I had barely swallowed the last crumbs of my breakfast before the telephone demanded my attention. The bush telegraph had swung into action, and I had to field a barrage of calls from friends and more distant relations, all anxious to know the latest on Ian's health. Most of the callers were genuinely anxious to hear that there was nothing serious amiss, although one or two seemed to be hoping for a more dramatic outcome. It was some time before I could call the ward again, and this time, I got through immediately.

The nurse told me that Ian was stable, and his angiogram was scheduled for the morning. I couldn't visit until early afternoon, but as I picked up the phone again, to cancel my morning arrangement to meet a friend, I hesitated. Some congenial company might be just what I needed to get me through the anxious hours of waiting.

Sophia and I had one of those friendships which comes and goes over the years. It hadn't begun well. She floored me with ease in our university days; her sharp wit and flamboyant personality always keeping her several steps ahead of the naïve girl from the provinces, but age and experience had toughened me and tamed her, so that we met now on friendly and compassionate terms. She had married late in life to a retired diplomat, and we saw one another often in London.

The day held enough promise of spring to encourage me to discard my winter clothes and select jeans and a linen jacket from my wardrobe. Sunbeams picked out and polished the stone curlicues of the Victorian buildings by the river as I walked, and the city bustle seemed more purposeful than usual, as though spirits were blossoming in the unaccustomed warmth.

There was no sign of Sofia when I reached the café where we agreed to meet – no surprise there, as she operated to her own timetable, and I was used to her tardiness. I chose an outdoor table, mentally bidding goodbye to the confines of winter, and settled down to people-watching.

Was there an upmarket version of a bag lady? If so, I decided that Sofia would qualify, with her flowing hair, her loose, brightly-coloured garments and clashing scarves. But she made it look acceptably individual and almost chic, whereas I would have resembled the parish jumble sale in a similar outfit. She sashayed up, kissed me with hearty delight, entranced the serving staff, and settled herself beside me with a satisfied sigh.

The tale of Ian's woes came tumbling out of me and her dark eyes widened in sympathy.

'Poor Ian – and poor you, darling! What a beastly experience for you both.'

There was real warmth and consolation in the hug she gave me, and the concern on her face pierced my defences. I had kept myself together up to this point, but now I was glad that my dark glasses allowed me the indulgence of a little weep. Sofia waited until I was more composed, and then summoned a waitress.

'Two of your hugest, stickiest pastries,' she ordered, and I wiped my eyes, managing a bleary smile.

'Sorry. It hasn't exactly been a fun time. I was so frightened, but I think he will be okay now.'

'Well, of course he will be okay! Ian is a tough old bird, and St Thomas's is an excellent hospital.' She sipped her coffee; contemplative. 'Isn't that where you ran across Nick again, when he had pneumonia after coming back from America?'

'Yes. That seems like someone else's life now.'

I had no desire to revisit those days of mingled pain and excitement and was relieved when an enormous croissant was placed before me, studded with flaked nuts and oozing almond cream. Sofia seized hers and nibbled at it with an approving growl.

'Eat, Eithne. You need to keep strong for Ian. Now is not the time to go soggy at the edges.'

'I don't intend to sog.'

I spoke sharply, but I couldn't maintain a dignified front with icing sugar coating my chin, and reluctant laughter overcame me as I caught Sofia's eye.

'That's better. Let us be thankful that there are ways of dealing with these problems. I know we take our health for granted, but time always catches up with us,' she said.

We finished our croissants, and lingered, wrapped in the welcome warmth of the morning. Sofia sighed, stretching, and flinging back the wayward edge of a scarf, looking as though she was about to make an important announcement.

'Getting old... that was never part of my plan,' she mused, and I thought back to her vibrant undergraduate days. Sofia would never lose her youthful outlook, and that was the basis of her attraction. 'Even so, I must admit that some things don't come so easily now. Do you remember that wonderful feeling when we were at Oxford; that we were immortal, and could achieve anything we wanted?'

I reflected on that liberating time. Perhaps I'd never achieved exactly what I wanted, or more likely, I hadn't really known what I wanted. 'Anyway, don't let's depress ourselves,' she continued. 'Have I told you where Michael and I are off to next month?'

She swept me along in her exuberant wake, and for a while, my own cares receded. But unease nagged at me as the time came to depart to the hospital again. I didn't like to think that Ian had undergone a painful, horrible morning while I lounged in the sunshine with a friend: it didn't seem fair. Sofia took my hand as I rose to leave and squeezed it emphatically.

'Eithne... you must be prepared for this incident to have shaken Ian. You will have to tread carefully with him when he gets home,' she urged, and I frowned, not understanding what she was trying to tell me.

'I know he will need a period of recovery,' I began, but she held my hand more tightly, as if anxious to stress her point.

'I don't mean that. He may need to make a psychological adjustment of some kind. I suspect he might feel he's looked death in the face, and that can be hard to come to terms with,' she said baldly, and I felt a chill whisper of unease.

'Ian is such a positive, sensible person. I think he'll be fine,' I said firmly, as if saying the words would make them happen. However, her caution stayed uppermost in my mind, and I walked into the hospital with barely suppressed anxiety – only to find that Ian had been moved again. At least we would be spared the toddlers from hell today.

Ian had been transferred into a much larger ward, which was buzzing with visitors. He was lying on his bed, very still and pale of face, and with a bandage wrapped around one wrist. There was a curious, dead-leaf look to his skin, as though it had suddenly been stretched too tightly, and I felt a little flutter of concern as I bent down to hug him. A lady at the next bedside gawped at us with ill-concealed curiosity, causing me to chafe at the lack of privacy in these personal moments.

'Darling... how was the angiogram? Will they let you come home now?' I murmured, hoping that the back I turned on the next bay didn't look too impolite. Ian shook his head, resignation clouding his eyes.

'I have had two stents fitted, because they found that a couple of arteries were almost completely blocked. They tell me I have been lucky in avoiding a fatal heart attack,' he said grimly, and I shuddered to myself as I thought of the narrow escape from a lurking horror. 'I don't think they will let me out today, because my blood pressure has soared, and my pulse rate hasn't settled. My chest hurts,' he added, sounding for a moment like a suffering child, and I stroked his head.

'At least they have dealt with the problem. You won't be in here for much longer, my love.'

I intended my cheerful tone to brace him, but he was determinedly gloomy. A pneumatic little nurse came to the bedside, brandishing equipment.

'Time to check your pulse and BP again, Ian,' she told him, and I held my breath as the cuff tightened and deflated around his upper arm, but she shook her head when she had finished. 'Better than last time, but still too high. I don't think you will be going home today,' she advised, and he drooped once more. I cast around for something to distract him.

'Sam and I went for a meal last night. It was good to catch up on all his family news,' I exclaimed brightly. Like Pinocchio, my nose should have lengthened dramatically with this huge lie, but Ian seemed pleased to hear this, and I massaged his unbandaged hand as we sat there, hoping that an affectionate touch would be soothing for him. I exerted myself to amuse, and an occasional wintry smile crossed his face, but I realised that Sofia had been right. It would take both of us time to adjust to this unlooked-for experience, and to the painful knowledge that other problems would be lying in wait for our ageing bodies.

I persuaded him to text his children to update them with the results of the angiogram, and then I visited the shop to buy some delicacies. However, before we could finish eating a bunch of grapes, we were interrupted by a curt greeting, and Sam graced us with his presence once again. Ian recounted the events of his morning, and Sam immediately vented his displeasure that his father was not about to be discharged.

'Who carried out the stent placement?' he demanded, pulling out his phone. Ian hesitated, but told him the name of the consultant, and Sam tapped away busily. Curiosity needled me.

'What are you doing?' I asked, trying not to let my irritation show. After yesterday's exchange in the restaurant, I wasn't feeling well disposed towards my stepson.

'I am looking up the rating of the consultant on a medical website,' he said grudgingly, and I prayed that he would have the tact to keep any adverse feedback to himself. Luckily, whatever he found seemed to satisfy him, and he snapped his phone shut without further comment.

'When you do get out, Father, we want to spend more family time with you. Ollie is at school of course, but it will be nice for you to see the little ones, and Emma says to tell you that she has been working on some exciting ideas for your flat. I worry that we have been so busy with our own lives of late that we've neglected you – and I intend to make up for that.'

Sam's voice was emollient, but I examined my fingernails, thinking angrily that this was a step too far on his part. Ian wasn't very interested in or enthusiastic about small children, and surely any decorative changes in our flat should stem from our own wishes? Perhaps this was another effort to make me aware that Sam considered me to be of little consequence, and I was pleased to hear my husband's response.

'That's good of you Sam. Tell Emma we'd appreciate her advice next time we are contemplating anything of that nature. But I will want a few quiet weeks at home now – I'm sure you understand.'

'Maudie is coming down with the twins very soon,' I added, with a cheerful lack of tact. 'We can get together for a family celebration.'

Sam's cold grey eyes contemplated me with ill-concealed irritation as he took in this information. '*You* are not family,' he was thinking. But he sensed Ian's lack of enthusiasm and adroitly changed the subject, seeking to interest his father in some business gossip before getting to his feet again.

'I'm afraid I'll have to go. I'm due in the City for a meeting with Wesendorps. Chin up, Father. Next time I see you, you'll be at home again, I'm sure.'

He hugged his father, waved a limp hand at me, and strode off down the room, sending waves of disapprobation in all directions. Ian and I sat in silence for a while after Sam had left; feeling perhaps that his visit was best left unremarked on. Eventually, Ian could stifle his yawns no longer.

'I meant what I said to Sam – the prospect of a few quiet days at home is very appealing. In fact, I feel knackered now, because I slept so badly last night. Would you mind if I took a nap, darling?'

'No, of course not. I think I'll go for a stroll on the South Bank rather than sit around here, though; it's such a glorious day.'

We held one another close; the embrace saying so much more than words. Then I helped him to settle down in the bed and watched quietly as he drifted into sleep. I cocooned him in with drawn curtains, and tiptoed away, certain that rest was the best thing for him after the trying procedures of the morning.

The South Bank made a welcome contrast to the subdued interior of the hospital. Everything was merry with colour and lively noise, and the river sparkled as the incoming tide slapped against the embankment. Little bursts of spray shot up and startled the seabirds as they perched on the grey stone walls, bringing a smile to my face as they squawked and jostled for position. I found a seat and checked my phone, and discovered messages of support from Louisa and Nicholas, which warmed and cheered me.

But a surprise was waiting when I returned to the hospital. Ian was talking with animation to a figure by his bedside, and as I hurried up, I saw that it was Alex, his elder son.

Alex jumped to his feet when he caught sight of me.

'Eithne!'

He kissed me with affection and I hugged him in return, really delighted to see him, although my pleasure was tempered by the sight of a huge bruise on his cheekbone.

'Alex! Whatever have you done to yourself?'

He grimaced, blushing painfully like an awkward adolescent.

'I walked into a door at home. Unfortunately, I didn't have the courage to borrow some of Chloe's make-up – I might have been able to make myself look less alarming. But I had to get down here to see Dad.'

His voice stuttered as he turned anxious eyes on his father, and I grasped his arm, giving it a reassuring squeeze. I hoped that Ian appreciated this genuine concern, because I suspected he was often unobservant about the finer points of his sons' personalities. Sam was, in many ways, a younger version of his father – career minded, forceful and energetic – but he lacked Ian's charisma, and his approach to personal matters echoed his mother's acquisitive and overweening nature.

I had never known Alex's mother, Jane, because she had moved to America after she and Ian divorced, but I understood that she was a reasonable, gentle woman, who had shaped her son in a similar mould. There were times when I found myself fighting for Alex's corner, because it was too easy for his dominant half-sibling to assume first place, and I didn't think that was fair. I knew that Sam loved his father, but he was also alive to the benefits which Ian could bestow, in a way which Alex would never contemplate. Being in Alex's company was far less stressful for me than when Sam was present, and I was very cheered by his presence at the bedside.

We spoke for a while about Ian's health, but during a lull in conversation, Alex turned to me with a shy eagerness in his face.

'Have you heard from Olivia recently?'

His eyes and voice softened as he spoke her name. I had seen a similar expression when he talked about his son Jack, but I could not recall him speaking of Chloe with equal warmth, and an old feeling of sadness nagged at me. I wished so much that Alex and Olivia had stayed together.

'You know what a wanderer she is. She's living in Italy, and she is involved in some restaurant venture. I have e-mailed her to tell her about your father, but she hasn't responded yet.'

'Give her my love when you next contact her. It's been ages since we met,' he murmured; reflective now.

'Tell me how Jack is getting on at school.'

I wanted to switch the talk to a less emotive topic. Jack was aged eight, and Alex beamed as he recounted Jack's prowess at primary school, and his enthusiasm for his extra-curricular activities. I couldn't help contrasting Alex's attitude with that of Sam towards poor Oliver – *'Ollie's been slacking; he'll be getting a tutor'* – and wondered which child had the more enjoyable life, despite the difference in household prosperity and status.

And it was only polite to enquire about Chloe, but Alex's face grew wary at the mention of her name.

'She's fine. She's extra busy just now, because she's got the chance to do some modelling work for a friend of hers. It means having a professional photographic portfolio done, and she's over the moon about it,' he said, trying to inject a note of enthusiasm into his voice. It didn't sound convincing to me.

Chloe was in her late twenties; much younger than Alex, but I was surprised to think she might be considered suitable model material, although she always projected a superficial, heavily made-up glamour. What sort of modelling might it be? I had a funny feeling that I didn't really want to know.

Chapter Four

Alex insisted on staying until the end of visiting hours. A doctor confirmed that if Ian's blood pressure stabilised he would be allowed home the next day, and so the mood was more buoyant as we said our goodbyes. I remembered guiltily that the Rolex was still in my handbag and made a mental note to remove it as soon as I was home again.

'Are you rushing to get a train back?' I asked Alex as we left the ward. He had been sending and receiving texts during the last hour, and he turned preoccupied eyes upon me; shoving the phone into his pocket as though he was irritated with it.

'I do have to get back tonight, but I can get a late train. I'd been hoping to hook up with Sam, but he says he can't make it.'

No surprises there – however, I sensed there was an underlying anxiety in the way Alex spoke, which wasn't just about his father. His face looked creased with stress, and whatever was worrying him tentacled out and snagged me too. I was sure that he needed to get something off his chest.

'How about a quick bite before you leave for the station? I saw a little Italian place by the bridge when I was walking today. On me, of course,' I added, in case the cost was a worry for him. He glanced down at his feet and then up at me, and there was a sliding hesitancy in his eyes.

'Okay. That would be nice. It will have to be quick, though. I'll be in for it if I miss the last train.'

His clumsy attempt at a smile left me in no doubt as to who would be dishing out the chastisement if he didn't get back on time.

The trattoria was homely and relaxed, and I had no embarrassment tonight about the way I was dressed. Alex hunched over the menu, frowning and distracted, but I didn't think he was worrying about what food to order. I poured him a large glass of wine and kept the chat light until he was looking a little less tense.

'Did you want to see Sam about anything special?' I enquired, and a painful flush rose to his face. He crumpled his napkin with nervous fingers, and took a deep, confessional breath.

'Promise me you won't tell Dad, Eithne. I don't want him bothered at present, for obvious reasons.'

I nodded; apprehension settling its heavy hand upon me – what could be coming? Alex sighed, and took courage from another mouthful of wine. 'I had no idea that this stuff Chloe is doing would cost so much to get off the ground. The clothes and the photography ... my overdraft is up to the limit, and I'd hoped Sam might be able to help me out in the short term.'

This statement incensed me. I had a fair idea that the overdraft was entirely down to Chloe's excesses, because Alex and Jack didn't have expensive tastes. Didn't she understand the family finances?

'Can't she get a job, to help out?' I asked, with ill-concealed impatience, but he shook his head.

'She says she has her hands full getting this going, and with Jack, of course. And I want to keep things happy at home, for Jack's sake.'

I could read all sorts of uncomfortable things into this statement. Alex gazed at me across the table, his eyes doleful, like those of a mournful dog. 'I know what you think,' he muttered. 'I wish I could give her all the things she wants. It's hard to say no, because we all suffer when she's upset.'

I repressed my first instinct, which was to retort sharply that Chloe needed a good smacked bottom and a lesson in economic realities.

'Alex – I have to say that I don't approve of what Chloe is doing.'

It was an effort to keep my voice sounding reasonable. 'You need to get it across to her that she can't behave like a spoiled child and hold you to ransom.'

He looked away again, but not before I had seen real unhappiness in his face. An idea floated into my head, and I seized it. 'But, thanks to your father, I am very comfortably off. I am happy to let you have a loan, although there are two conditions attached. One is that you don't let Ian know, and the other is that you and Chloe sign up for counselling, or guidance of some sort. Otherwise, I'm not sure I can see a future for your marriage.'

It was hard to sound admonitory when I really wanted to reach out and hug him. He was such a lovely man, but he was completely at the mercy of his avaricious wife, because there was a hostage – Jack. Would he be able to summon the courage to give Chloe the plain talking she needed?

Alex sat with his head bent, mulling over what I had said to him. After a while, he looked up, bleak and guilty.

'It's three thousand pounds,' he said, with a little gulp.

'Well, that's not chicken feed, but I can let you have it without too much difficulty. But Alex, you *must* start being tougher with Chloe. You have let her get away with things for too long. She is an adult: she should be able to understand that she can't spend what you don't have.'

The jolly little waiter was puzzled by our long faces. He served our pasta with smiling and vocal encouragement to eat and enjoy the food, and we turned to our plates as a welcome distraction.

'Lecture over. You know I just want you to be happy,' I said to Alex, picking up my fork and forcing a smile, although I felt hollowed by sadness inside. 'The money isn't a problem, but you need to man up, Alex. And for what it's worth, I'm glad you didn't mention this to Sam. I don't think he would understand.'

And neither would he have offered to help.

Alex was evidently unhappy, but he ate his pasta, and his brow cleared a little. He had always been attracted to women with a mind of their own – Olivia certainly fell into that category – but whilst he had made a working partnership with her during their time together, selfish, predatory Chloe could outwit him with ease. Feelings of anger pricked me as I ate. He was too nice a person to be taken advantage of in this way.

'I am sorry that I haven't got to know Chloe better,' I said, wondering if it was too late now to make a difference. 'It's always difficult when you live at a distance, but I know that isn't a good enough excuse. I feel that we could have helped in some way.'

Alex shook his head.

'It isn't your fault. I have tried often enough to get her to visit you, but she's terrified of Dad, and I can see that they have nothing in common. And the only time we went to Sam's, Emma was so bloody condescending... no; we don't fit in down here. But I'd like it if you came to see us sometimes, because I do feel a bit isolated.'

What a sad statement. Guilt stole over me, although I could see that there were lots of reasons why families could fragment in this way. Something more than mere goodwill was required to bridge the gaps when different social classes and aspirations clashed – it needed sympathy and understanding on both sides, and we had all fallen short. Perhaps the best we could hope for now was some sort of truce at a distance. Alex laid his hand on my arm with anxious pressure.

'Don't tell Dad,' he cautioned again, and I nodded. I didn't like having secrets from my husband, but this was something best kept between Alex and me.

We finished our meal, and I paid the bill. Alex was beginning to fret about making his train, and I summoned an Uber to take him to Euston.

'I'll arrange a bank transfer first thing tomorrow.'

I kissed him goodbye, wanting to smooth the trepidation from his forehead, and conscious that his own mother was very far away. 'Don't worry about paying it back just yet, because I'd rather you got to grips with your overdraft. And please don't worry about your father. I will take good care of him.'

'I know you will. Thanks, Eithne; thanks for everything'

Poor Alex. I understood from his hang-dog expression that he hated to take money from me, but he didn't have a choice. I gave his hand a little squeeze, and he exclaimed and winced. Turning the hand over, I noticed an angry looking gash on his palm.

'My God, Alex, that looks sore! What on earth did you do?'

He snatched his hand back, shielding it from my gaze with an awkward movement.

'I think I'm a bit accident prone at present. I'll get to the doctor if it doesn't heal soon.'

'Please don't ask me about it.'

That was what I read in his eyes, and I drew back, although a very nasty suspicion began to filter through to me. I stood on the pavement as his Uber pulled away, trying to reconcile the warring thoughts in my head. At least he hadn't gone to Sam with his request for money. I could just hear Sam's cool, derisory voice as he twitted his half-brother, and he would not have understood the situation one little bit.

I was pierced with remorse that we hadn't made more efforts to involve ourselves with Alex and his family in recent years. I began to hatch little plans for visiting Manchester or luring Chloe down to London, although common sense told me that things like that would need to wait until Ian was better. When I got back to the flat, I carried out a dutiful response to the e-mails enquiring after Ian's progress, but there was nothing from Olivia, and I was surprised at the sense of disappointment which lingered amongst all the other emotions of the day. I was worried about the children, and anxious about my husband, and the only glimpses of light on my horizon this evening were the watery gleams along the embankment; transient and intangible.

Next morning, the landline shrilled in my ear, and I struggled back to consciousness. A jubilant Ian announced that he was due to be discharged during the morning and was now in urgent need of suitable clothing. I made a hasty breakfast and took myself back to St Thomas's with the appropriate gear.

Ian greeted me happily, and promptly tented himself to shed his pyjamas. Once he was dressed in sports jacket and slacks he seemed to grow about three feet, and I was thrilled to have my husband back again, instead of a supine and querulous invalid. I wanted to relegate this whole episode to the past as quickly as I could; to make it into an anecdote to be taken out and exclaimed over at a comfortable distance, when time had drawn its sting.

However, we had reckoned without hospital procedure. Discharge didn't just mean strolling out with a cheery wave and heartfelt thank you to the staff. It was necessary to wait for the doctors' notes and instructions as well as a supply of medication, and I watched Ian's face settle into weary resignation as the minutes, and then hours, went by. I went to fetch us coffee from one of the outlets, and as I waited for the lift, my mind turned back to the previous night and my difficult conversation with Alex.

When had problems begun to surface in his marriage? I was certain that Chloe had been an easier, more supportive partner during their early years together. They had been very excited when baby Jack arrived, and we waited for news of baby number two – waited in vain, as things turned out. I had pleasant memories of Chloe in the later stages of her pregnancy, when she was a pretty, artless girl, who was delighted to have a new husband and a child on the way.

I suspected that the dynamics of their relationship had changed over the last few years. They had moved, with Ian's assistance, to a larger house in a more upmarket area, and Chloe attached herself to a group of ladies whose partners were wealthy men. Alex had once remarked, laughing, on the women's fanatical devotion to beauty enhancements and a complex social whirl, but I felt he wasn't comfortable with his wife's enthusiastic participation.

I knew that Ian could appear forbidding – he had no understanding of that sort of life, and it took time to adjust to his sardonic sense of humour – but it was noticeable that Chloe always had an excuse to stay in Manchester on the rare occasions when Alex and Jack paid us a visit. It was now some years since we had seen her, although Maudie reported disapprovingly on her appearance when she'd combined a recent marketing trip to a Manchester wedding fair with a call on her half-brother and his family.

'Chloe looked almost radioactive with that awful orange fake tan, and I could swear she's had a boob job. Trout pout, too. I can't understand why Alex lets her do it,' she sniffed down the phone.

Well, probably Alex had no say in the matter. I knew these procedures didn't come cheap, and then I wondered whether Chloe had become one of those women who think nothing of spending thousands on designer handbags and shoes. If she felt she had to keep up with the pack she was running with, there would always be problems in store.

'Cheer up, darling,' Ian admonished, as we were finally released from the hospital building and walked out into the next part of our lives. 'I thought you would be pleased to get me home, but you seem a bit down.'

His voice was accusing, as though I wasn't sticking to my part of a bargain.

'I'm sorry, Ian. You can't believe how much I want you back at home with me – everything has felt so empty without you. It's just that the last few days have been exhausting,' I hedged, assuming a brighter smile. There was no way I could tell Ian about the conversations with Sam or Alex. I pushed away the problems of my difficult stepsons and concentrated on my husband instead.

Once we were at the flat, Ian walked to the big window in the living room which overlooked the river. He pulled up his favourite chair, which was deep-seated and button-backed, and settled himself; gazing out at the world as though trying to find his place in it again. He wasn't conversational – he was markedly silent, but I thought that his introspection was understandable after the unpleasant experiences of the last two days.

I made us a light lunch, and then Ian slept in his chair. By the time I had caught up with the latest e-mail enquiries about his health, I was ready for a snooze as well. But I had only just dropped off, when the peal of the doorbell recalled me to grouchy consciousness. Sam had arrived to visit his father, and this time, his wife Emma was also in attendance.

Emma was one of those fortunate people in possession of high cheekbones, excellent teeth, and a surfeit of self-confidence. She claimed to despise yummy mummies, but I placed her firmly in that category, with her spin classes, her designer clothes and her resident au pair. She swanned into the room with understated elegance, her long dark hair pulled into a side ponytail, and Ian welcomed her with open affection. He had no complaints about this son's choice of wife.

She kissed Ian on both cheeks, and greeted me with smiling enthusiasm, although I didn't read too much into that. I had observed her over many years and noted that this cheery effervescence was her habitual display; designed to disguise a basic lack of interest in most people she encountered. Emma was, in her own way, a smooth operator, like her husband.

Sam fussed about with glasses and a bottle of champagne he had brought to toast his father's homecoming, and I stepped back to let him take over. I would have preferred to spend a quiet afternoon with Ian so he could acclimatise himself to home once again, but there was no stopping this showy onslaught. As we sipped the sparkling liquid, Sam dictated a list of things which his father ought, or ought not to do in the coming days, and Emma nodded in dutiful approval. I couldn't help looking across at Ian with a sceptical light in my eyes, and he frowned slightly.

'Thank you, Sam. I have full instructions from the hospital and will be following things up with my GP in the next day or so. You don't need to be concerned,' he said, in a voice which indicated the subject was now closed. But Sam was oblivious to the hint. He droned on about diet and exercise and specialists, and I grew fidgety on my husband's behalf.

'Why don't you come and convalesce at Rivermead for a while? My parents would adore to have you, and Eithne needn't come if she's busy in town,' Emma suggested, and now I was the one to frown.

Emma's parents, Dominic and Jocelyn Templeton, lived on a large estate in Hampshire, and were diligent in their offers of hospitality – to Ian. Dom was harmless enough, but Jocelyn was a social climber of the first order, and a little of her went a long way. I believe she had earmarked Ian for a friend after Laura's death, and she had never forgiven me for interfering in her schemes, especially as I lacked social status in her eyes. As a result, I was often omitted from invitations to Rivermead when it could be done without being too blatant. To be fair to Ian, he was usually aware of this, and didn't often go along with her plans. Now he smiled down into his glass.

'That's a very kind thought, Emma.'

I was waiting for his refusal of the offer, but the telephone summoned me. It was an elderly friend of Ian's late parents – God knows who had told her about Ian's hospital admission – and I knew she would be the last person Ian would want to speak to in his current frame of mind. I shrugged my shoulders and carried the handset into the kitchen, because the poor lady was hard of hearing, and it was embarrassing having to shout platitudes in front of company.

It took her a while to understand what had happened to Ian. I told her that he was sleeping, and would speak to her later, and after a lot of fluttery waffle, I finally got her off the line. But when I returned to the living room, everyone else was on their second glass of champagne, and I had the strangest feeling – almost as though I had interrupted something; some private business. They all stopped talking. Emma was perched on the arm of Ian's chair, murmuring into his ear, and his lips were curved in a slightly secretive smile which I was unable to interpret.

'That was your 'aunt' May,' I said tartly, and Ian groaned at the prospect of having to return her call. He and Sam began to reminisce and banter in a bitchy way about various relatives and friends on the fringes of their family network, and I sat quietly with my drink, because I couldn't contribute to this conversation. Frankly, I didn't want to. Sam could bring out something in his father which was at odds with the person I thought I knew, and it was unsettling.

I was relieved when our guests rose to go, pleading a dinner engagement, although Ian urged them to come again soon. This was a sentiment I felt unable to echo.

'Would you like supper now? I'm afraid that I wasn't expecting company, so I am rather behind with things,' I said, switching on the table lamps, so that the room grew homely with their cheerful glow. My husband was gazing out on the Thames, whose waters were fiery as they reflected the red glare of a fine sunset, and I crossed the room to put my hand on his shoulder. I was looking forward to having him to myself now, and a sense of peaceful happiness engulfed me. It was time to get back to our usual quiet life and affectionate ways.

'I'm not that hungry. Anything will do.'

Ian yawned, and looked at me with a question, his brow lowered. 'Have you fallen out with Sam? You are very prickly with him these days.'

His tone indicated a degree of disapproval. I paused, gathering up empty glasses, and choosing my words with care.

'It isn't a case of falling out. But I don't think Sam always appreciates what's best for you,' I said, making sure I sounded reasonable rather than someone passing judgment. 'You've had a trying time and need to rest. We should take things slowly at present.'

'Hmm... you must let me decide about that. And don't be silly about Dom and Jocelyn, will you? They mean very well,' he remarked, and I felt my face grow hot. We had always been of one mind about the Templetons in the past; what had prompted this sudden change? I frowned, tempted to challenge his reproof, but he turned his attention back to the window and the setting sun and the moment passed. Anyway, I didn't want an argument on his first night back. It was a time for quiet celebration, not hasty words which we might come to regret.

After picking at his supper, Ian declared his intention of turning in for the night.

'It will be a relief to have a comfortable mattress, and get away from all those snorers,' he remarked. Then, as I rose to assist him, he pushed me back down in my seat.

'It's all right, Eithne. I am quite capable of putting myself to bed, and I would rather you didn't fuss over me too much.'

This almost sounded unkind. Ian tousled my hair in passing. I think this was meant for an affectionate gesture, but he spoiled it by making a cool statement that he would understand if I wanted to sleep in another room, so we didn't disturb one another.

'I need a good night, after the sleepless hours I suffered in hospital. Lack of proper rest is a downer at our age.'

He took a shower, and I heard him cursing afterwards, as he yanked a little too hard on the curtains where a hook had become dislodged, but I didn't intervene. I sat alone in the sitting room, trying to read my book, but often finding myself staring into a darkening evening which matched the bleakness of my mood. This wasn't quite the happy homecoming I had anticipated, and I couldn't understand why.

Chapter Five

There was no way I was going to sleep in the guest room. The more I thought about the suggestion, the more it bothered me; as if it was somehow divisive and demeaning – for both of us. I longed for the familiar warmth and contours of Ian's body. I had missed the little groans and snuffles he made in his sleep, although after our awkward exchange, I felt almost shy as I slipped under the duvet; as though there was something proscribed about our proximity. He was deep in a slumber which felt impenetrable, but as I snuggled against him, my body relaxed and the day's tensions drained away. Ian was bound to be on edge after his frightening experience, and I hoped the morning would bring my affectionate husband back.

I wasn't aware of him waking in the night because I slept well, and it was a shock to reach out in the morning and discover the empty place beside me. Alarmed, I threw back the covers and padded into the sitting room; my bare feet soundless on the carpet. Ian was enthroned on his chair by the window, his eyes fixed on the mist-shrouded river and the first stirrings of life in the city.

'Ian? Are you feeling all right, my darling?'

He started like someone lost in deep thought.

'I am fine, thanks,' he said cautiously, clearing his throat as though his voice wasn't quite ready to be used. 'Umm... my sleep patterns got out of kilter in hospital, and I suspect they will take time to settle down again.'

It sounded as though he was searching for an excuse, and I wriggled on to his lap. This was something he usually accepted with an affectionate hug, but he kept his arms stiffly to himself; gripping the chair as if anchoring himself to it.

'Is anything sore? Do you need a painkiller?' I asked, kissing his forehead, and longing for a tender gesture in return.

'No – nothing like that. But I feel disconnected, somehow. You wouldn't understand.'

This hurt. Why did he think I was unable to empathise with his experiences of the last few days? 'I have had to face up to my mortality in a way I've never done before,' he continued, before I could protest. 'Perhaps it's fair to say... I feel anxious and depressed.'

'That's only to be expected,' I exclaimed, wishing I could warm him with my conviction that he was over the worst. 'But don't be pessimistic, Ian. You have been very fortunate that the problem was picked up before anything more serious happened. It's been fixed, and your recovery should be just a matter of time now.'

'Yes. I suppose that's true.'

He stared past me, leaving me on the fringes of his consciousness. I wasn't used to Ian being unresponsive, and this detachment left me confused. Normally, he was so full of life and self-confidence, but I didn't recognise this solemn stranger. My caresses went unreturned, and after a while, I relinquished the attempt and went to make a cup of tea.

His distant mood continued all day, leaving me floundering to find an acceptable stance. It was as if a stagnant mist had descended, which distorted the normal channels of communication between us. Ian stayed glued to his chair, toying with the papers, his i-pad and the small meals I prepared for him, but I suspected that none of them had his full enjoyment or attention. He was polite to me; courteous even, but the reality left me frustrated – somehow, I couldn't reach the person under the veneer.

And he would not countenance leaving the flat. Next day, our GP visited, and confirmed all the positive advice from the hospital, and so I urged little trips, meals out, meeting friends, even (God help me) Sam and Emma, but he stayed firmly rooted to the sitting room. Night time meant a cool, solid back, turned towards me with an air of reclusiveness.

After we had passed three days in this impasse, I rang Sofia, feeling on the verge of panic. Ian was dozing in the chair when she arrived, and I hustled her into the kitchen.

'It's awful – I don't know what to do with him! It's as if a different person came back from the hospital.'

Tears gathered as I spoke, and Sofia gave me a little shove.
'Stop that, Eithne. What did I tell you? Men find it hard to deal with this sort of thing, and he's coping by withdrawing until he gets his confidence back.'
'But he isn't in any danger now.'
I reached for a piece of kitchen paper, sniffing hard. 'I don't understand why he's so distant and unkind to me.'
'He probably doesn't realise that he's doing it. Get a grip, Eithne. It's only been a few days.'
'Eithne?'
Ian called irritably from the sitting room, and I blotted my eyes.
'Go and talk to him while I get us some coffee. He'll like that.'
Sofia thumped me on the back and went into the sitting room. Ian's voice rose in surprise, and then his deep laughter rumbled as he and Sofia exchanged greetings. When I went in with coffee and biscuits he was smiley and convivial, and even his posture seemed more upright and assured. Of course, he could always be relied upon to make an effort for a pretty woman – especially if he wasn't married to her.

Sofia kept up a bright flow of chat. Thanks to her confident personality, she could take liberties with Ian which he wouldn't accept from me, and I was grateful for the broad hints she inserted into the conversation which suggested that he could stop considering himself to be an invalid. She spoke breezily of friends who had suffered similar problems and who had seized life by the horns afterwards, and the room seemed to vibrate with pictures of energetic oldies dashing up mountains and making exotic voyages. I wasn't sure that we needed to emulate them, but I was sorry when she got up to leave us, and I know Ian was too.

'If he's difficult, I should just let him get on with it. He'll snap out of it eventually,' she advised me, as I kissed her goodbye in the hall. 'I'm sorry that we will be away on our cruise all next month, but I'll try to e-mail you to see how you are getting on.'

Colour and vitality seemed to drain from the air as her footsteps echoed down the corridor. I watched her draw back as the lift arrived, stepping aside to let a traveller laden with a heavy backpack squeeze past, and I wondered where the new arrival was bound. Then my heart gave a joyful thump.

'Olivia?'

I could hardly believe it, but the slim, tanned figure striding towards me was indeed my errant daughter. Impulsively, I reached out to hug her, but she evaded anything demonstrative and merely pecked me on the cheek. 'You might have warned us you were coming,' I added, remembering as I spoke that she always operated on spec.

'Well, I knew you would be here. How's the invalid? I hope you're looking after him.'

She barged past me into the hall, dumping her bags down without ceremony, and I debated whether there was a satirical edge to her voice, but she appeared to be sincere about the sentiment. Then she walked in to greet Ian, addressing him in Italian, which he spoke with fluency, and I was delighted to hear him responding in the same tongue. Anything which provoked her step-father's interest was welcome at present.

They had to switch back to English when I joined them.

'You've been very fortunate, Ian. Mum doesn't usually have much luck with her men. She makes a habit of losing them in unexpected circumstances,' Olivia said, with her customary bitchiness towards me, and for a moment my hand itched to give her a slap. I could see Ian beginning to frame a reprimand, but then his mouth quirked up as he savoured the sardonic humour in this remark. After all, he was a survivor.

'At least I keep them for a while first. How's Francesco?' I asked cattily, remembering the name of her Italian boyfriend just in time. Olivia's face grew guarded, and she picked up a cushion, hugging it to her chest like a barrier.

'Well, I think that relationship may have run its course. But I still have a stake in the trattoria. It's doing well. Our reviews on TripAdvisor are amazing,' she said, but there was a hint of something sad in her voice, as though once again she hadn't found what she was hoping for.

'Well, I'm going to start on supper – I assume you will be staying?' I said to Olivia, and she nodded. 'You talk to Ian then, and I'll call you if I need help.'

I thought that she could pay for her keep by entertaining him. Although they had never been close, I knew that each had a grudging respect for the other. They both possessed a hard-headed conviction of the validity of their individual views, and these were often poles apart, but I didn't think that mattered in the circumstances. Sparring with Olivia would be stimulating for Ian in his present low state of mind.

I was chopping vegetables in the kitchen when Olivia joined me again.

'Can you put me up for a few days? I won't get in your way,' she asked, and my mood brightened at the prospect of her company.

'Yes, of course. Maudie and the twins are coming to see us next week, but they will be staying in the other flat.'

'Really? I'd like to see Maudie again.'

She pulled out her phone, and rapidly thumbed a text.

'How do you think Ian is looking?' I asked, needing her opinion, and she hesitated for a moment, as though she didn't want to say the wrong thing for once.

'I don't think he looks ill, if that's what's worrying you. I'm sorry you had such a fright, but he seems to be doing well now. He is a bit craggy these days, though – after all, he is getting on.'

I wished she hadn't felt it appropriate to remind me of that. However, we made a pleasant enough supper. Olivia's presence was like an electric spark enlivening the recent solemn atmosphere of the flat, and Ian grew almost communicative, although he still retired to bed early, pleading fatigue. He kissed me goodnight, and then Olivia and I made ourselves comfortable with coffee and chat about our side of the family, and I was unexpectedly soothed by her company after my recent surfeit of Inglises.

'I haven't heard from Alex for ages. How is he these days?' she enquired, and I was sorry I didn't have better news to report.

'I think he's having a hard time.'

There was no point in hiding the truth from her, because I knew from experience that she was an expert winkler-out of secrets. 'We've always known that he and Chloe are not exactly compatible, but she has been impossible since she acquired all these new friends. Alex and Jack take second place to her clothes and her appearance, and I am afraid they've got into debt as a result. Alex can't face kicking up a fuss, because she takes it out on him – and more importantly, on Jack.'

A shadow fell across Olivia's face, and her sapphire eyes flashed fire.

'Alex is too soft for his own good. Always was,' she exclaimed, twirling a curling lock of hair round a finger. I wondered whether she was thinking back to the time when she and Alex had been close, because she frowned at me, as if wanting to apportion blame.

'I know, Mum. I know you wish I'd stayed with Alex, but we didn't have a long-term future,' she muttered, her voice sulky. 'Think how young I was. And after Dad died...'

The words sounded choky, and she swallowed hard. 'I couldn't bear to be around all the places associated with him. I had to get away. But I don't like to think that Alex is unhappy now.'

'Well, I have helped him out with a loan, but Ian doesn't know, and you need to keep this to yourself,' I told her. 'I advised Alex to start being tougher with Chloe, but God knows whether he'll manage to rein her in. She's hell-bent on some modelling opportunity, and it all sounds rather dodgy to me.'

'It's a shame you don't know her better – some of this might have been avoided. I wonder whether she's doing it because she's bored and looking for help or attention.'

Ouch. Olivia stretched her long legs, and walked to the window, scowling out at the twinkling skyline. She had hit on a half-truth, which I accepted with regret, because the last few days had shown me that we didn't really understand Alex and his family. Although Olivia had an abrasive personality, she believed in treating people with honesty and respect, and she was incensed at the thought of Alex suffering because of the immaturity of his wife. But could Ian and I have done more to help Chloe be satisfied with her lot? We anticipated that the latest house move would give them a more comfortable life but had not foreseen these new problems.

'We do ask them here, but she doesn't ever want to come. And it's difficult when we spend half the year in France,' I murmured. It wasn't much of a defence, but it was the truth.

'I wonder whether I should go and see him,' Olivia mused, and this prospect set alarm bells ringing.

'Olivia! You are the last person who should interfere! Alex needs to fight this battle himself, and you'd just make it worse. Please promise me you will stay out of things. And I really don't want Ian to know what's going on, because he mustn't get stressed at present.'

Olivia's shoulders were tense with irritation, but I hoped she understood the necessity for secrecy. She continued to examine the night sky, as though looking for celestial answers, and I wondered how to persuade her I was right. If only it wasn't so difficult to get under the prickly shell she had constructed for herself over the years! We understood one another better nowadays, and I didn't want to return to the hurtful time when she would barely acknowledge my existence. She would doubtless say that she felt no need of her mother, but I was suddenly conscious of how much I needed her. If Ian was going to take time to come to terms with the after-effects of his medical emergency, her brusque common sense might be invaluable in helping me to manage things – not least, my own expectations.

I remembered Sam's words in the restaurant and tried to repress a tiny stab of fear. If he carried out his threat to shatter the fragile relations with my daughter, it would be very hard for me to bear.

'Why did you finish with Francesco, darling? I don't mean to pry but I would love to see you in a happy and settled relationship.'

This was a bold move on my part, and Olivia gave me a chilly, sideways glance.

'We were good together – and then we weren't,' she said, after a reluctant pause where she debated with herself as to how much she could conceal from me. 'He showed that he could be a domineering bastard if he was thwarted. I'm not going to hang around if I'm not getting what I want, and unlike you, I find it easy to move on. Thank God I didn't inherit your faithful heart.'

'Or your father's,' I said coldly. She knew how to get under my skin, but I didn't find her argument convincing. Olivia was in her thirties now, and I felt this rolling stone existence would begin to pall as she grew older and her life choices narrowed. However, she wasn't about to give up her attack.

'You've had three relationships in your life, Mum. I assume that you've loved the men you lived with, and I suppose that's been enough for you. But you've never challenged the status quo or struck out on your own. Don't you ever regret the fact that you tied yourself to a man for most of your life?'

I couldn't let myself laugh, but this view sounded strangely old-fashioned to me, and it was certainly a blinkered one.

'I don't consider I have been tied to anyone – but I have been privileged to share loving partnerships. And what about children? Single parenthood may be fashionable these days, but it's a very hard life. Take it from me; I know.'

My voice trembled slightly, as I recalled the first months of my son's life, when loneliness and sorrow had been my companions every day. 'Don't you feel you would have missed out on a world of experience and love if your father hadn't been there for you when you were young?'

She couldn't argue with that, and her face crumpled in a grimace of pain. Olivia would never get over her father's death. They had shared a special bond, and he was the only person who could make her see sense when she flew off on a tangent. I sent a desperate thought winging to Peter's spirit; hoping for some assistance in helping our difficult daughter to make the most of her life. I longed for her to be happy, and I felt that she was anything but that, despite her confident front.

'Dad was the best,' she said quietly, after sitting, wrapped in a remote silence, for some minutes. 'I suppose I'm looking for someone like him, but I never find anyone who comes close. Perhaps I never will.'

I thought that Alex was cut from the same cloth as her father – loving, steadfast and open – but circumstances had dictated that their relationship could not progress to maturity. However, this was a thought I couldn't possibly voice without arousing more controversy.

'But don't you ever want to have a family of your own, darling?'

This was another risky question, but I might not get such a good opportunity again. 'You'd be a brilliant mother, and I know you would enjoy it. With luck, you might even be living in the UK, and I'd get to see more of a grandchild than I do now.'

Mentally, I ducked, waiting for a furious rebuttal. But although Olivia's shoulders were raised in a shrug, she continued to trace the patterns on a cushion with slim pink fingertips, as though the idea wasn't entirely new to her. Then she hit the nail on the head as usual.

'Well, Mum... you've just pointed out the desirability of having a father around, and I can't think of anyone in my life who'd be up for that role. Sorry to disappoint you.'

My mobile rang. I was annoyed to have this unusual and intimate chat with my daughter interrupted at this critical point, but appropriately enough, it was Alex calling. He enquired anxiously about his father, and I said that Ian was doing well – no point adding to Alex's woes by telling him my concerns. I added,

'Olivia has come to see us. She's with me now. It's lovely for me to have her here.'

He went quiet for a moment, and I pictured him sitting at home in Manchester; perhaps remembering old days.

'May I speak to her? I'd like that,' he said, suddenly sounding like the immature young man of years ago, and my breath quickened as I felt the tug of the past. It was only for a second, and I shrugged the feeling away.

'I don't see why not.'

I handed the phone to Olivia, and took myself off to the kitchen, busying myself with some small tasks because I didn't want her to think I was eavesdropping. She exclaimed with delight when she heard his voice, and I reflected that it was a strange coincidence he had rung at this moment. If only she would remember not to be tactless about Chloe...

I began to fold some washing, but my attention wandered, and I allowed myself a little daydream in which Alex and Olivia had stayed together. They would have a whole brood of children by now, and Olivia would be a super-efficient working mum, with a house and dogs and a happy husband... why was it that life never followed the course one wanted? Sighing, I wandered back to the sitting room, and Olivia transfixed me with bright eyes.

'Yes – okay. I'll meet you at Euston,' she was saying. 'Do you need to speak to Mum again? Fine. Till tomorrow then.'

She answered my quizzical glance with a nonchalant toss of her head. 'Alex wants to come to see Ian tomorrow. We'll have lunch together first – I hope that's all right with you.'

'Yes, of course. It will be good for you to catch up with one another,' I said, guiltily abandoning the daydream to the realms of fiction. 'But remember to go easy about Chloe, won't you?'

'I'm not daft, Mum.'

I knew that, but she was apt to become vocal in support of anyone close who was having difficulties. The last thing we needed was more family drama.

Chapter Six

Next morning, Olivia was up and around with the early sparrows. The sound of her singing in the shower floated through to where I lay in bed, and I found myself smiling at this cheerful beginning to the day, although Ian stirred irritably beside me.

'Why is Olivia so damn chirpy?' he growled, his face burrowed into the pillow, and I reached across to him, stroking his back with gentle fingers which ached for a loving response.

'She's always been a morning person. Don't complain. It's nice that she feels happy to be here with us.'

Ian shrugged away from my hand, and heaved himself on to one elbow, yawning like a disgruntled hippo. It was time for a few plain words.

'What is the matter with you, Ian? Since you have been home from hospital, nothing seems to please you, and you are horribly cold and distant with me. Have I done something to upset you?'

I knew very well that I hadn't, but I couldn't take much more of this harsh rejection. He sighed as though the weight of the world was upon him, and sat up, swinging his legs over the bedside. A shaft of morning sun illuminated his face. His skin looked fragile and papery, like something which has been deprived of sunshine and warmth, and I made a mental note that it was time to get him back to France.

'Don't be ridiculous, Eithne.'

How often had I heard those words over the years! It was my husband's stock response when he didn't want to pursue a subject, but I wasn't going to let him brush me aside like he usually did.

'Well, could you please try to be more cheerful? I appreciate that you have had a horrible experience, but you are on the road to recovery now. Why don't we go out for lunch today, to give us a change of scene? You are being such an old bear...'

I made myself give a little laugh, to soften the reproach implicit in my words, and he grunted.

'I'm afraid I forgot to tell you. Tom and I are meeting for the lunch we should have had at Simpson's. Let's hope I make it this time.'

He sidled off to our bathroom, closing the door behind him with a meaningful bang. So, he wouldn't be drawn into a discussion, but I hoped that my rebuke might filter through the layers of his self-absorption and shame him into better behaviour. Thwarted, I pulled on my dressing gown and joined a buoyant Olivia in the kitchen, where the comforting aroma of fresh toast hung appetisingly in the air.

'I hope Ian won't mind if Alex and I have lunch together. We'll be back quite early, so there will be loads of time for them to talk,' she said, rubbing at her damp curls.

'Ian's just told me he will be out, because he's meeting a friend. No need for you to feel guilty,' I replied, picking up the morning paper. It was fraught with gloomy headlines, which chimed with my own frustrated mood. Perhaps I ought to write to an agony aunt – 'please tell me how to cope with my husband's grouchy temper'. I could imagine the brisk, no-nonsense reply for myself, but advice always seemed easier when it was applied to other people. When I read the main section of the paper, it was filled with unhappy families in horrible situations, and I could see that my own concerns were trivial in comparison, but that didn't mean I wasn't exposed to pain because of Ian's detachment from me. I would have to keep working to find a way to break through the barrier between us.

Ian glanced suspiciously at me when he finally entered the kitchen, but he seemed relieved to escape further chastisement. He allowed me to press tea and toast upon him, while Olivia expounded on her plans for the day. She was a trifle hesitant, as though she had intuited discord in our relations and was testing the ground.

'I don't think that Alex is very happy these days,' Ian told her, surprising me with this sudden candour. 'Perhaps you can find out what's bothering him? Of course, if it has to do with Chloe, he'll have to sort it out for himself. Ghastly girl. What a terrible mistake he made in marrying her.'

'But Jack is a sweet child, and a lovely grandson for you,' I objected, feeling that someone needed to put a positive spin on things. Jack was a warm-hearted and sensitive little boy, and I instinctively preferred him to Sam's children, although this was undoubtedly unfair of me. But my views were coloured by the behaviour of their parents. Although I was a step-grandmother, Jack always called me Grandma, but Sam and Emma insisted that their children called me by my Christian name; correcting them when they tried to address me as Granny, and saying that I wasn't a real relation, which confused the poor little things no end.

Ian looked over the paper at me, and his face was smiling and placatory. This was a step forward. Perhaps my censure had hit the mark.

'Jack is a good boy. But last time we met, he wouldn't say boo to a goose. I'd like to see more spirit there.'

'He is frightened of you,' I thought. I wanted to say it but realised that it wasn't the time or the place to do so. Ian didn't understand how unapproachable he could appear to a small child, although I hoped this was a fault which would lessen as the children grew older, and his height and abrupt manner became less intimidating. I suspected that Maudie's twins' reaction to him would be much like Jack's – it would be interesting to see.

As I had a hair appointment, I left the other two to their own devices for the morning and contented myself with a lonely portion of sushi for my lunch. It would be more accurate to say I discontented myself with it, because I couldn't help feeling hard done by. My hopeful suggestion that we all go out for dinner had been dismissed by Ian, who said portentously that it would be bad for him to eat two large meals in one day. Well, yes, he had a point, but he didn't seem to recognise that I would have liked a family outing.

The afternoon was warm and bright, and I grew dozy as I sat by the window, struggling with a sudoku to pass the time. At length, I heard voices, and Livvy and Alex laughed their way into the room.

'Hullo, Eithne.'

Alex bent down to kiss me. 'I'm sorry you've been left here on your own. How's my Dad doing? Keeping you busy, I expect.'

Alex's face was bright and open, although he still bore traces of the blow to his eye. A glance at my daughter showed a similar happy flush, and my pulse quickened with a fleeting feeling of apprehension. But they chatted openly and eagerly, and the atmosphere was warm; suffused with past memories and present affectionate friendship. When Olivia disappeared to the bathroom, I turned a more serious countenance towards Alex.

'I assume you received the money from me. Have you been able to talk to Chloe?' I asked quietly, and a shutter seemed to fall across his face.

'Yes, Eithne, thank you so much. I have the money, but I haven't found the right occasion to speak to Chloe yet. I promise I will do it soon.'

His jaw tightened, and he became fierce and solemn. It was the only time I could ever trace a resemblance to his father in Alex, and the unexpected likeness to Ian made me start, but the return of Olivia cut our conversation short. She sent me a querying look which I ignored, and I scrabbled to think of a less controversial subject.

'When does Jack break up for the holidays? I remember you saying that he is very happy at school.'

I tried to make my voice light, but it came out bleating and artificial, and Alex stared at me in surprise.

'He loves school, but Chloe thinks we should be educating him privately. Most of her friends have their kids out of the state system.'

He hesitated, and I cursed myself for starting this hare running. 'Do you know if Dad helps Maudie or Sam with their children's education?' he asked me, his face puckered in a frown. 'The cost has gone up such a lot since we went to school. Chloe is badgering me to ask him, but I don't like to raise the subject. I don't think it would be fair, especially after all the help he gave us with the house.'

I could sense Olivia about to voice a critical opinion, and broke in hastily.

'Maudie's children attend their local primary,' I replied, glad that I could say this. 'I don't think that Ian helps Sam, although that might change when Sam has all three at school. But the Templetons may be willing to fork out for their grandchildren. After all, Emma's brother Crispin doesn't have kids.'

Nor was he likely to, as he showed no signs of wanting to marry or settle down, much to Jocelyn's displeasure. Rumours about his sexual orientation were rife, although Emma always dismissed them with an airy toss of her shining head.

'Darling Chrissy is so shy with girls, poor lamb,' she cooed, but she didn't convince me. I didn't think that shyness was a Templeton characteristic.

'Well, we all went to state schools, and did okay for ourselves. Surely the important point is that Jack is happy?'

Olivia sounded impatient. Then she hesitated. 'Does he look like you, Alex? You must have a picture of him on your phone.'

Alex's eyes rested on her with a wistful expression of mingled affection and regret. He picked up his phone, and scrolled through, until he found what he wanted.

'This is him, in his school uniform. He's growing a lot just now,' he said, his voice full of pride, and Olivia gazed at the picture for several long moments.

'He's lovely,' she said softly, and there was genuine warmth in her tone. Then the door opened, and Ian walked in, accompanied by Dominic Templeton, Emma's father – the last person I was expecting, or wanting, to see.

Dominic was my age, but there any similarity between us ended. He was a florid man of medium height; fleshy and ponderous in his movements. His shiny face was garnished with an absurd little moustache, and he exuded the cordiality of a hungry python. Now, he advanced across the room, and I braced myself for the dubious pleasure of his moist, wine-fuddled embrace.

'Eithne! Such an unexpected treat! But your hospitable husband – looking in very good shape, may I say, despite his recent adventures – insisted that I accompany him here, to wait for darling Jocelyn to finish with the dentist. And the thought of seeing you was just too irresistible.'

'Hullo, Dominic. How nice of you to call,' I murmured, with heartfelt insincerity, and Olivia gaped at me across the room. I avoided her eyes and extracted myself with some difficulty from Dominic's tentacles. Ian introduced him to our children and explained their position in the extended Inglis hierarchy. They would have met at Emma and Sam's wedding, but I don't think that Dominic remembered either of them, doubtless thinking they were insufficiently important for him to bother with.

An offer of tea was accepted, and I retired to the kitchen to make it. Ian followed me in.

'You don't mind me bringing Dominic here? We ran into each other at Simpson's, and for some reason, he was angling for an invitation.'

'No, of course not.'

I could lie very well when I chose. Ian lowered himself on to a kitchen chair, and I looked at him closely; worried in case he had overdone things.

'I hope the outing wasn't too much for you,' I said. He shook his head, and I noticed him smother a little yawn.

'It was good to get out. Tom seems to know a lot of people who have been through the same procedure, which is reassuring, even if they haven't gone on to lead the life of Riley like Sofia's chums.'

We shared a moment of amusement, which heartened me. But he couldn't conceal the fatigue in his face, and I urged him to return to the sitting room and a more suitable seat. Dominic had sequestered his special chair, but Alex fetched a footstool for his father and unobtrusively made him comfortable on the sofa.

It was always difficult to get a word in when Dominic was in full flow. Alex frowned down at his watch, and Olivia realised that he was being deprived of the chance to speak with his father. She took decisive action: pulling up a chair beside Dominic to divert his attention. I admired the way she responded archly to Dom's intrusive questioning about her life, in such a way that he could not have thought her rude, but which avoided giving away any specific information. He looked increasingly puzzled, and I was pleased.

Then the doorbell rang and I went to answer it. Jocelyn Templeton was perched on the doormat, with a social smile plastered across her face to greet me.

Jocelyn was a real contrast to her husband, being small and bird-like, with beaky features. Her dark hair was styled in a sharp, fashionable cut, which unfortunately made her look older than her years, and the brown dye she favoured didn't suit her skin tone. But her figure was good, and she always sported the latest fashions. I saw her run her eyes over my top and skirt and dismiss them instantly.

'Hullo Jocelyn. I hope the dentist wasn't too painful,' I said politely, as she air-kissed my cheek.

'Just a check-up.'

She walked purposefully into the sitting room, and exclaimed over Ian, embracing him with ten times the enthusiasm she had shown to me. Ian introduced the children again, and she was smilingly dismissive as she usurped Alex's place by his father. Poor Alex stood by looking awkward, until his father asked him to organise drinks.

Then I relieved Olivia from Dominic's attention, letting the wash of his inanities flow over me. But my attention was caught by an unexpected sentence.

'...and he said he'd like to come to our fishing weekend. Do him good, don't you think, Eithne? Chap needs a bit more colour in his cheeks.'

'He could borrow some of yours, and you wouldn't miss it,' I thought to myself, before the implication of what he'd said hit me. Jocelyn broke in, with a tight smile on her lips.

'Afraid it's a weekend for the menfolk, Eithne – hope you don't mind. They should have some good sport. Ian will know most of our other guests, and he certainly won't be bored.'

I turned a querying gaze on Ian. He dropped his eyes for a second, running a cautious hand through his hair to allow him time to frame his response. It was obvious to me he didn't care that I was excluded from the invitation.

'Is that all right with you, darling? It will be nice for you to have some time to yourself after nursing your poor old husband,' he remarked, in such a way that I couldn't possibly object, although I was surprised and somewhat peeved. Ian had never shown any previous inclination to go fishing, but perhaps some time in the country would do him good.

Once they had established that Ian would be going to Rivermead, the Templetons made moves to depart, and I didn't hinder them. I saw Jocelyn whisper something in Ian's ear which made him smile and raise an eyebrow and wondered what else she was plotting. At least I had the prospect of getting away from them for the summer once the visit was over.

'I didn't know you were keen on fishing,' I said to Ian later; after we had eaten, and Olivia had gone to see Alex off at Euston. I suppose that I sounded accusing, because Ian looked down at his empty plate, and a transient trace of guilt crossed his face, which puzzled me.

'I'm not. But it would have been churlish to refuse the invitation. I get the feeling that they have arranged this weekend for my benefit, which is very good of them.'

'Never trust a Templeton bearing gifts,' I thought. However, I couldn't think of an ulterior motive for their hospitality and chided myself for being uncharitable.

Ian went to bed, although I stayed up for Olivia. She returned from Euston looking remote and chastened; the happy mood of the earlier meeting dissipated after their goodbyes. Maybe it had been harder for her to see Alex again than she had anticipated. She shied away from my gentle attempts to pursue the subject.

'It's not very nice to see someone you care for so unhappy. But I'm not going to talk about it now.'

Olivia spent another two days with us, and then flitted off; promising to return when Maudie paid her visit. The weather remained fine, and Ian slowly began to pick up his old pursuits, although he continued to be very tetchy with me. There were times when I wondered whether his grave manner concealed an accusation of blame for what had happened to him. I had picked up enough of his conversations with Sam to understand that Sam's hints about my supposed lack of care continued to be inserted into Ian's consciousness, and it was difficult to remain aloof from this provocation.

It was even harder to hide my surprise when Ian returned from a shopping expedition with what was almost a new wardrobe. If I had to describe my husband, I would have said that he was a traditional English gent, who wore conservative clothes in expensive fabrics, and the colourful chinos and trendy tops and sweaters invading his cupboards were something I'd never seen him in before.

'Golly – is that a T-shirt, Ian?' I asked teasingly, walking into our bedroom as he was unpacking his haul. He scowled; not meeting my eyes.

'For heaven's sake! You are always nagging me to wear something more casual when we're in France. I thought you'd like it.'

'I do,' I said, pained at his tone. He rattled hangers aggressively, and then I noticed his head. 'And you've done something different to your hair!' I exclaimed, without thinking. 'Is Gino away?'

Ian had patronised the same barber for years, and I couldn't remember any variation in his usual style. Today, it appeared that the hair above his ears had been trimmed close to his head, while the top parts retained length and a certain floppiness. He glanced quickly at the mirror opposite and allowed a furtive smile to hover on his lips.

'No. But I thought it was time for a change. Gino says I'm lucky to have a good head of hair still, and I think it makes me look younger.'

'It's very nice,' I faltered, although I suddenly felt that I wanted to cry. There was no need for my darling husband to rejuvenate himself – I liked him the way he was. And there was something pathetic about this attempt to turn back time; as if he was trying to convince himself he had a viable future. It wasn't what I would have expected of pre-hospital Ian, and I remembered Sofia's warning with a premonition of further unhappiness.

Ian hummed to himself as he closed the cupboard doors, and I sat on the bed, trying to retain my composure in the face of this depressing development. 'Well, I'm glad your fishing trip is for men only. I think I might worry if there were a load of women going too,'

I ventured, trying to make a joke of the situation, and he accepted the remark with a smirk, as if he agreed with me. But the result of this makeover (I couldn't think what else to call it) was that he became more cheerful and outgoing, and somewhat less snide with me, so that at least was a bonus.

Maudie arrived to stay, with Elspeth and Ruaridh in tow. They were now six years old, with impish, pointed faces, and their father's sandy colouring. Both took one look at their imposing grandfather and buttoned their little mouths tightly shut.

Ian had no idea what made little people tick, and his attempts to be interested in them were unconvincing, because he found it impossible not to be bored, and show his boredom. In the end, I took them off to do some London sightseeing while gentle Maudie accompanied her father on more adult pursuits, and their visit passed off successfully. I loved being with the children, and hoped that they liked my company too, although I couldn't help feeling wistful because they weren't my own descendants.

The day before they returned to Scotland, we were invited to a lunch party at Sam and Emma's house. There was a certain show of ostentation on the part of the hosts, and the twins retreated to my lap at first, but eventually, the au pair coaxed them away to play with their small cousins.

The food was excellent. Emma always kept a good table, and Sam ensured that everyone's glasses were topped up. By the time the meal was over, Ian was overcome with drowsy yawns, and he excused himself to take a nap in the conservatory.

'Father is more like his old self,' Sam informed me, his voice expressing a grudging satisfaction. 'When is he seeing the specialist?'

'Don't know – you'll have to ask him,' I replied. I knew that Ian had done nothing about following up this instruction from Sam, because the GP had told him it wasn't necessary, but I didn't want to get involved.

'There's something else I have to tell you,' Sam continued, and I hoped my face didn't reveal the frisson of apprehension such remarks caused me after our recent restaurant dialogue. 'Emma's parents are renting a small chateau in the neighbourhood of Le Clos Fleuri for a month in the summer. They are hosting a large house party, and we intend to be there for several weeks. We thought it would be nice to spend time with Father this year, and this way, the little ones won't be under his feet.'

Le Clos Fleuri was our house in France. At first, I didn't know how to react to this surprising statement. The prospect of assorted Templetons on the doorstep was not one I found appealing, and despite the recent fraternisation over the fishing party, I wasn't sure how pleased Ian would be either. But I couldn't say that to Sam, whose smug face looked as though he expected to be congratulated on a breathtakingly good idea.

'That's lovely,' I managed to stammer out. 'I wonder which house it is? It was clever of them to find it at such short notice.'

'They were lucky – there was a cancellation.'

I could think of only one house in the neighbourhood which might accommodate a big group. It was an elegant building which always looked a little shabby and neglected: the crumbling stonework had an air of *tristesse*, as if it remembered better days. The grounds were beautiful, though, and there was a tennis court and outdoor pool. And it would be interesting to see inside – surely, I would have to be included in one or two invitations during their stay?

A few more questions confirmed that I was right. I longed to wake Ian and share the news, but he was deep in a slumber too peaceful to disturb. I also wondered why Sam had waited until now to tell us about these holiday plans, but he admitted that Jocelyn had only just texted Emma with confirmation of the booking.

'We didn't want to raise your hopes until we were sure we were going,' he explained, and I spluttered into my coffee.

I was called upon to console the twins from time to time, because the au pair was possessed of a strident and hectoring manner very unlike their mother, and they were uneasy in her presence. Ian finally woke and wandered back to where we were sitting.

'Sorry, Emma,' he said, giving her a peck on the cheek. 'You can blame Sam's excellent Chablis. I don't often sleep after lunch.'

What a fib! I opened my mouth to make a teasing correction to this statement, but Emma got in first; telling him about their plans for summer in Provence with the confident assumption he would be delighted at the news. And Ian did seem pleased: observing that it was important for families to spend time together. I thought about his tolerance of Elspeth and Ruaridh and tried not to smile.

'Why don't you come too, Maudie? It would be great for the little ones,' Ian said, but Maudie shook her head regretfully.

'July and August, Daddy – it's the height of the wedding season for us. And don't forget the grouse shooting starts on the twelfth. But it's kind of you to ask.'

'We could invite Alex and his family. They haven't been to France with us for ages,' I said, and was amused by the intake of breath and narrowed nostrils which indicated Sam's disapproval of this suggestion. But Ian didn't immediately dismiss the idea, and I began to do a little internal plotting. I thought it might be pleasant to have some more agreeable companions amongst the Templeton ménage, and perhaps we could help to dissipate some of the tensions between Alex and Chloe.

'Daddy seems quiet,' Maudie said to me, as I kissed her goodbye the next morning. Ian was doling out banknotes to the twins, who stood with solemn faces, hopping from foot to foot as their grandfather dispensed words of farewell along with the cash, and the sight made me smile. 'But I know you will look after him. I hope he will soon be back to normal.'

There was a hesitant note in her voice, as though she had noticed a change in her father, and I wished that she had felt able to talk to me about it before she left. I blinked away a tear as the taxi departed, because I would miss the cheerful prattle of the twins, and especially their easily bestowed affection – I wasn't getting much of that at home just now.

Chapter Seven

Next day, I reminded Ian to ask Alex and his family to visit us in France during the summer holidays. He needed his arm twisted just a little.

'You know I can't stand Chloe. A fortnight of her will seem like a life sentence,' he moaned, his face full of gloom. 'I shall rely on you to keep the peace.'

'I expect she'll want to lie by the pool all day, and you need only meet at mealtimes. Think of Alex and Jack – surely you would like to see them? I don't think they get too many treats these days,' I pleaded, hoping he wouldn't be difficult.

He grumbled for a while, but eventually e-mailed an invitation to Alex, which was promptly accepted. We planned to depart for Le Clos Fleuri ourselves the weekend after the Templeton fishing do, and I couldn't wait to leave, anticipating that once we were relaxed and settled in France, life would resume a more untroubled course.

Olivia had returned to us in time to spend an evening with Maudie. She seemed distracted, and when I got her to myself next day, she didn't need much persuasion to share her concerns. She had travelled to Cheshire to visit old friends and called on Alex before returning to London. What she discovered shocked and saddened her.

'I only saw Chloe for a few minutes. Alex said she was going to the opening of some new club, and she was tarted up no end.'

Olivia snorted at the memory. 'But, Mum – I am so worried about Jack and Alex! There's a terrible air of neglect about the house, and the pair of them. Alex evidently does what he can, but he's got a full-time job to worry about, and Jack's unnaturally quiet for a little boy, as though he's waiting for the next telling-off.'

My chest felt tight with tension, and I wished I could block my ears, because I didn't want to hear any more.

'Are you sure you aren't imagining things?' I whispered, and she shook her head, with her lips compressed in a grim line.

'I don't know how to put this, but I think that Chloe sometimes goes for Alex when she can't get what she wants – in a physical way.'

I remembered the bruise and the wounded hand, and suddenly the situation was illuminated with all the force of a tabloid headline.

'You mean that Alex is a battered husband?' I asked bleakly, hating the cliché, and the anxiety in her eyes confirmed that this was true.

'You know Alex. He's such a sweet and gentle person; not like Ian at all. He'd never bring himself to fight back.'

That made me grimace, but I let it pass.

'But why would she behave like that? Alex infers that she gets her own way all the time,' I mused, clutching at anything which might mean that we were mistaken. Olivia sat hunched in a ball, knees tucked against her chest, as though trying to ward off the unpalatable truth.

'I think it's a recent development, although from something Alex let slip, she's always had a terrible temper when she's roused. Mum – you can imagine I couldn't ask too many direct questions, but Alex had a long scratch on his neck which he couldn't explain, and as soon as Chloe left the house, both he and Jack seemed to relax and breathe a sigh of relief. What must it be like for Jack to grow up in that atmosphere?'

I didn't know what to say. This was something outside my own experience. It was the kind of thing you read about in the papers and trusted would never happen in your own family. I thought about the forthcoming visit to France, and quailed.

'Olivia – please don't say anything about this to Ian. I don't want him worried,' I said, echoing the words I'd used to Alex on an earlier occasion. 'Perhaps I can talk to Chloe when they are with us in France, and they can be persuaded to get proper, professional help. I hate to think that Alex and Jack are unhappy, but we might make things even worse by jumping to conclusions.'

There was contempt for this response in Olivia's fierce gaze.

'Why shouldn't Ian know? This is his son and grandson we're talking about!' she cried, striding about the room, and clenching her hands in a gesture I remembered from her childhood. But my instincts told me not to involve Ian until we were sure of our ground. He was supposed to avoid stress, and anyway, I knew his response would be blunt and unsympathetic, because he simply wouldn't understand how his son could let this happen. I didn't want schism in the family, on top of all our other problems.

It took some time for me to convince Olivia that it would be best to approach the matter with velvet paws. I promised to tackle Alex about his home life when we were in France, and in the meantime, I would do some research, so I could be armed with suitable advice.

Thank God Ian was out at his club. It was not an easy task to pacify Olivia, although she finally accepted what I was saying. But she couldn't bear to sit idle in London and packed her bags again. She decided to return to Italy, to wind up her business with Francesco. Her mood was combative, and I didn't give much for his chances in the debate.

The weekend of the fishing trip arrived.

I recalled a popular television ad of years gone by which featured an older man and angling and indulged in a little gentle teasing about this visit. Ian grew snappy with me as a result – any trace of a sense of humour was still noticeably absent – so it was almost a relief to wave him off on Friday. I planned to spend the time making final preparations for France and was confident that the days would pass quickly.

But my omission from the invitation and his ready acceptance still rankled. By Saturday afternoon, I was bored, annoyed, and beginning to feel sorry for myself. I threw the papers aside and walked to the window, only to observe that London was populated with happy couples strolling in the sunshine. The irony wasn't lost on me. I gritted my teeth, and the telephone rang.

Was it Ian, calling to say how much he was missing me? Not a chance – but it was something almost as good. It was Aurien de Groot.

Aurien was a business associate of Ian's from way back. He was one of those people who can never quite tell you how they have amassed their money, and who parry personal questions with a smiling, cordial vagueness, but he was always charming to me, and I cherished a very soft spot for him.

I recited the tale of Ian's hospital experience, which I was almost bored with by now, having had to recount it so many times. Aurien listened without interrupting me.

'I am so sorry to hear this,' he said, when I had finished. There was the faintest trace of an accent in his voice. Aurien was of Belgian descent, and he lived in France. 'I was hoping to see you both,' he added, sounding regretful.

'Well, Ian is down in Hampshire, staying with Sam's in-laws on some sort of fishing jolly,' I said, and Aurien's laughter floated down the line.

'With the terrible Templetons? My dear Eithne, however did you manage to escape this awful expedition?' he asked teasingly.

'I wasn't invited. I almost never am. Jocelyn doesn't like me,' I replied, not caring if this fact went further. Aurien stopped laughing, and I heard him give a happy sigh.

'But this is good news for me. If you have no other plans, perhaps you would dine with me tonight, Eithne?'

'That would be wonderful – I'd love to!' I exclaimed, thinking with happy anticipation that I could give a new dress its first outing. We arranged to meet for drinks at Claridge's, and now I could look out on the riverside strollers without envy. Aurien was always excellent company, and I knew from experience that dinner would be equally good.

I took care with my appearance and descended to the Uber with a light heart when I was ready to go. As I waited for the lift, I wondered whether I could hear our landline ringing, but I was tight for time, and didn't go back. Aurien rose to greet me when I arrived at the hotel and kissed me warmly on both cheeks.

'Eithne. You look charming,' he said, head to one side. 'I feel very privileged to have you to myself this evening.'

'Ian will be so sorry to have missed you,' I smiled, enjoying this easy flattery.

'He will be even sorrier when he hears where we had dinner.'

I raised my eyebrows, and Aurien named a restaurant where it was notoriously difficult to obtain a table, and which was one of Ian's top favourites. 'What do you suppose the Templetons are eating tonight?' Aurien continued, a grin of feline cunning illuminating his face. 'Hampshire... I imagine they have been fly fishing on the Test. Trout, perhaps? A very dull fish in my opinion, but suitable for a Templeton party.'

He made me laugh, and we chatted comfortably over cocktails. Aurien nodded to acquaintances from time to time, and I was conscious of a few curious glances coming my way.

'I bet people are wondering why you are here with a woman of your own age and not some trendy young thing,' I remarked, as we left for the restaurant. 'How are the glamorous mistresses these days?'

Aurien was fanatically private about his emotional life – he was singularly unforthcoming about all aspects of his intimate affairs, despite his expansive public person. Because we got on so well, and were of similar years, I sometimes wondered whether I could have fallen for him in younger days, but I think his instinctive reserve would have made him a difficult partner. He was rumoured to entertain a succession of beautiful ladies at his house in Paris, but he was rarely seen with a woman in public, unless he was escorting the wife of a fellow tycoon to a charitable event. The feline smile became a tigerish frown at the mention of glamorous mistresses.

'You are certainly reading too many gossip columns, Eithne. Please let's talk about something more interesting.'

When the time came to leave for the restaurant, I was surprised by a flashbulb as we entered a taxi, and a voice called 'Mr de Groot – which way will you be voting at the Godfrey shareholders' meeting?'

Aurien merely bowed his head, saying 'Good evening, gentlemen,' as he joined me; slamming the taxi door on the paparazzi clustered round the hotel entrance. I had imagined they were waiting for celebrities, but I realised that Aurien was a star player in the world of business and was also grist for their mill.

'What on earth is the Godfrey shareholders' meeting?' I enquired, my eyes round, but Aurien gave a dismissive headshake.

'Nothing for us to worry about tonight. Tell me what's going on at your place in Provence.'

He could be an oyster when he needed to be. Over dinner, we spoke about France and holidays, and then he turned the subject to Ian. My unhappiness at Ian's recent behaviour flooded forth, encouraged by the sympathy of my companion, and I could see Aurien thinking it all through.

'Not being in control – that's hard for a dominant personality like Ian. And I can understand that it was a shock to be forced to confront his years, and his limitations. Most of us still feel young inside, and reality is an unwelcome guest. We don't live for ever, much as we might like to.'

'At least he's had a decent shot at life.'

I thought ruefully of Nick and Peter, whose lives had ended so abruptly. Aurien reached out and grasped my hand.

'I'm sorry – was that very tactless of me? I spoke without thinking.'

I squeezed the hand, knowing that Aurien had not intended to cause me pain.

'Another thing... this isn't easy for me to say.'

I described Ian's recent experiments with trendy gear, and the new, sharp hairstyle. 'It isn't *him,* if you know what I mean, and I'm afraid people will laugh. I couldn't bear that to happen.'

Aurien and I exchanged thoughtful glances across the table. I knew that he understood, and it was a welcome relief to be able to express myself in this way.

'Poor Eithne...' he murmured, still holding my hand, and I felt the sting of tears in my eyes.

'I just want the old Ian back,' I muttered, blinking hard, and averting my head.

'And I am sure he will come back – but maybe not quite yet. You must be patient with him; patient and loving. That's not so hard for you, is it?'

His intuitive sympathy warmed my heart, and I began to feel better. Despite my worries, it was a happy evening, and I relished Aurien's flattering attentions after Ian's recent coolness towards me.

But after summoning a waiter to ask for the bill, Aurien surprised me by saying, 'Tell me about Sam Inglis. I think he's not such an astute businessman as his father. Am I right?'

This question left me frowning and puzzled.

'Well, I hardly know. Their expertise is in different fields. Sam is a banker, and Ian was an adman…'

'But an adman with a finger in many different pies, you must admit.'

He selected a card from a slim wallet and placed it on the plate. 'And I do hear things, Eithne. It sounds as though Ian isn't firing on all cylinders at present. Just make sure he does his homework very carefully before allowing Sam to talk him into anything. And for heaven's sake, don't let him get into bed with Dominic Templeton.'

A twinge of alarm shot through me and my mouth fell open in dismay.

'But, Aurien – I can't talk to Ian about business! Especially if other family members are involved. Can't you please speak to him if you suspect there is something risky in the offing? He won't listen to anything I say.'

I recollected another restaurant scene, and Sam's discontented face, as he talked of 'projects' – and other matters. Was this what Aurien meant? My tummy contracted, and apprehension traced a slow finger down my spine.

Aurien looked away, creasing his eyes; suddenly conscious that he might have said too much.

'It's better dealt with face to face, and I'm going away tomorrow. Just keep your ears open, Eithne, and if you have any real concerns, get in touch with me.'

He drew a card from an inner pocket, and handed it to me, with the merest hesitation. 'Please don't give anyone else this number. It's strictly for you.'

I was sorry that the evening was ending in this worrying and mysterious way. Aurien clammed up again behind his smiling façade, and I could get no further information from him about dodgy deals that the Templetons might be hatching. He kissed my hand very formally as he saw me into a taxi.

'Thank you for your delightful company, Eithne. I hope that Ian will soon be back to his old ways – and don't let him treat you badly. Tell him that I will carry you off for myself if he makes you unhappy.'

That was sweet of him, but I couldn't envisage such a scenario. On the way home, I checked my phone – I had switched it off out of politeness during the evening – and found several missed calls from Ian. I sent him a text to say I'd been out for dinner and would call him in the morning.

After this unaccustomed late night, I slept in, until the shrill insistence of the landline interrupted my dreams.

'Eithne?'

My husband's tone was anxious and reproving. 'Why don't you answer your mobile? How the hell am I supposed to reach you if you're out, and your mobile's going through to voicemail?'

Guilt wrestled with irritation inside me, and the latter won.

'Didn't you read my text? Anyway, I tried to call you yesterday afternoon, and your phone was off then. As you are staying in a house party, I didn't think I needed to be concerned about your welfare. It's not as if you are on your own somewhere.'

'I certainly wasn't out on the town with Aurien de Groot.'

I leaned back on my pillows, focusing on the sunlight making flickering, intricate patterns on the bedroom ceiling.

'What?'

'You're in the *Mail on Sunday*. 'The financier Aurien de Groot and a companion.' I never thought I'd see my wife gracing a gossip column.'

His voice rose with discontent, but the pompous sentiment roused me to delighted laughter.

'Oh, Ian… what a hoot! If you must know, Aurien wanted to ask us both to dinner. He hadn't heard about your heart. I didn't think you would mind if I went – you are off doing your own thing, after all.'

Ian growled, but I had nothing to be ashamed of. 'We went to Solus,' I added, knowing that this would add fuel to the fire, and he gave an exasperated groan.

'How on earth did Aurien get a table there?'

'He knows the right people, I suppose. He usually does.'

Ian was silent for a few moments, and then he uttered an unwilling laugh, as though he could appreciate the funny side of things, albeit from a distance.

'It's certainly improved your standing with Jocelyn. Breakfast was enlivened no end. Is Aurien in town for long?' he enquired. 'I'd like to see him when I get back.'

'Well, when are you coming back? You haven't seen fit to let me know.'

I didn't want to punish him, but I wanted him to understand that I wasn't happy with his attitude. There was a pause, while he dissected the tartness in my voice.

'I suppose that Sam can run me back tomorrow morning. There's a big lunch party here today, and you know how these things stretch on.'

'I look forward to reading about it in the paper.'

Another long silence.

'Are you all right, Eithne?'

'No, I am not all right!' I wanted to shriek. 'I am not happy that you accept an invitation which deliberately excludes me and cosy up with people I distrust. I don't appreciate your lack of support, when I've put up with you being difficult for days.'

But of course, I didn't say it. Instead, I made some anodyne remark, and we chatted briefly before he suddenly said he had to go.

'I'll see you tomorrow, then, but don't wait in unless you want to,' he said, sounding remote and almost unfriendly. I put the phone down with a mixture of annoyance and bewilderment, because I almost didn't recognise the person I'd been speaking to. Thank God, we would be leaving for France at the end of the week. I felt that I didn't want Ian to go to Rivermead again if this was the result of prolonged exposure to the Templetons and their set.

Chapter Eight

I passed a quiet day catching up with household business and making final arrangements for Provence. My first task was to write a thank-you note to Aurien at his Paris address, repeating my plea that he would find a way to speak to Ian if he heard anything else of concern about Sam's financial plans. Then I tried to put the problem to the back of my mind. I knew that the business world thrived on rumours and bluffing, and it was always possible that Aurien might be mistaken in his interpretation of events.

Ian spent two more nights at Rivermead. Whether this was by chance, or to annoy me, I wasn't sure, but it was Tuesday morning when Sam finally dropped him back at the flat. I happened to be glancing out of the window when Ian arrived, and was surprised to see a curvaceous female figure climb out of the car to bid him farewell. This involved hugs and many elaborate little kisses before the woman folded her elegant legs into the car and drove off with Sam. I sucked in my breath as I watched them. Despite his difficult ways, my husband was a desirable and attractive man, and I didn't plan on sharing him with anyone else.

Ian gave me a more perfunctory greeting when he came in; one which was suitable for a stay-at-home spouse.

'I see you have enjoyed yourself with the Templetons. Who was that I saw you saying goodbye to?' I asked; smiling to show I didn't mind. He paused, astonished, and a guarded expression passed across his face, like that of a child who has been caught with its hand in the sweet tin.

'Oh – that was Véronique Duhamel. Véronique Iglesias, I should say. She's someone I was friendly with after Laura died. She married a wealthy Argentinian, and I haven't seen her for years. It was a complete surprise to meet her again at Rivermead.'

'A nice surprise, I see.'

It was meant as a little tease, but Ian merely shrugged, and retreated with his case into the bedroom. Communication between us was becoming limited to these pinprick exchanges, and I was finding it increasingly difficult to bite my tongue.

'What are your plans for today?' I asked, trailing behind him to gather up the washing, and he hesitated for just a second.

'I thought I'd look in at the club at lunchtime, and I have to see the GP at four, to check I have enough medication for France. Was there something you wanted me to do?'

His back was turned towards me, and it sounded as though he hoped there wasn't.

'No. Just asking.'

I refrained from nagging, although I would have liked his assistance with a couple of small jobs. However, it was a relief to see him depart for the club clad in a well-cut grey suit and looking more like himself again. I wondered whether I dared to move some of his recent purchases to the back of the wardrobe and hope they might be overlooked when the time came to pack for France.

The day continued to be filled with niggly and unpleasant moments – such as finding Jocelyn on the doorstep that afternoon. With her face wreathed in a weaselly smile, she told me that Ian had left a sweater behind at Rivermead, and she had come to return it. The sweater was one of his recent acquisitions: cashmere, in a vivid lime green, and we were both lost for words as she handed it over, although the wry look on her face made me realise our thoughts were similar for once.

'It's so dreadfully hot today – I'm dry as a cork,' she announced, and I was obliged to take the hint and ask her in. Our conversation was punctuated by awkward pauses, and I wondered why she had wanted to spend time with me. Her disdain meant there was always a barrier between us, and I resented the way her gaze travelled around the room, as if she was pricing the furniture and ornaments. I cast around for a suitable subject.

'Ian tells me he met an old friend at Rivermead – a French lady,' I said, having forgotten her name, in the way I was apt to do nowadays. Obviously, the weekend hadn't been entirely for men, as stressed in the original invitation. Jocelyn grinned, showing white, pointed teeth.

'Yes – 'Nique Duhamel. She and Ian were very close after poor Laura died. He must have told you about her?'

'I'm not sure I remember,' I faltered, knowing very well that I'd never heard him mention her name until today. Jocelyn slid out a paw to snare a biscuit and nibbled daintily at its edges. Her eyes rested upon me; calculating and cunning.

'Dom and I always thought they made a lovely couple. But 'Nique had a rich Argentinian in tow at the same time, and she married him instead, and went to live in Buenos Aires. Ian said it's been amazing to meet her again.'

Instead? Had she been a contender for the title of the third Mrs Inglis? This was news to me. For a moment I was flummoxed, almost choking as I took a hasty sip of tea. Luckily, Jocelyn passed on to the engrossing subject of their holiday plans, and I found myself agreeing that she had been very fortunate to obtain the chateau booking. It was implied that Ian and I were very fortunate as well. On another level of consciousness, I was mulling over what I had just learned about Véronique Duhamel.

As she was on her way out, Jocelyn paused to adjust the strap of her handbag.

'Oh – and tell Ian that we've persuaded 'Nique to come to us for a while in France. He'll like that.'

Her beady eyes bored into me, and I thought quickly.

'What about the wealthy husband? Isn't he coming too?'

'Oh, no. Poor Ricardo died earlier this year.'

As ever, there were several last-minute panics before we left for France, and for a few days, Ian and I were ships that passed in the night. On the evening before we were due to depart, he didn't appear for supper, and I assumed crossly that he was dining with a friend. His mobile was going through to voicemail, and I was annoyed that he hadn't let me know his plans. He rolled in just before eleven, as I was becoming fluttery with worry.

'Sorry, darling – an unexpected invitation.'

He bent down to give me a conciliatory hug, and I took a deep breath.

'Let me see... it wasn't Johnny Marsden, unless he's developed a taste for Chanel No 5. And I think this shade of lipstick is a little too red for Tom.' I traced the imprint of lips on his right cheek. 'Who was the lucky lady?'

In my heart, I already knew the answer. Ian pulled away from me; frowning and irritable now.

'Don't fuss, Eithne. I happened to meet Véronique in town, and she was at a loose end. It's a while since she's been in London, and she doesn't know many people here these days.'

'Is she looking for another husband? You'd better tell her that she can't have mine.'

Our eyes met. Ian's scowl deepened, and the little shiver which fluttered down my spine told me that my question was unexpectedly close to the truth.

'Don't be ridiculous, Eithne. She's a very old friend. I hope you're not going to be jealous and silly about her, especially as the Templetons have asked her to stay with them at the chateau. I don't want any scenes.'

'Neither do I. But I would appreciate a little consideration,' I said sharply. 'Didn't it occur to you that I might be worried as to your whereabouts tonight? You could have let me know what you were doing.'

He tossed his jacket aside, as though the last thing he wanted was to have to explain his actions. I didn't know whether to be more narked by his lack of consideration, or the fact that he'd spent the evening with another woman.

'For God's sake! You've done nothing but nag and fuss over me since I came out of hospital! I'm not an invalid, you know.'

He stumped into our bedroom, leaving me speechless, and barely able to suppress a surge of fury. Why was he always so unreasonable with me? I wandered to the window, breathing hard and attempting to rationalise the very mixed emotions which burned in my brain.

Ian had slept with dozens of women in his younger days, and I knew from guilty experience that he didn't regard the marriage vows as sacred. Since we had come together after Peter's death he had given me no reason to suspect him of infidelity, but that didn't mean he wouldn't be open to temptation, despite his advancing years. And perhaps his recent experiences had prompted him to experiment once again. Illness could make one do irrational things: primed by the fear that opportunities were running short.

At the same time, I recognised that he was never in a hurry to change the status quo. He had shown no signs of wanting to leave Laura during our brief affair, (and I thought remorsefully of how little I had considered her feelings at the time.) He was a person capable of compartmentalising his life – sex with a passing fancy would stay just that – and so I did not worry that I had serious competition.

However, I didn't relish the thought of him flirting and spending time with this French siren; no doubt facilitated by Jocelyn's ill-will towards me. A voice from the past echoed in my ear – Laura, telling me in gently mocking tones, that I wasn't tough enough to deal with Ian. Maybe she had been right. I would need to find new reserves of strength if our time in Provence wasn't going to prove an unhappy experience for me this year.

We survived the tedious hours of travel next day without further contretemps. I think that Ian was ashamed of his harsh words, because he was attentive and kind to me, as if he wanted to atone for his recent distant behaviour. Le Clos Fleuri awaited, and when we inserted the key into the creaky, wooden door and our footsteps echoed on the sunshine-dappled flagstones, I felt as though the house threw its arms around us. We were home.

Kind Marie-Noelle, who looked after the house in our absence, had stocked the fridge with delicious treats, and it wasn't long before her husband Georges, the gardener, scrunched up the drive in a new pick-up truck. He immediately took Ian off for a technical conversation about the pool, helped along by a beer or two.

When I had unpacked our cases, I joined them on the terrace. A vine I had planted some years earlier provided a shady bower, and my favourite jasmine and bougainvillea drenched the air with musky perfume. A busy hum of insects made a cheerful chorus as we chatted, and my fingers couldn't wait to gather bright bouquets from the flowers which overflowed the borders with their trailing blooms. I thought briefly of noisy, crowded London, and counted my blessings.

We pottered for the first days. Local friends heard we were back and called on us, and Ian enjoyed regaling them with tales of his time in hospital. He slept peacefully in the garden after lunch, and his skin began to tan, and lost that stretched quality which had worried me in London. At the end of our first week, he woke me one morning with urgent caresses and murmured words, and we made love.

I'm not going to pretend it was the passionate congress of our early days together, but it was overwhelming to feel close to him once more, and I was overjoyed that he felt well and confident enough to resume our physical relationship. The problems of the last few weeks seemed to dissipate, burned away by the hot Provençale sun.

'That was lovely, darling,' I whispered, stretching beside him, and stroking his chest. 'Just like old times.'

I wanted to express my appreciation, even though something felt slightly askew, and I was disappointed when he turned his head away from me. But he sought for my hand and squeezed it.

'The doc says there's no reason I can't have sex, and I thought I'd been abstinent long enough. There's life in the old dog yet.'

'Cliché,' I teased, and he grunted. But the day was suffused with a happy sense of affection and certainty for me; things which had been lacking in my life, and which I had missed. That night, we visited some old friends for dinner, and I was very content to see Ian holding forth in his old assured manner.

'You must have had a terrible shock, Eithne.'

Elizabeth, our hostess, lowered her voice, as we ate our way through a huge fruit tart. 'Did you think that Ian was about to die?'

'Not really, because the ambulance arrived so quickly. But it wasn't an experience I want to repeat.'

'He's obviously fine now. Back to normal... in every respect, I trust.'

She nudged me, and I was pleased that my answering laughter was genuine. But at the same time, the tiny doubt which had assailed me earlier resurfaced, and I caught my breath as I thought back to the early morning. I had been in Ian's arms, but it hit me with a thumping clarity that he'd been thinking about an entirely different person at the time.

After this unlooked-for revelation, the rest of the evening passed in a kind of blur for me. I counselled myself that it wasn't exactly unknown to fantasise about other people during sex, but it wasn't a comfortable feeling, especially as I had a fair idea of the identity of Ian's imaginary partner. Should I challenge him? No. That would lead to embarrassment and resentment, which might destroy the recent fragile harmony between us. Better to put the subject on one side – but I knew I wouldn't be able to forget it altogether.

The days slipped past, languorous and lazy, and it became easier with every sunlit hour to dismiss the tensions of our last weeks in London, and file them under 'problem solved' in my mind. But one Monday, I was concerned to hear Ian spurning an offer of a walk with a friend, and he spent the afternoon bent over his laptop; his serious face and furrowed brow indicating that something critical was in the offing. When I took him a cold drink, he closed whatever he'd been perusing, looking harassed.

'It isn't like you to refuse a walk with Fred; particularly one scheduled to end up at the bar,' I said, sounding speculative. I knew I would have to approach him sideways on to find out what he was doing, and even then, he might choose not to tell me. He scrutinised me carefully, as if making up his mind whether I could be trusted to know his business. When he did speak, he dragged the words out with slow reluctance.

'Sam has asked me to invest in a buyout he's putting together with his father-in-law,' he admitted, swallowing his drink in several rapid gulps. 'It isn't an area I'm familiar with, so I'm having to do my homework, although Sam is very anxious to get things moving.'

The bomb had fallen. I wandered across to the mantelpiece, pretending to re-arrange flowers in a vase, but really thinking how I ought to react to this news. I could blurt out Aurien's warning, but that might backfire. Ian was touchy about anything reflecting on his professional competence, and I didn't want him to think I'd been gossiping. That could easily bounce him into a reckless decision.

'Don't let Sam hustle you into something you aren't happy about, Ian. You have been out of mainstream business life for some years now, and things change so rapidly. I expect Sam will be able to find another investor if you don't want to go ahead – he must know of other suitable partners he could approach.'

A cricket chirped loudly and ominously outside the window, and I heard a mocking note in its shrill song. 'Tell Sam you want to wait until he's here, and you can talk it over in person. That's perfectly reasonable. It's your money, after all. Sam will understand.'

I nearly said: 'It's your money *at risk*,' but that might be a red rag. It seemed an eternity before he answered me.

'I suppose you're right. It's too big a sum for me to throw away.'

So, Sam's 'little project', the one he'd mentioned in the restaurant, wasn't so little after all. My chest felt tight with apprehension. I could find myself in a tricky position, especially if Sam thought that I was associated with any hesitation on Ian's part to agree to his plans. I might have to choose between exposing my husband to financial jeopardy, or myself to unwelcome revelations for my children. If that choice was forced upon me, which way would I jump?

Chapter Nine

I lured Ian away from the computer with the offer of dinner in town, and the danger was averted – for the moment. At least I knew what was in the offing and could be alert for further developments. Little bursts of rage bubbled up inside me as we ate. I was furious that Sam was willing to put his father in an invidious position, and the worst of it was that I knew Ian wouldn't listen to me if I tried to intervene. Ian had an inflated view of Sam's capabilities, and was proud of his son's city career, his classy house in Notting Hill, and his elegant wife. I suspected that Sam's personal finances might not hold up to scrutiny, but Ian didn't appear to mind the requests for assistance, which came with some regularity. Alex would agonise before asking his father for money, but Sam had no such scruples.

My ammunition was limited, but I made sure that our social calendar was filled for the next few days, so Ian had no time to worry himself at the computer. Then it was high summer, and the Templeton party descended on the neighbourhood.

Jocelyn had hired domestic help for the period of their visit, including a cook, and there was much excited speculation about the wealthy English family renting the chateau. I tried to dampen this where I could. We were never sure how well-to-do the Templetons really were, and I was afraid that local traders might be in for a disappointment.

The estate in Hampshire had belonged to Jocelyn's parents, and on my infrequent visits there, I couldn't help noticing that the showy surface didn't always hide a lack of polish round the edges – shabby bed linen, rooms in need of redecoration, fraying carpets – that sort of thing. The food was often dull, and portions skimpy, although Dominic poured drinks with a generous hand.

Jocelyn certainly had a miserly streak. She dressed with a sense of style, although her clothes were from the high street, but her shoes were often in need of heeling, or her nails a good manicure.

'What a bitch you are, darling,' Ian exclaimed, when I pointed this out to him. 'Luckily, Emma always looks the real deal.'

In her own way, Emma was as high-maintenance as Chloe. It amused me that both women were so different to my own daughter-in-law; cheerful, laid-back Patti, who seemed to live in T-shirt and shorts, with her long locks scrunched into a casual topknot. Of course, the Australian climate helped...

'Are you looking forward to the Templetons coming?' I asked Ian, the day before their arrival. We were eating at a rustic café in the village square, enjoying the cooler evening air, and the sense of relaxation which infused the atmosphere after the heat of the day. Ian lolled in his chair, looking lazily replete.

'It will be nice to see Sam and his family,' he conceded, stretching his long legs. 'You know I have no great love for Dom and Jocelyn, but I daresay they will be a source of amusement. I'm anticipating a few fierce games of tennis, too.'

I toyed with my wineglass, feeling twitchy, because I was anticipating a different sort of game.

'And I expect you will be pleased to see Véronique again,' I said, wondering as I spoke why I couldn't resist needling him with this provocation. He raised his eyebrows, and crunched the tiny macaron accompanying his coffee.

'I have to say I like spending time with 'Nique. She's a very stimulating woman. I hope you'll feel the same way, when you get to know her. You mustn't be jealous; it's silly.'

There was exasperation in his tone, and colour rose to my cheeks.

'I'm not jealous. But I shan't sit by like a prune and let you flirt with her all the time. I want you to know that.'

Ian asked for the bill and drew his wallet from his trouser pocket.

'You have a flattering notion of my powers of attraction, my dear. I think I'm past the age of affairs, but that doesn't mean I don't enjoy the company of a pretty woman. You won't begrudge me that, I hope.'

There wasn't much I could say in response without sounding impossibly prissy. We agreed that we would let the families settle in before calling at the chateau, but two days later, Jocelyn, Sam and

Oliver, Ian's eldest grandson, turned up at Le Clos Fleuri. Ian was out walking with a friend, and I had just reached a climactic part of my novel, so the welcome they received was somewhat muted.

'Eithne, dear! So, this is your sweet little house...'

Jocelyn cast a cursory glance around her. My home was looking particularly lovely; its old stones buttered by the glowing Provençale sunlight, and I raised an eyebrow at her patronising tone. Le Clos Fleuri had four double bedrooms and the downstairs accommodation was spacious and airy, but I suppose it was small compared to Rivermead or the chateau. I gave her a duty air-kiss and turned to Sam and his son.

'Hullo Sam. Hullo Oliver. Are you enjoying your holiday in France?'

Ollie scuffed a toe in the gravel and muttered a greeting. He was a skinny, gawky child of eight, and so far, he showed no signs of emulating his confident parents. Sam's critical gaze rested on him.

'Stand up straight, Ollie, and remember your manners. God knows why I'm paying such a lot in school fees when they can't even teach you how to shake hands.'

Oliver's cheeks flushed, and he looked up at me with piteous eyes. I felt painfully sorry for the child.

'Jocelyn – why don't you and Sam make yourselves comfy on the terrace, in the shade. Oliver can help me with the drinks.'

I took his hand firmly in my own and led him into the house. Despite the hot day, his fingers felt cold, and there didn't seem to be much flesh on the bones. I hoped he wasn't bullied at school, because he was such a shrimp. 'Do you remember this house from when you were little, Ollie? It's been a while since you stayed here,' I said, trying to sound friendly and encouraging. The child gulped and nodded.

'I remember going in the pool with Mummy. It was nice.'

'You will have a wonderful time in the pool at the chateau – it's bigger than ours, I think.'

His shoulders relaxed as I chatted to him, and he began to lose the apprehensive look which shadowed his eyes. I asked him to arrange some biscuits on a plate, and he undertook this little task with care, ensuring that the biscuits were spread in an even pattern, which touched and amused me. He asked politely for apple juice, and, gaining confidence, began to question me about life at Le Clos Fleuri.

'Daddy says we mustn't bother Grandfather, because he's been ill,' he informed me, with a solemnity which belied his years.

'Well, he's better now. I know he will want to see you, but he's out with a friend at the moment.'

Ollie stared at me with cautious eyes, taking this in. He was dressed in knee-length shorts and a striped polo top with a designer logo. The garments hung loosely on his skinny frame, and I wondered crossly why Emma couldn't clothe her son in something which fitted, because the baggy shirt made him look like an urchin in hand-me-downs.

'I'm glad he's better,' he said, with a funny air of formality.

'Yes. Can you carry the biscuits for me?'

He picked up the plate and followed me to the terrace, frowning with concentration as he walked.

'Just the one biscuit,' cautioned his father as I passed the drinks round, and Ollie nodded obediently. I wished I could encourage him to scoff the lot but knew better than to interfere.

Jocelyn fired off several nosy questions about the house and its value, which I parried with a vague response. She subsided, looking a little grim in defeat.

'Where is Father? I hope he hasn't been overdoing things again,' Sam asked, his eyes drilling into me and a reproof hovering on his lips. He was disappointed to find that Ian wasn't at home.

'He's very well. I think you will be surprised when you see him,' I replied, pleased that I could give a positive report. 'He always thrives in this climate, and he seems to relax more easily than when we're in London. I'm sure you understand that it's especially important that we keep anything stressful away from him, after what happened earlier in the year.'

I didn't dare challenge Sam more openly, but I wanted him to realise that he should avoid pressurising his father about financial affairs. He opened his mouth to retort, and then shut it again. His frown told me he didn't like the implication of my words, but he was in no position to argue. He turned his attention back to Ollie, and began to criticise him for fidgeting, and now I grew cross.

'Ollie – your cousin Jack will be here soon,' I told him, cutting across Sam's nagging voice. 'I think you could have some fun together. Grandfather and I will take you both to the coast one day. Would you like that?'

His serious little face brightened as he stared at me over the rim of his glass.

'I'd like to play with Jack. Can we go swimming in the sea together?'

'Yes, of course. You won't believe how warm the water is, compared to England. And we know a café where they sell the most amazing ice-creams you have ever tasted.'

Sam interrupted me before I could expound further on these delights.

'That's all very well, but it will depend on how Ollie behaves. He is supposed to do two hours of study every morning, because his school report wasn't good enough this term. He won't be going on any trips unless he works hard first.'

Even Jocelyn looked appalled at this statement.

'Oh, come, Sam – let the poor child have some holiday,' she objected, and I felt relieved that Ollie seemed to have another ally. I registered Sam's displeasure, but I made a pact with myself that Ian and I would make sure Oliver got to enjoy at least some of his time in France.

Sam hung on, hoping that his father would appear, but eventually had to accede to Jocelyn's demand that they should return to the chateau.

'Come to dinner tomorrow night,' she commanded as they left. 'We have more guests arriving, and there will be quite a house party.'

'It's very kind of you,' I replied, wondering how many people she intended to fill the chateau with. Was she paying off arrears of hospitality?

'Well, we've been fortunate. Some American friends of Crispin's are renting Rivermead while we're away, so in effect, the chateau is costing us almost nothing.'

Her tone was smug. I hoped the Americans would overlook the deficiencies of an English country house – perhaps they would find its shabbiness authentic and charming. Ian couldn't help laughing when I told him of this development on his return.

'Typical of the Templetons. Always got an eye open to make a bob or two. Anyway, I expect you will enjoy dining at the chateau. You've always wanted to see inside.'

Jocelyn had dropped no hints about Véronique Duhamel being present at the dinner, but I spent more time than usual getting ready to go out. Ian also fussed over his appearance; luxuriating in a very long shower which left me with the miserly, lukewarm dregs of the hot water tank, and frowning over the shirts in his wardrobe, before he settled on one of formal white linen.

'It looks good with my tan,' he explained, catching my astonished glance as he preened before the mirror. He swept the silvery hair away from his face, and was liberal with his cologne, looking for all the world like a stock photo of an older man accompanying a feature on senior grooming, and I tried not to wince. I found it difficult to reconcile this latent conceit with the sensible man I had married and wondered whether the fabulous Véronique might be behind this sea-change. If she was, she had a lot to answer for.

When we arrived at the chateau, Dominic was serving drinks on the paved terrace, where small tables were decked out with gaily striped sunshades. It looked like an advertisement for some trendy aperitif, with lots of chat and swooping laughter as the guests exchanged pleasantries. The immediate family party was present, and we were introduced to Jocelyn's sister and her husband, then a local couple, and a retired colonel and his wife – 'a distant connection', Jocelyn explained fussily, making it sound like something out of Jane Austen.

And the svelte lady taking possession of my husband could only be Véronique Duhamel – Iglesias, I should say – whom I had heard so much about.

I took a careful look at her. She was smaller and slimmer than me, with long, caramel blonde hair piled on top of her head in that casual way which takes a lot of effort to get right. She had got it right, and resembled an older Bardot, with her high cheekbones and glossy red lips and nails. I was uncomfortably conscious of the assured and affectionate welcome she gave to Ian, before she turned to me, with an expansive, appraising smile.

'*Ess-nee*. How nice to meet you. Ian has told me so much about you.'

She had an attractive accent, and her English was impeccable. It occurred to me that she could easily have pronounced my name correctly, and the fact she hadn't done so was irritating – it felt like a deliberate snub. Dominic pressed champagne cocktails upon us, and then she detached Ian from my side with practised expertise and led him away to sit at an unoccupied table.

I took a deep breath and prepared to let my husband enjoy the company of a pretty woman.

It's hard to make social chit-chat when part of your mind is distracted. Luckily, Jocelyn was in full flow, and I tried not to keep gaping across at the table where Véronique's blonde head was bent unnecessarily close to Ian's silvered one. But I was relieved when Sam walked up to them and drew out a chair to interrupt their tête-à-tête.

I felt as though a caustic, biting insect had crawled inside my clothes as I watched Véronique deploy her charms. Ian could never resist the opportunity for a little flirtation, and I had grown accustomed to him seeking out an attractive woman at social gatherings, to practise his skills. I knew it was harmless enough, and his vanity was gratified. But this open appropriation of my husband seemed to be in a different league. I suspected that Véronique had her own special agenda, although I wasn't yet sure what that might be.

It was impossible to dampen my unease, and I was relieved when dinner was announced, and we drifted into the house. Véronique clutched at Ian's arm as though she was glued to him. He drew out her chair with a gallant gesture, and she thanked him with a sexy little look from beneath long, mascara-laden lashes.

The dining room was lofty and ornate; heavy with embellished plasterwork, glittering mirrors and a vast fireplace, and my attention wandered from my husband for a moment as I stared around. It was a room of cool formality – but I sensed there was something oppressive about its stateliness, and my feelings of discomfort wouldn't go away.

Jocelyn distributed the guests with her customary efficiency. Ian had a seat of honour at one end of the table, placed between his hostess and Véronique, but I found myself well below the salt, with the retired colonel and the unknown neighbour as my fellow diners. It looked as though the evening would be hard going for some of us.

I sighed inwardly and turned to the colonel as he addressed me over the vegetable soup.

'Do you know this part of the world well, Edna?'

'It's *Eithne!*' I snapped, wondering how many more people would be taking liberties with my name before the night was over. The man had the grace to look abashed when I corrected him.

'I beg your pardon. Rum sort of name: don't think I've heard it before.'

We began on the soup, which was surprisingly good, and I relented a little.

'I know the area very well. We have a house nearby, and always spend our summers here,' I explained.

'Very pretty spot. And that's a very pretty dress you are wearing, my dear. I do like to see women looking feminine, and you and the French lady get full marks tonight.'

We looked up the table towards Véronique, who had laid a caressing hand on Ian's arm and was addressing him in a husky voice. I was too far away to hear what she was saying, but it sounded cooing and intimate, and I could tell from the rapt expression on Ian's face that he was lapping up every whispered syllable.

'That chap certainly seems to be enjoying himself,' the colonel continued, tilting his bowl to capture the last drops of soup.

'Frenchwomen have such style, don't you agree? It's quite an education, watching her land her fish.'

'That's my husband.'

My neighbour began to crimson around the ears.

'Sorry. Don't mean to speak out of place. But Dom hinted to me that she might be looking around for a new chap. Apparently, her late husband in Argentina left most of his dough tied up in a family trust, and it's been something of a blow to her. Anyway, I'm sure your man is safe, seeing as he already has such a charming wife of his own.'

He sounded anxious as he spoke – I could feel him metaphorically wiping his brow, and hoping he'd dug himself out of a hole. Ian glanced towards us, sending me a small, remote smile, before returning his attention to Véronique, and I clenched my teeth. It was ludicrous to suppose she might have designs on Ian, but I wished she was safely in Paris, or London, or anywhere else but here.

Conversation with my other neighbour was far less controversial, and I was grateful for the respite. The man – Michael – had lived locally for many years, and we swapped gossip and information in a light-hearted fashion. He had a droll sense of humour and having someone to take my mind off the little love-in at the other end of the table was most welcome. Our chatter grew animated, and even Ian was roused to look at us from time to time as the meal progressed.

When she was at home in England, Jocelyn retained the old-fashioned custom of gathering up her lady guests after dinner, leaving the men to enjoy a glass of port. She pursued the same strategy here, and the women filed out of the dining room after her, while Dominic waddled to a sideboard in search of the decanter.

'Not too long, Dom,' she cautioned, and her tone was sufficiently astringent that I realised she was quite capable of returning to drag them all out if she felt they had overstayed their allotted time.

The drawing room was dotted with elaborate little tables and hideous lamps, as well as a plethora of sofas in the hard, satiny style beloved by the French. I found myself seated next to the colonel's wife and listened with half an ear to her inconsequential chatter, while the other ear was stretched to overhear what Emma and 'Nique were talking about, a little further away. They seemed to be discussing her life in South America.

'You must miss him,' Emma was saying, in a voice dripping with sympathy. I saw 'Nique stretch and yawn beside her.

'Ricardo? No; not really. I was a good wife, but it was never a great passion. And I can't forget his behaviour towards me at the end. I deserved a better return for my years with him.'

Perhaps the colonel was right. 'Nique's voice was disgruntled, and a shadow fell across her face, but my companion claimed my full attention, and I cursed at having to miss the rest of this interesting conversation. However, when the men came in to join us and Jocelyn was reshuffling people, I did hear Emma saying,

'Ma tells me you knew my father-in-law very well after Sam's mother died. It must be interesting for you to run across him again.'

'Nique smiled down at her feet, her pretty mouth demure.

'Oh, yes – it's been wonderful to see Ian once more! He and I were so close at that time, and it is good to resume our friendship. But I must be careful not to upset Mrs Ian, because she looks as though she would like to throttle me.'

They lowered their heads in conspiratorial laughter, and I turned away, my face aflame. 'Throttle' sounded quite pretty when uttered in a French accent, but she was heading in the right direction.

I don't think that anyone else was aware of my discomfort, but I was relieved that the rest of the evening passed without further obvious dalliance between my husband and his old amour, although she bade him a lingering and physical farewell when we left. We didn't speak much in the taxi home. I was determined not to be the first to mention Véronique, and I think my silence on the subject made Ian a little uneasy.

'That was a surprisingly good dinner,' he said, as we were getting ready for bed. 'Emma tells me they have some sort of cordon-bleu girl cooking for them. It certainly beats anything I've ever been offered at Rivermead.'

I was sitting at my dressing table, taking off my earrings and necklace. His comment reminded me of what Aurien had said about Templeton parties.

'By the way, Ian, I have never asked you… did you catch any fish when you went to Rivermead last month?'

He paused in the act of unbuttoning his white shirt.

'What a funny thing to bring up now! Yes; I did land a trout or two. The party accounted for a sizeable catch, and we had the fish for dinner that night, well gussied-up with a watercress sauce. They were quite palatable.'

He sounded as though he was trying to mean it, but I suspected it hadn't been a meal to remember.

'The old boy I was next to at dinner said he enjoyed watching Véronique landing a fish – by which, he meant you,' I said coolly. There was silence while he considered the implications of this remark, but his face tightened, and I had the impression he was mentally reviewing the evening, in case I had genuine cause for complaint.

'What's that supposed to mean?' he asked, with a corresponding chill in his voice.

'I'm merely reporting a conversation. You might want to be aware of how other people see things,' I said. I had been careful not to make a direct accusation, but there was a sub text which he couldn't miss. He threw the shirt in the direction of the laundry basket, but it fell to the floor, like a deflating balloon, instead.

'Don't be ridiculous, Eithne.'

Chapter Ten

The topic of fishing was off the agenda next morning. I forced Ian to accompany me to the hypermarket after breakfast, because Alex and his family were due to arrive and I needed to re-stock the larder. While we were queueing at the checkout, Ian's phone beeped. He scanned the message and sighed.

'Sam wants to come over this afternoon, to talk me through these financial plans,' he explained, looking anything but pleased at the prospect. I cursed, hoping that Sam wouldn't succeed in railroading Ian into an agreement, but I couldn't think how to intervene without arousing his suspicions.

'Remember what I said. Don't jump unless you are sure of a soft landing,' I urged, resisting the temptation to brandish a baguette like a weapon. The morning had been spoiled for us, as we drove home, both deep in thought about what awaited. I tried to work out ways to put Sam off, but short of staging a collapse, nothing useful occurred to me. The evil day would have to be faced sometime anyway; we couldn't get out of it.

After lunch, I stretched out in the shade to write postcards for the twins. I was snoozy and comfortable, and regretted the fact that Sam was coming to disrupt our afternoon. Then I heard voices and saw that Sam had brought a companion with him. 'Nique climbed gracefully from the car, and snaked her arms round Ian's neck, laughing kittenishly at his surprise in seeing her.

Double damn. I didn't want her here, invading my space! But it would look unacceptably rude if I ignored their arrival, so I put down my pen and sauntered over to the group.

'Ess-nee. I 'ope you don't mind. Sam tells me he is coming to see his father, and I could not resist the opportunity to visit Le Clos Fleuri again, to see all these wonderful changes you have made.'

'Nique greeted me with that dangerous smile of hers, and her words hit me with unpleasant force.

'I wasn't aware you had been here before,' I mumbled, trying not to sound ungracious. 'I expect you know that Sam and Ian have business plans to discuss, but I will be happy to take you over the house.'

How did she know our home? Ian and Laura had bought the property shortly before Laura's diagnosis with cancer, but they had spent regrettably little time here together before the illness claimed her. Perhaps 'Nique had visited Ian here during the year or so after Laura's death, before he and I had resumed our relationship.

A few more questions from me confirmed that this was the case. And I knew what that meant.

'Well, I expect you are already familiar with all the rooms, then,' I said, unable to keep a caustic note from my voice. The corners of her mouth curved up into a cheeky grin, and Ian shot me a warning look, before Sam chivvied him away to talk business. I knew that Ian would have preferred to stay outside with his harem, but his son was implacable.

'Nique and I were left standing on the gravel, and she put her head on one side to survey me. She was wearing a soft denim sundress with a matching scarf draped around her neck, and she looked cool and chic. I was sorry I was clad in old cropped trousers and a loose, sleeveless top which I kept for garden days.

'May I say something to you? I do not want your 'usband,' she purred, touching me on the arm with one beautifully manicured hand. 'I think you must know that he and I were lovers in the past, before life took us in different directions. But you mustn't mind, Ess-nee, if Ian and I enjoy sharing memories and spending a little time together now.'

These were horribly direct words, and despite her caressing tones, I felt as though she'd slapped me in the face. Why hadn't Ian been more upfront with me about their history? I traced a pattern in the dust with one toe, considering my reply.

'I don't mind,' I muttered untruthfully. I did mind very much, but there was nothing I could do about it. 'But I think you ought to be more discreet with one another in public. People talk; it's embarrassing.'

'Oh, la la!'

She shrugged, pulling a wry face, as if to show how little she cared for what people might say. We exchanged a very hard look. Then she smiled, and I was struck by how beautiful she was, despite her age. I guessed that she was in her sixties, like me, but she could have passed for a much younger woman.

'Okay, Ess-nee. For you, I will try to be discreet. But you may need to give Ian a little hint as well.'

A not-so-little thump would be more like it. We stood there, neither of us wanting to give ground, until I finally remembered my duties as a hostess.

'Would you care for a drink? And my name is Eithne.'

'Et-ne.'

Well, it was an improvement. 'Yes, please. And I want very much to see your kitchen, because Ian tells me you make great changes there.'

She followed me through the hallway into the cool interior of the house and exclaimed over the combination of old and new which made the kitchen such a pleasant place to live and work in. I was proud of it, because I had put a lot of thought into planning and updating the room, and it was gratifying to see her reaction. The tension between us lessened now we could talk about practical matters. She described the kitchen of her ranch in Argentina to me, although I had the feeling she had never cooked or worked in it herself, as Ricardo had evidently employed a household of servants.

'Didn't you want to stay there?' I asked, wishing fervently that she had, and her expression hardened. Tiny lines creased around the corners of her eyes.

'The house was left to my stepson and his family, and I am no longer welcome. I must begin again, back in Europe – not so easy at our time of life.'

Her tone was bitter, and I almost felt sorry for her. However, I didn't trust her, especially where Ian was concerned. Everything I intuited about her told me that she was the type of woman who looks for a man of means to fund her lifestyle, and she would have no scruples in spearing her prey. Why had Ricardo disappointed her when it came to the contents of his will? I longed to know, but I could hardly ask her.

We took our drinks outside. Her desire to see the rest of the house seemed to have evaporated, and I was very relieved – I really didn't want to find myself in the master bedroom with her. My cheeks grew hot at the thought, although I tried not to contemplate this shared experience. It had the potential to be horribly awkward.

However, I soon sensed that 'Nique was making a great effort to disarm me. She chatted easily about the Templetons and the chateau, and I couldn't help smiling when she poked gentle fun at some of Jocelyn's little economies. At the same time, I felt like a fly being trussed up by an efficient spider. I knew that she was a hard-nosed character who would always look out for herself, but she combined this with penetrating charm and intelligence of observation. It was difficult to keep her at a distance, and I realised, with a tremor of apprehension, that Ian was already imprisoned in her gossamer web.

Ian strolled out to where we sat after half an hour had passed; perhaps to check that I hadn't pushed her into the pool. He and I exchanged one of those meaningful husband/wife looks, which communicate so many unspoken things.

'Hullo, darling. How are you getting on with Sam's plans?' I asked, my voice sugary, and he frowned.

'We've hit a small stumbling block, I'm afraid. I just wanted to make sure you ladies had everything you needed.'

As if! He wanted to make sure we were not at one another's throats, and he seemed almost disappointed by the serene atmosphere which surrounded us.

'I can't stay for long, Ian darling. Jocelyn is coming to pick me up, to go to town.'

'Nique fixed seductive eyes on my husband, reaching out to stroke his arm. She really had some nerve. 'But I hope to see you at the chateau again very soon. Will you come to play tennis with me tomorrow?'

'He can't go tomorrow. Alex and his family are arriving, and Ian needs to be here to welcome them,' I interjected, before he could respond to her wheedling question. He hesitated, and then took her caressing hand in his own

'I'm afraid tomorrow isn't possible, but I'll try to get across the following day.'

'Be sure you do.'

She got up and kissed him farewell in a leisurely way, while I seethed at her tone of command. Ian returned to his paperwork, his hunched shoulders denoting more than a degree of reluctance, and then it wasn't long before Jocelyn rolled up. She lowered her car window but made no attempt to get out.

'Can't stay, Eithne. See you soon, I expect,' she said, sounding as if it was a chore she couldn't get out of, and I raised a limp hand in acknowledgement. 'Nique brushed her cheek against mine, and then they drove away, leaving me to speculate about the real reason for this social call. Was 'Nique hoping to know me better, and allay any fears I might have about her intentions regarding Ian? Or did she want to see for herself how things were between us at Le Clos Fleuri? Her motive was buried under an avalanche of Gallic charm, and I told myself that I had better keep a spade handy.

Ian accosted me in the kitchen afterwards. Sam had driven off with an impatient ploughing of tyres on the gravel, which led me to believe the discussion with his father had not gone as he would wish. I looked up from washing strawberries, but Ian's face wasn't giving anything away.

'Did you enjoy yourself with 'Nique?' he enquired, picking at some olives on the table. There was vigilance in the question, as though he was afraid I might have uncovered something unpalatable. Was he hoping we might become friends, or would he prefer us to dispute for his attention? Was he worried I might get stroppy because of their brazenly renewed flirtation?

'Yes, I suppose so.'

It was a deliberately vague response. He hesitated, and then tried again.

'What did you find to talk about?'

'Oh, this and that. She told me a bit about her life in Argentina. She liked our kitchen. And we talked about having sex with you, obviously.'

'*What?*'

Ian's brow contracted, and I suppressed a smile. I adored my husband, but I was aware that he lacked a sense of humour at times, especially where his *amour propre* was concerned. He glowered at me, not appreciating this pointed teasing, and I uttered a little sigh.

'I was joking, Ian. But as we are on the subject, I am curious as to why you have never mentioned her to me before these last weeks. According to her, she might have been the third Mrs Inglis, if she hadn't decided to marry Ricardo Iglesias. I can't believe you had forgotten her.'

He picked up a peach, and examined its furry skin with care, as if he was weighing up his answer.

'No. I hadn't forgotten. But she was out of the equation when we came together after Peter died. If you are wondering why I didn't ask her to marry me, it's because I didn't want to make a commitment at that time. Does that make you feel better?'

I put down the colander and walked over to him, putting my arms around his neck. His afternoon with Sam had brought strain and tension to his eyes, and I wanted to take them away.

'I will try not to nag you, Ian, but you need to cut back a bit on the flirty stuff. It makes me look pathetic, and I resent that,' I told him, feeling that honesty was required to make my point.

He shrugged, gazing over my shoulder, although he did plant a hasty, conciliatory kiss on my cheek. 'If she carries on with other men like she does with you, I can understand why Ricardo chose to leave her as little as possible,' I added, sounding virtuous, although I knew that would annoy him.

'What! A little private conversation or two? It's hardly carrying on, as you put it. You've had your nose in too many problem pages.'

'I don't think so. At the dinner party, you were almost her main course. Perhaps you don't realise that people feel bad on my behalf when she plasters herself all over you.'

I could hear my voice rising, and I knew my cheeks were flushed. Did he appreciate my frustrations in any way? He looked solemn, but I couldn't see guilt or understanding in his eyes.

'We don't seem able to communicate these days,' I added, my voice cracking on a sigh. It was a sad post-script. Maybe I was sensitive, but I was beginning to resent his self-absorption. He had always been selfish – it was a character flaw I had come to accept over the years, but I hated the feeling that he was closed off from me. He eased himself out of my embrace, as if shrugging off an old jersey which had become tight and restrictive.

'You have become dreadfully needy of late, and it's making you invent a situation which doesn't exist. I hope you'll soon get over it,' he stated, in a tone of righteous remonstrance, which made me seethe. He bit into the peach as though chastising it, and strode out into the garden – well, he always liked to have the last word. Ruffled, I returned to my preparations for supper, and when we met for a drink before the meal, we managed to find a whole range of subjects to discuss with an awkward formality, none of which concerned the chateau and its inhabitants. But I saw it was only a temporary truce, and I was desperate for the company of Alex and Chloe to lighten the oppressive atmosphere of our house, even though that might result in other problems coming to the surface.

'Please don't frighten Chloe more than you can help,' I said to Ian, as we awaited our guests next day. He nodded obediently, and I smiled on him as he kissed her warmly (and insincerely) on both cheeks as she stood in the doorway, adopting a selfie pose in front of a beautiful rambling rose. We had an early dinner, and Ian drifted off to his study while Alex and I did the dishes. Chloe excused herself, saying she had to put Jack to bed, but I caught sight of her lounging at the poolside, hunched over her mobile phone.

'I hope Chloe finds she's getting reasonable reception here,' I said to Alex, who was already looking far less uptight than when I'd last seen him. 'Young people seem to be incapable of coping with life without their devices.'

'Gosh, you sound about eighty, Eithne,' Alex said, laughing. He joined me in gazing out towards his wife and gave a little sigh. 'But I really don't know what Chloe finds to gossip about all the time.'

I took a quick look round. Alex and I were alone.

'Have you managed to talk to Chloe about money yet, Alex? I hope she understands where you are coming from,' I murmured, and he rolled his eyes at me, in a way which didn't indicate much success with this mission.

'I have tried, honestly. She has agreed not to commit herself to anything expensive, and I have to hope that she doesn't fly off on one of her silly schemes again.'

I wished his voice held more certainty.

'What happened about the photo shoot, and the modelling?' I asked.

'She's signed up for catalogue work, and she's been in an issue of *Cheshire Life*. It's small stuff, but she says she has to begin somewhere.'

And where did she think it would it lead to, I wondered? Chloe's pretty features were screwed into a mask of discontent, and she clutched her mobile like some sort of lifeline. She had dyed her brown hair into a pinky blonde colour, and her skin was so heavily tanned that she looked as though she had spent an entire summer here, and not merely a few hours. Ian had already commented on her artificially enhanced cleavage and flashy white teeth, and not with approval.

I guessed that Le Clos Fleuri had not been Chloe's holiday destination of choice from a remark she let slip earlier, when Jack was exclaiming delightedly about the pool and the garden.

'Mum! Do you remember seeing the lizards when we were on holiday before? I wonder if they still live here?'

'Ugh. Horrible, wriggly things. Yes, I expect they are still in that old bit of wall. Nothing seems to change here. I don't know what your father thinks I'm going to do with myself all day…'

Her voice tailed away in a whine of discontent, which was lost on her excited son. It was evident that Chloe was a reluctant guest, and I hoped Ian wouldn't latch on to her petulance, but at least there was no sign of any recent injury to Alex. Maybe things had improved. I was counting on the lazy, sun-filled days to relax the tensions between them, and hopefully, lead to a renewed understanding between the pair.

Later that evening, I was summoned to say goodnight to Jack. He was tucked up with a selection of magazines and playthings on the sheets and didn't look at all sleepy. He grinned at me, patted the bed, and I sat down beside him.

'Hullo, Grandma. Do you know your house is super-cool? I'm going to see if I can catch a lizard tomorrow and keep it as a pet.'

'I'm not sure a lizard would like that, Jack. And they are incredibly quick little creatures. Why don't you just watch them playing along the wall instead?' I urged. He considered this suggestion; head resting on his knees.

'But I'd like a pet. Mummy won't let me have one at home,' he replied, pulling a sad face. We chatted amicably about the things he wanted to do while on holiday, and I noticed that it was always 'me and Daddy,' and that Chloe didn't seem to figure in the plans at all.

'I hope that Mummy will be coming on some of these trips with you,' I said, repressing a selfish fear that I might get lumbered with a bored and sulky Chloe, and he shrugged his shoulders.

'I'm not sure she'll be here all the time. It's supposed to be a secret, but I think she's planning to see Si Barnabas. I heard her talking to her friend Tara about it,' he said, small lips pursed in disapproval.

'Si Barnabas... where is that?' I asked, mystified, and the bed shook with Jack's laughter.

'Not where, Grandma – who! Si Barnabas is a winger with 'City. Mummy met him at a club back home, and her picture was in the paper with him and some other players. Daddy didn't like it, but it made Mummy ever so happy.'

'He's a footballer?' I enquired, after making a few painful deductions. Ian was a rugby and cricket fan, so my soccer knowledge was inadequate, to say the least.

'Well, yes, Grandma. I thought everybody knew that.'

Jack's reproving tone left me in no doubt that I had been found wanting. He lay back on his pillows, turning his attention to a flashy model car.

'Is he a good player?' I asked, hoping to regain some lost ground.

'Yes, he is. I expect Grandpa knows all about him.'

'I will ask him for his opinion,' I said gravely. We sat in silence for a minute, and I processed this interesting snippet of information. Where on earth would Chloe hope to run across a footballer in rural France? It was all very puzzling. Alex put his head round the door.

'Time to say goodnight, Jack. I'll look in on you later but give Grandma a kiss now.'

Jack reached up and hugged me. He smelled of toothpaste and toys and felt tip pens, and I was transported back to the days of Nicholas's youth.

'Goodnight, darling. Sleep well,' I said, feeling a teary pang of nostalgia as I returned the hug. 'We'll find lots of exciting things to do tomorrow.'

'I know. I'm going to work out how to make a lizard trap now.'.

There was fond amusement in the glance that Alex and I exchanged as I crossed to the door.

'I don't think the lizards have much to worry about,' he murmured, and we watched as Jack sank back on a pillow lumpy with books and toys – how he could sleep amongst such a collection was beyond me, but I remembered the cluttered beds of my children, who had somehow made themselves comfortable amongst a similar hoard of precious objects.

'I hope we can get Jack and Oliver together during the holiday. I feel that Ollie could do with a friend,' I said to Alex as we went downstairs. Later, I asked Ian if he knew of a football player named Si Barnabas.

'Yes. He's a rising star, by all accounts. Why on earth do you want to know about him?' he asked, looking puzzled.

'It was just something Jack said.'

I felt disinclined to go into details. Probably, Jack had misunderstood the situation, and the meeting was merely speculative. Ian sat on the bed to remove his sandals.

'I'm going across to the chateau early on tomorrow, to get some tennis in before the day gets too hot. I hope that's okay,' he said, and I wondered how he would react if I said it wasn't. I wished he hadn't jumped so obediently to 'Nique's commands, but it gave me the opportunity to ask about another chateau-related topic; one which had more serious implications now.

'What have you decided about Sam's investment project? You are keeping very quiet about the details,' I said, and I sensed a stillness in him, as though he was reluctant even to think about the matter. Our eyes met, and I could see how far he was out of his comfort zone.

'As a matter of fact, I'm not convinced it's as watertight an opportunity as Sam and Dominic seem to think. It's hard to refuse to go in with them, though. I can't take my money with me, and I believe in helping the children where I can,' he explained, but his disquiet was palpable. He would not have hesitated to reject such a plan in the past, and I wondered again whether his health scare had left him more inclined to take chances, as though conscious of the possible limitations of his time. I contemplated his serious face, and decided he needed some pragmatic advice.

'Think, Ian. If you are not one hundred per cent convinced that this is a safe investment, you won't be doing Sam or Dom any favours by agreeing to it. You could all be at risk,' I argued. He half-turned his head away, but I knew my words had reached him. 'When Aurien and I had dinner, he made some reference to a business proposal he'd got wind of; something involving Dom and Sam. He told me 'Don't let Ian get into bed with Dominic Templeton.' That makes me very worried on your behalf, because Aurien is no fool in these affairs.'

I hoped that by implicating Dom rather than Sam, Ian would not over-react to this overt criticism. He sat very still, as if contemplating an escape route from a frustrating maze, and I was relieved that he hadn't immediately dismissed my concern.

'Why didn't you tell me this before?' he asked, after a long silence.

'I was afraid you would think I was interfering. Sam is your son, not mine,' I added. Ian sighed, looking bowed down by an unacceptable burden.

'Aurien and Dom have some history, you know. Way back: there was an accusation of insider trading, and Dom's reputation in the City has never fully recovered. Aurien almost got burned, and he can be an old woman at times – but I wish you hadn't told me this. I will sleep on it a while longer,' he said, and I knew that I would have to be content with that. At least I had tried to alert him to the danger, although I was still unsure of what was going on.

Chapter Eleven

The next morning, Ian's alarm shrilled out, and I stirred groggily in bed as he plunged into the shower. He hummed to himself as he towelled his body, in anticipation of a pleasurable day ahead, and he dressed rather fussily in tennis whites, ignoring my comment that no-one else would be expecting Wimbledon. I heard the whirr of the coffee machine when he went downstairs, but he drove off to the chateau before the rest of us were ready for breakfast. I tried to gloss over his absence as best I could, because I knew that Alex was disappointed not to be with his father.

'He is playing tennis with a friend, and it gets too hot to be on the court after mid-morning. I expect he will be back with us for lunch.'

However, Ian didn't appear at midday as he had promised. Our morning was spent around the pool, and I prepared cold cuts and salad, which we ate in his absence. I hoped this wasn't going to set a precedent, because Ian needed to spend time with his guests at Le Clos Fleuri as well as those at the chateau. I could imagine him complaining that Chloe had frightened him off, and I would have to remind him that he was her host if he offered this as an excuse. However, Jack was happy enough wrestling with a prototype lizard trap, for which he had raided the contents of the gardening shed, and in the afternoon, Alex and Chloe took themselves off to visit the nearby town. I was pleased that they were spending time together, although it was difficult to detect any signs of empathy or affection between the pair.

When Ian did roll up shortly after tea, he devoted himself to Jack in such a way that it was impossible for me to utter any remonstrances, and the remainder of the day passed in relative harmony. But he couldn't escape the sharper edge of my tongue when we were alone in the bedroom.

'I hope you are not planning to spend all day tomorrow with the Templetons. Alex and Jack want to do things with you too,' I said frostily, conscious as I spoke that the Templetons were unlikely to be the main attraction for Ian at the chateau. He was slumped on the little sofa by the window, too tired to contemplate his usual bedtime routine, and I was worried about the after-effects of his strenuous day.

'You look exhausted. How many games did you play this morning? I can't believe that it is sensible for you to over-exert yourself physically in this heat. 'Nique is being very selfish, and very thoughtless, too, if she thinks you can cavort about the courts like a young man.'

This might have sounded spiteful, but I was genuinely concerned for him. We were experiencing a period of debilitating and sultry heat, which left everyone drained, even without taking exercise. As I surveyed the weary lines around his eyes, I wished that I had objected more strongly to him falling in with the request for tennis today.

Ian shifted his long frame on the couch; his face screwed up in an irritable grimace. He knew that he had overdone it, but as ever, he wasn't prepared to admit that he was at fault.

'Don't fuss, Eithne. We didn't play for long, but then Dom collared me, and one thing led to another. I promise I will take things more easily tomorrow.'

I wondered what other things he had been led to, and whether I would be allowed to know how he had spent the rest of his time at the chateau. I had the disagreeable sense that whatever was happening, there was no inclination to involve me, and that I was viewed as an outsider by this select party. These cogitations were interrupted by my mobile, and my heart jumped as I realised the lateness of the hour. I didn't want to be confronted by more bad news. But it was Olivia, calling from Italy.

'Mum? How's things? Will it be okay if I come to see you? I've finished wrapping things up here, and I fancy a few days lying by a pool.'

I hoped she didn't notice my momentary hesitation. In normal circumstances, I would be delighted to see her, but the presence of our other visitors meant that a quota of sensitivity and tact would be required if she joined the party, in order to avoid reviving old feelings and awakening petty jealousies. Tact wasn't one of Olivia's strongest points.

'Well, yes. You know I would like to see you... but Alex and his family are with us,' I said slowly, and there was a pause, while she considered the implications of their company.

'I understand – but I wouldn't make trouble. And I do need to talk something over with you, Mum. Please say yes.'

Olivia hardly ever consulted me about her affairs, and this request immediately plunged me into a whirlpool of worries.

'Are you ill?' I asked sharply, and I could hear her sighing down the line.

'No. There's nothing to get uptight about, but I really want to come.'

'Well – all right. I don't suppose Ian will mind,' I added, almost as an afterthought.

'That's good. We don't want to put Ian out.'

She reverted to her usual sarcasm, and this made me feel reassured rather than annoyed. She told me to expect her in three days' time and rang off abruptly. Ian had been listening to the conversation.

'What won't I mind?' he demanded, and I recounted Olivia's request. He whistled between his teeth.

'More to the point is whether Chloe will mind. I know that Alex will be delighted to see Olivia, but I hope she isn't plotting marital discord.'

'No. Other people are already doing that,' I said, unable to keep my grievances from bubbling up. Ian frowned at me, knowing very well who was in my sights.

'You mustn't be so judgmental about 'Nique,' he said, stretching again, and rubbing his calf muscles. 'She's not had an easy life.'

An easy life! I was infuriated by this throwaway sentimentality.

'Which of us has?' I challenged, thinking that this was no excuse at all for underhand behaviour. 'I haven't been without troubles; neither have you, for that matter. I don't feel that the vicissitudes of marriage with a rich South American are in the same class as being a refugee, say, or keeping down a job while raising a host of kids and struggling to pay off the mortgage. Please don't tell me that she deserves my pity.'

My voice ended on a high, angry note, and we exchanged an antagonistic glance; aghast that we were so quick to spark conflict these days. A faint scented breeze stirred the air through the open window, bringing memories of summer nights which had once been full of laughter and affectionate words. Now, I felt sad, and unloved. Something in my face, some evident distress, must have pierced my husband's conscience, because he levered himself from the sofa and came across to take me in his arms.

'I don't want to quarrel with you, Eithne.'

He pressed his face against my hair, and I wished we could stay in this close embrace. I wished that I'd never heard of Véronique; that Ian had never been taken ill; that I could somehow unpick the silly little incidents which had gradually built a barrier between us. But I didn't know how to proceed.

'You have nothing to fear from my friendship with Véronique. For God's sake, Eithne. You must trust me,' he said, sounding reproachful, and I smothered a little gulp of panic. I wanted to say that it was the lady I mistrusted but feared that might be taken the wrong way. It was better to accept this olive branch, although I wasn't sure how leafy it really was. 'I have said that I will entertain Jack tomorrow, and I think Alex will want to be involved. Will you be okay here with Chloe if we go off somewhere?' he added.

Chloe had plans of her own, which had entirely slipped my mind.

'I meant to tell you – Chloe is taking the train to the coast. She has a girlfriend staying there, and they want to meet up.'

Chloe's French was non-existent, and I was worried about her ability to cope, but she assured Alex that she would be met at the station by her friend at the other end of her journey.

'Which friend is this, Chloe?' I asked politely, and a faint flush rose to her pretty cheeks, as she adjusted her large hooped earrings before the hall mirror.

'Oh – Tara is a pal from home. Her hubby is loaded, and they're renting a yacht for a few weeks. It must be great to be able to spend what you want like that.'

The discontent in her voice grated on me. I realised that a free holiday in the country wasn't the same as a maritime adventure in a trendy tourist hotspot, but she never expressed any gratitude for the good things she did have. Alex looked at me with warning eyes, but I couldn't restrain my tongue.

'Having lots of money isn't the answer to everything. You have a nice house, an easy lifestyle, and a wonderful family. Lots of people would envy you, Chloe,' I said, and she threw me an irritated look which said: 'a fat lot you know.'

'Well, my friends don't seem to have such a bad time. Sometimes I wish I hadn't got tied down so young with a man and a kid,' she retorted, and stalked away on perilously high heels.

I hadn't relayed this little scene to Ian before. Now, happy that we were in sympathy for once, I leaned into him, and repeated what she had said.

'We can't interfere, Eithne. Alex and Chloe are adults, and either the marriage will last, or it won't. I wish things would come to a head. Neither of them appears to be happy,' he replied, looking at me for confirmation of this diagnosis.

'But what about Jack? He won't want his parents to split up. His life will be turned upside-down, and it could affect him very badly.'

'Thanks for reminding me.'

Ian pushed me away with a rough gesture, his voice sour, and I bit my lip; furious with myself for spoiling the conciliatory mood. He was alluding to the early years of Alex's childhood, when the hostile divorce from Jane resulted in Ian losing contact with his son for a period of years. I hadn't meant to be tactless. The sentiment was genuine, but I had spoken without thinking.

'I'm so sorry, Ian. That wasn't intended to be a dig at you. Whatever happened in the past, you know very well that Alex thinks the world of you now.'

But there was cold reproof in the way he shrugged me off, and I couldn't recall seeing such real dislike in his eyes. I was appalled that my careless comment had wounded him so deeply.

''Nique was asking about our history today,' he said, in a tight, measured tone. 'It reminded me that I don't have the monopoly on bad behaviour. You might want to bear that in mind before you criticise me again.'

I couldn't contradict him. The unfeeling way I'd thrown Ian over when Nick returned to my life still made me feel flaky when I remembered the harrowing episode. I'd tried to make reparations since our marriage; not by any direct apology, because Ian knew that I was sorry for hurting him, but by concentrating all my affection and care on my living partner. Of course, he hadn't been very nice to me in the aftermath, either. Suddenly, it seemed imperative that we shouldn't waste emotions in scrapping when our remaining years together were numbered, but that night, the back he turned on me seemed more implacably cold than ever. I lay in a miserable fug, wishing that I could revoke my words, but the damage had been done. Next morning, he treated me with a studied politeness which only made me feel worse. Alex seemed confused by the tension between us, as we breakfasted in an atmosphere of forced civility, marked only by curt requests and terse replies.

'Eithne tells me that Chloe is going travelling today. Is that wise? She won't be able to cope if things don't go to plan,' Ian said to his son.

'She has her mobile in case she gets stuck. If we put her on the right train, I can't see that she's likely to get into trouble,' Alex replied. He sounded indifferent to the affair; helping Jack to brioche and jam and pouring himself a large mug of coffee. Chloe was still upstairs, preparing for her expedition.

'Why don't you go too? It would be really interesting to see a superyacht at close quarters,' I suggested, but Alex raised his eyebrows, apparently resigned to a bad deal.

'I don't think I'm included in the invitation. The guest list will be moneyed Mancs, and a few C list celebs, if I know Tara. Chloe's only invited because she's pals with Tara back home, and she happens to be staying nearby.'

'It doesn't seem very fair on you, or on Jack, for that matter.'

'Leave it, Eithne.'

Ian intervened, warning me to drop the subject. I got up from the table and began to busy myself with a series of small, unnecessary jobs, wondering whether Chloe would be content to spend the rest of her holiday with us, or whether she would try to wangle a longer invitation with her friend. Any hopes I had harboured of bringing her closer to her husband had long since disappeared. It was clear that she and Alex were growing away from one another – no, had already grown distant, and neither seemed motivated to save the marriage. Ian was right, and it would be better if they made up their minds to separate as amicably as they could. We would all do our best to help Jack accept the situation.

After breakfast, Ian and Jack set off together to go boating on a nearby lake. I agreed to accompany Alex and Chloe to the station – my French wasn't wonderful, but it was better than theirs, and I could certainly cope with purchasing the correct train ticket.

Chloe kept us waiting, and Alex grew impatient, tutting and striding to the foot of the stairs.

'You'll miss the bloody train!' he bellowed. A door slammed, and Chloe's heels clicked snappily on the floorboards above. Her face was alight with child-like excitement as she lugged a pull-along case down the stairs behind her, and her hair and make-up were immaculate, although I could never see her heavily plumped scarlet mouth without repressing a little shudder, because I thought she had spoiled the naturally pretty lines of her lips. She was wearing a mini-dress with cheeky, cut-out panels around the midriff, which exposed startling amounts of smooth, tanned skin. Alex surveyed her, expressionless.

'Are you planning to spend the night, then?' he enquired, heaving her case into the boot, before slamming it shut, with an air of annoyance.

'Yes. You won't mind, will you? Tara says she needs some help with the entertaining, and I'm not much use here, am I?'

That much was true. The ride to the station was passed in a stifling silence. When we arrived, Alex dragged the case along, and I bought the ticket, and we accompanied Chloe to the appropriate platform.

'I would just like to make sure she's on the right train,' Alex muttered in my ear. Chloe wore a Cheshire Cat grin at the prospect of escape from Le Clos Fleuri, and she attracted glances both admiring and censorious from her fellow-travellers as she teetered in her strappy sandals. At least she bestowed a careless kiss on her husband's cheek as she boarded the train, although the grim way he wiped the lipstick off afterwards was hardly an advertisement for marital affection.

I opened my mouth several times on the ride home to ask Alex how he was feeling about his marriage, but somehow, the words stuck in my throat. It wasn't as though my own partnership was so very wonderful at present – I felt that I could hardly offer advice when Ian and I were so often at cross-purposes. But as we pulled up outside the house, Alex turned to me, and I was struck by the look of resignation in his face. He seemed tired and frazzled.

'I'm going to take myself off for a long walk, Eithne. There's so much I need to get my head round, and I think I'm better by myself. Do you mind me leaving you on your own here?'

'No, of course not, Alex. Are you sure you wouldn't like company, though? Can't I help in any way?'

I hated to see him so solemn and miserable. He shook his head, looking away over my shoulder.

'Thanks, Eithne, but no. But I would like to spend some time talking to Dad on his own tonight, because he's – well, he's my Dad. I'm sure you understand.'

I nodded, and watched as he took off across the garden, striding, head down, into the dusty hillsides beyond. Things were coming to the boil. I wondered what malevolent spirit had settled on Le Clos Fleuri for the summer, because this wasn't turning out to be a peaceful and restorative holiday for any of us.

Chapter Twelve

At least Ian and Jack spent a pleasant day together. They returned from their boating trip replete with laughing anecdotes, and Jack didn't comment on his mother's absence; not even once. He was tired after a day of fresh air and activity and submitted to an early bedtime without complaint. I excused myself from the kitchen not long afterwards, knowing that Alex wanted a heart-to-heart talk with his father. The walk seemed to have perked Alex up, but I suspected that he was putting on a cheerful face for everyone else's benefit. Ian went to fetch a bottle of cognac, and I left them to it.

As I sat at my dressing table, I wondered idly whether Chloe was enjoying herself on the yacht. Visions of bikini-clad girls draped over tanned and muscled young men floated unbidden into my mind, and I decided that she was a modern and scaled-down version of 'Nique, although I'm not sure that 'Nique would have agreed with me. It was apparent that Chloe put in hours of effort to make herself look good, and I was sure that my French rival did the same, although the results were very different. There was a subtle sophistication in 'Nique's public persona which was totally lacking in Chloe's in-your-face presentation.

That made me pensive. I removed my make-up, and examined myself in the mirror, wanting to gauge how well I compared with the glamorous 'Nique. I decided that my skin was clearer, and less lined than hers – after all, I hadn't spent years living in a hot climate – but she was adept at disguising and camouflaging any little defects, and there was no denying her sense of style. Maybe I needed to up my game in the face of this competition.

An idea wavered at the back of my mind. After a momentary hesitation, I threw my usual cotton nightdress into the laundry basket and rummaged in a drawer for a present that Maudie had given me some time back, after a visit here. I'd never worn it, thinking it unsuitable for my years, but now I welcomed the pretty lace and clingy pink silk of the sensuous garment as I slipped it on. I was lucky in that I rarely put on weight, and my figure was still good.

I hoped that Ian would like it and look at me with renewed appreciation – it was a sending a clear signal that I wanted him to do so. Then I climbed between the cool sheets, waiting in pleasurable anticipation for him to join me. The soft murmur of voices drifted from the kitchen, and I picked up my book. It was a warm, scented night, and my eyes grew heavy as I shuffled the pages. An owl hooted, and the incessant chirping of crickets serenaded the moon, soothing and sonorous…

The next thing I knew, the nightly noises had been replaced by shrill and insistent cockcrows from a neighbouring farm. It was morning. I yawned, stretched, and became aware that Ian wasn't in our bed, but was seated in a chair by the window, seemingly waiting for me to wake. He didn't look as though he'd spent an agreeable night. His face was as rigid and stony as an Easter Island statue, and I feared an uncomfortable scene was about to burst over me. What awful thing had happened now?

'Why didn't you tell me you had lent Alex money?' he burst out, as I struggled to sit up in bed. 'I don't appreciate you going behind my back, especially where *my children* are concerned.'

I wasn't expecting this! Alex must have admitted the fact during their conversation last night, despite my plea for him to keep it a secret. The timing of the revelation was unfortunate, to say the least.

'It happened when you were in hospital, and I didn't want to worry you,' I stuttered, thinking that he must understand my reasons. I rubbed my eyes, striving to clear the fog of sleep from my brain, and desperate to avert a row. 'It wasn't very much money, and I can assure you that no deception was intended. I simply wanted to help Alex. Can't you appreciate that?'

He made an impatient gesture, indicating that he had no intention of heeding what I'd said.

'You seem to think that the heart attack robbed me of my wits. Ever since it happened, you've been ludicrously over-protective – do you think I'm incapable of rational thought? Why do you feel it's necessary to keep me out of decisions which affect our family?'

He sat there, implacable, passing judgement on a penitent. 'And the constant nagging – don't visit the Templetons, don't get involved with Sam, don't play tennis with 'Nique – it's beginning to get me down, and this is the last straw!'

Waves of his fury washed over me. Then my own anger began to surface, as I realised what he was implying.

'You are being horrible, Ian. I've only tried to do what I thought was best for you. Just think back to when you came out of hospital... you were really worried about yourself; you hardly stirred from the house for days. Of course, I've been concerned for you, too. Don't twist things into a false perspective.'

Energised, I jumped out of bed, hoping that a caress might calm him, but a sudden contemptuous light in his eyes stopped me halfway across the room.

'What on earth are you wearing? You look like some cheap tart. It's bad enough having to watch Chloe strut her stuff without you following suit.'

I had forgotten the pink nightie. I glanced down at its slinky folds: now, the thought that my husband might find it attractive suddenly seemed shameful and embarrassing. Why hadn't I seen it was the same silly aspiration to revitalise a mature body that Ian had attempted, with his natty clothes and modish haircut? My legs trembled, and I reached blindly for a tissue, because tears were inevitable after this cruel jibe.

'Oh, don't turn on the waterworks!'

He turned his back on me, and began to dress, slamming drawers and pulling on his clothes with angry, rapid movements, as though he couldn't wait to get away. His feet clattered on the stairs, like so many gunshots, and the kitchen door banged shut with stark finality. The sound of the car engine told me that he intended to do without my company – for how long?

I felt as if I was dissolving in misery, and half expected to find myself in a soggy heap on the bedside rug. But eventually, my breathing calmed, the sobs hiccupped away, and I forced myself to get a grip on things. I pulled a dressing gown over the offending nightie and struggled downstairs, then tottered from the kitchen to the terrace, where the morning air was cool and sweet, like a refreshing tonic. I gulped it down. This was a favourite time of day, but I was almost heedless of the beauty around me.

What was wrong with Ian? His testiness and lack of judgement pointed to a crisis of some kind, as if he was blindly determined to prove that he was still an alpha male charging his way through life. Sofia had talked about a psychological shift, and I could only speculate that a deep insecurity had surfaced after Ian's brush with death, which was prompting him into irrational reactions to things which he didn't understand or couldn't control. He didn't realise that he was precious just as he was to those of us who cared for him, and I was scared that he was risking more than his physical well-being by allying himself with people and schemes which he would normally have rejected. And I had no idea how to return him to his old, sagacious self. What worried me most was that he might have no desire to return.

I sat there in stillness, stunned into a sorrowful meditation on all that was important in my life. After some time, Alex and Jack appeared, obviously wondering why we weren't at breakfast.

'Has Dad gone out already? I thought I heard wheels,' Alex asked, rubbing his head, and smothering an inelegant yawn. No doubt the cognac bottle had taken a hammering the night before, and maybe it could also accept a portion of the blame for Ian's behaviour this morning. There was a tiny crumb of comfort in the thought.

'He's taken himself off somewhere,' I said carefully. I needed to remove Jack from the scene before I could tackle his father.

'Jack, would you be a darling, and fetch my book for me? It's on the little table by my bed.'

Jack skipped off obediently, and I motioned to Alex to sit down. 'Alex – your father and I have had a terrible row this morning. Why on earth did you tell him about the money? He's furious with me,' I said baldly.

Alex gasped, and leaned against the trellis post, looking in need of support.

'God, I'm so sorry, Eithne. I'm afraid we talked into the small hours last night, and both of us sank more than few cognacs.'

He lowered himself gingerly to the chair next to me, grimacing as though he regretted the over-indulgence. 'I was feeling so close to Dad, and somehow, things came out before I could stop them. I certainly didn't expect him to blame you for anything.'

'He's in a real temper, and my guess is that he's gone to find more congenial company at the chateau. And he's taken the car, so I'm afraid you will need to do the shopping with me today.'

And was 'Nique taking advantage of this opportunity to smooth his furrowed brow? I could imagine those soft, elegant hands dispensing comfort to her aggrieved former beau, and hear the delicately murmured words which would distract him from domestic cares. 'Please don't let him tell her about this morning,' I prayed silently, burning with heated shame that Ian might recount his reaction to the pink silk nightwear. They would put their heads together and laugh ... and she would be clever enough to turn it all to her advantage.

Jack returned with my book and asked hopefully about breakfast. Alex rose to his feet staggering as if slightly unsure whether they belonged to him – I hoped he would be feeling better when the time came to visit the hypermarket.

'Can I fetch you anything, Eithne?' he asked, bending over to kiss my cheek with affectionate warmth. I knew he was mortified by Ian's behaviour, and my own feelings of annoyance abated a little as I observed his stricken face.

'A nice strong coffee would be good. Help yourself to croissants; you know where everything is.'

They disappeared inside. A little later, Jack came to fetch me. They had laid the kitchen table with care, and a special place was set for me, with a peach-coloured rose adorning a napkin. This unlooked-for thoughtfulness made me weepy again.

'Look, Grandma! We cut the rose specially for you, and it smells really sweet,' urged Jack, ushering me to my chair, and I reached out to ruffle his shiny head.

'It's lovely, darling. Thank you so much. What a shame Grandpa isn't here to see it.'

I swallowed down a sob and accepted these ministrations with gratitude. I knew that Alex was trying to atone for his father's rage, even though I didn't blame him for the morning's scene, and I managed to force down a slice of brioche, although I felt that there was an obstruction in my throat and I had little appetite. But if I didn't eat, I would feel terrible later – as if anything could make me feel worse than I already did.

Alex looked more human after a shower and a shave, although he seemed to be wary of sudden movements. The three of us set off for the hypermarket, and Jack was in ecstasies because his father had promised to buy him a net, ostensibly for lizard-trapping.

'It will have to be a fishing net, so I hope that will do,' Alex cautioned, and Jack nodded, eyes glowing at the prospect of catching a reptile for himself.

'If I don't manage to get a lizard, we'll take it to the river and go fishing,' he announced, and I thought how lovely it must be to live in a world filled with such simple joys. As I delved into my bag to find the trolley token, I realised I'd left my phone at home, but I was deluding myself if I thought that Ian would want to contact me after the morning's scene.

Once we were inside the shop, the boys went in search of a suitable net, and I began to load my trolley with bottled water and soft drinks. The mundane business of shopping was strangely calming, and I began to feel more hopeful that the cloud of Ian's rage would pass. I threw in bags of crisps for the boys, followed by a selection of breads and patisserie, because I had forgotten how much healthy young men could eat. The trolley groaned under the weight of delicious and calorific treats, and Alex joined me as I was checking the final items off my list. He was speaking into his mobile, and I thought it must be Chloe calling.

'Yes… no problem. She's here now: hold on.'

He handed the phone to me. 'Dad' he mouthed, and I nearly dropped it.

'Ian?'

I could feel my heart thump. What was he going to tell me? Perhaps he had decided to take off somewhere; to give himself some time away from the wife who had annoyed and upset him so comprehensively.

'Eithne. Look: I'm sorry about this, but is there any way we could feed the chateau crowd tonight? Their caterer is down with a bug. It's just the family, plus Véronique, because the little ones will stay with the nanny and have fish fingers, or whatever it is they eat.'

I was tempted to tell him to sod off, but that would result in more anger and scenes, and I wanted to avoid that possibility. I certainly didn't want the Templetons to know how bad things were between us.

'Well... all right. I suggest we have a barbecue, though. It's far too hot for me to do a lot of cooking inside, and then we can eat on the terrace. You are lucky that I'm in Super U with Alex, because I wouldn't be able to shop otherwise,' I said stiffly, alluding to his disappearance with the car. He made no apology for this.

'A barbecue is a good idea. Alex and I can do our chef routine and spare you some of the bother. Thanks. See you later.'

He ended the call before I could ask him where he was, or how he intended to spend the day, and I shrugged my shoulders.

'Did you get the gist of that?' I asked, handing the mobile back to its owner.

'Yes. Dad spoke to me first. Don't worry – we'll all pitch in to help.'

We had to fetch another trolley for the extra wine, charcoal and food we needed to cater for such a large party. Although I wasn't pleased with the last-minute nature of the occasion, we owed a debt to the Templetons for their recent hospitality, and this was a good opportunity to reciprocate without too much effort on my part. Jack was jumping at the prospect of visitors.

'They will bring Oliver, won't they? I want to play with him,' he exclaimed, and I asked Alex to text his father to make sure that Oliver was included in the party.

There were some benefits from this unexpected social invasion. The mental and physical demands of the preparations stopped me from brooding, and I knew that Ian would have to be civil towards me in the presence of guests. After lunch, Alex prepped the large built in barbecue area and cleaned the outdoor furniture, while I assembled salads and marinated steaks.

'It's about time Dad was here,' Alex said, shooting me an anxious look as we paused to refresh ourselves with cold drinks. The afternoon was shading into evening, and a car crunched up the drive as he spoke. Ian emerged, standing to attention as 'Nique's slender body and legs unfurled from the passenger seat. I hoped that my greeting to the pair was cool and dignified, and 'Nique embraced me in her usual charming fashion.

'So much to do! You must let me help, Et-ne,' she drawled, before sinking into the comfortable swing seat on the terrace and lighting a cigarette. I reflected that she only needed a cigarette holder to be a latter-day Hepburn, and Ian hurried off to fetch her a drink.

'Nique was her usual glamorous self. She was wearing a silky jumpsuit, in which she looked both sexy and on trend, and her *maquillage* was perfect, emphasising huge, smoky eyes. As she placed her handbag on the table, I couldn't help noticing that it was one I had recently admired in a local shop, and she followed my gaze.

'Do you like my new bag? This Valérie in town, she has good things, *n'est-ce pas*? Quite unexpected, for the provinces.'

She stroked the soft leather with an appreciative hand, and I was suddenly convinced that Ian had bought it for her.

'It's lovely. I'm afraid that Valérie's stock is usually too pricey for me,' I said truthfully, then wondered if that made me sound pathetic. 'Nique looked down demurely, and a tiny smile of satisfaction crinkled her cheeks.

'Good accessories... they are important,' she murmured, blowing out smoke. 'I say this always to Jocelyn, but she ignores my advice – as she does on many things.'

For the first time in my life, I felt a twinge of sympathy for Jocelyn. It wouldn't last long. Ian loomed over us, two ice-topped glasses in his hands, and I remembered my unfinished preparations. I didn't think the second drink was meant for me, and I certainly wasn't going to play gooseberry with this pair of old *amants*.

'Will you please excuse me? I have a few things still to do for supper,' I said, turning away. It was galling to hear her gaiety echo behind me, and Alex glanced nervously at me as I returned to the kitchen.

'I will try to get Dad on his own as soon as I can, to make sure he understands about the loan,' he muttered, and I grimaced.

'Better leave that until later, Alex. There's enough to think about with the Templetons about to descend. Can you wash those radishes for me?'

We worked in silence, both of us conscious that matters were topsy-turvy and threatening to get out of hand. Jack wandered in and out and didn't improve the mood by remarking that 'Grandpa was laughing a lot with the French lady.' With impeccable timing, Ian strolled back inside as we were clearing up.

'Shouldn't we light the charcoal? The Templetons will be here any minute. What are we cooking?'

This was addressed to Alex rather than me. I left Alex to explain the menu and retreated to my room; keen to extinguish all traces of my afternoon's hard labour. There was nothing in my wardrobe which could match the allure of 'Nique's attire, but I selected a decorous shift dress which I knew that Ian had liked in the past and refreshed the small amount of make-up I wore. If I couldn't be glamorous, I could at least be natural. Ian was alone in the kitchen when I went back downstairs.

His ill-temper of the morning still rankled with me, and I wasn't going to speak first, or even look at him. I hoped that he could read reproach in my stiff movements as I banged cutlery and plates about. He seemed to be casting around for a suitable opening, and then he cleared his throat.

'I'm sorry about this evening. Jocelyn didn't give me much choice,' he muttered, gazing down at the table, and I felt like grabbing his shoulders and shaking him. He knew perfectly well that the constraint between us was due to the discord of the morning, not the social plans for the evening. But I didn't want to rake that argument up again.

'We would have to entertain them at some point. This is a relatively easy way of doing it,' I said, carefully impassive. We had to communicate; there was no way we could get through the evening otherwise, but I didn't feel like extending a helping hand.

'Yes; I suppose that's true.'

We looked at one another without smiling, but I think we were both relieved to have taken a tentative step towards an understanding, no matter how fragile. He fidgeted with the corkscrew, and strode back to the garden, and as I followed behind with a bowl of potato crisps, I watched him slide into the seat next to 'Nique with an air of relief, like someone who has dodged a bullet.

There was possession and celebration in the affectionate smile with which she welcomed him, and her eyes darted towards me to check that I was looking at them. She leaned against Ian's shoulder with an artless, confiding movement, and ran her tongue around her lips in an overtly sexual way, as though sending a message, and I gulped. For the first time, I began to consider the possibility that my marriage was in danger.

Chapter Thirteen

Before I could pursue this thought to its unappealing conclusion, I heard wheels on the gravel, and the Templeton party arrived. I cranked my face into a welcome and went to greet them. Jocelyn barely paused in her running commentary about the house, the weather, the astounding inconvenience of the caterer's illness, and the novelty of a barbecue (something apparently unknown at Rivermead). While she was talking, she managed to bestow her usual perfunctory kisses before appropriating Ian's place next to 'Nique on the swing seat. Dom enfolded me in a sweaty embrace, which felt like an elephant rubbing me against its rumpled hide, but Sam and Emma greeted us with their customary cool distance, and I was thankful for that. I looked round for Oliver, but Jack had already grabbed his arm, and was leading him off to the lizards.

'Don't go anywhere near the pool!' Sam called after them, and Jack turned to give him an incredulous stare.

'We're not babies,' I heard him retort.

Ian opened champagne – only the best would do for these special guests – and then he and Alex got to work at the barbecue, which was glowing hot and ready for the food.

'And where is Chloe?' enquired Emma, as she helped me set out the bowls of salad and bread on the long table.

'She's visiting a pal on the coast. The pal's husband has hired a yacht, and they are having a party on board,' I said, enjoying Emma's ill-concealed surprise at this news. Jocelyn pricked up her ears and demanded more information, but I couldn't satisfy her curiosity.

'Darling Chrissy will be staying there next month, seeing some old friends,' she informed us. 'It's such a shame we haven't managed to overlap our visit.'

I doubted that darling Chrissy was equally upset. It wasn't long before the first savoury offerings from the coals were ready. The steaks were charred and appetising, but deliciously bloody inside, and the merguez sausages oozed piquant, oily juices when their skins were pierced. It was gratifying to see our guests eating with hearty appreciation. Ian sat by 'Nique, of course, and was assiduous in his attention to her needs, but I noticed that she toyed with her plate, and a very small amount of food actually passed her lips. No doubt this was how she kept her willowy figure.

'Mummy knows a lot of footballers. Some of them will be on the yacht with her,' Jack piped up unexpectedly. I don't know whether he thought this would impress our visitors, but the amused glances between the Templeton party were anything but admiring.

'Oh, that's nice for Mummy. Why wasn't Daddy invited?' asked Sam, sending a snide glance towards his nephew, and I heard Emma giggle.

'It isn't fair to leave Dad and Eithne to look after Jack,' Alex replied calmly, and I was pleased he had not risen to the bait. But Sam couldn't leave things alone. He contemplated his half-sibling with mocking eyes, before saying,

'I never knew you moved in such exalted circles. I'm afraid we aren't lucky enough to count footballers among our intimate friends.'

His tone oozed contempt. Alex's face crimsoned as he bent over his plate, and I frowned at Ian, hoping he would put Sam in his place, but a counter-attack was mounted from an unexpected quarter.

'In Argentina, we often invited players from the top teams to visit when we entertained. Ricardo was a huge football fan; he would always attend the big matches of Boca Junior,' 'Nique informed the little boys, and the awkward moment passed. Ian smiled his gratitude upon her, and I saw him give her hand a surreptitious squeeze. I knew he didn't like it when Sam tried to put one over on his half-brother in public, but I felt cynical about 'Nique's motivation. Did she want to save Alex from embarrassment, or was she hoping to score points with his father by this timely intervention?

Despite all the disquiet which rumbled under the surface, it wasn't such a bad evening. Platters of local cheese and patisserie followed the barbecued meats, and our guests were loud in their compliments about the food. But I felt as though I was viewing everything through a lens which distorted my vision of events. On one hand, I was hyper-sensitive to every communication, every glance between my husband and 'Nique, but Jocelyn's snide conversation, which would normally have been an irritant, washed over me and left me unmoved. Ian barely addressed me; speaking only when his duties as host demanded it, and I began to dread what awaited me in the bedroom. Perhaps he would decide to sleep elsewhere, or even make some excuse to return to the chateau. I looked on without comment as he devoted himself to our guests; knowing that he was keeping me on the fringes and wondering if they knew it too.

At the end of the meal, Alex made coffee, and I tilted my chair, trying to lose myself and my worries amongst the shimmery stars which dotted the darkening sky above the trees. Conversation was lazy and voices languid, and I snatched a moment to relax, feeling sorry that the unwelcome task of clearing up after the meal awaited me.

'Eithne!'

Jocelyn's sharp tone recalled me to the present, and I sat up, startled. 'We'll be leaving shortly. It's way past Oliver's bedtime. Don't you worry about such a late night for Jack?'

'I'm not his mother,' I replied, yawning. 'And we are on holiday. It's too lovely a night to worry about bedtimes, and besides, I like to see the young ones enjoying themselves.'

Ollie and Jack had devoured sausages and strawberry tart, before making off with Jack's net for a moth and beetle catching expedition. Their happy shrieks of laughter echoed through the groves, and I was delighted that Oliver was enjoying little boy pursuits for once. There was a moment of immense excitement when they managed to trap a lizard baby who had been rash enough to linger in the last rays of sunshine, but Sam ignored their protests, and released the little creature back into the rocky crevices of the garden wall. Jack's fury was boundless, and his father had to intervene.

'It isn't fair on the lizard, Jack. Leave him where he's happy,' Alex said, giving his son a consoling hug. I could see the disappointment on Jack's face, but he stuck out his chin, and disappeared amongst the trees again, with his new pal in pursuit.

'I hope you will let Ollie come and play with Jack again. They get on so well,' I said to Emma, but she frowned as she rose from the seat and shrugged her shoulders into her pashmina.

'I just hope that he isn't ill in the night. He's had far too much to eat,' she said in accusing tones, as though I had been force-feeding my young guests like so many fledglings. As I had been sitting at the other end of the table from the boys this seemed unfair to me, but I hoped for Ollie's sake that no such catastrophe would occur. I thought he would be all the better for making a hearty meal.

Despite the desire to get Oliver home and into bed, our visitors hung around making lengthy farewells. I began to long for them to go. There was no hired help to wash the dishes in my house, and I was tempted by a mischievous urge to invite the chateau ladies to come in and assist me, but I wasn't brave enough to voice the request, although I knew that nothing would send them packing more quickly. At last, the red lights of their people carrier faded into the night, and I turned my attention to the debris of the evening.

Ian's face showed the ravages of over-indulgence, but at least he was still with us. He and Dominic had drunk with careless excess during the meal, and exhaustion had crept up and snared him. Alex and I exchanged glances, and then he took his father by the arm.

'You look awful, Dad,' he said quietly. 'I think you and Jack should get to bed. I'll help Eithne to clear the worst of this away, and we'll do the rest in the morning. It was a good party, but you need to get some rest.'

Ian looked directly at me, for almost the first time that evening. I read guilt and apprehension as well as tiredness in his eyes, and that didn't make me any more comfortable.

'I do feel knackered,' he admitted, wiping a hand across his face. 'I'm afraid that Dom always encourages me to drink more than I should, and I had no idea they would stay so long. Is that okay with you, Eithne? I promise I will do my share in the morning.'

I shrugged. I was in no mood to let him get away with things, but neither did I want him to overtax himself, and I didn't know how he had spent the earlier part of the day. If 'Nique had lured him on to the tennis courts again, he would be genuinely exhausted by now.

'Alex is right. Go to bed, Ian, and you can muck in tomorrow morning,' I said. Part of me was relieved that this would lessen the chance of awkward bedtime conversation, or what would be worse, of hostile and pointed silence. Ian trod wearily upstairs, accompanied by a somnolent Jack, and Alex and I were left to contemplate the wreckage of dinner.

How had we accounted for such a mound of dirty plates and glasses? We surveyed the table and began to laugh. 'This is awful. I think we'll leave as much as possible,' I decreed. 'I don't see why your father should get out of his share. Let's clear everything inside, put a load in the dishwasher, and worry about the rest tomorrow.'

'Agreed.'

We worked in bleary and distracted silence until the mess was stacked in the kitchen. Alex went to rake over the dying embers of the barbecue, and I leaned against the doorpost, almost too spent to appreciate the mysterious life of the night garden. All the usual smells were intensified into a heady bouquet of fragrance, and a bat dipped low over my head. I remembered how Chloe had screamed a night or so ago, when she had ventured out for a ciggie and encountered nature at uncomfortably close quarters and was relieved to find I could still muster a smile at the memory.

'Have you heard from Chloe?'

I felt guilty that we had almost forgotten her in the bustle of the evening.

'I had a text message. Apparently, the yacht is *mega*. Don't feel you have to worry about her, because I'm not.'

There was a complete lack of interest in the way Alex spoke about his wife. The debris of the evening also contained the remnants of broken relationships and family ties, and it was a struggle to remember a time when the future held warmth and affection rather than cares and enmity. Alex scrutinised my sad face.

'Please don't look like that, Eithne. Tomorrow, I will straighten things out with Dad, and this awful atmosphere will blow over; I'm sure of it. And I am beginning to see what I need to do about Chloe.'

There was a question in my eyes, but we were both too tired to pursue the subject. 'I'll lock up,' he continued. 'You get to bed now; you look all in.'

Ian was a snoring hump under the bedclothes when I entered the bedroom. I had a sketchy wash, slipped on a nightie – not the reviled pink one – and crept under the sheets to lie beside him. He was only an inch away from me, but I felt as though it was no longer possible to bridge that tiny gap. I was in that state of exhaustion where you long for sleep, but the mind refuses to switch off.

I couldn't get comfortable. When I closed my eyes, I could see 'Nique's serene and confident face, as she insinuated herself into my husband's psyche. Sam's drawling voice throbbed inside my head, and despite the wash, my skin felt permeated with smoke. After some time of restless, unhappy cogitation, I slid out of bed, and retraced my steps downstairs. The old sofa welcomed me like a friend, and I pulled a throw over my body as I sank down on the cushions, to ward off the night-time chill. It was better to curl up on my own than be lonely next to the man I loved.

Jack's bright morning face bent over me, and I woke from a troubling sleep with a gasp. For a moment, confusion claimed me, but then I realised I was still lying on the couch, and explanations would be demanded from me before long.

'Grandma! What are you doing here? I've brought you a cup of tea, and Daddy says to stay put while he and Grandpa get the kitchen sorted out after last night.'

I struggled to sit up, because my limbs were cramped from lying on the sofa. Ominous bumps and clattering assailed my ears, and I knew that I would find it impossible to go along with this request.

'Thank you, darling. Perhaps you could help them too,' I suggested. He skipped from the room, and I limped upstairs with the tea to my bedroom, where I pulled on a bathrobe, and made a hasty toilette. I didn't look too bad, despite my unconventional night, although the muscles of my back felt stiff and creaky. Then I descended again, hoping to find that order had been restored in the kitchen. A glass smashed on the tiled floor as I walked in.

'Blast!'

Ian sucked a finger, then looked up and met my gaze. 'You are supposed to keep away until we've finished,' he said, scowling, but I chose to ignore this.

'I hope you haven't cut yourself badly,' I remarked, looking round for the dustpan. Shards of glass had flown everywhere, glinting evilly in the sunlight on the tiles, and I told Jack, whose feet were bare, to stay out of the way.

Alex brought the brush and pan and began to clear up the fragments. I walked across to Ian and took his injured hand in mine. Somehow, he had acquired a deep gash, and blood was flowing freely. He glanced at it and shuddered. He hated the sight of blood.

'Come and sit down.'

I led him outside, and he sank unsteadily on to a garden chair, while I knelt by him, applying a clean tea towel and pressure to the cut. A bird chided us noisily from a nearby bush, complaining that we were disturbing his morning routine. Ian gave a little groan, and after a minute or so, I checked the wound. 'I don't think we will need an ambulance today,' I said, attempting a gentle tease. 'But you had better let me bandage this. I'll need to clean it, so stay put while I get the First Aid kit.'

He grunted, keeping his head averted from the sight of his finger, but I saw that colour was seeping back into his cheeks now the first shock was over. When I returned with the necessary materials, he allowed me to clean and dress the cut, wincing as the antiseptic stung his skin.

'That was careless of me,' he observed. His gaze slid up from his hand to my face, searching for the answer to something which puzzled him. 'Why on earth were you on the sofa this morning? I couldn't think where you'd got to.'

'I couldn't sleep. I went back downstairs and must have dropped off.'

I could see from his pursed lips that this explanation wasn't satisfactory, but he nodded, and commented briefly on the success of the barbecue. I wanted to capitalise on this docility and I seized the opportunity to speak my mind.

'Please don't disappear today, Ian. We must talk. I am not happy about your continual visits to the chateau, and neither do I appreciate the unpleasant things you said to me yesterday morning. I can't think why you are behaving like a moody schoolboy – it's not very dignified.'

I knew that would hurt. His eyes widened, and he sucked in his breath, but I had to make him see reason.

'Yes – we should talk,' he murmured. 'But the boys want me to take them on that coastal drive today – Ollie's coming, too. Could it wait until this evening? I would hate to disappoint them.'

He reached out and ran a tentative finger over my forearm, as if he was mollifying a wary animal. It sounded a reasonable proposition, and I didn't want him to disappoint the boys. But it would have been a welcome change to spend the day together, just the two of us, and I was sad to feel that he was pleased at the prospect of escape.

'If that's what you want.'

My voice was grudging. I was anxious to straighten things out, so I knew where we stood, and it meant another day wrestling with my worries until we could be alone. 'Don't forget that Olivia will be here tonight,' I added, wondering how successful I would be in concealing my fears from my forthright daughter.

'Well, I can ask Alex to take her off for a drink in town if necessary. Do we expect Chloe back?' he asked, a faint tremor of exasperation in his tone.

'I would be most surprised to see her. My guess is that she intends to stay there for a few days.'

'That's something to be pleased about, at any rate.'

At least the omnipresent 'Nique didn't appear to be included in the day's plans. Alex hovered with restorative tea for his father, and then we spent an hour submerged in soapsuds, until we finished clearing up. It was a relief to see the kitchen back to normal, and nothing else got broken.

I waved my menfolk off a little later – Jack bubbling with excitement about being with Ollie again – and I promised myself a lazy day. There was plenty of food in the house, and the prospect of a swim and a proper sleep after lunch was very appealing after my uncomfortable night.

However, my mid-morning coffee was interrupted by the sound of wheels on the gravel, and I uttered a prayer that it wouldn't be any of the chateau crew, because I'd had my fill of them for the time being. Then I saw my friend Elizabeth hovering in the doorway, and my spirits leapt. She was always good company, and I was out of touch with the neighbourhood news after my preoccupation with domestic issues. With luck, she would have some juicy titbit about the local views of the Templeton household to amuse me.

'Eithne... I'm not disturbing you, I hope?'

Elizabeth peered around furtively, as if fearing an auditor in the bushes, and I wondered why she seemed so jumpy and distracted.

'No. I'm on my own today. The boys are having a road trip, and I'm recovering after entertaining the mob from the chateau last night.'

I made her a coffee and we retreated to the shade of the veranda. She took a sip of her drink, and blew out her cheeks, as though she'd just run an enervating race.

'I'm so pleased to find you on your own.'

Her fingers plucked nervously at a tendril of vine, and she didn't seem able to meet my eyes. 'Bill told me not to come, and that I should mind my own business, but I felt I had to see you. Please don't think I'm prying – but I thought you ought to know.'

I sat very still; impaled upon apprehension. After such an introduction, I felt that what she had to say wasn't going to be easy to hear, and I guessed what it would concern. 'You know I always get my hair done at that little place in the square in town,' she continued, her fingers still shredding the leaves. 'Bill usually drops me, and afterwards, we do some shopping, and have lunch out. It's just that yesterday, we were there... and we saw Ian. I'm sorry to have to say this, but he was with another woman, having drinks outside the Hotel Lion d'Or, and it looked as though they were more than just friends.'

Her voice cracked, and she took a hasty gulp of coffee. 'I don't know who it was, but the woman was draped over him, and he was enjoying it for all he was worth. Hand-holding, little whispers and kisses... it was all I could do not to march across and give him a piece of my mind, but Bill dragged me away. You've been such good friends of ours. I hate to think there's something going on behind your back.'

As I remained silent, she added, 'I asked myself what I'd want in your place, and I would need to know. Please say you don't hate me for passing this on, Eithne!'

She reached across the table, grasping my hand in hers, and I returned the anxious pressure of her fingers.

'It's all right,' I murmured. 'I mean: it's not all right, but none of this is a surprise to me. I know exactly who it was. She's a French lady Ian knows from way back – an old flame. She was widowed at the beginning of the year, and she seems to have taken up with the Templetons. I have it from her own lips that she isn't after Ian, but I am beginning to wonder if that's the truth. Her late husband hasn't left her in funds, and she needs another source of income, because she's obviously a high-maintenance woman.'

Elizabeth was goggle-eyed with amazement at this information. She opened her mouth to speak, but the words wouldn't come.

'Ian is flattered by her attentions, and his judgment is all over the place at present, after the shock he suffered in April. What can I do? I'm hoping he will come to his senses, but right now, I think he's enjoying himself too much to stop.'

I was surprised by how cool I sounded. Was I really accepting that my husband was in public pursuit of a glamorous rival? Elizabeth gaped, scarcely able to believe what I'd said.

'You know about her? Why aren't you fighting her off, then? Surely you won't sit back and let her walk away with your husband?'

'It isn't quite so black and white, Elizabeth. Ian tells me that he's merely enjoying the company of a pretty woman, and you know he practically has a degree in flirting. I won't believe that he wants to end our marriage. Our lives have been intertwined for so many years, and we have been very happy together. But he hasn't been himself since he came out of hospital, and I don't know what is driving him at present.

'We had sharp words yesterday, and I've told him we need to talk things over when he gets back tonight. I don't know how to tackle things. Do you have any advice?'

'Tackle things! I'd let him know that you won't put up with this public display of infidelity. People are talking, Eithne. He's not unknown in the area, and you know how people love to gossip. Does he like that?'

'I think he'd be flattered, in a funny way. It shows that he's a person who matters, and that's what's important to him at present.'

The gathering cloud on Elizabeth's brow told me exactly what she thought of my analysis. I had to seal my lips while she lectured me; saying that Bill was appalled by the indiscretion of his old friend, and the expat community was seething with speculation and rumours. It didn't make pleasant hearing. But at last, she wound down, and I tried to dampen the flames. I assured her that we were not about to part, and that I hoped the little affair would fizzle out before too long.

'I don't see how my rival can stick around once the Templeton's tenure of the chateau is over, and that has only two weeks left now.'

My voice wavered. Despite these brave words, I wasn't confident that Véronique would take herself off when they left, or that Ian wouldn't be tempted to follow her if she did. She might even try to get herself invited to stay at Le Clos Fleuri – she possessed the nerve to do anything to further her ambitions. It looked as though a showdown was inevitable, and I didn't relish the prospect.

'Tell Ian that Bill wants to have a round of golf with him tomorrow. Bill will tell him what's what,' Elizabeth said, sounding determinedly pleased at the idea, but I shook my head.

'No, please not, Elizabeth. Ian hates feeling he's being boxed in or hectored, and that might make him more likely to do something silly. He isn't rational these days.'

A little breeze sprang up and tousled my hair. The distant skies had grown clouded, and I shivered, sensing we were in for a shower. Elizabeth was brooding; thinking over my explanation for my husband's behaviour.

'I know men can get silly over women. Bill made me awfully unhappy once, over a very glamorous secretary he had, although I don't think it ever came to anything.'

Her voice wobbled as though she wasn't quite sure of that, and it was painful for her to think back on the memory. 'But it's such a disappointment to see Ian acting like this. I've always looked up to him, and he's the last person I would expect to lose his head. It isn't as if she's a young girl, either.'

Now she sounded accusing, as if I ought to have repelled the piratical boarder of my matrimonial ship more swiftly, and I asked myself if I should have taken a firmer line with my husband at the start. It was too late now. I squeezed her hand again; comforted by a friendly touch.

'Listen, Elizabeth, I am not at all offended by what you've told me, and I am grateful for your concern – Bill's, too. But I must figure out a way to get through this, and I need time to think.'

There was a tremor in my voice, as I contemplated a difficult scene ahead. 'I do know that Ian won't react well if he believes that we're all out to chastise him, and bring him to heel, so can you ask Bill to back off for the moment? Let's hope it will blow over – like this shower.'

But a curtain of rain fell across us, and we had to retreat to the shelter of the house. It was a sad and doubting Elizabeth who kissed me goodbye, but I hoped I had convinced her not to interfere further at present. I wasn't upset that she had reported what she'd seen; in her place, I would probably have done the same. However, it was chastening to have confirmation of the overt and unheeding nature of Ian's flirtation, and maybe I had been naïve in letting things go so far.

Chapter Fourteen

I was too miserable to face eating lunch; contenting myself with fruit and a morsel of cheese to quell internal rumbles. Although the rain had cleared, there was something grating about the brilliant azure sky which followed the downpour – it was too blue, too perfect, and I would have welcomed grey clouds, which were more in tune with my feelings. I settled myself on the sofa with one of Chloe's glossy magazines, but not a page was turned. The words blurred when I tried to read them. I could only picture the intimate proximity of two heads, the silver and the blonde, laughing together under the colourful parasols outside the hotel. The vision filled me with an aching sadness. When was the last time Ian and I had spent time together in such a carefree way?

Then a sudden noise startled me, and I sat upright in alarm. The house was unlocked, and I remembered that burglaries were not uncommon in the summer months, when heat and wine distracted careless holidaymakers. I was uneasily conscious that I was alone, and at the mercy of any intruder, and I doubted whether I could reach the fire irons by the inglenook in time if I had to act.

It was almost a relief to see Sam stride into the room. He stopped short when he saw me, and I clutched the magazine to my chest, in an involuntary defensive gesture.

'Eithne. Good. I wanted to catch you when Father wasn't here.'

He placed himself on a chair opposite, and I struggled to attain a more dignified position. My heart was thumping as if I'd been jumping hurdles.

'You frightened me,' I murmured, and he made a small, scoffing sound.

'It's asking for trouble to leave the house open like this. What would you do if a felon broke in and attacked you? You wouldn't stand a chance.'

I couldn't summon a suitable response. His pointed disapproval always robbed me of my ability to speak clearly and with intelligence at the best of times. We gazed dispassionately at one another, and he scratched a mosquito bite on one calf. 'Listen, Eithne. I've been very patient so far, but I need Father to let me have the money to complete my deal. You've been bleating about Aurien de Groot, and it's put the wind up him. You'd better back off, because if you don't, your life is going to get difficult. Olivia's due here today, isn't she? And Father's getting very friendly with 'Nique. At least she's more helpful than you are.'

Sam rose to his feet, looming over me like a threatening shadow. He was scowling, but there was a hint of panic in his eyes, and I realised that his position wasn't as strong as he was making out – perhaps fear had prompted this visit. 'Tell Father that you're mistaken about your pal de Groot, and you'll be left in peace. That's all. I'll see myself out.'

He turned on his heel, slamming the door behind him. I rubbed a hand across my eyes, wondering for a moment if I'd dreamed the entire episode, but the sound of his car engine brought me back to reality, and tears began to sting behind my eyelids. Sam was a horror, and I couldn't stomach the way he was prepared to batten off his father, like a loathsome, bloodsucking insect.

There was no way I could relax with my magazine now. I trod wearily up the stairs to my bedroom, brushing at my wet face as I contemplated the net which was closing around me. I was trapped, like the lizard, but Sam wouldn't be so ready to undertake a release this time.

And I must have wept myself to sleep, because when I awoke, it was to find the tanned, frowning face of my daughter bending over me.

'My God, Mum, what's the matter? Where is everyone? You look terrible!'

Olivia sounded frightened, an emotion I didn't associate with her, and this shocked me back to life. I pulled myself into a sitting position, and she put her arms round me in a gentle hug. This was so unexpected, and so little like her usual distant stance, that I found myself weeping all over again. Olivia reached for a tissue and handed it to me.

'Please don't cry, Mum. Can you tell me why you are in such a state? Would you like a drink?'

I contemplated tea, then rejected the idea in favour of a stiff brandy. That might give me the courage to spill some beans – maybe not all of them, though.

'Do you know where the drinks are kept? Perhaps a brandy would be good,' I sniffed, and she nodded, evidently relieved to be able to offer practical help. She whisked from the room and I heard cupboard doors bang, and then she reappeared, carrying a balloon glass for me and a bottle of beer for herself.

'Here you are. Drink some of this, and then please tell me what the fuck is going on.'

Her voice had an edge of exasperation now that the first fright was over. I raised the glass to my lips, and took a shaky sip, spluttering as the fiery liquid hit my throat.

'Urggh. It doesn't taste right at this time of day ...'

I forced a trembly smile, pushing back damp tendrils of hair and stretching my limbs. Puzzled anxiety crumpled Olivia's brow, as she tried to work out what had reduced her mother to this soggy mess.

'Where's Ian? Has he been taken ill again?' she demanded, and I shook my head.

'He's out with Alex and Jack and little Ollie. I'm sorry to alarm you, my darling – you weren't expected until later.'

'Well, I'm glad I was early, then. I can't remember the last time I saw you in tears.'

'It's complicated,' I muttered. I would have liked to deflect her concern with some trivial explanation, but I knew that her inbuilt bullshit detector would kick in now she had seen me like this, and only a full account would be acceptable to her. For a moment I deliberated, wondering whether I could explain the full force of Sam's threats, but I shrank from revealing a truth which would wound us both, perhaps irrevocably.

'Mum?'

I swung my legs round to the floor and tottered to a standing position, concentrating on gathering my strength.

'Could we go downstairs now? I'd like to wash my face, and I think I'd feel better outside,' I said, playing for time. The shock of cold water on my inflamed eyes made me gasp, but I could see the swelling beginning to subside as I dried them, and I took a few moments to try to regain a semblance of self-possession. I knew I would need to proceed with the greatest care.

Olivia had waited for me, and we walked in silence to the terrace, where the tangled profusion of the flowerbeds, refreshed and fragrant after the morning rain, soothed and consoled my bruised spirit. Suddenly, I wondered how much longer I might have left to enjoy the garden. The house belonged to Ian, and I would have to surrender any claim on it if we separated. It was a shockingly painful thought.

'I do love it here,' I said, gazing over the trees and shrubs to the retaining wall where the lizards basked; safe from the attentions of small boys for the moment. 'I would be unutterably sad if I had to leave Le Clos Fleuri.'

Olivia choked on her beer at this bald statement.

'Why should you have to leave? Ian isn't planning to sell up, is he? He loves it, too.'

'I know he does. But things aren't very good between us, darling. It's a silly story; a culmination of lots of little things – and one or two bigger ones. I don't know where to start.'

'The beginning is usually the best place.'

I gazed at my matter-of-fact child, envying her ability to deal with life in black and white terms. I had never been able to separate emotion from circumstances, and I reflected that my path might have been smoother if my nature had resembled hers. But conjectures were of no help in the current situation.

I told her briefly that I thought Ian's heart problem had given him a lasting shock. His ability to make decisions was compromised, and he would not listen to those who were closest to him.

'He's been very tetchy and unkind, but he doesn't seem to care how much he upsets me. Sam is trying to involve him in a suspect business deal, and my advice to steer clear hasn't been well-received. But the worst thing – he is conducting a public flirtation with a French widow he knows from some years back. She's a guest of the

Templetons, and Ian has contrived to spend most of his time with her recently. People are beginning to gossip about them, and I think that he's trying to prove something to himself.'

My words tailed away on a tiny sob, and Olivia frowned, drumming impatient fingers on the table top.

'Sod his illness – what an arse! You never could deal with him,' she stated, and I winced at the vehemence in her voice. 'He always does what he wants, and you just go along with it. I've seen it ever since you got together after Dad died, but I thought if he made you happy... you don't always choose your men very wisely, Mum. Thank God you had some good years with Dad.'

This statement stupefied me for a moment. It was true that both Nick and Ian were dominant personalities, and I had never been able to resist being swept along with their plans and wishes. Peter's gentle, more measured approach to life had made him an easier partner, although I hadn't always appreciated this during our marriage. I hesitated; struggling to marshal a defence, but Olivia's face suddenly drooped and grew pensive.

'Do you ever think about Daddy?' she asked, in the merest whisper.

'Yes, of course I do.'

It was true. Peter had been part of my life for so many years, and I wished that I had such a stalwart person beside me now. Faced with the wiles of 'Nique, Peter would have been politely baffled. If I shut my eyes, I could picture the look of courteous perplexity spreading across his face. Olivia reached out and grasped my arm, her fingers digging painfully into my flesh.

'I'm so glad. Sometimes, I've worried that you live such a cushy sort of life with Ian, and you wouldn't ever want to look back on your years with Daddy, when things were harder. Please don't ever stop thinking about Daddy, because it helps keep him alive for me.'

This unexpected emotion almost overpowered me on top of everything else I was having to deal with. Had my life been more difficult then? Different, certainly, but I was never tempted to draw comparisons between my husbands: I couldn't see the point.

Poor Peter. He certainly hadn't deserved his untimely fate, and neither had Nick. I felt guilty that, with the passage of time, the memories of my all-consuming early love had grown disjointed and fringed with sepia, like a fading photograph album. But thinking about the past made me even more painfully aware of the problems I was facing in the present day.

I took another swig of brandy, and this time it made me choke and splutter.

'Sorry, darling. I think that tea would be better after all. I'll put the kettle on,' I said, but Olivia forestalled me.

'No, you stay there, Mum. You need to think about what you want to happen. My instinct says: tell Ian to get lost and take him for as much as you can, but I know you'd never be up for that.'

Her determined stride demonstrated exactly how she would deal with an errant partner, but it wasn't that simple. I didn't want to lose my husband. He was behaving very badly, but the thought of being on my own was daunting, and I loved this flawed, exasperating man. My life would be a blank without Ian and all the shared joys and sorrows of our past, and I felt that the difficult times we had endured ought to weld us together in an unbreakable bond. I could understand only too well why 'Nique was keen on establishing a new partnership – but snaffling someone else's spouse was out of order. Why couldn't Ian see what she was trying to do?

A car hooted, and I realised it was the boys returning from their day out. That meant postponing my discussion with Olivia, and I was relieved that my dark glasses were to hand, to hide the last traces of tears on my cheeks. Jack and Ollie clambered out, and ran across to me, bursting with news of their exciting day. Both looked flushed and dirty, like happy little boys should do.

'Hi Grandma! We drove along these cool cliffs! Ollie thought we'd fall off the road it was so twisty, but I said it would be okay!'

Jack hit his cousin playfully on the arm, and after a little start, Ollie lunged at him in return. Then they raced off towards the lizard wall, and I was pleased that their noisy cries gave the reptiles a good chance of escape. Alex strolled towards me, but Ian made for the house, merely giving me a sketchy wave of acknowledgement as he passed through the door.

'Hullo, Eithne. I hope you've had a good rest, because you deserved it.'

Alex settled beside me, fanning his face with his cap. The day was sultry, and small beads of sweat glistened on his skin. I wanted to ask him whether he had explained to Ian about the circumstances of the loan, but Olivia reappeared with my drink and the opportunity was lost. There was enough intimacy in their greetings to make me feel superfluous, and so I wandered back to the kitchen, nursing my mug. Ian was leaning against a worktop, texting laboriously with his uninjured hand.

The sight roused me to fury. Was he contacting his beloved? I was suddenly tempted to seize his phone and smash it on the floor – that might shock him into awareness that I wasn't going to tolerate his selfish behaviour any longer. All my recent grievances kaleidoscoped inside me, and I knew it was time to begin the fight back.

'Who are you texting?'

My tone was biting, and surprise sharpened his features.

'Sam... he wants to know when to collect Ollie. Are you all right, Eithne? You are being very abrupt with me.'

'You know I am not all right,' I snapped in exasperation, and he bit his lip, examining his mobile as though he hoped it might contain the answers to our current dilemma. His eyes showed strain and tiredness after a difficult day's driving, and I had to repress a fleeting desire to show sympathy or tenderness towards him. He didn't deserve either emotion. 'As you see, Olivia has arrived. Please don't take yourself off anywhere, because I would like us to eat as a family tonight. That doesn't include Sam.'

I stomped from the room, aware of his astonishment. But I was tired of being the one who had to be conciliatory; who had to tiptoe around being careful not to upset him. Olivia's combative spirit was sparking in me, and Elizabeth's visit provided an urgent incentive to fight for my husband. I thought I knew where to begin.

Upstairs, I rummaged in an inner pocket of my handbag. The card Aurien had given me was still there, and I picked up my phone...

It wasn't a lengthy call. When I returned to the kitchen, Sam had arrived to collect his son, and we exchanged a cool greeting, although I was secretly exultant when I thought of the conversation I'd just finished. Sam smiled at his father, turning his back to me in his usual impolite and dismissive way.

'Would you come and dine with us, Father? The caterer is back on form, and everyone would be so pleased to see you.'

He stressed the word 'everyone', as if wanting to make a point, and it needled me into a quick reaction.

'We are eating here *en famille* tonight, Sam, so I'm afraid your father is otherwise engaged. Perhaps you'll see him another evening.'

Ian opened his mouth, but a glance at my determined face made him close it again. He made no attempt to contradict me, and Sam had to accept the situation. He departed with a reluctant Oliver, and Ian turned to me, reproach kindling in his eyes.

'I do wish you wouldn't treat Sam as if he was an enemy. You aren't helping matters,' he stated, pulling the cork from a bottle of wine with an aggressive pop, but I merely smiled in response. I was pleased to have asserted myself – it felt good.

'We'll see about that. Pour me a glass while you're at it, please. I didn't get a chance to try that Chablis last night.'

He snorted but did as I asked before stalking outside; his demeanour that of an aggrieved innocent. On the way, he brushed past Olivia, but he merely nodded at her and I was relieved that Olivia hadn't sprung at him on my behalf.

'Olivia – please leave me to deal with Ian,' I said rapidly when we were alone, and she sighed, irked at having to suppress her feelings.

'I'll find it hard not to give him a real dressing-down. Tell me what I can do to help with supper, then.'

She moved to the table and picked up a melon. 'I'm pleased that pig Sam isn't staying, because I can't bear the way he speaks to Alex. And Emma's not much better. This melon isn't ripe,' she added, squeezing it with unwonted force, as if she wished her hands were around Sam's neck.

'I know. We don't need it tonight.'

Should I risk telling her about Sam's devious attempts at blackmail? I began to consider how I might skirt round the subject, but Jack skipped in, and I was relieved to abandon the attempt. Olivia smiled at him, and her ill-humour drained away. Jack had an endearing, rumpled little boy look in his grubby T-shirt and shorts, and his skin was glowing after several days' exposure to the sun. He clutched his net in one hand and waved it in the air with a proprietorial gesture.

'Look, Olivia. This is my lizard net I was telling you about,' he explained, pride shining in his wide grin. 'Ollie and I managed to get a baby one, but Sam made us let it go. I'm glad he's not my dad,' he added, and the grin disappeared at the sudden, unwelcome idea. I exchanged a complicit glance with Olivia, and I knew we were thinking the same thing. She took the net from Jack and examined it with approval.

'My brother Nicholas and I used to fish frogs out of the garden pond when we were little, with a net like this, but Mum would never let us keep them. Once, we brought a big, warty toad in to show her and it got loose in the kitchen. You should have heard her shriek!'

Jack's little face puckered up with laughter as he pictured the scene, and it made me smile too.

'I'd forgotten that. It was bad enough dealing with the mice and the birds the cat brought in, and the toad was a step too far,' I replied, and a sudden memory of the pine cupboards and shabby Aga in the kitchen at the Old Rectory swept over me, leaving me weak with nostalgia. We had spent so many happy years there. Olivia's rapt face looked as though she was sharing the sensation.

'Who is renting the Old Rectory now, Mum? Do they have a long-term lease?' she enquired, and I wondered fleetingly why she wanted to know.

'The Busbys. He works in Warrington, and they've been there for a couple of years. They are good tenants, and I hope they stay a while yet.'

An expression of calculation in Olivia's eyes gave me the feeling that this answer didn't please her, although I couldn't think why. She paused, and then turned her attention to the pile of vegetables she had chopped.

'I'll simmer these, and bung in a handful of orzo pasta, if you have it. It makes a good soup, especially with loads of Parmesan on top,' she explained.

A comforting scene of culinary activity reigned in the kitchen, and I found it very soothing after my rollercoaster day. Jack petitioned for a handful of olives and a chunk of cheese, and I was struck by the easy way he chatted with Olivia. He hadn't asked for his mother and showed no signs of missing her. Alex grinned happily when he came in and found us at work.

'Something smells wonderful. We didn't eat much at lunchtime, because we all felt a bit carsick,' he explained, and I felt thankful I had not been in the party.

My husband was skulking in the garden, still annoyed by the peremptory way in which Sam had been dismissed. Alex went to fetch him when supper was almost ready, and Ian surveyed our open, laughing faces, looking a little grim, as though he had been left outside a particular joke. He helped himself to more wine, perhaps to fortify himself, and his mobile rang.

He grabbed at it with a furtive movement, and I assumed it was 'Nique on the line, but his face was puzzled as he read the display. I held my breath, forcing my gaze away as he began to speak.

'Hullo... *Aurien?* How on earth did you get this number? I certainly wasn't expecting to hear from you!'

He strode off to take the call in private, leaving a pulsating sense of enquiry behind him. I explained to Alex and Olivia that Aurien was an old business connection; trying to keep my voice calm and unconcerned, because I didn't want it to appear that the call had anything to do with me.

'Do you mean Aurien de Groot? He's a big guy in the City,' Alex told Olivia, to whom the name meant nothing. 'I wonder what he wants with Dad?'

'We will soon find out,' I replied, concentrating my attention on the fruit I was hulling for pudding. But it was some minutes before Ian returned, smoothing back his hair, and with a reflective gleam in his eyes.

'What do you think? Aurien will be down this way the day after tomorrow, and wants to pay us a visit,' he announced, and the glance he sent me contained a definite hint of suspicion. 'This doesn't have anything to do with you, by any chance, Eithne?'

'Me? What makes you think I would know Aurien's plans?'

I arched my eyebrows, and an actress couldn't have produced a more demurely innocent tone of voice. 'I haven't had any contact with him since the time he took me out to dinner when you were at Rivermead.'

Not actual contact in person, I added mentally, discounting the telephone call I'd made earlier. Ian surveyed me with a noticeable lack of conviction, but he couldn't argue with this statement.

'Your mother and Aurien are great mates. They even feature in the *Daily Mail* together,' he informed Olivia, who paused at the stove, looking startled. Then she grinned, pleased.

'Good for you, Mum. It must be fun, rubbing shoulders with the jet set,' she said, and Alex laughed. Ian sat heavily on a kitchen chair, pondering the details of his conversation with Aurien.

'Aurien is brokering on behalf of a new investment company who need a toe-hold in the UK. He wants me to set up an urgent meeting with Dominic and Sam, because he thinks they might be a fit. It's very short notice, but I've texted Sam, to make sure they are available.'

He looked both puzzled and relieved by this request, but I was invigorated by the sense of stepping back from a crumbling cliff top.

'Well, that's good news, Ian. You can see if they might be interested in Sam's current proposition, and get Aurien's advice, before you commit yourself any further.'

This was said in a neutral, matter-of-fact manner, but I still felt Ian's wary eyes on me as I turned back to my cooking. He clearly thought that I had a hand in this somewhere, and I tried to move the conversation on. 'Does Aurien want to stay with us? If Alex and Jack could share a room for a night or two, we could manage.'

My mind began to turn to housekeeping matters, but Ian shook his head.

'No. He's putting up at that boutique hotel which has had such rave reviews recently. I'll ring Sam when we've eaten, and we can agree a time when we can get together.'

'Can't I get to see Aurien too? Perhaps we could go for a meal out when the business discussions are over,' I suggested, thinking that I could do with basking in Aurien's gentle admiration after days of Ian's cool neglect.

Jack interrupted the conversation with a request for Alex and Olivia to accompany him to the lizard wall, and the room grew quiet. Ian sat slumped at the table, apparently lost in thought. I sent grateful vibes to Aurien for his swift reaction to my request for assistance – after speaking to Ian, he had obviously realised the urgency of the problem. In any case, it was having the desired effect.

I was relieved and surprised that Ian hadn't already acquiesced to his son's demands, and then I wondered whether 'Nique, though nominally in the Templeton camp, might also have urged caution. If she hoped that Ian might provide her comfortable future berth, it would be preferable for his capital to remain untouched, because I was quite sure that she didn't give a hoot for Sam and Dom and their shady speculations. Did she already have more influence with my husband than I did? I turned my head away, grimacing, as I suddenly visualised her taking my place, not just in Ian's life, but in the charming kitchen here which had given me so much pleasure over the years. Then I felt sad, as I realised that if she were the chatelaine of Le Clos Fleuri, the kitchen would probably fall into dusty disuse. Domestic skills were foreign to her, and I wondered whether Ian would appreciate this, once the gloss had worn away from their relationship. Despite his sophisticated surface, Ian was a person who liked his home comforts, and I had always enjoyed fussing around him. I couldn't envisage 'Nique behaving in a similar fashion. Her power was in a different sphere.

Sighing, I wandered to the hob and gave Olivia's soup a perfunctory stir.

'I suppose I could see whether I could get a table at Les Quatres Saisons,' Ian said, referring to an up-market restaurant at a town not far away. 'I think Aurien would like it there, even if it isn't anything like the same class as Solus.'

Supper was ready, and I put my head outside to call the children. Olivia dished up her soup and looked gratified when the men fell on it with appreciative appetites. It came as a surprise to me, because I had always thought her culinary skills were limited, but she confessed that she had grown enthusiastic about cooking after her experiences with the chef in Italy. I had been so full of my own troubles, that I had neglected to ask her what agreement she had reached with Francesco, and I reminded myself to raise the topic with her later in the evening.

Before he could finish his soup, Ian's mobile interrupted us once again, and I frowned, irritated by the interruptions.

'Let it go through to voicemail,' I mouthed, but he shook his head, glowering at me.

'Sam... yes, that's right. I was going to call you after supper.'

He made no move to leave the room this time, but sat, drumming impatient fingers on the table, obviously harassed by a lengthy exposition from his son. I stole a glance at him and noticed irritation and resignation flash across his face. Every time he tried to speak, Sam cut over him, and Olivia dug me in the ribs to express her amusement. Sam finally wound down, and Ian expelled his breath with a tense little sigh.

'It seems like a lot to ask, but if you're sure she wants to do it, it could be helpful. I'll tell everyone here. Give our thanks to Jocelyn. I'll be seeing you beforehand, obviously.'

We sat there like pupils in an expectant silence as he put down the phone and returned to the last dregs of his soup. He seemed to take ages over it, and I was bursting to know what Jocelyn had cooked up now.

At last, he put his spoon down. 'Jocelyn wants us to have dinner at the chateau when Aurien is here,' he explained. 'We're all invited.

At least that solves the restaurant problem, and that chalet girl or whatever she is can be relied on to produce decent food.'

He gazed at me, a tiny hint of apprehension wrinkling his eyes. 'Is that all right with you, Eithne?'

It wasn't all right. I was annoyed that Jocelyn had hijacked our guest, although it was hardly a surprise. Aurien was someone she would love to have at her table, and I could imagine the capital she would make of it when she returned home, but I couldn't say this in the circumstances.

'Perfectly all right.'

The lie slipped out smoothly. 'But will Aurien be happy to dine there? You know how he likes his privacy,' I added, and Ian grunted.

'I'm sure that Aurien is capable of coping with the Templetons for an evening, and it may be an astute move as far as the business is concerned,' he said.

'And perhaps Dominic can root up a paparazzo, so Jocelyn can be in the paper too,' Alex said unexpectedly, making everyone laugh. The atmosphere relaxed, and the rest of the meal passed off in a comfy, family way, which I would have appreciated if I hadn't been so uneasy about my husband's wandering ways.

Jack requested that Olivia went to see him in bed, so he could show her some of his most treasured possessions, and their laughter lit up the house. Alex helped me with the dishes, and Ian enquired abruptly whether Chloe's return was imminent.

Alex shrugged his shoulders, drying glasses with elaborate care.

'She's texted to say she's staying on for a bit. You don't mind, do you? Olivia and I thought we might take Jack to the sea tomorrow – Ollie too, if Emma and Sam will let him come.'

Ian appeared relieved to hear this. He said no more on the subject, but when Alex followed the others upstairs, he turned swiftly to me.

'That's a relief. Chloe would be a fish out of water at the chateau party, and it could be uncomfortable for everyone. I wish that Alex would take some decisive steps and end that relationship while he still has the chance to find happiness with someone else.'

Then he caught his breath and his face reddened painfully, as though the import of what he'd said had struck him in another context, and I was so stunned, I thought I might pass out.

Chapter Fifteen

I gripped the back of a chair, my knuckles showing white, and took a shuddery breath.

'Will you come and sit outside with me, away from the others? We have got to clear the air. I don't understand what is going on with you, Ian.'

He lowered his head, as if accepting that he was to blame for this confusion and was almost anticipating a blow, before giving a little nod of assent. Once we were on the terrace, we settled ourselves in the peaceful and balmy dusk, and I braced myself for yet another difficult conversation. The vine leaves tangled in my hair with clinging tendrils, seeming anxious to eavesdrop on our deliberations, and I reflected with a wry shiver that I seemed fated to rehearse my problems in this pretty spot.

Ian wouldn't – or couldn't – look at me. He slumped on the seat, half-turned away, and his body language was taut and defensive. This barrier had to be dismantled before I could begin, and I reached across to take his hand in mine. It felt cool and unresponsive, but I pressed on.

'I am frightened by what you just said, Ian. Are you trying to tell me that you want to begin again, with somebody else? You don't seem very happy with me at present, that's for sure.'

Oh God – I hadn't intended to be so direct, but there didn't seem to be a way of avoiding the question. Ian expelled his breath in an enormous sigh, hugging his other arm across his chest.

'I'm sorry, Eithne. I know that I've been moody and bad-tempered with you of late. I am not saying that I want our marriage to end, but I think I need some space. Can you understand that?'

His eyes sought mine unhappily, and I felt my world collapse around my ears with an echoing thud. He said he didn't want our marriage to be over, but I had read enough agony columns to know that any request for personal space and freedom was usually a precursor to the breakdown of a relationship. I wanted to scream out loud and slap him – and then I wanted to kill 'Nique.

I didn't know how I was going to fight my corner, but I needed to understand how things had begun to go wrong for us.

'I am sorry for not telling you about the loan to Alex,' I began, but he waved this aside.

'No. I have to apologise for over-reacting about that. Alex explained all the circumstances to me today, and I do understand why you kept the matter from me. I will repay you the money tomorrow, and that can be the end of it.'

This was now a minor issue as far as I was concerned.

'Ian – it isn't about the money. That's almost incidental. I just need you to understand how the transaction came about; that's the important thing. And I wanted to avoid you getting stressed, because we were all worried about your health.'

I choked slightly on the last words. The background chorus of noisy insects intensified as a slim moon stole over the horizon, and I blinked at the vision through teary eyes, remembering past nights when I had sat here, carelessly happy and secure with my husband, and never dreaming of a scene like the present. Ian gave my hand a tentative squeeze.

'I do know that, Eithne. I am afraid I am no spring chicken, despite what the paramedic said at the beginning of all this.'

He didn't drop my hand, but his touch felt alien and unwilling, as though it was being tugged in another direction. There were still so many things I was struggling to understand.

'When you talk about wanting space, Ian – do you mean you want my permission to have an affair with 'Nique? Or are you already involved with her again? You must know that people are gossiping about the two of you, and I find it embarrassing and painful,' I said, boldly grasping the nettle, although I was afraid how much the stings might hurt. He shifted awkwardly in his seat, and shrank away from me, needing distance before he could go on.

'Look, I do enjoy being with 'Nique. She doesn't nag me, or remind me that I'm an old man, in fact, she takes me back to a time when I was capable of living life to the full,' he admitted, and I

156

recognised with an electrifying clarity that this was the nub of the matter. It was easy to be swayed when life was a matter of pleasing little personal episodes, and boring old reality was kept at bay. 'I told you at the beginning of the holiday that I enjoyed the company of a pretty woman – I always have done. Can't you let me reconnect with her now?'

'It depends on what that means.'

A sharp pain almost stopped my speech. I felt that he was deceiving both himself and me. And once someone like 'Nique had her claws embedded in a victim, I was sure she would be very unwilling to let go. 'You are risking everything we have been to one another,' I muttered slowly. 'I can just about accept you spending time with her, but I don't think you understand that she sees you as her next meal ticket. Maybe you should explain to her that you may not be such an attractive prospect if you decide to divorce me. I can tell you now that I won't give you up without a fight, and things could get tough.'

I repressed a hellish vision of lawyers and courtrooms and friends taking sides, knowing I was taking a chance by issuing such a challenge, but feeling it needed to be said. Perhaps Ian understood this too, because he wriggled in his seat, and this time, his sigh contained a hint of irritation.

'But I am not about to ask you for a divorce, Eithne. And don't you think I would know if 'Nique was using me? I'm not stupid,' he retorted, and waves of enmity swirled round us. I was almost overwhelmed by the sadness of it all.

'No, of course you are not stupid. However, I do think your judgment is impaired, and I wish you would take a step back to see what you might be letting yourself in for – with 'Nique, and with Sam. I wish you could accept that I am on your side.'

My voice tailed away in a suppressed sob. But something in my tone, or in my words, finally aroused a response in Ian, because he sat up and put his arms around me, although I still sensed a reluctance in his embrace. I buried my head against his chest, wondering whether we could ever get back to the happy days we had taken for granted before the upsets of this difficult year. Perhaps I had been naïve in thinking that the turbulence of our past had been erased by the calm which succeeded our marriage, because I was tortured by dramatic memories from our long history. I recalled the angry and violent man who had found himself passed over for another, and the middle-aged lover who had not been prepared to lose the world for love. Nothing ever ran smoothly for us. Maybe this was just another phase of our tangled relationship, and it, too, would be succeeded by a different order.

'Please don't cry, Eithne. Don't you want me to be honest with you? You need to give me some time to sort myself out.'

Now Ian sounded more like himself, and I swallowed down the tears which had come, hoping that the crisis had passed. 'Let's not quarrel in front of the children,' he added, his voice soft and persuasive, as if he had suddenly seen an escape. 'I have difficult business ahead with Aurien's visit, and I will need to concentrate on that for a few days. Afterwards, I hope I will have a better idea of what I want to do.'

'I hope that you will come to see that you are happiest with me, Ian. Think of all that we've been through – and everything you would lose if we are not together. And promise me that you won't do anything in a hurry. You owe me that.'

I swivelled round to gaze at him, my eyes demanding assent. He looked guilty, and there was a restless excitement in his face which didn't make me feel better about my chances. I could sense him being pulled in two directions, and I knew how hard it was for him to resist temptation. I knew that – but at least I knew what I was up against.

Voices echoed in the night air, and we drew apart, realising that our discussion was about to be curtailed. I would have to live with the uncertainty as best I could. 'Will you be seeing 'Nique tomorrow?' I asked quietly, and he shrugged his shoulders.

'I'm not sure. She was visiting an old friend today, but I think she will be expecting me to be available for her. I will have to spend some time at the computer, though, so either way. I'm afraid you won't have much of my company.'

'Well, I'm getting used to that.'

I couldn't keep the bitterness from my voice. Alex came out to speak to his father, and Ian seized the opportunity to excuse himself, saying he was tired after the drive, which was undoubtedly true. He stumped off to bed, and left me to make a distracted third in company with Olivia and Alex, before we all turned in.

My emotions had been skittled by the day's events, and I fell into an exhausted torpor as soon as my head was on the pillow. Next morning, Ian and I skirted around one another with careful politeness as we got dressed. I couldn't decide whether this was better than the angry confrontations of recent days, but it was at least restful.

The seaside trip had to be postponed, because Ollie was required to do penance for some misdemeanour, and Jack would not countenance going without him. Alex took Jack for a nature walk to try to lessen his disappointment, because Jack had been looking forward to seeing his cousin again. Ian lurked in his study – I was surprised that he wasn't already off somewhere with 'Nique – and Olivia and I went shopping.

This gave me the opportunity to tell her an expurgated account of my conversation with Ian, and she was incensed that I had not taken a harder line with him.

'I know how he works, darling. Telling him what he ought to do never gets a result, but I am hoping he will gradually come to his senses, before he does anything irrevocable.'

I knew this was putting an optimistic gloss on things, and Olivia ground the gears, frowning and muttering under her breath.

'Can't you get off with Aurien de Groot? I know the guy likes you,' she suggested, but this idea brought a rueful smile to my face.

'Aurien has his pick of women in Paris – young, beautiful women. I'm afraid I'm long past competing, even if I wanted to.'

'Mm.'

She drove neatly into a parking bay, and sat motionless for a moment, busily thinking through the unexpected complexities of life at Le Clos Fleuri. 'I have to confess that I'm longing to see this French dame for myself. She must have something well out of the ordinary,' she added, and reluctantly, I had to agree with her.

Her wish was granted sooner than either of us could have anticipated. When we returned to the house, I saw Jocelyn's hire car in the drive, and noticed two heads together in the pool. Closer examination proved that they weren't Alex and Jack. One of the heads belonged to Ian, and by a process of elimination, I realised the other was 'Nique's. She seemed to be taking care to protect her elaborate coiffure from stray splashes, and one arm hung around my husband's neck, keeping their bodies intimate and close. Alex was beside himself with embarrassment and could hardly meet my eyes when he came to help unload the shopping.

'That French woman has come to see Dad, and they've gone for a dip,' he muttered, trying to apologise, although it was hardly his fault.

Olivia glanced towards the amorous duo in the water, and her eyes grew cold. She thrust the bag she was carrying at Alex and disappeared to her room, emerging shortly afterwards in a striped bikini, which gave the impression of revealing more than it covered. Jack was trailing behind her, and I heard her tell him to keep back. She strode purposefully to the pool, standing above the point where the two heads were close, and executed a perfect swallow dive, which drenched them in a fountain of spray. I caught Alex's eye, and we began to laugh.

'Oh dear. That won't have gone down well,' I predicted.

Olivia commenced an energetic backstroke, managing to displace a surprising amount of water as she traversed the pool. Her dive had resulted in a sharp feminine shriek, and after a minute or so, Ian and his companion extricated themselves from their watery punishment. Olivia was left in sole possession, and I sucked in my cheeks with glee as 'Nique picked her way across the lawn, her elaborate coiffure plastered to her head, and a smeary mess of eye make-up disfiguring her cheeks. Ian's flushed face radiated annoyance and embarrassment, although it was difficult for him to exert authority wearing dripping wet bathing shorts.

'What the hell is Olivia playing at?' he snarled, and Alex and I assumed expressions of wide-eyed innocence.

'Oh dear... perhaps she didn't see you. Would you like a shower?' I offered, as 'Nique shook herself like a sleekly outraged poodle.

'I would. And a 'airdryer,' she said; terse and unsmiling. I showed her to a guest bathroom, supplied her with towels, toiletries, and the requested equipment, and returned downstairs. Ian had stretched himself out to dry off on a sun lounger, while happy shrieks from Jack and Olivia resounded across the garden. He frowned at me, scowling and suspicious.

'Did you put Olivia up to that?' he demanded, and I shook my head with a clear conscience, although giggles tried their hardest to erupt from me as I spoke.

'Of course not. I'm afraid she must have mistimed her dive,' I said sweetly. But back in the kitchen, Alex and I exchanged a rapid high-five, to celebrate the event. We stowed the groceries away and returned to the action in the garden. I was eager to see what would happen next. Jack climbed out of the water and ran across the lawn to accost his grandfather.

'Olivia's teaching me to dive. She's ever so good,' he enthused, and Ian grunted. He was so blinded by 'Nique that he had eyes for little else, even the enjoyment of his grandson.

A long time elapsed before 'Nique joined us again. She had retrieved her poise, but the finished article was not nearly as polished as the one we were used to seeing. Long strands of hair straggled on her shoulders, and without the camouflage of skilfully applied make-up, she looked every year of her age. I felt my spirits rising as I realised she had imperfections just like the rest of us.

'She's not so bloody marvellous. I can't think what Ian sees in her,' Olivia whispered to me later, as we stuffed wet towels in the washing machine.

'She has a very seductive way with her, darling. That dive was naughty, but I must say I enjoyed the results.'

'Yeah – me too!'

Olivia grinned. I looked at my wayward child and felt a surge of affection warm me.

'You still haven't told me about what you agreed with Francesco,' I reminded her. 'I am afraid I've been so caught up in my own troubles, that I haven't asked you what you wanted to talk to me about. Has the settlement been difficult?'

She didn't appear to be anything but her normal bumptious self, but I wanted confirmation on this issue.

'No, nothing to worry you, Mum. But the time isn't right; it can wait. At present, I'm just enjoying chilling with Jack and Alex.'

'Don't get too close to them.'

The words were out before I could stop myself. Olivia wheeled round, her eyes blazing, and ready to put me in my place.

'For God's sake, Mum! I'm not a child, and you can't even deal with your own relationships.'

'Maybe not – but Chloe will be here any day, and you'll have to back off when she's around, unless you want to cause trouble for Alex.'

There was an uneasy silence. Olivia wandered over to the windowsill, and loitered there, picking some dead leaves off a geranium. Despite her confident words, she was unsure of her ground.

'How do you think things are between Alex and Chloe?' she asked, carefully keeping expression from her voice. 'She doesn't seem to be in a hurry to get back here. And Alex and Jack have hardly mentioned her. It's as though they exist in their own little bubble.'

I was about to agree with her when Ian interrupted us. For a moment, I thought he was about to reprove Olivia because of her dive, but he caught my eye and changed his mind.

'I'm going to shower and dress now. Will you please see that 'Nique has everything she wants?'

This sounded more like an order than a request. I trailed back outside, thinking I would have to motivate myself to be civil to my rival after all I had learned in recent days. But she seemed to have recovered her usual aplomb and greeted me with an outward show of affection.

'Jocelyn will be annoyed with me, because I take her car!'

'Nique uttered a tiny, trilling laugh. 'I return from my visit, and I mean only to call in to say *bonjour*, but Ian, he insists that I stay. You don't mind, Et-ne?'

'Why should I mind?'

She glanced up at me swiftly but rearranged her face to indicate composure almost at once.

'You are a good 'ostess. Jocelyn could learn from you, I think.'

I did not respond to this unlikely flattery, and she changed tack with an adroit expertise. 'Some very close friends, who knew us in the old days, they are touring nearby. Will you let me take Ian to visit them tomorrow? It is not so very far away, and I know they would adore to see 'im again.'

She rolled the 'r' of 'adore' in a slightly sinister way, and her sharp eyes bored into me to gauge my reaction to her proposal. Something told me that the 'friends' were a figment of her imagination, and I was relieved that I had excellent grounds for refusing this invitation on Ian's behalf.

'No, I'm afraid that won't be possible. Of course, if you've been away, you won't have heard – an old business contact of Ian's is coming to have a meeting with Sam and Dominic tomorrow afternoon. Aurien's staying for dinner, too – we're all invited to the chateau,' I told her, and she became very still as she digested this information.

'Aurien... Aurien de Groot? The man I see you with in the paper?' she asked, her voice rising with surprise, and I nodded.

'Yes. He and I are old pals.'

It gave me a little thrill of satisfaction to be able to say this – she wasn't the only one to enjoy quality time with desirable members of the opposite sex. 'Nique lolled in her chair, gazing over the garden with her red lips parted as she considered this news. After a few minutes' silence, she roused herself.

'But Jocelyn will need my assistance, I think. I know that she will.'

She stood up swiftly, gathering her wrap and bags, and stubbed out a freshly lit cigarette on the gravel.

'Et-ne, will you please tell Ian I 'ave to go? I will speak to him very soon.'

By now, she was marching to her car, with an air of excited abstraction. I almost felt indignant on my husband's behalf as she switched on the ignition and wrenched the steering wheel round. He had suddenly been relegated to the second division of her attention, and I couldn't understand why it was so important for her to get back to Jocelyn, although I was delighted to see her leave.

Ian came out of the house in time to receive the brief wave of her hand which was her only farewell, and he turned to me with a look of surprise and accusation. I gave a Gallic shrug, worthy of my rival.

'Nothing to do with me, Ian. I simply told her that Aurien was coming tomorrow, and she seems to feel it's necessary to get back to the chateau to lend Jocelyn a hand. Perhaps she's worried that Jocelyn won't be going to enough trouble for such an important guest,' I said, and he gave a little exclamation of irritation at the thought.

'Well, maybe it's for the best,' he said, after a pause. 'I need to prepare for the meeting, in any case.'

I could sense his disappointment in the slow measure of his gait as he walked back into the house. By contrast, I felt nothing but relief. I knew that Olivia's behaviour towards the guilty pair would border on being rude or challenging if we were in company together, and it was difficult enough for me to play the gracious hostess while my husband paid court to another woman. I didn't want the additional role of peacemaker thrust upon me. It might prove to be something which finally sent me over the edge.

Chapter Sixteen

The sun went down on an uneventful evening at Le Clos Fleuri for a change. The surface was calm enough, but I thought that we were all putting on a stalwart front of some kind, to mask an emotional turmoil which rumbled away under the surface. Alex had his own demons to contend with, and I was beginning to realise that Olivia was far from happy with her life, despite her earlier attempts to put my mind at rest.

As a rule, she drank very sparingly, but tonight, she matched Ian glass for glass. She was outwardly in high spirits after vanquishing 'the old French dame' as she insisted on calling 'Nique, and Ian grew tetchy as she passed a number of pointed and tactless comments about his inamorata. I had to kick her under the table to get her to shut up.

When we had eaten, Ian announced that he would spend the rest of his evening with his business plans in the study.

'I'd appreciate a coffee a little later, when you're making one,' he said to me and I nodded. Olivia regarded his departing back with a sardonic gaze.

'He does like to be waited on. Do you always have to run around after him, Mum?' she enquired with a snigger, and this time, Alex began to look nettled by her criticism.

'Don't stir, Olivia.'

I was anxious to defuse the situation and rose to clear the table. Jack wandered off to bid goodnight to the lizards, and Olivia drained yet another glass. I started to say that she had consumed enough, but she cut across me.

'Do you know, Alex, I'm pretty sure your father has narcissistic personality disorder,' she announced, tilting back in her chair in a precarious manoeuvre. Alex stopped short on his way to the fridge and frowned.

'What on earth do you mean?' he asked, and there was marked hostility in his tone. I suppressed a gasp, worried about what was coming next.

'*Narcissistic personality disorder.*'

Olivia rolled the words around her tongue, savouring them like a tasty morsel. 'I think Francesco has it, too, although I can't be sure. I'm not a passive person like Mum; that's why things didn't work out between us. But someone with the syndrome has...' she hesitated, ticking the descriptors off on her fingers. '...an inflated sense of their own importance, a need to be admired, and a lack of empathy for anyone else. That's your father to a T.'

I was gobsmacked by this frank and unflattering analysis of my husband, and Alex's brow grew thunderous. 'Of course, he could just be a bastard. Most men are,' she added, giggling, but not exactly improving matters.

I saw Alex's hands tremble as he placed a bowl on the draining board, and he averted his head as though she had struck him. A doom-laden silence threatened to become embarrassing.

'I think you need to apologise, Olivia,' I intervened, anxious to lower the tension which had ballooned into the room. 'All that wine has loosened your tongue. I know you believe in plain speaking, but you are out of order here.'

Alex didn't pass any comment. He left the room in search of his son, and a small flicker of apprehension crossed Olivia's face for the first time.

'Well, I could be right. Ian's been behaving appallingly with that old French dame, and we all know it,' she muttered, pulling a sulky face.

'You aren't helping matters. Go and find Alex, and say you are sorry. You know how much he adores his father – how could you speak to him like that?'

At least she hadn't assassinated Ian's character to his face, because that could have resulted in fireworks that none of us would ever forget. Olivia flounced from the room, perhaps feeling ashamed of herself now, and I reflected that even a dinner spent in 'Nique's company would have been less controversial than this conversation stopper.

Footsteps on the stairs heralded the departure of Jack to his bed, and then I heard Olivia's bedroom door bang shut. I assumed that meant her attempt at an apology had not been well received, and the evil spirit of dissension continued to stalk through the house.

Ian was still brooding over his computer screen when I finally took him some coffee. He looked up as I entered and rubbed his eyes.

'Thanks. I'm almost finished here,' he said, and I stared at my husband, wondering whether Olivia was right in her bleak assessment of his personality. I hoped that she wasn't. I couldn't deny that a life bolstered by good looks, wealth and intellectual capacity had rendered him complacent and often selfish in his attitude to others, but I could cope with that. I recalled the scene at dinner in Solus, telling Aurien that I wanted the old Ian back, and that was still true for me.

What I didn't want was the man he had become in recent weeks – vain, lacking in judgement, and not caring if he hurt those close to him.

'Are the children still up and about?' he queried, beginning to close the files on the screen.

'No, I don't think so. I'm off to bed now, Ian. Please don't be late; you have a long day ahead of you tomorrow.'

Everyone was subdued the next morning. Breakfast was a dilatory affair, avoiding eyes and personal contact, and passing the butter with cool, exaggerated politeness. Olivia's bleary face showed that she had been weeping, and I was astonished, because she never allowed such weakness to overcome her as a rule. Only Jack seemed unaffected by the sombre mood. He was fizzing with excitement, because he was accompanying us to the chateau in the evening for a sleepover with his cousins.

Alex pushed back his chair when he had finished eating.

'Jack and I are going out for the day, but we'll be back in good time for the festivities,' he informed his father, ignoring the rest of us. Olivia lifted her head with hopeful eyes, but he left the room without returning her gaze. She looked down at her plate and pushed the remains of a croissant away.

Ian strolled off to de-bug the pool, a job which he claimed to enjoy, and Jack trotted by his side. My daughter sat on at the table, lost in thought, and my heart contracted with pity for her.

'Olivia... is there anything special you'd like to do today?' I asked gently, pulling on one of her long curls on my way to the sink, and she shook her head away from my caress.

'No. I may not come to this shindig tonight, Mum. In fact, I may take myself off again. There doesn't seem to be any point in my staying on here now.'

She evidently regretted her tactless intervention of the night before, but there was no going back. I had to find a way to help her.

'Livvy – go and find Alex and give him a big hug and say you are sorry all over again. You must find a way to clear the air, because it's making things awkward for everyone else,' I said, thinking that at least Ian and I had managed to keep a civil face in company despite the many disagreements between us. I wasn't sure whether Olivia would take my advice, because she hated to admit she was in the wrong, but she seemed to latch on to my words like a lifeline.

'You're right for once, Mum. This is silly, and we've already wasted far too much time.'

She was gone from the room before I could ask her what she meant. But a short while later, I heard voices outside, and found Alex, Jack and Olivia stowing supplies in the boot of Alex's car. Alex and Livvy's movements around one another bordered on the tentative, but I was relieved they were on speaking terms once more.

'We won't be late back,' Alex told me, grimacing slightly at the thought of the evening. I knew he wouldn't enjoy massed Templetons who were out to impress.

'That's fine. Enjoy yourselves.'

I waved them away, relieved that a truce had been brokered, and Ian returned from the pool.

'I'm not happy about the filter,' he remarked, brushing a few leaves from the front of his shirt. 'I'll ring Georges to ask him to look at it. Do you have anything special planned for today?'

'No, nothing much. I assume you will be tied up with Aurien?' I asked.

'Yes. I'm going over to the chateau now to prepare for the meeting and will take a change of clothes for the evening. Alex will drive you there tonight.'

It was mundane, unimportant chat, but it had the welcome effect of making me feel he was still involved in daily life at Le Clos Fleuri and was not about to commit to anything elsewhere. I allowed myself to nurture a tiny hope for a positive outcome. Such a lot was riding on Aurien's intervention; I was desperate that he wouldn't let me down.

Ian had scarcely left the house, when Jocelyn's car screeched to a halt on the gravel, and I swore under my breath, tempted to hide myself away. What did she want now? Was she hoping for a comprehensive list of Aurien's likes and dislikes? There wasn't much I could tell her. But it was 'Nique, not Jocelyn, who slid from the driver's seat, and greeted me with a suspiciously friendly smile. She couldn't seem to leave us alone, and my temper began to ferment.

'Ian isn't here...' I began crossly, but she stopped me with an imperative gesture.

'Et-ne. *Bien.* Get your bag, because we are going to town.'

'What?'

'We go to town, because there is work to do. And you may wish to change your clothes for something more *comme il faut.* 'Urry; there are appointments to keep.'

She gave me a little shove, and I turned, as though mesmerised, to do her bidding. How did she always manage to get people dancing to her tune with such ease? I hesitated for a moment once I reached the bedroom, wondering whether to fabricate an excuse, but curiosity urged me to go along with this peremptory request. I swapped my shorts for a skirt and top, and ran a brush through my hair, before adding a pair of sunflower earrings to my ensemble. She looked me over as I came back down the stairs and sighed.

I scrawled a note for the children to explain my absence in case they returned before I did, locked the front door, and climbed in beside her. The car scrunched down the drive, and 'Nique accelerated around a corner, her face set and determined.

'Where exactly are we going?' I demanded, as she cut in sharply before a lorry, causing the driver to lean from his cab and vent a volley of Gallic oaths. It was just as well I couldn't understand a word. She muttered at him under her breath and turned to me with a calculating look in her smoky eyes.

''Ow long you been married to Ian, Et-ne?'

'Eight – nearly nine years.'

She exhaled sharply, gripping the wheel as if fighting it.

'So long... and you wonder why he does not see you?'

This stumped me; I didn't have a clue what she meant. She sighed again and sent me a pitying look. 'A man like Ian, Et-ne; you need to make sure he keeps seeing you. Otherwise...'

She snapped her fingers in a dismissive gesture, and then I understood what she was implying, although I thought this demonstrated breath-taking cheek, considering her own recent masterclass in appropriating other people's husbands.

'That doesn't sound very liberated,' I retorted, and she shrugged her elegant shoulders.

'You will not appreciate being liberated when 'e leaves you for another woman.'

She became very French in her efforts to get her views across to me, and her accent thickened. Was she referring to herself? I was puzzled by these gnomic utterances, and sat in resentful silence for a while, until the outskirts of town came into view.

When we rolled up in the main square, 'Nique parked illegally in a disabled bay. She pulled a face when I pointed this out to her, grabbed me by the shoulder, and steered me into a boutique whose doors I had never darkened in all the time I had been coming to the area. A single, simple, fiendishly expensive dress was draped with casual artistry in the window.

Madame, the proprietress, came forward, and greeted my companion with restrained but multiple cheek kissing, and I prayed I would not have to follow suit, because I could never remember how many times the kissing ought to go on for. But Madame merely shook my hand, while 'Nique let fly a torrent of chat which I had no hope of following. They turned towards me, and Madame cast a critical and rueful eye over me as I stood there, clutching my bag and feeling inadequate in some unspecified way.

She produced a tape measure, and ran it around my bust, waist and hips, and there were more exclamations, accompanied by hand waving and dramatic gestures. It was certainly different to shopping in John Lewis or Marks and Spencer. No-one consulted me, but Madame disappeared into the depths of the shop, and an underling crept out, bearing a tray with two tiny cups of black coffee. I felt in need of a boost and swigged mine down in one gulp.

'What is going on?' I asked 'Nique, as she sipped at her cup with a more fastidious air, and she looked at me from under her eyebrows, as though repressing a desire to smile.

'You need to surprise them tonight. When I 'ave finished with you, Et-ne, you will be the belle of the ball.'

'But what about you?' I blurted out, astonished, and she gave me her sassy grin.

'Oh, me, I am always a belle. Today, though, it is your turn to shine.'

I was at a loss to understand her motives, but Madame bustled back, carefully carrying a silky garment of an unusual jade green colour as if it was almost too precious to be handled.

'Oh – I never wear that colour,' I exclaimed, but they ignored this, ushering me into a changing room which was accoutred in the way I imagined the tent of some glamorous houri in a desert romance; embellished with floating drapes and multiple mirrors. The lighting was subtle, and skilfully sympathetic. I was wearing one of my better bras, but Madame regarded it with a disdainful sniff, and went to fetch a replacement. I must say the one she brought for me to try was feminine and pretty and fitted in a way I wasn't used to.

The jade silk dress looked very plain to me as I slipped it over my head, but it seemed to meet with 'Nique's approval.

'*Pas mal,*' she muttered, as Madame tweaked and patted the fabric until she was satisfied. 'With some better shoes, it may do...'

I took a surreptitious peep in a cheval glass while they were talking, and I had to admit I did look nice. A slow smile spread over my face as I turned before the mirror, and I could hardly believe that something which appeared so devoid of shape on the hanger could transform itself into such a flattering garment. The dress wrapped round my body, revealing a delicate hint of cleavage, and although the hemline finished just below my knee, my legs looked longer and shapelier than usual, and my waist a whole size smaller. The jade colour complemented my skin tone and brought out the blue of my eyes, and when Madame produced a necklace and earrings of tiny flowers in a similar shade, it gave exactly the right finishing touch.

'*Parfait, Madame. Elle va les prendre.*'

'Nique shooed me back into the houri closet, and I put my blouse and skirt back on with some reluctance – I had enjoyed peacocking in the jade dress. When I emerged, Madame's assistant was packing it into a large, flat box, folds of tissue paper billowing around, to prevent the precious fabric from creasing. Then I uttered a little squeak of horror. I had not asked the price, and the bill presented to me was stupendous; outrageous for such a simple piece of material! I started to say I could not proceed with the purchases, but 'Nique placed a forbidding hand on my arm.

'Your 'usband is a wealthy man, Et-ne, and this dress will please him. Get out your credit card, and don't think about the money. I am willing to bet that Ian will not even notice the amount.'

I wasn't so sure of that, but I did as she instructed, thinking that I wouldn't hesitate to lay the blame at her door if Ian threw a wobbly when the statement arrived. This time, I was kissed goodbye along with my companion before we returned, blinking, into the sunlight of the square. It was quite an effort to keep my mouth shut, and not gape, because I felt stunned by the whole experience.

'Nique laid the box carefully on the back seat of the car and motioned to me to climb in again.

'Now, we 'ave bookings at Maison Nicole. You are lucky she can take us, because a client has cancelled due to illness. You know it?'

'No; I've never been there.'

I took a short, gasping breath, worried that this would be another pricey visit. Maison Nicole was a chic beauty salon, and I had often driven past its gleaming windows, adorned with pictures of shapely French bottoms flaunting their freedom from cellulite, without feeling courageous enough to go inside. 'Nique hummed a little tune under her breath as she drove, and I wondered if she was deriving some perverse pleasure in educating a frumpy British matron in the ways of the modish French.

It was past midday, and I was beginning to feel the growling protests of my stomach. I tended to grow faint if my blood sugar dropped, and I wondered whether it would be acceptable to suggest a quick snack before we entered the sacred portals, but this proposal was met by a swift headshake and an exasperated shrug.

''Nique – I simply must eat something, otherwise I'll pass out.'

I could be firm when I needed to be. 'Nique uttered a swift reproof, telling me that eating at midday was merely a habit which could be broken, but I was insistent, although I felt rather like a small child being indulged as she screeched to a reluctant stop at a drive-through patisserie and allowed me to purchase a savoury croissant. She refused to partake of anything herself. However, the flaky pastry was delicious, and when I had devoured it, I felt that I was suitably fortified for whatever rigours might await us in the beauty salon.

We arrived at Maison Nicole. I was led captive to a cubicle, gowned and stretched on a bed, and a beautician began to give me a vigorous facial massage. It was surprisingly painful, and I couldn't help emitting a little yelp from time to time, although the woman never stopped her kneading and stretching. My eyebrows were waxed, and tiny hairs plucked from my chin and upper lip before the session was over.

Afterwards, I found myself in another part of the salon, where a different young lady applied make up to my face and eyes. It took her a long time, and I reflected that it would be a bore to have to do this every day. When I was ushered back to the main reception area, I saw that 'Nique had been undergoing a similar treatment, because she looked refreshed and toned and sultry as always.

'Et-ne. It is good. You look one million dollars, and so much younger.'

There was calculating satisfaction in her perky smile. I reached for my credit card again, uttering a quick prayer that the cost of treatment would be less than the dress, but she put out a hand to stop me.

'*Non.* It is on the chateau account. Emma and Jocelyn come here,' she said, with a sly wink, but I shook my head.

'No – I can't have Jocelyn paying for my treatment.'

'Don't worry, Et-ne. I will sort it out.'

She prodded the small of my back and ushered me out to the car. 'Tonight, Et-ne, the dress – you have shoes to suit? And clip your hair behind one ear, so.' She reached up to demonstrate before we got back in. 'Ian will be thrilled with his new wife.'

What was 'Nique up to now? I realised that I had enjoyed this pampering, although the amount I had spent on the dress still gave me the shivers. Why this sudden amity, this volte-face, when she had spent the last weeks trying to detach my husband from me? I gazed after the car as 'Nique sped away from Le Clos Fleuri with my thoughts in a whirl, and went inside the house, to survey myself in various mirrors with increasing satisfaction. Olivia gave a gasp when she arrived back at the house and saw me.

'Mum! What have you done to yourself? You look fabulous.'

'Eithne always looks beautiful,' Alex corrected her, sending me a sweet smile. They seemed to be happy in one another's company again, and I was pleased I had forced Olivia to make her peace with him.

''Nique took me into town, and we had our faces done. I bought a dress, too.'

Olivia gave a little snort of surprise, although she didn't pass any comment – perhaps the events of yesterday had shocked her into more circumspect behaviour for once. We had tea; an unwilling Jack was forced into a bath, and then it was time to leave for the evening's entertainment.

'Where did you get the dress? It's nothing like your other clothes,' Olivia murmured, as we waited by the car for Jack to retrieve a favourite toy. 'You look so elegant – and your hair's nice like that.'

I had followed 'Nique's instructions and was delighted with the result.

'The dress is lovely, but it cost a fortune. I hope Ian likes it,' I replied, smoothing its folds with guilty pleasure. I found that I was looking forward to the evening. My new dress and make-up provided me with a confidence which I badly needed, and it would be a treat to see Aurien again. But my tummy gave a little lurch when I thought about the business discussions. If things had gone badly, I would have to cope with the fallout from Sam, but I hoped he wouldn't be silly enough to carry out his threat to expose me in such a public forum, where his father might also be damaged by hurtful disclosures.

The evening was humid and cloudy, and drinks were served in the drawing room. Alex took Jack off to be with his cousins, and Olivia and I made our way to the assembled company, where chatter was loud and assertive. The first person I saw was Aurien. He gave a cry of pleasure when he noticed us and detached himself from the knot of people he'd been talking to, taking my hand and grazing my cheeks with his.

'Eithne, my dear! You are looking very French tonight, and it suits you,' he exclaimed, and I laughed nervously, hoping that 'Nique had not felt it necessary to give everyone the details of our day in town. 'And can this beauty be your daughter?' he continued, bending his head as he kissed Olivia's hand. She almost snatched it back, not being the type who responded to flattery of this kind.

Aurien's gaze lingered upon her, and the appreciative smile on his lips indicated that he liked what he saw. Olivia returned the look with her usual defiant stare, and I thought it was a pity that there was such a discrepancy in age between them. They would make a well-matched, if sparky, pair.

'Will you excuse me, please? I have to speak to Emma,' she said politely, and moved away. Aurien regarded her departure with approbation.

'An interesting young lady... Eithne, you need worry no longer about your silly husband. I have sent Sam in another direction, and Ian's capital is safe. But I don't guarantee I can always be around to pull him out of a hole. You must make sure he steers clear of Templeton schemes in future.'

The room suddenly seemed fringed with radiance as I breathed a sigh of relief at this news, and I could only press Aurien's hand to express the depth of my gratitude.

'But will Sam catch a bad cold?' I murmured. I had no love for my son-in-law, but I didn't want him to face financial meltdown. Aurien kept my hand between his, and I felt reassured by his firm grasp.

'No; because I have been able to dangle a different carrot before his nose. He won't get the return he was hoping for, but it will suffice. And in case you are worried about me, I can assure you that I stand to do rather well out of the transaction. It's complex, but I'll tell you all about it one day.'

He broke off as Dominic waddled towards us, and stood there, grinning, as I was forced to endure Dom's usual too-familiar embrace. Dom didn't appear to be out of countenance, and I could only assume that Aurien had worked his magic on all concerned. Jocelyn peeked over Dom's shoulder, her beady eyes taking in every detail of my dress as though she was required to commit them to memory.

'Eithne... whatever have you been doing to yourself? You look positively chic.'

Her tone implied that this was something unexpected, and I noticed Aurien's mouth twitch. But before I could muster a suitable reply, my husband joined us, and I breathed a little faster, hoping that I might read approval in his eyes. He kissed me in a grave manner, putting a hand on my shoulder.

'Hullo, darling. I like the dress. Have I seen it before?'

'No. It's new,' I faltered.

'Et-ne is elegant tonight.'

'Nique gave me the merest wink as she inserted herself between us, and I prayed she wasn't about to spin a laughing account of the ugly duckling's transformation at her hands. That would be a cruel thing to do. But she changed the subject at once, imposing her personality on the group, and ensuring that all eyes turned to her. Her hair was caught into her usual Bardot updo, and a filmy, strappy dress accentuated every curve of her body. I knew that I could never radiate such brazen and alluring sex appeal, and that she would always be the stealer of every scene, but tonight, I felt so confident in my own right that I didn't care.

There was a proprietary air in the way Ian gazed upon her, and my heart squeezed in a vice as I watched them. She made some whispering remark to him, and he bent down so that their heads were close, in the way I had so often seen them in recent days. But this time, she didn't lead him captive to a table for a private audience. She moved skilfully round the group until she was at Aurien's elbow, and he was the favoured one selected to receive her special attentions.

I felt a tap on my shoulder. Emma was standing there with more guests to be introduced, and I realised that I was speaking to the real owners of the chateau, Monsieur and Madame DuPlessis. It was another feather in Jocelyn's cap that she had managed to snare these rare birds, because their local reputation was one of unapproachability and snobbishness, even though they spent large parts of the year living in a cramped cottage on the edge of their family estate. They rented out the chateau to provide a necessary income for them, and rumour was that they were sensitive to their reduced circumstances.

I quickly discovered that they were either reluctant or unable to speak English, and I hastily assembled such French as I possessed, hoping I would not get stuck with them at the dinner table. Jocelyn's way of coping was to blare forth her native tongue even more loudly than usual, and a frosty carapace formed over Sylvie DuPlessis as Jocelyn harangued her about the need to resurface the tennis court.

Luckily, Ian's French was very competent, and he staged an emollient intervention before there was further damage to Anglo-French relations. The glacial glint in Sylvie's eye began to thaw as Ian paid graceful compliments about her family home, although it was painful for me to see the yearning glances he sent after 'Nique, who was now settled cosily on a chaise longue with a smiling Aurien.

Sam and Alex strolled up to join us. I was prepared to defend myself against a disappointed and aggressive Sam, but he merely gave me a curt nod. He was too well brought-up to argue with his in-law's guests, although his eyes were spiteful.

'Can I see the little ones before they go to bed?' I asked, but he shook his head.

'Renate follows a strict regime with them, and she won't want them to be disturbed. Another time, perhaps.'

Renate was the au pair, whose domineering manner had frightened the twins in London. Perhaps you had to be tough to survive in Sam and Emma's regulated household, but I felt sorry for the children in her care. No wonder little Ollie behaved in the way he did.

Michel DuPlessis bent towards me, with questions about Le Clos Fleuri, and I had to concentrate hard to reply in passable French. He was more smiley and less formidable than his wife, but it came as a relief when Jocelyn announced that the meal was ready. We began to move towards the dining room, and I had to suppress a little jump as Michel's guiding hand settled briefly and appreciatively on my left buttock. Was this an unlooked-for result of my new jade dress? I wondered what other surprises the evening would hold.

Chapter Seventeen

I found that I was seated between Alex and Michel DuPlessis at the dinner table. One side was no problem; the other would be more of an effort for me. It was disappointing that I wasn't within talking distance of Aurien, and he looked down the table towards me with a rueful glance as he took his place as guest of honour between Jocelyn and 'Nique.

Tonight, the little smiles and eyelash fluttering were directed at another victim, although I was pretty sure that Aurien would be more resistant to the flirtatious techniques than my husband had been. 'Nique laid her hand on Aurien's arm with a stroking gesture which was very familiar to me, and I admired her chutzpah all over again.

Ian, slumping gloomily between Emma and Sylvie DuPlessis, gazed up the table towards them with narrowed eyes. He had the mournful look of a dog who has been relieved of his bone, and I almost felt sorry for him. 'Nique had discovered a bigger fish in the water, and she was angling for all she was worth.

That had been the motivation for the trip to town. Now she was tempted by a more desirable prospect, one with considerable means, and without a pesky spouse in the background, 'Nique wanted to extricate herself from Ian's attentions, and thought that presenting him with a gift-wrapped version of his wife might help her to do this. For a moment, I felt duped, used even, but the feeling soon passed. I was happier and more optimistic than I had been for a long time, and 'Nique's makeover had a lot to do with that.

I had eaten very little all day, and so I fell upon my crab mousse with indecent haste. Michel DuPlessis was murmuring a lengthy tale about his ancestors in my ear, and I was relieved to find that he liked the sound of his own voice. This meant I only had to provide little expressions of encouragement or surprise rather than full replies, although it was disconcerting when he emphasised the salient points of his discourse with little squeezes of my thigh.

Olivia sat opposite us, and she noticed my disquiet. I permitted myself the briefest of eye-rolls, and she understood what was happening. She leaned across the table and distracted my assailant with an enticing display of cleavage, and Alex gaped at her, not realising how women unite to deal with the attentions of over-familiar gentlemen.

But all too soon, I had to concentrate on the terrible injustices inflicted on the DuPlessis family by successive French governments and their punitive tax laws. It was a struggle for me to keep up, and I was very relieved when plates of succulent lamb cutlets succeeded the mousse, and etiquette demanded that Michel DuPlessis had to turn to his other neighbour. Alex and I exchanged an understanding smile.

'That chap sounds like hard work,' he muttered in my ear.

'It would be difficult enough in English, but it's almost impossible in French. I always mean to take some conversation classes when we're back in England, but somehow, I never find the time.'

Alex nodded, spearing his lamb with relish. 'I am so glad you and Livvy have made up. I'm sorry about last night; I don't know what got into her,' I continued, wanting him to know that I didn't approve of her behaviour, and his face grew serious.

'Trouble is, I felt there was an element of truth in what she was saying. Dad isn't the easiest person, is he? Do you think he might have this syndrome, or something like it? It would explain some of the things about him which I struggle to understand.'

'Oh, Alex... I am no psychologist, so I can't interpret people's personalities. But my instinct is that he is someone for whom life has fallen readily into place, if you know what I mean. Do you appreciate what I'm saying?'

He nodded, dark eyes round with entreaty. I felt he needed words of comfort and reassurance, and so I struggled on, not exactly sure whether my analysis was sound. 'Of course, I'm not suggesting everything has always gone to plan for him.'

There would have been occasional setbacks, such as my breaking off our engagement all those years ago. 'However, he's never had to struggle to achieve success in business or attract women – it's always been handed to him on a plate. When you live like that, it must be easy to think that you are the most important being in your universe; virtually invincible. Then when something unexpected hits you; something which you can't control, you might fall apart in a way which a normal person wouldn't, because they are used to bumbling along and things not always working out for them. Perhaps that explains why he's been so erratic in recent weeks.'

We gazed up the table at Ian, who was eating his dinner with a remote and abstracted air. He didn't seem to be enjoying the evening.

'That woman...'

Alex was referring to 'Nique. 'Do you think she will take herself off now, and leave Dad alone? It must have been awful for you recently.'

There was affection and sympathy in the squeeze he gave my arm, and I rubbed my face against his shoulder.

'Well, it hasn't been easy. I have been very worried that he would get carried away by the excitement of the moment and do something daft. But I am hoping that she will retire from the field now, because something tells me she can scent a juicier prey.'

'Poor Aurien. He seems nice; do you think he's in danger?'

'He is one of the shrewdest people I know, and I think he can watch out for himself. But with 'Nique, you never know.'

We were interrupted by her trilling laugh as it echoed down the table. Ian turned his head to catch her eye, but she didn't return his glance, and he raised his glass to his lips with gloomy resignation. He had grown used to basking in her fulsome attention, and he didn't like being passed over.

I wondered how Aurien would manage affairs. I had mentioned Ian's devotion to the lady during our telephone call, and maybe Aurien was deliberately offering himself as bait. It would be wonderful if he paid her enough attention to raise her hopes of a kill. Then she might take herself back to Paris in pursuit, and Ian would be forced to realise that he was out of the running. He would be mortified, but that feeling would pass if we all took pains to help him rebuild his ego.

'My mother always says that Dad was the most charming, and the most selfish person she's ever known,' Alex mused, looking with fond exasperation at his parent despite this statement. 'She admits that they would never have married if she hadn't found she was expecting me. It's not very nice to go through life thinking that your parents hadn't planned to have you. That's why I've tried so hard with Chloe, for Jack's sake. I would hate him ever to feel he hadn't been wanted.'

This gave me a lot to think about, but before I could respond, I was conscious of Sam at my shoulder, topping up my wine glass. I turned to thank him, and he gave me a snide glare.

'How very convenient that Aurien de Groot was visiting friends in this neck of the woods just now,' he almost spat at me. 'He timed his appearance very well.'

His grim tone left me in no doubt of his annoyance that his original plans had been derailed, but I smiled sweetly in his sour face.

'Yes, wasn't it a good thing? I understand that he's been very helpful, and you must be delighted that you have the green light for your project.'

My eyes challenged him to deny this. He grimaced, muttering to himself as he moved on to my neighbour, and a little tweak of agitation intruded into my enjoyment of the evening. Although Aurien had assured me that the crisis was over, Sam might still cause me trouble, even if Ian's money was safe from his machinations.

The caterer had excelled herself with the dinner menu. An exquisite peach and strawberry confection followed an elaborate cheeseboard, and everyone could appreciate that the Templetons had spared no expense to entertain this special guest. Jocelyn's cheeks were flushed as she held forth to Aurien, who had temporarily freed himself from 'Nique's predatory attentions. I could tell that Jocelyn was loving playing hostess to such a big name. She may not have been privy to the details of her husband's business dealings, but she was making the most of her captive lion.

'But Aurien, you simply must come to us at Rivermead when you are next in England. Dom would love to take you out for a day's sport on the river.'

Whoops – she was not going to get very far with that one. I caught an indefinable expression passing over Aurien's face as he considered this tempting invitation.

'So very kind of you...'

I longed to hear the end of this exchange, but a DuPlessis hand descended on my thigh again, and this time, I removed it. Luckily, Jocelyn chose that moment to summon the ladies, and I contrived to make my escape.

'What an old lecher! I wouldn't be surprised if my leg is bruised tomorrow,' I grumbled to Olivia as we returned to the salon.

'Well, it's only your leg, Mum. In Italy, it could be any part of your body.'

'Maybe – but I'm hardly a young girl,' I replied. Olivia shrugged, affecting a woman-of-the-world attitude.

''You're female, Mum, and that's usually enough for any serial groper.'

Jocelyn pounced on me before I could take my coffee, gripping my arm with unwonted force, and I feared another bruise would be forming.

'Aurien is such delightful company! It's very naughty of you and Ian to keep him to yourself all these years,' she purred, and I forced an artificial smile to my lips.

'He isn't in the UK very often. And of course, he's very much in demand,' I responded, wondering where she was headed.

'Well, we will be seeing a lot more of him in future. I've invited him to Rivermead,' she said, with smug certainty that the invitation would be accepted. I was willing to bet that the visit would never take place, but I merely smiled and nodded. Olivia and I perched uncomfortably on one of the slippery sofas, and across the room, 'Nique and Sylvie DuPlessis conversed in quick-fire, unintelligible French. Alex's earlier revelations were still heavy on my mind.

'Alex said something rather sad tonight,' I mused to my daughter. 'It was about feeling unwanted. I expect you know that his mum and

Ian were only together for a year or two and would never have married in the first place if she hadn't become pregnant. It's just struck me that Alex repeated the same pattern with Chloe. He's desperate for Jack to grow up feeling loved and secure, and that's why he puts up with Chloe's nonsense. But I wish with all my heart that he could be happy, too.'

Before Olivia could reply, Emma swished up to us, her eyes bright and angry.

'Renate says that Jack won't go to sleep. It's late, and Ollie should have gone off hours ago. Can you come and tell him to stop being so naughty?'

This was addressed to Olivia rather than me, and we both gaped at her in astonishment.

'I'm not his mum. Hadn't you better speak to Alex?' Olivia said, a red spot beginning to glow on each cheek.

'Mummy doesn't like the men to be disturbed over their port.'

I didn't dare catch Olivia's eye. Before she could tell Emma what she thought about the men and their sacred consumption of port, I got to my feet.

'I'll go,' I said, but Olivia restrained me with a quick push.

'No, it's all right. I'll come and speak to him.'

I watched her accompany Emma from the room, thinking it was difficult to judge whose back was most rigid with annoyance. There was no doubt Renate was a martinet in the nursery, and Jack wasn't accustomed to hard words and commands. I hoped that any conflict wouldn't jeopardise the friendship between the lads, because it was important for them both. Ollie was in desperate need of a pal, and Jack was sometimes lonely without siblings, despite all that Alex did for him.

They were gone a long time. I was left to drink my coffee in isolation, as Jocelyn was trying her hardest to infiltrate the French-speaking enclave, although neither 'Nique nor Sylvie appeared very welcoming. Finally, she abandoned her efforts, and plumped down next to me on the sofa.

'You'd think they might make more of an effort to speak the language of their hosts,' Jocelyn complained, and I noticed 'Nique throw an old-fashioned glance in her direction.

'Well, I suppose we are in their country,' I said feebly. Raucous laughter was coming from the dining room, and Jocelyn pursed her lips. It wasn't acceptable for the men to enjoy themselves too much, and she glanced at her watch, calculating when she might expect their revelry to end.

'That Michel DuPlessis has very wandering hands,' I told her, thinking she might find it funny, but she merely raised her eyebrows and pouted.

'With you, Eithne? I find that hard to believe.'

I couldn't summon the energy to argue with her. The door opened, and Olivia flounced in, her tight lips indicating that the bedtime drama hadn't been easy to resolve. Emma followed in her wake, and Jocelyn called her across to assist with a leaky cafetiere.

'Honestly! That au pair is a complete pain,' Olivia hissed in my ear, angrily pushing the hair back from her face. 'Poor little Jack was frightened, because he'd been dumped in some grotty cupboard of a room away from the other children, and not surprisingly, he crept back to find Ollie. Anyway, I've insisted that she makes up a bed on the floor in Ollie's room, so he'll sleep now. Emma thinks it's naughtiness, but I know it isn't. Fancy treating the child like that!'

'Oh, poor Jack. I'm glad you sorted it out,' I said, feeling indignant in my turn. 'But we won't say anything to Alex, because I don't want him to be upset or worried. He's already uptight tonight.'

'That's because Chloe texted him just before we came out, to say she'll definitely be back tomorrow.'

Olivia sounded as if she regarded this as a challenge, which was the last thing I wanted to hear. However, we couldn't pursue the topic, because the men were now ambling in to join us; their faces flushed and smiling. Aurien immediately came to sit by me, displacing Olivia with a polite nod.

'Oh, good. I've been wanting a little conversation with you, Aurien,' I murmured, and he patted my hand.

'Let's get to the point. Do you have your husband back again?' he asked, and I shook my head.

'No. Apart from the business issues, he's been behaving like some sort of love-struck teenager with 'Nique Iglesias, and God knows where that's going to end. I'm more grateful than I can say that you've averted the financial crisis, but I'd love it if you could spirit her away with you when you leave,' I said candidly, and he roared with laughter.

'Don't you think I am likely to fall for her in the same way? The lady is charm personified,' he declared, and I gave him a wry glance.

'I'm aware of that. But I don't think you are...' I hesitated, searching for the right word, '*vulnerable*, in the way that Ian is at present. It's been very difficult for me to sit by and watch him be so flaky.'

Aurien was thoughtful now, looking away towards the flickering lights glowing in the twilight garden.

'I was friendly with Ricardo you know, a long, long time ago. He was a nice man; one of nature's gentlemen. The death of his first wife left him very cut up, and I don't think that marrying 'Nique was the wisest thing he ever did. I can believe that they were not well suited.'

'I understand she didn't get much when he died, but no-one will tell me the details.'

'Perhaps it's better not to know them,' he replied, with unexpected diplomacy. 'Well, Eithne, I can see that you may need my help to open your husband's eyes. But you owe me a little dinner *à deux* when I am next in town.'

'Won't you be going to Rivermead?' I queried saucily, and he uttered a heartfelt groan.

'You know my feelings on the subject of trout. Now, on a different topic... your daughter is a complex personality, I think. Is she in love with Ian's son?'

'They were in a relationship some years back, but Alex has been married to someone else for a while now, and they have a child.'

'Trouble ahead there, then. Poor Eithne. The good life in Provence is proving to be elusive this year, I can see.'

'Tell me about it...'

Ian was making his way towards 'Nique, still helpless in the tight silken bonds of her spinning, but she rose to her feet when she saw him coming, and skilfully deflected him into Jocelyn's orbit, before crossing the room to where I sat with Aurien. She looked at me with narrowed eyes, as if to say, 'my turn', and I automatically rose to my feet. As she slid on to the sofa, she began to address Aurien in honeyed French, and an enigmatic smile slowly crept over his face as her words caressed him.

I understood that I had been dismissed. I put down my cup and wandered across to where my husband stood. He looked tired and dispirited, and I longed to take him home and console him. He had behaved badly and shown a sorry lack of wisdom in recent weeks, to the extent of making himself look very foolish – but he was my fool, and I hated to think he was unhappy.

I detected embarrassment and irritation in the glance he gave me as I approached, but I ignored them both. His day had been full of difficult revelations, and he was fragile.

'Let me know when you want to leave, darling,' I said quietly, taking his hand in mine. 'You can come with us, and Alex can run you over tomorrow morning to collect your car and Jack at the same time.'

'Yes, that's a good idea.'

He looked brighter at the prospect; perhaps thinking that he would be able to see 'Nique then and bask in her undivided attention once again. However, he made no attempt to drop my hand, and smiled at me in a way I hadn't seen for a long time – it made me feel hopeful, as though he was looking at me through eyes which had been opened to the real world again. 'You really do look nice tonight, Eithne. I hope the effort wasn't all for Aurien.'

'Not at all. I'm glad you like my dress.'

I wished I could capture the mood and keep it as we stood there, in harmony after the days of clashing expectations. Alex caught my eye and wandered across the room to us. 'I think we should be going, Alex. Will you round up Livvy, and we can make our farewells?' I asked him.

Olivia had begun an argument with Sam, and their voices were rising on a discordant note above the social chat in the room. It wasn't a surprise to me. They had never liked one another, and usually managed to pick some silly quarrel when they met, which, thankfully, wasn't often. However, I didn't want people to think my family lacked manners, and I was pleased that Alex managed to detach Olivia without apparent difficulty, so we could thank our hosts and depart. I kissed Aurien with more than gratitude.

'I can't thank you enough, Aurien. Tread carefully with 'Nique,' I whispered, and he hugged me a little harder.

'Don't worry about me, Eithne. Concentrate on your husband. He needs you,' he replied.

'Nique embraced us all with apparent affection, but I thought that Ian held himself a little aloof from her. And he didn't appear to be on anything but the best of terms with Aurien – that was important for me.

'I will call you soon, Ian. Enjoy the rest of your summer here, with your charming wife,' I heard Aurien saying, but I couldn't catch Ian's response.

With dexterous sleight of hand, Michel DuPlessis contrived to pinch the side of my bust during the farewells, and it was painful and embarrassing for me. I was very glad that it was unlikely we'd ever cross paths again.

Chapter Eighteen

Olivia sounded off on the drive home, mainly on the subject of the Templetons' many deficiencies. Under normal circumstances, Ian would have intervened and requested that she hold her tongue, but he didn't seem to be listening, and it was left to me to suggest that she was lacking in both tact and gratitude by criticising our hosts so roundly.

'Sorry. But I am still mad about that awful Renate, and her jackboot methods. Why can't Emma employ someone with a bit more sensitivity, for the sake of her children?' she complained, giving a disapproving sniff.

'I popped upstairs before we left, and Jack was sound asleep. He'll have forgotten all about it by the morning,' said diplomatic Alex, and I had the feeling he had reached across to take Olivia's hand.

'I suppose it was a good dinner, anyhow. I'd like the recipe for that mousse,' she said, grudgingly apportioning a little praise. 'Your pal Aurien seems a good guy, even if he is a bit scary. Did you have fun with Madame DuPlessis?' she asked Ian, and he roused himself from his reverie.

'I wouldn't describe it as fun, but it was interesting to meet the owners of the chateau. I don't think they find their life is a bed of roses,' he said, and I realised his ear had been bent in the same way as my own.

'Her husband was all over Mum. Horrible old lecher,' Olivia commented, and I tried to laugh it off.

'Perhaps I should be flattered. Anyway, Jocelyn was delighted with the evening, and she's already hatching plans to become best buddies with Aurien when she's back home. It will be interesting to see how that develops.'

When we arrived back at Le Clos Fleuri, the children went straight to bed, but Ian and I lingered in the kitchen. There was a sense of unfinished business in the air.

'I haven't had a chance to talk to you about the details of the financial discussions. Did Aurien's intervention find favour with Dominic and Sam?' I asked, hoping this would now be the end of the matter as far as we were concerned. A huge moth battered with demented wings at the bright temptation of the kitchen light, and it made me wince, remembering my own frantic attempts to stave off financial catastrophe. Ian's face was carefully non-committal, but I could tell from the relaxed posture of his shoulders that a burden had been lifted from him.

'Very helpful. It's fortuitous that these contacts of his were looking for exactly the opportunity that Dom and Sam had identified. I'm afraid that the result will not be as profitable for Sam as he was anticipating, but I am very relieved I don't have to go in with them this time. It became apparent during the discussions that Sam has either been careless, or a little economical with some truths.'

The subtext was clear. Sam would be out of favour for a time, but at least he could not accuse me of scuppering his plans entirely.

Ian and I were not at ease with one another. It felt to me as though there was a sticky mire of conflicting emotions to be struggled through; almost a re-negotiation of our relationship, before firmer ground could be reached once again. I was more than content with my evening, but he was brooding on the defection of his admirer, and I knew he would be sensitive about a public loss of face. It seemed prudent not to mention the lady at all, and the rest of our conversation was entirely concerned with dull practicalities before we went to bed.

He seemed to fold himself into a protective cocoon, and although I longed to give him a cuddle, I worried that might make him feel even more sorry for himself. But soon, his steady breathing reassured me that he wasn't agonising too much about the situation, and I was able to drift off without counting over my worries for a change.

The next morning, he returned to the chateau with Alex immediately after breakfast, and Olivia and I lolled on the terrace, each occupied with our own thoughts. We were a little scratchy in the way that late nights and excitement make you feel out of sorts the next day, and Olivia was still incensed about the way Renate had treated little Jack.

'I can understand why poor little Ollie is so cowed all the time. The combination of that bitch and his father stops him from expressing anything he really wants. I know Alex and Chloe's relationship is far from perfect, but at least Jack has a chance of growing up without being scarred for life.'

'Yes darling. You are probably right.'

I was only half-listening; wondering on one hand whether 'Nique would still be keeping her distance from Ian this morning, and on the other, hoping that Chloe's arrival wasn't going to provoke a different kind of disruption in the household.

'As for your mate 'Nique... she made it clear that her sights were set on a different target last night. No wonder Ian looks pissed off today. The old French dame will be saying *adieu*.'

She sounded pleased at the thought, and I felt a tiny pang on Ian's behalf – God knows why, because he had got himself into this messy and unfortunate tangle without any encouragement from me.

'I don't think you should call her that, Olivia. Ian doesn't like it, and she is my age, you know. Do you usually refer to me as an old dame?'

She laughed in a catty way.

'Let's just say that you don't expend so much obvious effort on pushing back the march of time. But that facial she made you have was a great idea – your skin still looks amazing this morning. You ought to get one on a regular basis.'

I began to think that I would. It was nice to be pampered, especially when the results were visible. Perhaps I would cosset myself with some different treatments, although it was probably far too late for me to start worrying about cellulite. 'By the way, Mum, have you noticed the scar on Alex's right palm? He must have had a terrible cut there recently. Is that Chloe's doing?' she asked.

'I suspect that it is. I remember it being quite a fresh wound when Ian was in hospital, although Alex wouldn't let on how it happened. But I'm not aware of any quarrelling or violence since they've been in France,' I said, glad that this was true.

'That doesn't mean anything. Chloe's hardly been here.'

A sparrow hopped on spindly legs to filch a crumb or two from the paving stones. He was joined by his mate, and I watched them divvying up the spoils, before fluttering away together to perch in an olive tree. I envied the lucky birds, whose simple life didn't contain difficult spouses or unhappy children.

'I am beginning to think it would be better for them to go separate ways,' I said, after a reflective silence. 'The more I see them together, the more I find it hard to believe that they have anything in common. It will be painful for Jack at first, and I must make sure we are available for him more often than we have been.'

'It's such a pity.'

It was all such a pity. Why was it that we had almost been derailed by marital problems, when the horrible Templetons always presented a united front to the world? I couldn't go so far as to wish ill-fortune on them, but I did think that we were due some better luck, and bluer skies ahead.

Ian's car turned back up the drive. He was home sooner than I had expected, and my spirits lifted, because this implied either the absence, or the disinterest, of my rival. His face was morose as he walked towards us across the gravel, and it was hard for me not to make my smile too bright in response.

'Hullo, darling. How's life at Chateau Templeton today?' I trilled, and Olivia made a snuffling sound, as if concealing a giggle. Ian's head was down, and he looked dispirited and resigned.

'Everyone is fine. Sam is flying back to London for a day or so, because he wants to get things moving with the new investors. Jocelyn won't stop bleating on about Aurien, and Dom hadn't surfaced. Alex is bringing Ollie back here for the day, to play.'

'And what about 'Nique?' I wanted to scream, but something restrained my tongue. Olivia opened her mouth, saw my face, and for once, discretion prevailed.

'Coffee, Ian?' she carolled, jumping to her feet, and I seized the opportunity to accompany her back to the kitchen.

'Please don't twit him,' I said, sotto voce. 'He's feeling bruised; let him lick his wounds in peace.'

'Serves him right, silly old fool.'

I let this go by. Olivia took Ian his coffee and went off to do some serious laps of the pool, complaining that she was growing fat after a surfeit of heavy meals, while I stood and watched the disconsolate figure of my husband lounging on the veranda. The sight pierced my heart, and I went in search of my mobile.

'Elizabeth? How are you? Good... look, I know it's short notice, but is Bill free today? I can't really talk, but I hope the danger is blowing over here. However, Ian's at a loose end, and in need of some congenial male company.'

I smiled to myself as Elizabeth exclaimed excitedly at this news. She agreed to ask Bill to call Ian and suggest a round of golf, although I had to make her promise that Ian would not be scolded for his recent indiscretions. 'I want things to be as though this silly episode was gone and forgotten,' I said; my voice emphatic.

'I do understand, Eithne. Bill will be as relieved as I am that Ian has come to his senses. I knew it would all come right in the end.'

It could easily have gone the other way, I thought, as I finished the call, and it wasn't very reassuring to think that I'd had to call in outside assistance to repel the attack. I would never know whether Ian would have chosen 'Nique, if forced to decide between us. I didn't even know if he'd slept with her in the last weeks, but that didn't seem to matter somehow. A discreet visit to a local hotel... it was certainly a possibility. I thought that even 'Nique would have hesitated before taking Ian into her bed at the chateau.

I decided that I would never ask my husband how far he had been tempted.

Louisa had sent me a long e-mail with all the news from the States, which was overdue a reply. As I settled myself at the computer, I began to give her a heavily expurgated account of recent events in France. There was no point in exporting worries to someone so far off, and I had Olivia if I needed a shoulder. She was an unexpected comfort to me, and I hoped that the return of Chloe wouldn't drive her away. Ian strolled in when I was half-way through my task.

'I've just had a call from Bill. Would you mind if I joined him for lunch and then a round of golf? I told him I would need to check with you first, in case you had other plans,' he said, and I was amazed at this sudden consideration for my feelings.

'No, of course I don't mind. You haven't seen much of your old pals recently. Off you go and enjoy yourself.'

He looked brighter already. As he moved towards the hallway, he reached out and tentatively caressed my curls. I decided it was a friendly gesture; a way of expressing an apology which he couldn't yet bring himself to voice.

'You should wear your hair like you had it last night more often. It suits you,' he said, as he went to fetch his clubs, and I decided that was a request I could happily comply with.

When Alex returned with Jack and Oliver in tow, he was pleased to hear that his father was spending the day with a friend.

'What was 'Nique up to this morning? Was she off in pursuit of Aurien?' I asked Alex, and his face split in a wide grin.

'Didn't Dad tell you? She has gone back to Paris. Apparently, she claimed that sudden business needed her attention... well, I think we can guess who that involves. Jocelyn is most put out. Anyway, I managed to spirit Ollie away with me. It's much easier to negotiate with Emma when Sam isn't there.'

I looked fondly at the two small heads bent over a tablet. Their game was punctuated by shrieks of laughter, and it made me very happy to see the developing friendship between the cousins.

'Why don't we go out for lunch? I'll pay.'

'Nique's extravagant ways were rubbing off on me. 'And then we could drive to the lake, and you can take the boys boating,' I added.

Everyone acclaimed this suggestion. We drove to a little auberge I knew, where the cuisine was rustic and hearty, and even little Ollie ate with enthusiastic appetite. I could almost see him filling out before my eyes. Afterwards, we floated happily on the blue surface of the lake, and I lay back, letting Alex and Olivia take over the hard work of rowing. A delicious sense of relaxation filtered through my limbs, and I felt that worry and tension were dissolving into the waters beneath us, to be buried forever in the silty lake bed. My only regret was that Ian wasn't sharing our day, but I knew he would be receiving a different kind of solace on the golf course, renewing bonds with a supportive friend.

Afterwards, we sprawled at the lakeside café, guzzling enormous ices. The boys soon ran off to pepper the water with stones. Olivia finished her cornet and wandered amongst the wild flowers which fringed the lake, where Alex joined her. They looked peaceful and contented, as I remembered sometimes seeing them in former times, and it was impossible for me not to hope that they might revive their old attachment. If only Chloe could stay on her yacht for good...

Then I felt guilty at trying to wish Jack's mother away. Chloe wasn't a bad person, although I couldn't forgive her physical abuse of Alex, and her lack of interest in her son. But she didn't fit in with the rest of our family, and I suspected this made her as unhappy and frustrated as her husband. She would have been bemused and bored by last night's dinner, because it wasn't the kind of society she understood, or wanted to belong to.

And perhaps we were part of the problem. We all had different aspirations, and we ought to accept this without condemnation. Jocelyn's dismissive brand of snobbery came into my mind, and I shuddered to think that I might react with a similar lack of vision. Social inflexibility was nothing to be proud of, and I told myself that we must try to be more sympathetic towards my step-daughter-in-law, and far less judgemental, if we were to achieve a happy outcome for everyone.

My mobile trilled before I could think about this more deeply. Ian had finished his round of golf and asked if I would object to him staying on for dinner with his host and hostess.

'Elizabeth would like you to come too, Eithne, although she says to warn you it's pot luck,' he told me, and I deliberated for a moment.

'I'd like that. Alex can drop me on the way home, if Elizabeth won't mind me not being smart.'

It was difficult to tear ourselves away from such a beautiful spot. However, the boys began to complain of hunger again, and we stopped at the hypermarket to buy supplies for Alex to barbecue.

Ollie had been given permission to stay the night, and his meagre face glowed with sunshine and excitement – he looked like a different child compared to the waif of the previous week. I popped in to the shop to buy flowers for my hostess and hoped that they would make amends for my casual appearance.

'You could be wearing an old sack for all that I care, Eithne,' Elizabeth exclaimed after I had apologised. 'I'm just so relieved that things are back on track for you. It's so unsettling when good friends break up.'

'You should have seen me last night, when I was all dolled up. Remind me to give you the details some time,' I said, laughing. I could make the tale of my transformation into an amusing anecdote, but I wasn't quite ready to share the story. It would be easier when I knew for certain that the threat of 'Nique had faded into an insidious memory, and I couldn't yet be confident if that would happen.

Bill and Ian were stretched out in deck chairs by the small stream which divided the garden. They looked comfortable, like two old gaffers putting the world to rights, and I could tell from the way Ian was chaffing his pal that he was in better spirits.

'I'll drive home,' I offered, as Ian held out his glass to be refilled, and then we sat gossiping gently and enjoying the relaxing company of our neighbours. It was a welcome contrast to the formality of the previous evening. Elizabeth was avid for more details of the Templeton party, and lured me back to the kitchen, so I could describe the event to her.

'There's been a lot of comment about the awful English family renting the chateau – your pal Jocelyn has managed to get up quite a few French noses,' she said, looking almost envious. 'Can't you wangle us an invite before they leave? I'd love to see this gorgon for myself.'

'I could arrange for you to meet them on our territory, I suppose.' The thought wasn't very appealing, but I felt I owed Elizabeth a favour after her concern for us. 'However, they usually behave better away from home, so you might be disappointed.'

I gave her a synopsis of the encounter between 'Nique and Aurien, and her eyes were round and shiny with amazement.

'What a woman! And she's followed him to Paris? What do you think will happen next?'

'I don't know. For the moment, I'm happy that she believes she's on to something better with Aurien. He's much richer than Ian; younger too, and he isn't married, so she doesn't have to worry about the disposal of an inconvenient spouse. Aurien knows how to play her game, but I hope that even if 'Nique does reappear, Ian's eyes have been opened wide enough to realise she really did have an ulterior motive.'

'Oh, the poor lamb. I hope he isn't too hurt and embarrassed by it all.'

I reflected wryly that the last time we met, she had been fulminating about Ian's appalling behaviour – it hadn't taken long for her to range herself on his side again.

'You might have had her for a neighbour, although I imagine she would never want to spend much time here. There's not enough going on to keep her interested,' I said, and Elizabeth laughed.

'That goes for your daughter-in-law too, I believe. Ian was telling us that she skipped off to the coast as soon as she could. You do have a complicated life, compared to us old dullards.'

It was said with mock admiration, but I thought I detected complacency in her face.

'It's been a bit too complicated recently, Elizabeth. I'd like a few uneventful weeks now,' I said, thinking gloomily that the return of Chloe might make that an impossible target.

'Well, whatever happens, I am so glad that you and Ian are friends again.'

Friends, yes, but not yet back on more intimate terms. I wouldn't push Ian, but I hoped fervently that he wanted us to stay together, because I hadn't stopped loving him. But guilt was a hampering emotion, not easily dispelled, and there was no guarantee that it wouldn't delay a lasting reconciliation between us.

The starry sky provided a classically romantic background when we drove home, but Ian was nodding beside me, tired out after exercise and a good dinner. The little boys had been tucked up for some time, and Alex and Olivia were relaxing on the terrace, laughing and happy. Their bright faces caught at my heart.

'Where is Chloe? I thought she was coming back this evening?' Ian asked, and his son grinned, as though amused at a private joke.

'She missed her train, apparently. She'll be here tomorrow morning.'

No-one commented on this reprieve.

'It's been a lovely day,' I said to Alex, sinking down on an adjacent seat as Ian yawned his way upstairs. It was wonderful to be able to say this and mean it, after the turmoil of recent weeks.

'By the way, I nearly forgot,' Alex said, turning apologetic eyes upon me. 'Sam left a message for me to give you this morning, before he left for the airport, and it slipped my mind – sorry. He said 'Tell Eithne that I'm looking forward to spending time with her and Olivia when I get back from London.' That was nice of him, wasn't it?'

Chapter Nineteen

I didn't think it was nice of him at all. My stomach heaved, and I felt as if I'd received a belting blow. There was a veiled meaning in Sam's words which would not have been apparent to innocent Alex, and my face must have revealed the full depth of my apprehension, because Alex's eyes grew puzzled.

'Are you feeling okay, Eithne? You look bushed.'

I dredged up a shaky smile from somewhere, hoping it would seem convincing.

'I'm fine... but I think I had too much sun today. Perhaps I'd better get a glass of water.'

'Goodnight, then. I'm so glad to see Dad picking up his old pursuits. Let's hope that we've seen the end of the French sexpot.'

He reached out and encircled me with affectionate arms before going upstairs, and I stumbled off to the kitchen. So, Sam meant business after all. I had interfered in his plans; he didn't like the result, and now he was plotting his revenge.

I stood immobile in the darkness for a minute, and then fumbled for a chair. Could I pre-empt matters, and tell Olivia the truth? The affair was such ages ago! It seemed to me to have been the indiscretion of another couple, who bore little relation to Ian and me in the present day. The immediate aftermath had hurt me rather than Peter or Laura, and they were beyond reach or reproach. But the simple fact was that Olivia's beloved father had been betrayed by his wife and her current husband.

I pictured the furious comprehension creeping across her face as I stuttered out the story. She would blow up, and never speak to either of us again, and I couldn't risk losing her now.

What if I asked Ian for his advice? It would mean telling him that his son was not averse to blackmail, but how would Ian react to that? I worried that he was already pricked by remorse because he'd not given Sam the financial backing that he wanted, and for all Ian's relief at not getting involved, he might begin to speculate that I had an entirely selfish motive for encouraging Aurien to re-route Sam's original plans.

And there would be no point in appealing to Sam's better nature – I didn't think he possessed one.

The air was still, and the inky blackness of my surroundings felt claustrophobic. The walls seemed to close in on me, like those of a prison cell. I comforted myself by deciding to sleep on the matter, hoping that morning would bring inspiration to my fuddled brain.

It was no surprise that the night was made ugly by nightmare scenarios of Sam's sneering face, but I felt unusually fuzzy when I unglued my eyelids in the soft light of morning. My head pounded, and my mouth was rancid and dry. The walk to the bathroom seemed to have grown longer in the night, and I flopped down afterwards in the tumbled bedding, because even that small activity had been an effort.

Cheerful breakfast noises floated up from below, but no-one seemed to be missing me, and I allowed a small tear to dampen my cheek, feeling abandoned and unloved. It seemed an age before Ian came upstairs. He barged into the room, loud and surprisingly jocular.

'Hullo, darling. You are having a long lie-in today! I suppose you'll be expecting me to bring you a cuppa now.'

But his expression changed as he came closer to the bed and saw my dishevelled state. 'Are you feeling okay, Eithne? Your face is very flushed.'

He put out his hand and felt my forehead, and I squeezed out another tear.

'I feel awful – hot and shivery,' I croaked, and he sat on the bedside and stroked my hair.

'Poor old you. Bill said yesterday that some bug is doing the rounds; perhaps it's that. Anyway, you'd better stay in bed. Can I get you something to drink?'

'Yes – a long, cold drink, and paracetamol.'

I sank down amongst the pillows, smothering a pang of disappointment, because I had planned to get Ian to myself today. However, I knew from experience that he was hopeless with illness.

He could dispense drinks and medications, but that was about his limit, and he had always shied away from soothing a fevered brow.

He left the room in search of the requested items, but they were brought to me by Olivia. At least she was a better nurse than Ian. She fluffed up the pillows to make me comfortable, and bathed my face with cool water, and I began to think I might be human after all.

'Don't worry about anything domestic, Mum. Alex and I can cope,' she said, opening a window to encourage a soft little breeze. 'Ian's going off to buy a new filter for the pool, and Alex and I will shop once we've run Ollie back. It's all under control.'

I knew that with Olivia in charge everything would run smoothly.

'What about Chloe?'

I remembered that her arrival was imminent. Perhaps the day wouldn't be so problem free after all.

'She's coming later. Don't worry, Mum.'

She whisked round the room, folding untidy garments away, and then she brought a little posy of scented blooms from the garden to brighten my bedside table. 'You need something cheerful to look at,' she said. 'I'll run the shopping list past you before we go.'

The drink and the paracetamol revived me just enough to give Ian a bleary smile when he put his head round the door again.

'Do you need me to stick around? If all you want to do is sleep, I'll take myself off to Casto to buy a new filter. Oh – and Frank Henderson suggested lunch, because he's had some heart issues like me, and we thought we'd swap notes. But I won't accept the invitation if you'd rather I came back here.'

I considered the alternatives. It would be a treat to have a little fussing from Ian, but the reality would probably be very different, and we would both end up frustrated. I decided it was better for him to continue to pick up the threads of our everyday life, and I knew that Frank would give him a good lunch.

'No, darling, I don't mind at all. It would be great for you to get together with Frank. Olivia has already taken charge, and I hope a quiet morning in bed will sort me out.'

His face was pensive, and he hesitated for a second, before crossing the room to the bedside. I could almost see the confusion of thoughts crossing his mind, as though he wanted to begin to clear away the obstacles which had come between us during recent weeks but didn't know where to start. I fumbled for his hand, and even that simple contact made me more buoyant. Surely, we could emerge from this drama with our partnership intact? He raised my hand to his lips, with an unexpectedly gentle touch.

'Well, if you're sure. Get better quickly, darling – I don't like it when you are ill.'

That was a pleasant thought to hold on to as I drifted back to sleep. When I woke again, it was past two o'clock. Little screams and splashes sounded from the garden, and the sun had moved round to the side window of the bedroom. I stretched and realised thankfully that I was no longer running a fever.

The stairs creaked. Alex tiptoed in and came across to the bedside when he saw that I was awake.

'Eithne? How are you?' he asked, his pleasant face puckered in concern.

'Not nearly so flaky, I think.'

I levered myself into a more upright position. 'I could murder a cup of tea.'

'You shall have one. Olivia and Jack are in the pool, but I'm a dab hand with a kettle. Is there anything else you would like?'

'Just tea, thank you.'

While he was brewing the tea, I tottered to the bathroom to splash my face with water and brush my hair. I was back in bed, taking deep breaths and relishing a growing sense of restored health, when he returned with a huge mug and a little plate of my favourite biscuits. Alex was solicitous and chatty, and I was very ready for company now.

'Jack is having a wonderful holiday. I'm so grateful to you and Dad,' Alex said, his eyes bright. 'And he's loved seeing so much of Ollie. It's been good for them both, I think.'

I nodded. The tea and biscuits began to have a restorative effect, and I felt relaxed and comfortable. My mood soared, and I wanted everyone else to feel the same way.

'Ollie is such a solitary little soul. We must make sure they see more of one another when we are all back in England. You know you are welcome to visit us any time at all, and I will try to think of an outing to tempt Chloe to come as well,' I told him.

My eyes met his, and then we both glanced away, conscious that this might be an impossible task. Alex looked at his watch, and grimaced.

'Talking of Chloe, I must be off to meet her train soon. I gather that her trip was amazing – no doubt she'll be full of it when she gets back.'

'Have you missed her?'

This was an unfair question, but I wanted to see his reaction, and he flushed, surprised to be put on the spot. He had been carefree and relaxed in her absence, more like the Alex I knew from the past, and I was apprehensive about Chloe's reaction when she arrived to find Olivia so embedded in her family's daily life. Like Aurien, I could see storm clouds on the horizon.

'Well... we've been busy here, so I haven't really had time to miss her. It's not like being at home,' he muttered, his voice wary. I drank some more tea and pressed on.

'Is it inappropriate for me to ask about your marriage, Alex? I know I'm not your mother, but I love you, and worry about you,' I said, watching his face grow shuttered. His lips compressed, and I floundered, unsure whether I was going too far. 'That awful scar on your hand, for example... I have a sense that's connected to Chloe. I get the feeling she loses her temper physically, and it's hard for you to stop her. Does it happen often?'

This time, he looked shocked at the direct question. He clenched his hand, but I held out my own, until he reluctantly placed his fingers in my grasp. I turned his hand over, and traced the raised, red scar on his palm, which still looked angry in places. After a few seconds, he gently withdrew it, and walked to the window, gazing fixedly at the greenery outside, before acknowledging a difficult memory.

'She went for me with a pair of scissors, and that happened when I tried to get them off her,' he admitted; miserable now. 'She's always sorry afterwards, but I don't know what to do for the best. I don't seem able to give her what she wants, and I've stopped caring enough to try. If it was up to me, I'd simply walk away. But there's Jack... I can't deprive him of a parent, because I know how traumatic that is. That's why I won't be the one to make a break, even though I think that Chloe might welcome it. Jack must come first.'

Jack's shrill treble floated up from the garden, sounding excited and carefree. An expression of pain passed across Alex's face as he listened to his son, and I felt sick as I wondered what he would be going back to when the time came for them to return to England.

'Tell me about when you were little, Alex, if it isn't too painful,' I asked, wanting to understand more fully. 'Ian never talks about that part of his life, and for different reasons, it's a time that we would both prefer to leave in the past.'

For a moment, I faltered, choked by a vivid memory of my beloved Nick and our short period of happiness together. 'Of course, I know that I must shoulder some of the blame for Ian rushing into marriage with your mother, but he's always led me to understand that you had a good relationship with your stepfather. I know how upset you were when he passed away.'

'Yes. It was a real blow. He accepted me without question, and with real kindness, and when I was older, I appreciated everything he did to make my mother happy. It took her a long time to get over Dad's rejection,' he said, his face sorrowful. 'My stepfather was a good person and I will always be grateful to him, although it actually made it harder when Dad began to take an interest in me again. I remember Dad visiting us in the USA, and because he was more settled himself by then, after he married Laura, he could finally begin to be a proper father to me. He was adamant that I should go to his old school in England, and you know that he usually gets his way. I hated it at first, but later, I was grateful, because that's when I got to know him better. In the end, I found it was easiest to put my life in two compartments. I was one person when I was in America with Mum, and another when I spent time in England with Dad.'

I thought that must have been impossibly difficult for a growing boy to deal with.

'Ian loves you very much,' I murmured, and Alex flashed a grateful smile at me.

'I know he does. And I don't just love him – I admire him for everything he's achieved in his life, which is why it's been so painful to see the way he's behaved these last few months.'

He came back across the room and sat on the end of the bed. 'Do you think you can forgive him for this stuff with 'Nique? I don't believe he seriously thought of leaving, Eithne. I don't think he could do without you.'

'I love your father, Alex, and I don't intend to go anywhere. I think we all understand why he hasn't been himself, and it's essential that we're here for him while he comes to accept that, despite the cardiac problems, his life hasn't really changed. Do you think we'll be able to look back and laugh about this in the future?'

Tears surprised me as I spoke, because I hoped fervently that the shenanigans of 'Nique would one day be consigned to history. I had dealt with the pain of the episode on a superficial level to get by from day to day, but it had gone deep, and my heart was still very sore. Then the door opened, and the subject of our recent conversation strode in, looking alarmed as he registered our solemn faces.

'Oh dear – are you really poorly, Eithne?' Ian demanded, stooping over my bed, and I hastily blinked the tears away.

'No, Ian. I've had a good sleep and feel much better. Alex is a great nurse.'

I managed to smile at Alex, and he grinned back at me. 'Did you have an interesting lunch with Frank? I bet you weren't allowed to have more alarming symptoms than he had,' I said.

'I'm not sure about that. But he didn't get rushed off to hospital in an ambulance, so I'm ahead of him there.'

Ian almost sounded proud about this. We chatted about Frank's health, before Alex got up to leave for the station, leaving an electric charge of tension behind – we were all apprehensive about Chloe's return.

'Have you heard from Aurien today?' Ian asked suddenly, and I shook my head.

'No. I wasn't expecting to. Have you heard from 'Nique?'

Now I read reproach in his eyes, but I considered that it was a fair question.

'No. I wasn't expecting to,' he parroted back, and left me to consider whether I'd overstepped the mark. That subject was still off-limits, then. But I hoped he was telling the truth, and when I got up to take a shower, I stood with head bowed in the warm water, feeling as though the cascade was washing away the unkind words of recent weeks as well as the day's ailments.

A delicious, savoury smell came from the kitchen, where Olivia was busy amongst the pans. She smiled at me as I came in, but I thought a shadow hovered around her eyes.

'I'm glad you are on the mend. Hope you don't mind me taking over the catering for once,' she said.

'I'm delighted to see you so domesticated,' I teased, and she grunted.

'I'm not the world's greatest cook, but after Florence, I know what to throw together for a passable meal. Jack has put in certain requests, and I'm doing my best to give him what he's asked for.'

I thought that was probably more than he got at home. Jack hadn't wanted to go to meet his mother – he was playing table tennis outside with Ian, and it was apparent that any lingering nerves Jack might have harboured about his grandfather had vanished long ago. This was another benefit of the family holiday, and I couldn't help smiling to myself as I heard Ian meekly submitting to his grandson's peremptory instructions.

'Please let things be all right with Chloe,' I prayed silently, as a car drew up outside. Olivia heard the wheels and scowled. She banged a pan with suppressed violence, and Ian put his head in at the window.

'Alex and Chloe are here,' he announced darkly, like someone announcing a death in the family, and I hoped her presence wouldn't ring a knell for our fragile harmony. Moments later, Chloe shimmied in the doorway, casting suspicious looks at Olivia and me as we paused in our kitchen tasks.

'Hullo, you two. Ooh, Eithne, Alex says you've been ill. I hope what you've got isn't catching.'

Not the most gracious of greetings, I thought, forcing a smile rather than a grimace in reply.

'I don't think it's anything serious, and I'm better now. Did you enjoy yourself with your friends on the yacht?'

'Yeah, it was mega. I felt like a real celeb!' she giggled, and I caught a look of weary resignation on her husband's face. Jack loitered behind, bat still in hand. He wasn't at all excited at his mother's return.

'Come on, Grandpa. I was beating you,' he exclaimed, and he and Ian disappeared outside again. Olivia bent over the stove. She became monosyllabic when I tried to engage her in conversation, her tight lips indicating a desire to be left alone, so I wandered out to join the others.

Early evening was another favourite time of day here. The garden seemed to breathe more easily after the fierce heat of the day, and I searched for an old watering can. It was soothing to potter amongst the geraniums and other flowering plants, refreshing the earth in which they grew, and renewing their special fragrance. I pinched the leaves of herbs in my little *potager* and relished their pungent odour on my fingers. If ever there was a cure for being under the weather, the garden could provide one.

Jack saw me and decided that he wanted to help. He seized the watering can, staggering slightly under its weight, and I noticed that more water was sloshing on the path than the plants, but he was enjoying himself too much to earn a reprimand. He grabbed a ripe tomato from a sturdy plant, studded with red jewels, and crunched it happily. Warm juice trickled down his chin.

'Why do tomatoes here taste so much nicer than at home, Grandma?'

He wiped the juice away with a grubby hand, before swamping a courgette plant with the remains of the water in the can.

'It's the sun, darling. The plants here get much more warmth and light than they do in England, and they thrive on it.'

His face grew reflective as he pondered this, and then he yelped, as a tiny frog dived for cover underneath some nasturtium leaves.

'I love your French house. I don't want to go home.'

I bit my lip, watching his small face grow despondent. A sudden desire to say he could stay on here until the end of his summer holidays had to be repressed as quickly as it had arisen, because I couldn't make the offer without consulting his parents and grandfather first.

'I hope you will come and stay again very soon, Jack.'

This was the best I could do, although the sentiment sounded hollow to my ears. We continued with our watering, until a shadow fell over the path, and Chloe joined us.

She had changed into a crop top and a miniscule pair of shorts and looked very fashionable and pretty – prettier than Olivia, I had to admit. Jack gazed at her with a hesitant expression, as if he was calculating what sort of mood his mother might be in.

'Would you like to come for a swim, Mum? Olivia's been teaching me to dive, and she says I'm doing really well.'

His tone was hopeful, but Chloe shook her head with decided reluctance.

'And wreck my hair? No thanks.'

Her son's disappointment washed over her, and she turned to me, looking and sounding pouty.

'I hope Jack's been a good boy while I was away. His Dad lets him get away with murder when I'm not around.'

This wasn't true at all, but it didn't seem worthwhile to begin an argument. I contented myself with saying,

'He's been no trouble whatsoever. And he's had a great time getting to know his cousin Oliver better – it's been a treat for them both.'

Now the pout trembled on her lips, and she whacked at a passing honeybee, needing to take out her ill-temper on something. I was pleased she missed it.

'I don't want him spending time with that snobby lot. I can't be doing with posh people,' she stated, and little Jack scowled at her from under fierce brows.

'Ollie isn't posh or snobby. He's my friend,' he retorted, and Chloe shrugged her shoulders, implying that she couldn't care less. I had hoped she would be pleased to hear about the little boys and their happy relationship, but she couldn't see past her own opinions.

Jack dropped the can and ran off towards the house, and Chloe gave me a defiant glare.

'You lot have been getting at Jack,' she muttered, her face grown sulky and petulant. 'Giving him ideas... I'll have something to say to Alex about that.'

Well, I thought it was time that I had something to say to Chloe.

'Walk down to the pool with me, Chloe,' I said quietly, and her eyes grew round and wide at this request. Things were coming to a head, and I uttered an internal prayer that I would be equal to the occasion.

Chapter Twenty

I set off for the pool, and Chloe trailed half a step behind me. A pair of loungers were set out on the paving at the deep end, taking advantage of a pretty view through the garden to the house, and I settled myself on the furthest one. Chloe perched on the edge of its neighbour, with her knees drawn up under her chin.

'I suppose you want to have a go at me,' she scowled, sounding exactly like a recalcitrant teenager waiting for a reprimand, and I quickly put her right.

'Not at all. But I would like to say how sorry I am that you don't seem comfortable with us and ask what we could do to make your stay here more enjoyable.'

This took her by surprise. Years of experience had taught me that a soft approach was often the best way to tackle a tricky subject, and my pacific attitude caused her mouth to gape slightly, as she sought for a hidden subtext to my words. Her cheeks flushed angrily, and there was a defensive hunch to her shoulders.

'*You're* all right.'

She spat out the words in a grudging monotone. 'But the others... just because I didn't go to a posh school, or come from a rich family, it doesn't mean I'm stupid, or worse than they are.'

'I agree. For what it's worth, the Templetons often make me feel as though I'm a lower form of life, although I do my best to ignore them, and I certainly don't feel they have the right to judge anyone else. But Chloe, I am quite sure that you and Alex are struggling to get along at present, and it makes me sad to see the two of you so unhappy. Would it help to talk to me about things? I'm not Alex's mother, and I don't have any axe to grind.'

'*What are you doing?*' I asked myself, as I spoke. I could imagine Ian being very angry with me at what he would see as unwarranted interference in his son's life. But I had the sense of coming to a crossroads in all our lives. With luck, Ian and I were back on the same path now, and I hoped so much that Olivia still had a fruitful journey ahead of her, although I couldn't see where she was headed. And I simply wanted to remove the hurt, defeated look from Alex's face, which he wore whenever he was faced with the antics of his wife.

Chloe surveyed me with a kind of suspicious dread. I tried to smile at her, hoping to disguise my apprehension about the risks I was taking with this confrontation. She fiddled with a flashy ring on her right hand, which was something I hadn't seen before. If the stone winking in the sunlight was real, then it would have cost way more than Alex could afford, and my heart quailed at the consequences of further extravagance.

She let out a gusty sigh, and I sensed that she had decided to lower her defences just a little.

'I know that Alex is a good husband. I'm not daft,' she added, her eyes bright and searching. 'When we first met, I thought he was everything I ever wanted. And then Jack came along.'

For a moment, her voice softened, and I understood that she did love her son. 'But I can't give Alex what he needs. We're too different, and it's got too hard for me. That's why I've been wanting to spend time with my girlfriends like Tara, because I don't have to try when I'm with them; I can just be myself. And I wasn't going to tell you… but I think I've met someone else.'

She couldn't prevent a triumphant smile blossoming as she spoke, and she glanced down at the ring, extending her hand with a familiar gesture of pleasure. I hoped that meant *someone else* had paid for it, but how would Alex react to this news?

'Is this someone a person you think you'd like to be with? How does he feel about the fact that you are married?' I asked, unable to decide what kind of response I wanted to hear. Her face seemed to open out with delight, and she gave a tiny giggle.

'He's amazing. And he couldn't give a monkey's if I don't know what fork to use, or how to speak foreign words properly. We like the same things – we have a good laugh, and he's important because of what he does, not because of his family.'

Her choice of examples amused me, but I was also ashamed when I remembered the condescension which had surrounded her trip to the coast, and our assumption that she couldn't cope with the rail journey. 'He wants me to leave Alex, and move in with him, and, Eithne, I really, really want to be with him, too. He can give me the kind of life I've always dreamed about. Do you think Jack will be ever so upset if I split with his dad? Of course, I'll still want to see Jack most of the time, and my boyfriend is cool with that.'

It was my turn to be astounded. I had no idea that things had progressed so far, and I was sure that Alex was equally ignorant. Before I could even think how to reply, Chloe's phone rang, and her eyes sparkled as she identified the caller.

'Won't be a min,' she mouthed at me, and I watched her come alive as she jumped to her feet, intent on her conversation. I guessed it was the special someone. The call gave me the chance to review everything that I'd learned, and I wondered how to answer her question. Of course, Jack would be upset and unsettled if Chloe and Alex parted, but on the other hand, it wasn't good for a child to live with parents who could barely tolerate one another, and he would only become more aware of trouble as he grew older. I had observed that his behaviour was much more relaxed when his mother was absent, and I knew that Alex would always be there for him. And Alex wouldn't be at risk of physical assault if Chloe left. Perhaps we should grab this opportunity while we could... then I reminded myself that I wasn't the person who ought to be taking the decisions here.

Chloe was a long time speaking to Mr X. Olivia appeared at the door, shading her eyes against the evening sun, and I heard her shout that dinner was ready. Chloe stopped in mid-gush.

'I'll be there in a minute. Keep schtum about all this, Eithne,' she hissed, and I nodded. I wouldn't know what to say, in any case.

When I got back to the house, I fought down a latent feeling of dread. I hoped that there wouldn't be a scene waiting around the corner, especially as Olivia had gone to considerable trouble over dinner. The places were neatly laid, and there was an attractive centrepiece of a ceramic bowl, overflowing with bright nasturtiums, on the table – she had an artistic eye, and it was delightful to see her handiwork. When the others came in, Olivia sent Jack out to wash his hands, which still bore traces of his gardening efforts. He didn't seem to mind her telling him what to do.

'Ooh, is that chicken, Olivia?' he demanded, as she hoisted a heavy casserole to the table, and she nodded.

'Wasn't that what you asked for? I hope I didn't make a mistake,' she exclaimed, and he crinkled up his eyes in amusement.

'No, that's just what I wanted. It looks yummy.'

It tasted good, too, and the men went back for second helpings. Chloe ate with the same spartan discipline as 'Nique, requesting a tiny portion, and making a petulant gesture when she thought there was too much food ladled on to her plate. I had a suspicion that she put on weight rather easily – she was curvy in all the right places, but she lacked Olivia's supple elegance.

As a result, Chloe was the first to finish, and she sat back, looking as if she needed a cigarette, although she knew we didn't like anyone to smoke in the house.

'We ate in some awesome places on the coast,' she boasted, feeling perhaps that she had been out of the spotlight long enough. 'And the people we saw! One night, Liz Hurley was in the Ladies, and I almost bumped into an actor from *Game of Thrones* – I forget which one, but he was really fit.'

We couldn't compete with this. I didn't think Aurien would count in her world.

'Were any of your footballing friends there?' I asked idly, and she frowned at me.

'A few of them were around,' she admitted, turning her head away, and I realised my question was too close to *someone* for her comfort.

'What about Si Barnabas? Did you see him?' piped up Jack, and now she scowled fearsomely at her son.

'Never you mind who I saw! Bedtime for you, you cheeky little b – monster.'

She darted a quick look at Ian, but he wasn't really attending to this exchange. Before anyone else could react, Chloe scraped back her chair, yanked at her son's T-shirt, and hauled him from the room.

Alarmed, I rose to my feet, but Alex laid a restraining hand on my arm.

'I'll go up in a minute and calm her down. And don't even think about clearing the dishes. You've been ill today. We'll bring you coffee in the sitting room when we've finished here.'

I wasn't going to argue. Although I felt much better than in the morning, my limbs were still heavy, and I sank gratefully into the sofa cushions. Upstairs, the sound of a noisy and argumentative dialogue indicated that Jack wasn't taking kindly to his enforced early bed.

Ian came in, carrying two brandy glasses with exaggerated care.

'This may help you to sleep. It's an aged Armagnac, which Frank recommended,' he told me, and I nosed the amber liquid, feeling a glow begin to warm me deep inside as I inhaled the spicy fumes. He took a chair opposite, and we smiled at one another over the glasses, feeling domestic and comfortable. The rest of the household was apparently in chaos. A thump overhead was followed by a wail, and I flinched at the sound.

Ian frowned down into his Armagnac.

'I don't want Alex and Jack to leave, but I don't know how much of this I can take,' he murmured, indicating the racket above us. 'What do you think Chloe really wants, Eithne? I'm tempted to give her a good talking-to, but I don't suppose you would encourage that.'

Perhaps this was as good a moment as any to tell him what I had learned by the poolside.

'I think she has another suitor lined up; one much better equipped to give her what she wants than Alex is. Obviously, we can't tell her to go, but if things are going to come to a head, maybe we should have it out with the pair of them, so we can help Alex and Jack to deal with the aftermath,' I said. 'It won't be easy, but we know that Alex has reached the end of the road with her. Sometimes, the only answer is to accept the need for everyone to move on.'

Ian shifted a little in his chair, perhaps thinking this was a dig at his recent behaviour. At least we had stepped back from the precipice ourselves.

'You may be right. I hope to God you are right – it would be the answer to a prayer.'

Both of us had uneasy ears stretched towards the chastisement taking place above. Then I heard footsteps on the stairs and hoped that Alex was on his way to intervene, before any real harm was done. 'How do you think we can open the dialogue?' Ian continued, and I shrugged, not knowing what to suggest.

'Maybe tomorrow we can all sit down and talk calmly. I don't feel up to dealing with family squabbles tonight. Anyway, I think the first approach must come from them.'

The house fell silent, and I suppressed a fleeting worry that Alex's patience had finally snapped. 'Husband kills wife in row over son…' The headlines loomed blackly in my imagination. It was a relief when the voices started up again, and finally, the noise level decreased, although I thought I heard the occasional sob. I breathed a little more easily, and Olivia came in with our coffee.

'Poor old Jack. I wonder why Chloe lost her rag with him at dinner?' she mused, but neither Ian nor I could answer her. She twirled a lock of hair, shooting a speculative glance at her stepfather.

'Ian – could you spare me some time tomorrow? I need your advice about the stuff I thought I'd agreed with Francesco. He's been sending me some scary texts,' she said, and he raised his head, surprised to be asked for his guidance. But as her words sank in, he looked almost pleased at this request.

'Of course. If you think I can be of help, I would be delighted,' he responded, with an air of old-fashioned courtesy, and Olivia nodded, evidently relieved at the prospect of sharing a problem. I thought wryly that suffering from narcissistic personality disorder didn't appear to be a hindrance in certain circumstances.

Alex didn't reappear, and it looked as though an early bedtime was on the cards for everyone. As I rinsed the brandy glasses in the kitchen, Ian fidgeted at the table.

'Sam called earlier, to say that things are progressing in London. He will be back late tomorrow, and the following day, he and Renate are organising a treasure hunt for the children in the chateau grounds, and we're all invited.'

My head went down, and Ian noticed. He added, 'Try to get along with Sam, won't you, Eithne? It's bad enough having Alex's life disrupted – I would feel much happier if I thought that relations between you and Sam could get on to a better footing.'

What could I say to that, in the circumstances?

'I don't want to be on bad terms with Sam,' I told Ian, reassuring him with a smile of considerable artifice. 'I can assure you that the animosity doesn't originate with me. But I am nerving myself for a day of awkward discussions tomorrow with the others. I hope we will have a clearer idea of a way forward for everyone afterwards.'

It was as well that I had no inkling of just how awkward the day would turn out to be.

Chapter Twenty-one

Next morning, I was woken from deep slumber by the throaty roar of a growling car engine, followed by sharp, peremptory rapping on the front door. Had we overslept? I picked up my watch from the bedside table and saw that it wasn't quite eight o'clock.

Ian was struggling into groaning consciousness beside me.

'What on earth…?' he muttered, and I crawled out of bed to peep from the bedroom window, in an attempt to identify the early caller. A smart, low sports car glinted in the sparkling morning sunbeams, and I could just make out an equally flashy male figure standing on the gravel; dark-haired and dressed in a striped business shirt. The figure gazed at the unyielding door, shrugged, and drew a phone from his pocket.

'It's a young man, but no-one I recognise,' I said, halfway to the bathroom to fetch my dressing gown, but Ian forestalled me.

'No; I'll go down. Something about that knock tells me there's trouble in store.'

He grabbed his bathrobe and stumped down the stairs, and there was a grating sound as he fumbled with the keys. I was suddenly stricken by the suspicion that something bad had happened to a family member, and my heart began to pound as I reviewed potentially horrible scenarios. However, although Ian's voice sounded stern as he addressed the visitor, it was succeeded by mellifluous Italian cadences, and I relaxed – but only for a moment. Italian! Was our early morning caller anything to do with Olivia?

This time I did fetch my dressing gown, and opened the door to discover Olivia on the landing, pulling a baggy sweatshirt over her rumpled shorts. Her hair was wild, and from the clomp of her feet on the stairs as she descended, I could tell that she was anticipating a row.

'Is that your Francesco?' I hissed at her, but she merely waved a hand in exasperated dismissal.

Ian was already ushering the young man through to the kitchen. Our guest caught sight of Olivia, and turned to her, his arms open in an expansive plea, but she flounced past him without acknowledgement. Ian turned to me, his face wary.

'Better stay out of this for the moment,' he cautioned, and I wavered on the bottom step. Then the door banged, and I was left outside. I listened fearfully to the sound of sharp, raised voices for a few seconds, before retreating to the sanctuary of our bedroom, tense and worried what might be taking place below. After another minute there was a tap on the door, and Alex peeked in.

'Is everything okay, Eithne?'

He sounded puzzled, but I couldn't reassure him.

'I don't know. Our early visitor seems to be Olivia's ex from Florence, but it doesn't look as though it's a social call. Your father said to leave them to it, so perhaps you could ask Chloe and Jack to keep out of the way for a bit.'

'Chloe's in the bathroom doing her usual beauty routine, so it's safe to say she won't be out for some time. Those false lashes are the devil to put on straight. Jack's still asleep.'

That reminded me of poor Jack's early banishment to bed the previous evening, and Alex read the question in my eyes. 'He was a bit upset last night. Chloe and I have had words,' he said, although I thought that was probably putting it mildly. Alex gazed past me, contemplating a dusty beam of sunshine spilling across the bedroom floor, and his shoulders drooped. 'More than words, really... we've agreed we can't go on like this. I am so relieved, but Eithne, I can't bear to think what a separation will do to Jack.'

'Oh Alex!'

I reached out and hugged him, pleased that he and Chloe were confronting their marital differences, but the thought of Jack's unhappiness was like a painful sting, and I was desperate to help soothe the hurt. 'Children are much more resilient than we think. You survived your parents' divorce without too much damage, and we will all help Jack to come to terms with this. I am sure it's for the best, in the long run. You deserve to be happy, too, and I know you haven't been happy for a long time.'

They were platitudes, but what else could I say? And although the words were commonplace, I believed they were true, and that everyone would be in a better place once the immediate tears and drama were over. Alex's face was weary, but there was a spark of something in his eyes – a sense of returning to life after a period of miserable stagnation, and I was optimistic because I could see he was already looking to the future.

'Chloe has been the brave one here. She has faced the fact that we've grown apart, and there is no going back,' he said, his generous nature allotting credit to his wife which I wasn't sure that she deserved. 'Of course, there will be practical stuff to sort out, but she has said she wants Jack to live with me during the week, so his schooling doesn't suffer, and that's a huge relief. Maybe we can be better friends at a distance – and better parents, too.'

I knew that no-one could be a more devoted parent than Alex already was, and it was difficult not to voice the thought, but I had a strong feeling that he didn't want us to take sides.

'Do you think that anyone else is involved?' I asked, my voice carefully casual. I wondered whether Chloe had confessed to the existence of her mysterious suitor, or whether he was still being kept under wraps. However, a sardonic smile appeared on Alex's mouth, which indicated he knew exactly what was going on.

'Well, yes. Chloe has confessed that she has a new fella in tow. I don't mind, honestly,' he added, seeing my surprise. 'It makes things easier, really. For me, that is. I don't know how Jack will react.'

Before I could reply, there was a patter of feet on the landing, and a small, rumpled head appeared round my door.

'Dad? What is it? Where is everyone?' Jack asked, frowning, and I hoped he hadn't heard the latter part of our conversation. Alex bent down and hoisted his son into his arms.

'Olivia's had a friend come to call a bit early, that's all,' Alex told Jack, pushing back a frond of his hair. Jack's face remained blank and mutinous as he processed this information.

'Well, why can't we go down? I want my breakfast,' he stated, and I was conscious of wanting mine too.

'Your grandpa thinks we should wait a little while,' I told him, thinking that I couldn't explain a situation of which I was ignorant. 'We will give them fifteen minutes or so, but I promise we will have breakfast after that. Come and see the blackbirds' nest from my window. They are raising a second brood of babies, and mum and dad blackbird are very busy keeping up with the demand for insects.'

Jack was distracted by the frenetic activity in the apple tree outside for a few minutes, but soon began to complain of hunger again.

'We can't lurk up here for ever,' I decided. 'Let's go down, and I'll suggest that whatever they are discussing can be dealt with in Ian's study, if it isn't for public consumption. I hope there isn't anything disastrous in the offing. Olivia didn't seem very pleased to see the young man.'

'I understand from what she's told me that he was a real brute, and she was glad to get away from him.' Alex informed me, and a little pang of regret stung as I wondered why Olivia would never fully confide in me. Her father had always been her preferred parent, but after the revelations of recent days, I had hoped that she was more sympathetic towards me, and more in tune with my own feelings, and I didn't want that tentative link to go away. We went downstairs with a hesitant tread, but Jack ran on, bursting the kitchen door open and greeting the occupants with his usual childish enthusiasm. I paused in the entrance, my eyes searching first for my daughter, and then for the Italian who had caused such a commotion.

He was a very handsome young man, dark and lightly bearded, and he wore his good looks like a lazy challenge to less fortunate mortals. He rose to his feet, darting a quick look at Olivia, and exclaiming something I didn't understand, before pressing my hand with intimate lips in a gesture more suited to the dance floor than to a woman about to serve breakfast wearing her dressing gown and mules. I managed to give him an uncertain simper in response to this effervescent greeting.

'I'm afraid I don't speak Italian,' I apologised, and Ian translated, managing to look amused and irritated at the same time. Then I turned to Olivia, and she shrugged.

'It's all right, Mum. We're dealing with things,' she said, but her eyes were fixed on Ian, and I could tell she was anxious for support. Ian fired off some more Italian, and the visitor nodded, ushering Olivia into a chair with another flamboyant gesture.

For a moment, the rest of us stood transfixed by the strange situation, but Ian turned his attention to the coffee machine, and I began to rout out croissants and brioches from the cupboard – there hadn't been time to pick up fresh bread from the patisserie. Jack noticed the sports car and ran to the window, pointing and asking questions, and although it was an awkward dialogue, with Olivia and Ian having to translate back and forth, his boyish enthusiasm meant that the tension in the room grew less oppressive. Francesco drank his coffee, but he didn't seem to enjoy his croissant. He kept trying to engage Olivia's attention, although it was evident to the rest of us that she wished he wasn't there. After a while, I couldn't keep my curiosity concealed.

'Can you tell me why he's come here?' I said in a low voice to Olivia, when Jack was in full flow about the car. She stared down at her plate and angry colour flew to her face.

'I thought we'd agreed everything in Florence, but now the pig says I'm trying to pull a fast one on him, so after breakfast, Ian is going to sit down with us to go through the accounts. I've been straight with Francesco, Mum, but his ego is the size of Mars, and he's only doing this to make my life difficult. I can't think why I got involved with the bastard in the first place.'

I stared at the personable Italian, comparing his striking features to the homely Alex. Alex had an open, good-natured face – it was the kind of face that you could turn to in a dilemma, or trust with a confidence. I didn't think I would like to get on the wrong side of Francesco, who had a slick, mafioso air in his flashing eyes and confident bearing, and I crossed my fingers that Ian would be able to broker an acceptable solution. Despite all his years of experience, I suspected he would not have run across such a situation before. And when we retired to the bedroom to dress, Ian intimated that he was anticipating a difficult morning.

'I don't think that Olivia has done anything wrong, but there appears to be some discrepancy in the accounts, and this young man is nursing an almighty grievance. I need to impress upon Olivia that she has to leave things to me,' he said, buttoning his shirt and compressing his lips. It wouldn't be easy for him to ensure she restrained her temper, but I felt relieved that there was sufficient distance in their relations to force her to listen to his advice, knowing that he would speak from a position of authority.

'If it's a question of him wanting more money, you know I can help her, providing it isn't tens of thousands.'

He grinned at me as he fastened his belt, because he had seen the flash of apprehension in my face.

'Leave it to me, darling. I won't commit you to anything too painful,' he said drily, and I had to be content with that.

Chloe had come down by the time I returned to the kitchen. She was in high spirits, and Francesco made it clear with meaningful murmurs and gestures that he admired her figure, attired today in a silly little playsuit, which struggled to cover her generous curves. Her giggles echoed through the room as the Italian ogled her, and I reflected that it was lucky Olivia had gone to get dressed, because she would be sickened by the spectacle. Even Jack's face was set in a disapproving scowl. He was beginning to be old enough to understand when behaviour or appearances were not appropriate, and this breakfast flirtation was overt enough to arouse his condemnation.

'I don't like your – what it is you're wearing, Mum,' he said, trying to catch my eye for support. There was no way I was going to get involved, and I bent my head over the sink, wishing the horrible Italian was back in his native land.

'That's not nice, Jack. Mummy got it in Marseille, and it's a designer label,' his mother said, with a petulant toss of her cloud of hair. This didn't impress her son one bit.

'Well, I like it when you wear a pretty dress, or trousers. I liked those jeans Olivia had on last night; the ones with a little rip in. Can I tear a hole in my jeans, too?'

A rapid succession of emotions played out across Chloe's pouting face. Astonishment was followed by chagrin and then irritation, as she absorbed the full import of her son's criticism.

'No of course you can't, stupid. You're getting above yourself, and any more cheek, and you'll be spending the day in your room!'

I didn't dare say anything. Jack's biggest mistake had been to express approval of something to do with Olivia, because I knew that Chloe would resent any comparison with a person she considered to be far less fashionable than herself. The Italian raised a well-groomed eyebrow as he watched this exchange, and I had the feeling he was concealing laughter, although he would not have understood the dialogue. But Chloe was exactly like a puffy, discontented hen as she bridled before her son, and it was impossible not to be amused.

'Serves her right,' I thought, picking up jars of jam, and stowing them in the cupboard. I wondered if her new man had helped with the purchase of the playsuit, because it didn't look like the kind of thing Alex would approve. Jack pulled a mutinous face, and Olivia put her head round the door, motioning to her ex-boyfriend. He got up to follow her into the study where Ian was waiting, and the door closed behind them, a creaking hinge adding an ominous portent to their deliberations.

'Would you like something to eat, Chloe?' I asked, guilt tweaking me, because I had almost forgotten my determination to avoid passing judgement upon her person and her desires. Jack ran off outside, in search of his father, and Chloe and I were left alone. She flashed me a radiant smile; her ill-humour diminishing now we were alone.

'Boys! Who'd have 'em?' she demanded, and I understood that she would have preferred a daughter, who could be primped and tweaked and fashioned into a smaller version of herself. Perhaps it was just as well she had a son. 'I'll just have a yoghurt,' she added, and opened the fridge door to survey the shelves. Would she be as open with me today as Alex had been? I was very keen to understand her version of events.

'What was all that racket about this morning?' Chloe asked, delving into the pot with her spoon, and I explained the few facts I knew. She couldn't prevent a tiny simper as she considered the implications; pleased in a perverse way because Olivia might be in trouble.

'I hope that Ian will be able to help them come to an agreement,' I murmured, thinking that he would need all his powers of diplomacy to bring this about.

'Ooh, dear. It doesn't sound great.'

Chloe put down her spoon and batted her false lashes towards me. Her moment of amusement had been replaced by wariness, and I was conscious of a quick, speculative glance, but my quiet demeanour appeared to reassure her. She sat on at the table, examining her nails, and I could see that she wanted to talk, so I fussed about, putting china and utensils away, until she was ready to off-load. 'Alex and I had a long chat last night,' she told me, fiddling with her flashy ring, and I tried not to look too avid to hear the details.

'Really? Was it a ...' I hesitated, not wanting to alarm her, '...a friendly sort of talk?'

'Yes. Yes, it was really, after he'd had a go at me about telling Jack off after supper.'

The red lips swelled in brief annoyance at the memory, but there was an irrepressible satisfaction in her eyes which wouldn't be kept down. 'Eithne, I could suddenly see that we might as well be arguing about something more important, because there only ever are arguments these days. Anyway, I need to have my say in what happens. So, I 'fessed up to Alex about my boyfriend – it didn't faze him at all. I think he might have been expecting something like that.'

She sounded almost aggrieved by Alex's ready acceptance of her bombshell. 'Later, we talked about what would need to happen for Jack. I don't mind if Alex and Jack live together during the week, because it's more convenient for his school, but I shall want Jack every other weekend. Jack will like coming to the matches with me; we get to sit in the box with the other players' families!'

Her voice rose triumphantly and I expelled an exasperated breath, wondering whether Jack would think this was sufficient reward for a family split in two. The boyfriend was a footballer, then, but was he really cool with this proposition, as she had claimed yesterday?

'Are you sure your new man is up for this, Chloe? Doesn't he have children of his own?'

'No, not yet. He's a bit younger than me, but he doesn't give a f- ... he doesn't mind. He likes kids, and he wants me to be happy. Ooh, Eithne, I really wish you could meet him, he's ever so fit!'

I uttered a silent prayer that the boyfriend liked her enough to accept the baggage of her life, because I suspected he'd only ever spent time with her on social occasions – no doubt they had slept together, but that wasn't the issue here. It was difficult to restrain the desire to rush to my computer and google 'City players, because Chloe was still reticent about naming the special Mr X.

'Well, perhaps I will meet him some day. What is he expecting to happen now?' I asked, thinking that this was a strangely detached way to be discussing the end of a marriage and the beginning of a new relationship. Was this conveyor belt procession of partners typical of the way young people conducted their lives? Chloe looked down at her ring as though it symbolised escape and a new beginning.

'He wants to come and pick me up so we can go back to England, because he's already overdue for pre-season training. He's been injured, but he's better now. I'll move in with him, as soon as I've collected what I want from home – you should see the penthouse he's renting! All the girls are well jealous, I can tell you.'

'And what about Alex and Jack?'

Chloe was panting to move on from her old, apparently repressive life. It sounded as though she was disposing of unwanted pets instead of her husband and child, and although I tried my hardest, I couldn't help disapproval dripping from my voice.

'They can finish their holiday here. There's not so many days left now. I know Jack likes it, and there's no point in spoiling their plans. When we're all back in Manchester, we can sort stuff properly, with a solicitor, I suppose. Alex will know what to do.'

Chloe didn't seem to appreciate that she was about to spoil a lot more than holiday arrangements. She pushed back her chair and then hesitated; a look of disquiet displacing her previous complacency. 'I don't want Ian to have a go at me,' she muttered, and I felt this was an appeal for me to rein in my forthright husband. I was sure that Ian would have plenty to say in the circumstances, but he wouldn't interfere if his son asked him to leave matters alone.

'Well, he will be sorry to hear that your marriage can't be saved, but he would never express anger with you in public. Obviously, his priority is to make sure that Alex and Jack don't suffer too much because of your decision to leave. You know Ian is sensitive about what happened with Alex after his divorce from Alex's mum, and you can't expect him to be very sympathetic – but he won't try to stop you, if this is really what you want.'

Chloe appeared to be thinking this through. She put her head on one side, looking at me with craftily assumed innocence.

''Course, you know what it's like to change your mind about people, don't you Eithne? I heard you dumped Ian for someone else once, ever so long ago. That can't have been a good time.'

My heart contracted – why did she feel it was necessary to make me an accomplice in a drama of her own making? It was hardly a comparable situation, and I was infuriated by her attempt to drag me in.

'We weren't married and there were no children to worry about,' I said, with cold reproof. 'But it isn't something I'm proud of, and I would advise anyone to think very hard before behaving in the same way. Please make sure that you really want to go down this path, Chloe, because it won't be all sunshine and roses, no matter how wonderful you think your new life is going to be.'

I wondered whether Chloe had any real understanding of the psychological drama of Alex's early childhood, but in any case, it was too late for this to make a difference to her decision. 'What have you said to Jack?' I asked, and she sucked in her cheeks, looking as if she was chewing a pear drop.

'Alex and I will talk to him later this morning and try to explain what will happen next. Jack won't want his mummy to be unhappy. He's a good boy like that.'

'I will make myself scarce, then. But on second thoughts, perhaps it would be a good idea for you to go out somewhere, because there seems to be enough drama here with Olivia's Italian friend.'

They took my advice, and Alex told me quietly that they were driving to the lakeside to tackle the subject of their separation with their son. It almost broke my heart as I watched Jack bouncing around before they left, unaware of the shock which awaited him. I hoped that they wouldn't return with a child who was distraught and broken, because I didn't think I could bear to see that. Jack had been so happy with us here.

The energetic rise and fall of voices from the study punctuated the morning. I made a quick trip to the shops in the nearby village, not knowing whether Francesco would still be with us at lunchtime, and it was almost one o'clock before Ian came to find me in the kitchen. I scanned his face, anxious to hear what had transpired.

'Well, it's been an interesting discussion,' he said drily, collapsing on a chair and blowing out his cheeks in mock exhaustion. 'I don't want to have to go through that again – I'm horrified by how rusty my Italian is, for a start. Anyway, we have reached an agreement. I'm afraid there will have to be a small financial adjustment in Francesco's favour, but I can take care of that.'

'I don't think so, Ian. That will be down to me. Don't you remember how annoyed you were when you found out I'd lent Alex money?'

He gazed at me, smiling, as if he'd almost forgotten that disagreement, and I felt aggrieved when I remembered the pain it had caused me. 'Olivia is my responsibility, not yours,' I added.

'I would like to think that she is our responsibility,' he corrected me, and I caught my breath, because I thought I heard something in his voice which belonged to the Ian of old times. 'But the money isn't a problem. Olivia has consented to go for lunch with Francesco in town, and I suspect he may be hoping for a renewal of their relationship, but I think that Olivia has other ideas'

'I do hope so.'

I didn't fancy welcoming Francesco as part of the family. Apart from other considerations, I was clinging to a hope that Olivia might be planning to return to live in England, so we could see one another on a more frequent basis. But I bade the Italian a polite goodbye, giving Olivia a warning look from under my eyebrows as they roared off in the sports car, trying to plead with her not to commit to anything irrevocable, or become involved in any further scenes. There was a haughty remoteness about the tilt of her head which I found reassuring. She was no fool, keeping herself aloof from the Italian's blandishments, and I had to be content with that.

Chapter Twenty-two

'Where are the others? The house is so quiet that I assume Alex and Chloe have gone out,' Ian said, and I braced myself to be the bearer of dramatic news. I sat him down with a full glass of wine and gave him a brief resume of my conversation with his daughter-in-law. It was difficult to gauge whether he was relieved or appalled as he listened to my hesitant recitation, although his brow contracted when I outlined Chloe's proposed living arrangements.

He was silent when I came to the end of the story, gazing into the distance as he pondered the outcome.

'So, they have gone off somewhere to enlighten Jack? Poor little beggar. I wonder whether he would like to stay on with us here for a while when Alex returns to England? He may be grateful for our support.'

I remembered making a similar wish during the garden watering session, but things had moved to a different stage now.

'I think he will want to be with his father, Ian. You know I would be delighted for him to stay here, but they need one another. Alex is the fixed point in Jack's universe, and I suspect that they will want to keep each other close.'

We sat there in sombre, reflective mood; two parents wondering how to assist their children in negotiating the difficult dilemmas in their lives. Ian and I had only just survived a challenging diversion in our own personal journey, but perhaps we could draw on that experience to help.

'Chloe is worried that you will 'have a go' at her,' I continued, and he gave an impatient shake of his head. 'I know you are anxious and annoyed, but please don't roar at her, darling. It won't change anything, because she is determined to go off and live this footballers' wives' kind of life. And you understand how unhappy Alex has been with her – it's an easy escape for him, I think. We can worry about the legal process when the dust has settled.'

'I won't roar at Chloe, but you must promise not to get shirty with Olivia, because I have undertaken to settle matters with the avaricious Francesco. Don't worry; it's a small enough sum. It will be worth it, to get him off Olivia's back. He isn't a person you would want as a son-in-law,' Ian said, and the grim edge to his voice made me shudder on my daughter's behalf.

'No roaring from either of us, then. That's more than okay with me.'

The effort of the morning's negotiations had etched itself on Ian's weary face, and I bent down to give him a hug, feeling a happy renewal of love and gratitude for my husband. 'I hope that Olivia appreciates your help today as much as I do,' I murmured, and he turned his head to nuzzle his cheek against mine in a way that expressed a genuine bond which went deep, and despite the morning's upsets, I felt quietly content.

'Well, I know that Alex has come to depend on your support in his troubles, so I guess we are quits. Thank goodness there are no problems between Sam and Emma. That marriage seems good and solid, at any rate,' he said.

Wham! My heart plummeted at the thought of the Templetons and the forthcoming treasure hunt, but I couldn't bring myself to augment Ian's difficult day by unveiling my blackmailer. We ate a simple lunch, and I wasn't surprised when Ian retired to take a nap after we had finished the meal.

Later, I sat with a book on the swing seat, and raised my head when a taxi breasted the drive, depositing Olivia in its wake. She saw me there and trailed along the path, looking washed out and exhausted by the events of her day. I patted the cushion beside me.

'I hope this means that Francesco accepted his dismissal?' I queried hopefully, and she sank down, pushing back her hair in a gesture of weariness. Her eyes were veiled in fatigue, and there was a passivity in her slumped posture which made for uncomfortable viewing.

'Yes, thank God. I don't really believe he wanted to get back with me – it was all part of the act to squeeze some more cash from our split. I'm as sure as I can be that he will leave me alone now.'

Her shoulders twitched in a little shudder as she contemplated her release from the Italian's tenacious grasp. 'Mum – it pains me to say this, but I am so grateful for Ian's help today. It wouldn't have been possible to reach a compromise without his guidance, and he really put Francesco in his place. He isn't so bad, you know.'

She meant Ian. The words came out slowly, as if they were being forced from her, and my heart hardened a little.

'For someone with narcissistic personality disorder you mean?' I asked drily, and the corners of her mouth crinkled in a wry smile as she accepted my rebuke. She took a deep, restorative breath of the jasmine's musky perfume, and shook out her curls, as if that might banish the toxic memory of Francesco's presence.

'I still think Ian is a selfish old git, but I'm grateful that he plays hardball where family business is concerned. I am afraid that I'll need to borrow money from you, but I promise I'll pay you back when I can. It may take a bit of time, though.'

'We'll talk about that later. I'm just pleased that you can move on. Which reminds me...'

I took the opportunity to impart the information that Alex and Chloe were on the verge of separating, but this didn't come as a surprise to her at all.

'Alex and I have talked about this over the last few days, and I know he'll be relieved that matters have come to a head. I don't think that he and Chloe have been singing from the same hymn sheet for years now. But I wish there was something we could do to soften the blow for Jack. He is going to be upset, Mum, and no amount of football matches will compensate for losing his family.'

'Do you know the identity of the man Chloe is seeing?'

'No; only that he plays football and has a high profile in sporting terms. But she'll have to come clean today, because Alex will want to know where they stand.'

She paused, and a flash of amusement lit up her face. 'I suppose she'll be a WAG now. I can just see Chloe in one of those reality TV programmes; all fake tan and tits. She'd be in her element. I hope to God that her new man is up for this too, because I'd hate her to be disappointed. She might decide that she wants Alex back...'

The faint flush which accompanied this statement made me wonder whether Olivia intended to pursue her own agenda with Alex, but I didn't get the chance to follow my line of thought, because the others arrived home after their day away. Chloe disappeared indoors, accompanied by her son, and Alex wandered across to where we sat. His expression was austere, as though he'd been turned inside out and squeezed dry by his recent experiences.

'Oh, Alex...'

I stood up to embrace him, wishing that he really was my son in that moment. 'Please tell me that Jack hasn't taken the news too badly,' I murmured, wondering as I spoke how the little boy had reacted to his mother's decision. I knew that Alex was resilient, but it was too much to hope that Jack would not be devastated by the events of the day.

But before Alex could respond, Jack appeared from the house; stumping out with a ponderous, adult tread. He was carrying his lizard net, and his small face was serious and remote.

'I don't want this any longer, Dad. You told me that it wasn't fair to take a lizard away from where he was happy... and I understand that now.'

He placed the net on the table, very gently, and with a sad sense of finality. I heard Olivia stifle a gasp, and I think we were all on the verge of tears. However, Ian had followed his grandson from the house, and he held out an encouraging hand to the little boy.

'Can I come and see the lizards with you, Jack? I'd like you to show me where they live,' he said, and Jack grasped his hand, looking as though he appreciated its strength. We watched in silence as they walked away, and through my blurred vision, it appeared that the olive trees swayed in the breeze, bending sympathetic branches over them as they passed, in a protective embrace. And at that moment, I think I began to find the first real glimmerings of forgiveness for Ian for all his unreasonable behaviour of the previous months.

Alex brushed an arm over his face; embarrassed at expressing what he was feeling.

'Dad will know what to say to him,' he murmured, relieved, and Olivia stretched out to caress his shoulder.

'I'm so sorry,' she said, in a voice warm with affection, and I suddenly felt in the way. If anyone could find words to comfort Alex, it would be Olivia, so I left them to one another, and tiptoed back to the house.

Chloe was singing loudly and untunefully in her bedroom, and her careless happiness jarred upon my nerves. Didn't she feel any responsibility for what she was doing to her family? I climbed the stairs and knocked irritably at her bedroom door.

She opened it, and I saw from the heap of clothes on the bed that she was already packing her cases. My eyebrows disappeared into my hairline, and reproach stiffened my resolve to speak out.

'What are you doing?' I said sharply, although it was obvious she was getting ready to take her departure. I resented her cheerfulness, but her gaze was limpid and devoid of any culpability.

'Well, my fella is coming to get me. Like I said, he needs to get back for training, and now everything's out in the open, there's no point in me hanging around here. None of you want me, do you?'

This was hissed out like a challenge.

'Your little boy might. He's had a big shock, and I thought you would want to make sure he's coping with things before you abandon him.'

She shrugged and turned back to her suitcase, evidently unwilling to pursue this line of thought. Her focus was on a more glittering future now.

'I can't believe that your new man is happy to come here and just drive off with you, as if we're handing over a parcel or something. Do you think Alex will let that happen?' I demanded.

'Oh, Eithne... you might not have realised it, but Alex handed me over months ago. We've been living separate lives for ever such a long time. Why are you making all this fuss? I know he's happy that we are splitting – and your daughter can muscle in all she wants now.'

There was a sarky edge to her voice, and my temper began to heat up. None of this mess was Olivia's fault.

'Just one piece of advice, Chloe. I'd be very careful not to be physically aggressive with your footballer if you ever get into an argument with him. There are very few men as gentle as Alex, and you might be in for a nasty shock.'

I caught a glimpse of real malice in her eyes as she realised what I was implying. For a moment, she hesitated, coat hanger in hand, and I had a horrible feeling that she was tempted to retaliate with some sort of physical assault on my person, but then she flounced around the bed again.

'Go away, Eithne. I'm done with you lot. Anyway, I don't know why you think I should take advice from you. Sort your own marriage out first – if you can.'

We were both furious now, and nothing was to be gained from further discussion. I banged the door shut and returned downstairs, finally feeling that her departure would be a real relief.

It was difficult to pick up normal routines again after all the drama. The day had disappeared into a confusing maelstrom of clashing people and events. I had thrown the ingredients for a casserole together during the morning, and now I began to assemble a salad and boiled some Camargue red rice to accompany the dish. We always took greedy advantage of the local produce in France, especially the cheese and patisserie – I knew I would return to England with my tight clothes showing the effects of over-indulgence – but there was so much going on in our lives at present, that food was almost a secondary consideration.

However, the family members drifted in one by one when I shouted that dinner was ready. I hoped that the lizards had proved to be sympathetic companions, but Jack insisted on sitting between his father and grandfather, as if he needed the comfort of their closeness. Chloe yelled down the stairs that she wasn't hungry, and so we started without her. I think we were all relieved at escaping further embarrassing confrontation.

The drama of the day had caused me to sublimate my own worries, but a wonderful idea came to me as I was dishing up the casserole.

'Perhaps we should give the treasure hunt a miss tomorrow. You could ring Emma later, and explain that there's too much going on here,' I said to Ian, trying to suppress a rising eagerness in my voice. Unfortunately, Jack had other ideas.

'But I want to see Ollie! He said I could play with his new tennis racquet. And we're going to do the hunt together.'

His shoulders drooped with disappointment, and I knew that chance of escape had vanished. Ian looked at me in open surprise.

'I think a change of scene will do us all good,' he said firmly. 'I'm sure you will enjoy yourself, Eithne. Just sit back and let someone else get on with entertaining the troops.'

How could I argue with that? And then I realised that absence on one occasion would not stop Sam confronting Olivia at another time. It could even make things worse, because I might not be there to try to soften the blow with an attempt at explanation.

A faint air of unreality hung over the meal. Jack's eyes were blotchy, but he didn't say anything about his mother, or the anticipated changes to his home life, and when we had finished eating, he asked Ian to play table tennis with him in the garden. Alex, Olivia and I sat on at the table, laconic, while the dishes went unwashed. Occasional thumps and bumps floated down from overhead.

'When does Chloe say she's leaving?' I asked, thinking we needed notice of her departure, and Alex shrugged.

'She says that the boyfriend may well be here to pick her up this evening. As you will have guessed, he was in the party on the yacht, and now they are going to drive back to England together. I had better remind her to take her passport. She's quite capable of leaving it behind.'

Olivia and I exchanged stupefied glances as he left the room.

'He seems so calm,' I muttered, and she shrugged.

'It wasn't a surprise for him. Better get it over quickly, and then they can all move on. Alex says that Jack has been very good about it, although I think it would have been a different story if it was Alex leaving home.'

'But it's all so sudden!'

'Is it? You know this has been brewing for a long time.'

That was true, but I had not expected the door to be bolted with such rapid finality after the departure of the horse.

As things turned out, there was a minor hiccup, and Chloe had to spend another night under our roof. For a second day, the early morning was accompanied by the arrival of an expensive car, but it wasn't a slick Italian knocking on the door this time. A chunky, well-muscled young man, with smooth chocolate-coloured skin hugged Chloe in a laughing, laid-back embrace, and her excited shrieks rivalled the dawn chorus in shrillness. I wanted to stay in my bedroom until she had taken her departure, but Ian, who had descended to take stock of the situation, soon returned, with a faint amusement crinkling his eyes.

'You had better come down. Chloe is adamant that we should meet her new man, and I think she is anxious that we should give a nod to the arrangement, if not our blessing. It's hardly conventional, but if Alex has accepted matters, who are we to cavil? I know you might not want to, but Alex says it's important for Jack for everyone to part on reasonable terms,' he told me, and I nodded in grudging agreement as I pulled on my dressing gown, because I resented having to go along with this charade. But I was also agog with curiosity to see this improbable pairing for myself.

It was the most unlikely scenario I could imagine. When I went outside, I found Jack and Ian admiring the cream-coloured Porsche, while Alex and the young man – it was indeed the famous Si Barnabas – were engaged in agonisingly polite conversation, as if they were merely discussing the weather. Chloe hovered, her gaze flashing from one group to the other, and more nervous than I'd seen her before, but unable to prevent her excitement bubbling through. She exclaimed when she saw me and came across to throw her arms round my neck. After our spat of the night before, I wasn't expecting, or desiring, such an enthusiastic embrace. One of her hooped earrings snagged in my hair, and I flinched as she disentangled it with her vampiric fingernails.

'Ooh, Eithne, thanks for being here for me. I hope Ian behaves himself for you now.'

I sucked in my breath, narked by this whispered criticism, but Chloe gushed on without waiting for a response. 'You must meet Si; he's dying to know everyone. He never had a proper Mum or Dad, and he likes big families. He wants everyone to know that he'll look after me and Jack, as well.'

I peered more closely at the footballer. He wasn't especially handsome, in fact, his face showed distinct traces of youthful immaturity – perhaps that was why he was attracted to Chloe's child-like personality. I guessed his age to be around twenty-four, but there was a marked physical confidence in the way he moved, which was reflected in candid eyes and a ready grin. He didn't parade his star status, and despite all my reservations, I could feel myself warming to him. Now he squatted down to talk to Jack, and I watched the little boy's face change from surly shyness to wondering surprise. But Si was mature enough to know not to push things with his girlfriend's child, and I felt unexpectedly positive about the situation as I watched them together.

Then my eyes rested unhappily on Alex, but his demeanour seemed to be almost unnaturally cheerful. I could have sworn that he gave me a wink, before he turned to his wife and asked her some practical questions, to check that she had the documentation and money that she needed. His voice sounded matter-of-fact; he could have been sending a maiden aunt off on a shopping trip.

Olivia didn't appear, and I thought that was just as well.

'I wasn't sure how one is expected to say goodbye to a daughter-in-law and her paramour,' Ian said to me later. 'But I thought we all behaved very well, in the circumstances. Jack will have to grow up quickly, but Si Barnabas seems an uncommonly pleasant young man, and I believe he'll make a responsible stepfather. I think that's the best we can hope for.'

There was tacit agreement that this new development would not be revealed to the inhabitants of the chateau. Jack shed tears when his mother departed, but Ian and Alex worked hard to distract him with promises of visits and treats, and there was an electrifying moment, when Jack realised that he would be just like his best friend at school, whose parents also lived apart. That was important for the little boy, and it became clear that he knew of many other children with unconventional family arrangements. I could see him beginning to relax as this knowledge took root, and he could see that he wasn't alone.

Despite Chloe's departure, I think that Jack was the person most pleased to be leaving for the treasure hunt. He had the promise of playing with Ollie, and the excitement of a new event, and he was also looking forward to demonstrating his diving in the swimming pool. Olivia had expended much time and effort in teaching him during recent days, and he had grown very confident in the water.

When I saw the resolute way that Jack was facing up to his issues, I felt ashamed of myself. If Sam did tell Olivia about our past infidelity, I would need to tackle the problem with similar courage. But my tummy felt as though small animals were fighting inside it, as we swept up the drive to the chateau where our friends – and an adversary – were waiting.

Chapter Twenty-three

The first person to greet us on our arrival was Emma, who was wearing a flowery apron, and an expression of exasperated frustration. The young lady who had been cooking for the chateau party had fallen out with Jocelyn and flounced away into the night, leaving the unfortunate Emma to cope with kitchen duties.

'Perhaps you'll lend me a hand?' she said to Olivia, smiling in a wheedling way. 'Ma is no use at all, and I am up to my ears in food. Sam got back so late last night, that he's only just up and taking a shower.'

Olivia gave a polite nod of assent. The bitchy side of me hoped that she would be able to discover what had caused the rift, because I looked forward to sharing the story with Ian when we were at home again.

Renate strode up and herded Jack away to where the other children were waiting – I almost expected her to lead him by the ear. The treasure hunt was scheduled to take place after lunch, but she had organised a game on the patio to occupy them before we ate. Jack gave his dad a brave look as she marched him off, like a prisoner awaiting sentence, and I repressed a sympathetic smile.

The au pair had enviable legs, glossy auburn hair and a patrician nose, and I wondered whether Emma ever questioned the wisdom of sharing her home with such a fine specimen of womanhood. It was very easy to view Renate as a Wagnerian heroine, but the children in her care didn't seem to thrive under her strict discipline.

We sat on the patio, where the air was still and almost stifling – the day was sultry, despite the unusual presence of threatening clouds. Jocelyn was tight-lipped about her spat with the chalet girl, and Dom plunged into business talk with Ian, so conversation had a staccato momentum. Chloe's absence was noted, but Ian batted the subject away, merely saying that she had been called back to Manchester because of family matters. As the Templetons had little interest in her, the subject was dropped.

Jocelyn revived after her first drink. When the men wandered inside to look at something on Dom's computer, she began to lecture me about Ian's health, saying that he looked run down and seedy, and wasn't I concerned that he had lost weight? I thought of Dom's sweaty and rotund person, and my hackles rose.

'I'm not aware of anything like that. Ian usually puts weight on when we're in France, because he enjoys his food so much. I can see that Dom likes it, too,' I replied, leaving her in no doubt that there was a critical undertone to this remark. Alex got up abruptly and wandered towards the little lake. He was sensible enough to avoid becoming involved in Jocelyn's brand of sniping.

A door banged and Sam strolled out. His hair was still slick from the shower, and I wondered whether I was imagining an ominous deliberation in his gait because of my apprehension about what he might do. However, I forced myself to meet his eyes, where the usual light of disapproval shone brightly.

'Good afternoon, Eithne. Where are your young ladies today?' he enquired in a silky way, which immediately aroused my suspicions.

I explained that Chloe had returned home and Olivia was helping Emma in the kitchen, and he made no further comment, merely remarking to his mother-in-law that she was lucky no more guests were due before they left for home again.

'I told you that girl was sensitive and wouldn't take kindly to being criticised all the time. Now I suppose poor Emma will be a slave to the kitchen for the rest of our holiday,' he grumbled, and Jocelyn's eyes grew steely. It occurred to me that there might well be a lack of sympathy between Sam and his mother-in-law – their personalities were alike in many ways, and it was satisfying to think that they deserved one another.

'You can always go out for meals. And doesn't Renate know how to cook?' I asked, thinking I would add to the debate, but my remarks had the effect of closing the topic down. Jocelyn began to catechise me about Olivia's life and aspirations, and I could only reply that her plans were uncertain.

'Olivia has always done her own thing. But I'm hoping she might come back to England again, because it is hard not having more contact with my children,' I explained, and a brief light of sympathy flickered in Jocelyn's eyes.

'It's lucky that you can see Sam and Emma, then. Maudie and Alex too, I suppose,' she added, grudgingly granting them equivalent status with her son-in-law and his wife.

'I'm looking forward to having a proper talk with Olivia after lunch. We have some catching up to do.'

Sam's words fell on my ears with the impact of a stone dropping down a well. We locked eyes, and he sent me a small, secret smile, which I could not return. Then, as if on cue, a sudden rumble of thunder shook the heavens, and giant, painful drops of rain spattered down in a heavy assault.

'Inside!' screeched Jocelyn, and we picked up our drinks and ran to the house. I was conscious of a commotion with the children – Amelia was wailing, rooted to the spot with fright, while Renate dashed inside with baby Simon. By the time she returned to scoop up Amelia, the pair looked as though they had been in the pool with all their clothes on.

Jocelyn tutted, annoyed that the weather had the temerity to interfere with her arrangements, but Jack and Ollie were excited by the wild storm and had to be restrained from venturing outside again. By now, the garden was being lashed by a steamy torrent, and Jocelyn told Renate that she would take Amelia upstairs to change her wet clothing.

'Leave Simon with his mother – he needs to be fed before we eat, anyway,' she instructed, and the au pair bore the little boy off to the kitchen. I took the opportunity to find a loo. Although I had escaped a soaking, I wanted to rearrange my hair, which tended to over-curl like a chrysanthemum when damp.

As I washed my hands, I surveyed myself in the shabby mirror above the basin. My eyes were heavy with worry, and I thought that if anyone looked run down, it was probably me. I applied more lipstick; not because I needed it, but because I was armouring myself to face lunch and what was coming after. Then I quietly opened the door and slipped into the passage – and came to an abrupt halt.

At the far end of the corridor, Sam and Renate were twined around one another in a passionate embrace. His hands clutched her buttocks as he rubbed himself against her, and she moaned; her arms tight around his neck. Sam began to kiss her with rapid, slobbery movements, and then he caught sight of me.

There was a moment of agonised recognition, before he pushed the girl away. She began to protest, but he caught her by the wrist, and she turned to face me where I stood, twisting the strap of my handbag in my embarrassment. But a fire of exultation was beginning to kindle inside me. Unexpectedly, I had a weapon with which to fight my stepson, and I would not hesitate to use it.

Renate disentangled herself and pushed past me, her eyes sullen and wary. She disappeared into the hall, and Sam and I were left alone, staring at one another as if frozen in time. He cleared his throat.

'It's not what you think.'

He forced the words out, and I widened my eyes, indicating that I understood what was happening only too well. Sam was his father's son, after all.

'No? How do you know what I think, Sam?'

It would be satisfying to let him dangle on the end of a hook for a change. I turned away, but he strode after me, and caught at my arm, pinching the flesh in his urgency.

'Please, Eithne... it was just a stupid impulse; it doesn't mean anything. We're not having any sort of affair. Emma...' his voice broke and blood suffused his cheeks, while I allowed myself to taunt him with a smile.

'You mean Emma doesn't know you're shagging the au pair? Oh dear, Sam. I hope that no-one tells her, because I feel she might not be very happy about it. Jocelyn and Dom might find it the tiniest bit upsetting, too.'

I savoured the power he had so carelessly tossed into my possession, and he swore under his breath; still holding my arm. It hurt, and I removed myself from his grasp with disdainful fingers.

'What are you going to do?'

I could see how much it pained him to be reduced to entreaty, and I relished the fear in his face. For a second, I hesitated. Ought I to tell Emma what I had seen? She was probably unaware of this predilection for infidelity, which Ian and his second son appeared to share. I wasn't especially fond of Emma, but I was on her side in this situation.

However, that would mean Sam had nothing to lose, and would retaliate in the way he had threatened. I decided that it was better for certain secrets to remain undisclosed.

'Well, Sam... I think we can come to an understanding,' I said, keeping my gaze fixed on him. He had turned a strange, blotchy colour, and his usual air of self-satisfaction was conspicuously absent. 'You have been implying that you will reveal certain facts about my past to my children, although you have no reason to act in such a spiteful way. I won't tell Emma, or even Ian, what I've seen today, but I expect your silence in return. And I advise you to think very hard about what you are doing with Renate. Life is much simpler when you stick to what you signed up for. You have a lovely family; don't throw it all away! I know that's a cliché, but you would regret it afterwards – I can tell you that from experience.'

Now it was my turn to feel pained, as I remembered the deceit and anguish which had resulted from my affair with Ian all those years ago. Sam expelled a spluttering breath and dropped my arm. He leaned against the wall, and I could see him testing himself, trying to keep things afloat, because he had almost been dashed against jagged rocks. There was an uncomfortable silence, and then his gaze dropped to his feet.

'It's a deal.'

The words were whispered, as though he regretted he had so little room for manoeuvre. However, I reached out and grasped his hand.

'Shake on it, then, Sam. Do the decent thing. And while we're here, let me tell you that your father would prefer us to be on better terms. We may not like one another, but let's try not to let that show so much in future.'

I left him standing, head down, in the passage, and walked in to join the others with my own head high. I felt as though I could look at the world clearly again. Fear had clouded my vision in recent weeks, but now I was free, and my heart rejoiced. Ian glanced at me, perhaps surprised to see the bounciness in my step.

'Are you okay, darling? I hope you didn't get soaked,' he began, and I hastened to reassure him.

'I am fine, thank you. And I'm looking forward to my lunch.'

The little boys were kneeling on a window seat to observe the storm, which was still punishing the garden. I joined them and enjoyed their excited shrieks when a thunderclap burst directly overhead, and the house seemed to shake on its foundations. Ollie was worried that the treasure hunt would be ruined, but I felt able to reassure him.

'These storms pass over very rapidly, Ollie. Soon the sun will be out again, and you will hardly know there's been a storm. And I am sure that Renate can salvage matters, because she seems to be a most efficient person.'

Very efficient – she had certainly worked her way into the heart of this family. When we finally sat down to lunch, Renate busied herself with Amelia and the boys, although from time to time she sent me a veiled, flickering glance, as if anxious to read my thoughts. I assumed that Sam had snatched a moment to inform her of my silence, but her manner was quieter and far less bumptious than usual.

Ian enquired about Sam's trip to London, and Sam worked up a positive response, although a sulky set to his mouth revealed he still harboured feelings of resentment over the way he'd been circumvented.

'Things are moving. Obviously, I was very disappointed that you didn't want to be involved, but I can see that Aurien could be a useful contact for me in future. There's something else on the horizon which he may be able to help me with, and I plan to meet up with him next time he's in London.'

'Yes, you should do that Sam. And don't forget he's promised to come to us at Rivermead,' interrupted Jocelyn. I concentrated on my food, feeling that Olivia was suppressing a snigger, and knowing that if I looked at her, I would find it hard not to laugh too. But Jocelyn was such a determined character that maybe she would get her way, and Aurien would be added to her bag of desirable guests. It was a shame that I would probably not be invited to witness the occasion.

The sun soon dissipated the last straggling grey clouds, and we were able to take our coffee outside. Renate bustled round to resurrect the treasure hunt, and the party began to fragment. I leaned back in a deckchair, listening to the sounds of birdsong and the excited, shrill voices of the children, and felt relaxed and more content than I could have imagined.

Olivia lowered her slender body into a chair by my side.

'I'm sorry you were drafted in to help with lunch,' I said, and she laughed.

'I didn't mind. Emma and I understand one another,' she replied, and I was pleased to think that there were some amicable relationships in this disparate family group. Things would be so much nicer if we could have genuine enjoyment in each other's company, but the rosy picture of a united and supportive clan was unlikely to be painted anytime soon.

We drank our coffee, and Olivia stirred in her chair.

'Mum… things have been so chaotic that we've never had that talk. Let's do it now. Do you remember Terry at the Three Feathers?' she asked, and my mind raced back to our old home village, and the half-timbered pub, where Olivia had worked as a waitress during her teenage years.

'Terry! Well, yes, of course I remember, although I haven't given him a thought for ages.'

A vision of Peter sitting in the pub garden, pint in hand, crept up and taunted me with a pang of sadness. 'I thought he had retired years ago,' I added, screwing up my face so an unexpected tear couldn't escape down my cheek.

'No. He's talked about it, but now he's really decided to pack it in. We've always kept in touch, and we've been floating a few ideas around recently. My Italian experience has sharpened my appetite for the catering trade, and I wondered how you would feel if I took over the lease? I've got lots of ideas,' she continued, sitting upright and sounding almost breathless in her earnestness. 'If things really took off, I might expand to a B and B as well – there are a number of bedrooms which Terry never did anything with.'

'So why did you ask me about the tenants of the Old Rectory?' I asked, remembering an earlier conversation, and she looked away into the distance.

'I just thought that I'd like to live there again. All those years of travel were what I needed after Dad died, but I think that's out of my system, and I would give anything to be back with my old, happy memories, rather than trying to brush them away. I suppose I've grown up,' she said, and I was struck by her quiet acceptance of this fact.

'But could you run the pub if you were living at the Old Rectory?'

'Yes; provided I had a resident manager. Obviously, that wouldn't be for a while, but Alex has been telling me that the area has been developed a lot, with tons of new housing at the other end of the village, and people have always come out from Chester, because of the great walks nearby. I think there's a great potential clientele, and the chance of developing a really profitable business.'

'How about the financial implications? Surely this would need a cash injection to get you going?'

'I need a proper business plan to take to the bank. I was hoping that Ian could help me put something together, and Alex says he's willing to be involved, too.'

My mind raced forward to a happy scene of Alex and Olivia living together at the Old Rectory, while a baby brother or sister for Jack lay peacefully in a pram under the maple tree. Then I shut the scene away. It wouldn't do to get ahead of myself.

'I have no objection in principle, and I'd be delighted to get you back in the UK. It would be lovely to think of a family member living at the Old Rectory again. But I won't be in a rush to give notice to the Busbys until your plans are a lot further forward.'

I saw Jocelyn beckoning and reluctantly rose to my feet. The treasure hunt was about to get underway, and we were required to observe the children and their quest. And despite my unenthusiastic feelings about Renate, I had to admit that she was an excellent organiser, because the game took in almost every part of the park and some of the house as well. There was no absolute winner, but all the children came away clutching a new toy, and their happy faces showed that the event had been an exciting treat for them.

After tea, we began to say our farewells, but were interrupted by the arrival of Michel DuPlessis, requesting access to carry out a small repair to one of the bathrooms. We all shook hands, but he didn't appear to remember me, and I was faintly miffed, considering the intimacy he had forced upon me at the dinner table.

'I'm afraid that you're just another thigh to him, Mum,' Olivia murmured, as we climbed into the car, and I couldn't help laughing. The day had threatened to overwhelm me, but I was more than happy with the way things had turned out.

Chapter Twenty-four

The thunderstorm heralded the end of conflict for the inhabitants of Le Clos Fleuri, as though everything bad was cleansed with the rain, and, like the lizards, we could bask peacefully in the sunshine and calm skies which ensued. Ollie was allowed out for another sleepover with Jack, and Sam took noticeable pains to be civil to me when our paths crossed. Olivia, Alex and Ian spent almost two days debating a business plan for the Three Feathers; deep in strategies and finance, and I enjoyed hearing the complicit laughter which accompanied the deliberations. It was wonderful to be blessed with an overwhelming spirit of harmony, and even some unexpected visits from Dom and Jocelyn, who seemed to be at a loose end after the departure of their other guests, didn't spoil the relaxed atmosphere.

One day, as we were sitting by the pool watching the children splash and shout in the water, Jocelyn confided to me that 'Nique had called her from Paris the previous evening.

'I think she was hoping that Aurien might have been available – you know what I mean,' she said, sounding almost human for a change. 'Anyone could have told her that was unlikely to happen. But now she has run across a very suitable man whose family own a vineyard, and she is busy planning a future in Burgundy. Poor 'Nique. She deserves some happiness after the way Ricardo treated her.'

The cause of the rift between 'Nique and Ricardo was still shrouded in mystery, and I realised that it was likely to remain so. This didn't bother me now, and I was sufficiently magnanimous to wish that she could find happiness – or at least, access to a satisfactory bank account – but I hoped it wouldn't be with any of the men in my life. I was extremely relieved to think that Aurien had shaken her off without apparent difficulty.

'I trust the vineyard owner doesn't have a wife already,' I murmured, thinking of the way she had behaved with Ian, and I was surprised to see faint colour vying with the rouge in Jocelyn's cheeks. There was no doubt that Jocelyn had encouraged 'Nique in her pursuit of Ian, but now that game had failed, it behoved her to restore amicable relations with me. She changed the subject abruptly and we parted on outwardly good terms, although I was pleased to think the Templetons would be leaving for home at the end of the week.

Then it was time for Alex and Jack to return to England. Chloe had telephoned her son every day, and Jack was slowly coming to accept his changed family circumstances, although we still had a few tears at bedtime. The topic of football was discussed between the boys with a new solemnity, and on one occasion, I found Jack at Ian's computer, poring over the latest sporting headlines. He frowned at me over the top of the monitor, his brow crumpled with the effort of reading.

'It says here that Si is going to be in the first team this season. I'm looking forward to seeing the matches when we're back home. Freddie will be dead jealous, because he's mad keen on football, and I don't think he knows any players.'

Freddie was his best friend from school, and Jack's eyes grew bright at the thought of his new, important status, as someone who was in with the stars.

'I expect all your pals will be longing to tag along with you,' I said carefully, putting an arm around his shoulders. There were times like this when he reminded me very strongly of my small Nicholas, and I liked to savour these singular moments. He put up a hand and patted my cheek.

'Can we go and water the garden, Grandma? I like helping you outside.'

'Yes, of course. Now would be a good time, if you're ready.'

Later, when the flowers and vegetables were reeling from an enthusiastic soaking, he heaved a sigh of satisfaction as he watched the trickles of water tracing their way through tiny cracks in the path. Then, abruptly, he put the can down, and turned to put me on the spot.

'I don't think Mummy and Daddy were very happy together, Grandma. I'm sad, but I do want them to be happy. Do you think things will be all right?'

I didn't want to fob him off with empty promises. I lowered myself on to a wormy old wooden bench, hoping that whatever I said would make sense to him.

'It is going to be strange at first, Jack. When you get home, you may be upset because Mummy isn't there all the time, like she used to be. But you will still see her, and Daddy will be living with you at your house. Sometimes grown-up people make mistakes and decide they will be better apart. It isn't anyone's fault, and I'm sure that you will all be happy again before too long.'

I saw a glimpse of pain in his eyes and pulled him towards me for a cuddle. He burrowed his face against my shoulder, and I tried to soothe some of the sadness away.

'Grandpa and I will make sure we come to stay with you very often, and you can visit us in London, to get together with Ollie from time to time. You would like that, wouldn't you?'

He nodded, head still hard against my chest, and his shoulders shuddered. Then he broke away, a sudden gleam of delight forcing its way through the gloom.

'I'd love to see Ollie, and I know he likes playing with me. It's horrible for him, having to be away at school. Why does Uncle Sam make him go?'

'Well, some mums and dads think it's good for their children. Don't worry, because your father would never, ever send you away,' I counselled, and I felt relief tremble through the small body as I held him close. After a minute, he sat up, the little interlude of introspection at an end.

'Dad says we can go and see Olivia when she comes to live in Cheshire, and help in her pub. I'll like that, too,' he remarked, and I nodded, wondering where this new venture was headed.

'Life will be different, but you are a big boy, Jack, and I know you will manage. Would you like Grandpa to give you your own mobile phone for your birthday, if Daddy says it's okay? Then, if you ever feel miserable or worried, you can always ring me or Grandpa and have a chat.'

This suggestion was met with a succession of whoops and jumps. I wasn't silly enough to think this was due to the prospect of being able to contact his grandparents, because I had seen too many children hypnotised by playing games on their phones and texting friends, but it was another small thing for him to look forward to.

Olivia was the first to leave us; headed north to begin negotiations with Terry and the bank. I searched for signs of special affection between her and Alex as they said goodbye, but they avoided any overt demonstration of their feelings. Both had been burned by their recent experiences, and it wouldn't do for them to rush things now. However, it didn't stop me hoping in a foolish, sentimental way that they would find love again before too long.

Then I kept a promise made to Elizabeth and Bill and invited them to lunch with Dom and Jocelyn. It was irritating that Jocelyn behaved perfectly well on this occasion, merely taking the opportunity to lecture Bill over coffee on the undesirability of expatriate life, and I felt as though I had been guilty of bitchy over-exaggeration where her character was concerned. But any irritation was transient, because the Templetons were returning to England the very next day.

'We have enjoyed ourselves here,' Jocelyn conceded, as she kissed me goodbye. 'I am so disappointed that we haven't seen more of the area, but we've been martyrs to our guests.'

There was an appraising look in her eyes as she glanced up at our house, and I had the feeling that this was an enormous hint for me to issue an invitation for them to stay with us at some future date. I had no difficulty in ignoring the feeling, and even Jocelyn wasn't brazen-faced enough to force the matter.

It was much harder to bid farewell to Alex and Jack. They had grown very close to us during their eventful visit, and I was determined that we would get to see them more often when we were all back in England.

I had to promise to keep a special eye out for a large lizard with half its tail missing. Jack had become fond of it during his holiday, and I was instructed to send regular updates on the creature's health and activity.

'You can be really creative there,' Ian murmured, amused, and I tried to stifle a smile, because I didn't want Jack to think I wasn't properly concerned about the improbably named Spiky.

'He likes that bit of wall by the peach tree,' Jack was saying, as he climbed reluctantly into the car on their way to the airport. 'Don't forget to visit him, please, Grandma.'

'I won't,' I assured him, and then a strange silence fell on Le Clos Fleuri as they departed. I wasn't sorry to hear it, but for a few days, the house felt cooler and emptier; almost lacking in heart, until it became our own once again.

Ian visited the local barber and returned looking like the man I'd married. I was careful not to pass any comment, especially as his newer items of clothing were languishing unworn at the back of the wardrobe, but I hoped that I had seen the last of the would-be youthful person who had surprised me at the beginning of the summer. The vintage specimen was the one I appreciated.

Some days later, I wandered into Ian's study to take him a glass of wine before supper. We were comfortable with one another these days, although there remained a degree of constraint in our relationship, like something that has been twisted out of shape and is still in the process of bending back. He gave a little gasp as he scrolled down the screen.

'What are you looking at?' I asked, walking behind him so I could see too.

'The credit card statement... I hope you aren't planning to make too many visits to that boutique in town.'

Guilt forced a rosy blush to my cheeks. He had spoken with satirical resignation, but I debated whether I should reveal that 'Nique was an accessory to the crime. I leaned over his shoulder to see the evidence for myself, and then it was my turn to gasp.

'Well, it isn't so very much compared to the cost of a handbag from Valérie,' I retorted, and he stiffened in the chair. He closed the screen down abruptly, but not before I had seen another item which jumped out at me as if ringed in red. A room charge at one of the local hotels... during the time that 'Nique was in residence at the chateau.

It couldn't have been an overnight stay, but I remembered all too vividly what Elizabeth had seen, and the French custom of conducting adulterous affairs in the late afternoon – they even had a name for it: *le cinq à sept*. A suffocating sense of distress rose up inside me.

'I don't remember us staying at the Hotel Lion d'Or,' I said sharply, and he knew I'd seen the evidence. The atmosphere in the room vibrated with a heavy, uneasy silence, and then Ian reached for my hand, separating and stroking my fingers with his own.

'Have I been a complete prick?' he asked softly, after some moments of painful reflection, and I looked down at our joined hands and saw the glint of a wedding band.

'Yes. A five-star, gold-plated prick,' I told him, resentment burning like acid in my voice. I thought of all the little hurts and insults I'd suffered over the summer; of how he'd done nothing to intervene when other people put me down, and how he'd rushed heedlessly after a shinier new toy to play with. But at the same time, I knew that my Ian had been absent for a long period and was only just in ascendance again.

'I don't know what to say... I've behaved like a complete idiot. You must know that I really regret the whole sorry business.'

He kissed my hand with remorseful tenderness, and I could not resist the pull of my deep affection for him. I knew he was telling the truth. I pressed my lips against his head, and he caught me round the waist, drawing me on to his lap. We exchanged a look of wry and loving understanding; honest with one another after the weeks of temper and deception, and in this embrace, I finally found the security which I had been longing for.

'I wasn't thinking straight for a while after I came out of hospital,' Ian confessed. His voice was surprised, as though he'd only just realised this, and I nodded in agreement. He frowned, staring out at the garden with puzzled eyes, and I felt that he was computing everything that had affected him in the last difficult months. 'I was adrift – I don't know; there was a certain fear and I needed to validate myself. I can see that I didn't always react to things in the most sensible way.'

'I think that's true.'

I put a hand to his face, turning his gaze towards me so I could try to convey my belief that we still had a future together. 'Life has taken us on a stony old path at times, hasn't it? But if you feel now the way you did before your heart attack, then let's put these last months behind us, and forget all the upsets of this summer. Do you think you can do that, Ian? Do you *want* to do that?'

'I don't want to lose you, my love. We waited so long to be together, and I'm desperately sorry that I have hurt you,' he murmured, his cheek pressed against mine. I thought ruefully of Sam and the au pair and wondered if his life was unavoidably set on the same course as his father – and whether Emma would be as willing to forgive as I had been. I could see some difficult times ahead, but at least there was a sense of coming home to roost for the two of us.

It's never possible to go on exactly as before after this kind of upheaval in a marriage. But we wanted the same outcome, and life seemed far less complicated now the truth was out, and Ian had recovered his equilibrium. There were moments when the ghost of 'Nique hovered between us; when the memory of her caressing ways and rippling laughter could disturb my peace of mind, and we still had to face some uncomfortable discussions.

Then we spent a quiet, happy, loving September, enjoying Provence and renewing our partnership, and I think we were even sorrier than usual when the time came to return to the autumnal mists of London.

I don't know whether he was prompted by guilt, but Ian began to plan a trip for us to visit both Nicholas and Louisa after Christmas, and I was very excited at the thought of seeing my family again after such a long absence.

Georges arrived to drive us to the airport on the day we closed Le Clos Fleuri for the winter, and I took a last sentimental look at the shuttered windows, knowing that the house was wrapping itself up for a long hibernation. Ian loaded our cases into the boot, but then I remembered something I had forgotten to do during the last days of packing.

I almost ran down to the lizard wall, fearing I would be too late. But the sun still warmed the higgledy-piggledy stones, and as I scanned them with anxious eyes, I was overjoyed to glimpse the blunt end of Spiky's tail as he whisked into a crevice. Jack would be delighted. Spiky had survived the summer, and I took that as a good omen. He was a living demonstration that life goes on, even when beset by the most unexpected problems.

On the way to the airport, I told Ian what I'd seen, and he reached for my hand.

'I suppose you're going to tell me that Spiky was sending a message to us,' he commented, as the car sped along the autoroute, and I saw his lips curve in a tiny, teasing smile. The cheek of it! I wondered how to respond, then remembered his favourite admonition. I had been waiting a long time to say it, and this seemed as good a moment as any.

I took a deep breath and gave the hand a reproving squeeze.

'Don't be ridiculous, Ian…'